I0822868

eBook ISBN: 978-1-964457-29-1

Paperback ISBN: 978-1-964457-71-0

Hardcover ISBN: 978-1-964457-31-4

Hardcover Wrapped Cover Edition ISBN: 978-1-964457-74-1

Cover design by: Warren Design & Persephone Entertainment Inc.

Printed in the United States of America

Published by Persephone Entertainment Inc.

Texas, USA

IN THIS VOLUME

PRAISE FOR THE WORST SHIP IN THE FLEET

If you like stories of heroes in need of redemption, this is the story for you. ...by the end, you will definitely want to read more.

TAMMY RUGGLES, READER VIEWS

...filled with humor, heartbreak, and mystery, The Worst Ship in the Fleet takes you on an exhilarating interstellar adventure you won't want to end.

PIKASHO DEKA, READERS' FAVORITE

Brad's story can serve as a message of hope to those who might have given up on life due to one or more bad occurrences that they feel responsible for.

ABRAHAM OZO, ONLINEBOOKCLUB.ORG

PRAISE FOR ROGUE AGENT

Rogue Agent is a compelling murder mystery that will force your brain into overdrive from the moment you start reading it. If you enjoy watching films like Black Widow, Wonder Woman, and Hanna, you will love reading Rogue Agent.

ALIJA TURKOVIC, READERS' FAVORITE

PRAISE FOR THE GALAXY'S WORST MERCENARIES

> …maintained a fast pace and was full of unexpected twists with no dull moments. I recommend it to readers who love adventurous sci-fi novels blended with humor.
>
> ISABELLA HARRIS, READERS' FAVORITE

DUMB LUCK & DEAD HEROES TIMELINE

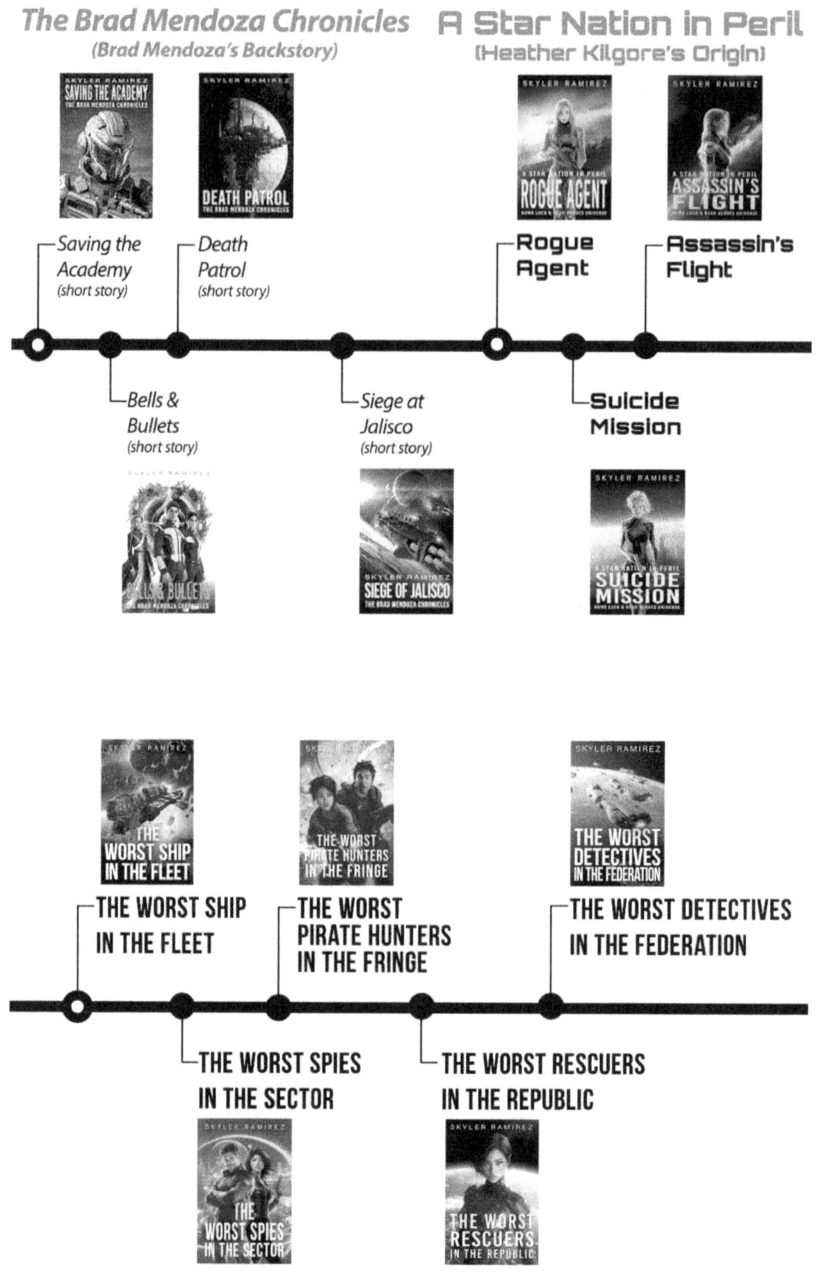

AND CHRONOLOGICAL READING ORDER

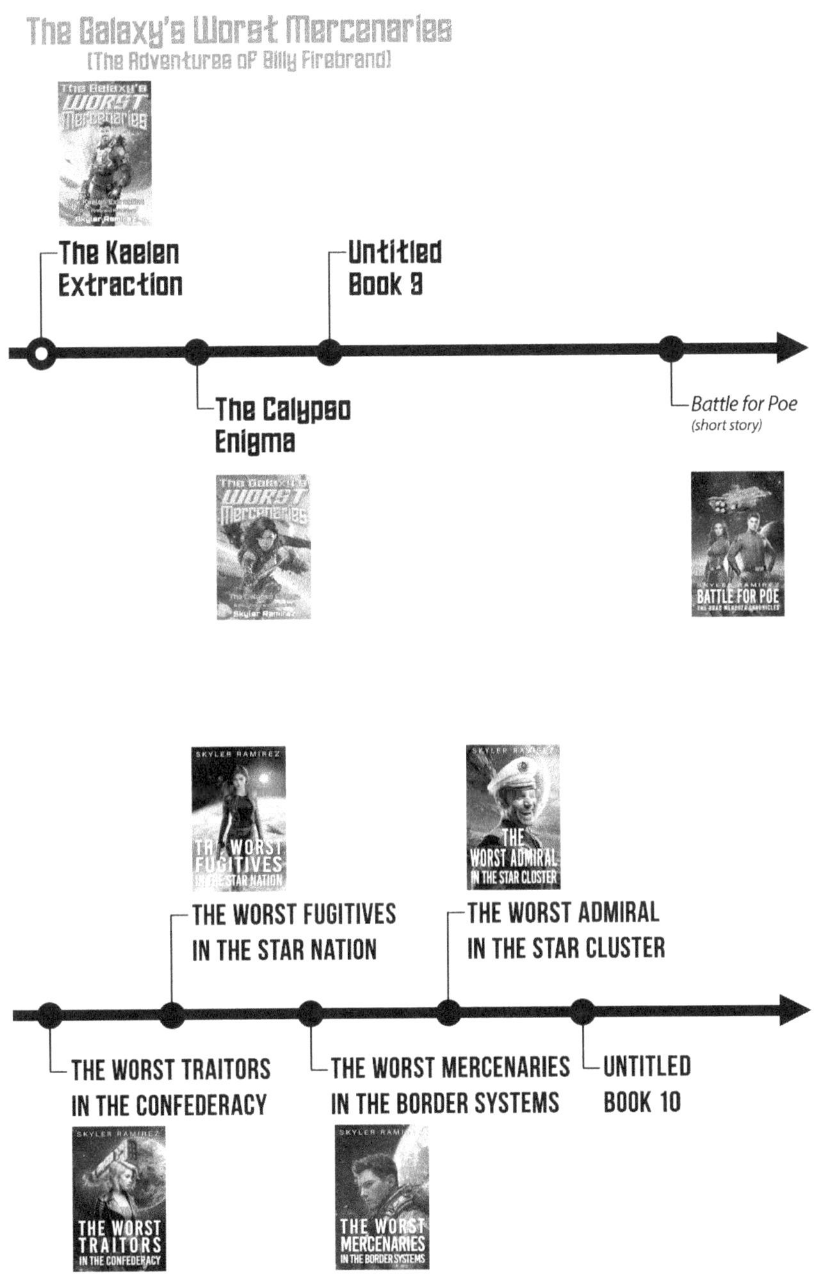

CONTENTS

THE WORST SHIP IN THE FLEET

THE WORST SPIES IN THE SECTOR

THE WORST PIRATE HUNTERS IN THE FRINGE

THE WORST SHIP IN THE FLEET

BOOK ONE

ONE
DEAD-END ASSIGNMENT

"Brad, you're an idiot."

I looked at the lined face of Admiral Terrence Oliphant. His crisp blue uniform held so many ribbons that I was idly wondering how he kept from hunching forward under their weight all the time. I wanted to argue with his statement; I really did. But you didn't argue with Terrence 'Terrible' Oliphant in the Promethean Navy unless you had a death wish.

But that alone didn't stop me from vocally disagreeing with the man. I had to admit I actually did sort of have a death wish, and not strictly in a figurative sense. The last six months had been the worst of my life in more ways than I could count…in no small part because of the man sitting across from me. But even so, I chose not to argue with his assessment of my intelligence, mostly because he was right.

I *was* an idiot. If the last six months had taught me anything, it was that my stupidity was an incontrovertible fact. Oh, sure, after this meeting, I would grumble about how Old Man Oliphant had screwed me over, but I honestly knew I deserved every bit of his criticism. That was the problem.

"You know, I should just kick you out of the Navy." He let the statement hang there as if he expected me to finally rise to my defense or beg for my job. As with his earlier insult, I didn't engage with him on this either. Part of me was absolutely terrified that he might follow through with his threat. But the other part of me wanted it to happen. It would remove the one final excuse I had to try to be…well, anything.

In my mind's eye, I pictured myself leaving the Promethean Naval headquarters building in street clothes, my rank and station stripped, and my fate sealed. I knew what I would do if that happened, and it involved a large bottle of cheap whiskey and my service sidearm. Maybe I would leave a note; maybe I wouldn't. Who would read it?

Obviously seeing I wasn't going to give him the satisfaction of begging to stay in the Navy, the Admiral frowned deeply. Then he shrugged and continued. "I would kick you out if it were entirely up to me. But it's not." He seemed incredibly disappointed in that fact. "Besides, I think you'll find yourself wishing I *did* drum you out. Maybe you'll even save me the paperwork and resign your commission." Now he sounded hopeful. But despite my fatalistic musings, I wasn't about to resign—no way would I give him that satisfaction.

"Your new assignment is being sent to your implant now. We're sending you to Gerson."

Hmmm. Maybe I needed to reconsider that whole resignation thing. Gerson was the hole of the spacelanes, the armpit of Promethean territory. And it was on the edge of human-controlled space. It literally bordered on *nothing*. So, *nothing* ever happened there. It barely even rated a naval station. Still, maybe it was better than eating a bullet… just barely.

"You'll be taking command of the *Persephone*," he continued, a smile breaking out on his too-good-looking features for the first time.

And there it was. Now it definitely wasn't better than just ridding the universe of my pathetic existence. The *Persephone* wasn't a command; it was the butt of a joke. It was the last of the Poseidon-class missile frigates, a failed experiment in building smaller warships to extend the Promethean Navy's patrol area, an experiment that had lasted just long enough for the first Poseidon classes to show their stripes in their shakedown cruises. They were horrible. Not only had their experimental ion drives proven so unreliable that they were never put in another Navy vessel afterward, but their meager armament and small missile magazines made them next to worthless in a fight with anything larger than a garbage scow. And even then, it was preferable if the garbage scow was already damaged and running on autopilot to give the Poseidons more of a fighting chance.

Persephone had been old when I graduated from the Academy. And her reputation back then had already been secured. No matter what assignment my classmates and I had received for our first post-graduate cruises, the common refrain had been: 'Well, it could be worse. At least it's not the *Persephone*.'

Worse, *Persephone* was such a small ship, with so small a crew—even at capacity, the Poseidons only held two dozen spacers—that she barely rated a lieutenant commander in the command chair. And I was a full captain.

The message was clear. The Navy wanted Brad Mendoza out. But they weren't going to just discharge me and let me fade to obscurity in peace. They wanted to *embarrass* me on the way out.

Still, I said nothing, and Oliphant's Cheshire Cat smile eventually faded as I refused to take the bait. It was a small victory.

"Get out," he finally said. "I expect you off planet and en route to Gerson within the hour. Dismissed."

I stood, threw a sloppy salute—going through the motions but too numb to be either respectful or overly disrespectful—and turned to leave.

"Oh, and Brad..." his voice stopped me in my tracks. I turned back around to see a hard look on the old man's face. "Stop calling Carla. She wants nothing from you ever again. Understood?"

Words failed me, so I just nodded and turned again to leave. It really sucked to have one of the most senior admirals in the Navy hate your guts. It was worse when he was your father-in-law...well, *ex*-father-in-law.

TWO
MY NEW BOSS HATES ME

"Sir, we'll be docking at Gerson Station in twenty minutes."

I opened one eye to regard the young spacer third class who had nudged me awake. I hadn't actually been sleeping, but pretending to doze was an excellent way to avoid interaction with the crew and few other passengers on the small transport that had carried me the three days through jump space to the outer limits of human territory.

They were judging me—all of them. I had caught a few of the enlisted spacers whispering and casting glances at me early in the journey. And sure, they could have been talking about my unshaven appearance or my wrinkled uniform. But I couldn't shake the feeling that they *knew* about my latest assignment and were having a great joke at my expense.

Because as much as it would be a drag to serve aboard a naval transport like this one, each and every one of the spacers and officers on this bucket could still say the same thing: 'At least it's not the *Persephone*.'

Or translated another way: 'At least I'm not Brad Mendoza.' But *I* was, and it wasn't fun at all.

I mumbled something back at the spacer who had roused me, and he went off to wake up the transport's other two remaining passengers on the final leg to Gerson. One of them was an older enlisted man wearing an engineer journeyman's patch, telling anyone who saw him that he might be enlisted, but his unique skillset made him pretty much immune to the orders of any mere mortal officer below the rank of commander. Shiny new ensigns who made the mistake of trying to issue an order to an engineer journeyman usually learned quickly the very narrow extent of their true authority over such men and women.

He had ignored me the entire flight in such a pointed way that I was one hundred percent certain he knew exactly who I was and where I was headed. It simply wasn't natural for him to have never once looked my way in three days.

The other passenger was a civilian, or at least she wasn't in uniform. But she was very pretty, with long auburn hair and a lithe build that showed curves in just the right places and reminded me a bit of my ex-wife. She had caught me looking *her* way a couple of times on the first day in transit, letting my imagination run a little free. Her sour return look quickly put an end to my fledgling fantasies. Since then, I had made it a point not to look at her; every time I did, even by accident, she met my gaze with a hard stare that told me she wouldn't want my attention even if I weren't the biggest pariah in the Promethean Navy right now.

I sat, studiously trying not to see or be seen by either the engineer or the redhead while the transport neared Gerson Station. At least, as the ranking officer on board the ship, I was granted one of the few seats near a virtual portal. It was the one and only concession to luxury that the spartan naval transport provided—the bathroom didn't even have a shower, just a full-body disinfectant and deodorant sprayer that made me crave the bottle of cheap scotch I'd smuggled in my footlocker—but the portal gave me a video view of the approaching station.

Unfortunately, it also gave me my first look at my new command.

HMS Persephone probably hadn't started life as the spacecraft visual equivalent of a flounder, but she sure had evolved into it over the decades. Where once her paint scheme might have been a uniform gunmetal gray or even the matte black of a Navy warship, now she was a patchwork of discolored hull plates that were evidently being held in place by chewing gum and maybe a few toothpicks. She looked like a kindergartner's wild drawing of what a warship might look like...if that kindergartner was terrible at art and hated the Navy and everyone in it and wanted them to collectively die from embarrassment.

My new home in space was shaped roughly like a long box, with an unevenly tapered front end and a flare at the back for the ion drive nozzles. On her dorsal hull, she had a small conning tower with an observation pod at the top of it. As with most warships, that observation pod had the only windows on the ship. It was designed as a last-ditch place for the ship's officers to visually target enemy craft if their entire AI targeting system failed or their external sensors were all fried. Of course, that was ridiculous; anything that could take out both the AI and the ship's external sensors would surely take out the thick glass enclosure of the observation pod well beforehand.

It was the same basic structure of most human warships—function over form. But somehow, *Persephone* made it look so much uglier than any ship I'd ever seen. And it wasn't just the patchy paint scheme. There was something depressing about her lines, as if the hull plates themselves weren't aligned properly to each other, making her look like an old beat-up car one of my buddies had in high school that I swear started life as parts of four different vehicles.

I was frankly surprised they even let *Persephone* keep the *HMS* prefix. I very much doubted His Royal Majesty wanted the ship in front of me to be associated with his name, his Navy, or even the same galaxy he lived in.

When the transport docked at the station, I wordlessly grabbed my day bag and returned a hasty salute from the spacer at the airlock before disembarking. I had very few privileges left to my rank, but having the transport crew unload my footlocker and bring it to *Persephone* for me was at least one thing I could still count on as a captain in His Majesty's Promethean Navy.

No one from the station had come to greet the transport as it docked, so I stepped out into an empty corridor. The cute but mean redhead and the aloof engineer journeyman would disembark after me—another supposed privilege of my rank. It didn't matter that even the lowliest spacer third class had a better chance of being in the Navy six months from now than I did. The military was nothing if not securely tied to tradition and ceremony.

I absently rubbed at the stubble on my chin as I hefted my day bag over my shoulder and walked down the short corridor to wherever it led. Most stations were designed the same, so the door at the far end would probably empty me out into a customs and immigration entry point, but maybe Gerson Station would surprise me with something different.

It didn't. The bored-looking man at the customs and immigration desk eyed me with just enough interest for me to know that he knew who I was and why I was there—the lack of respect in his tone also made that clear—before he waved me through.

"Oh, Captain Mendoza," he said, almost as an afterthought. "Captain Wainwright has asked that you present yourself at the Naval Commander's Office on level three before you board your ship."

I eyed the man dubiously. I had no idea who Captain Wainwright was. His or her name was probably in the orders and briefing packet stored in my implant, but I hadn't even been tempted to read them beyond the first few sentences. Those had made it clear I was to report to *Persephone* in the Gerson system and end my naval career, with the admiralty's compliments, of course.

Shrugging, I walked out the far door and into a larger open area than I'd yet seen. It looked like the interior of any other station, with a few shops and moderately narrow corridors between them, interspersed with intersections that led to other docking airlocks. Except, being a Fringe system, the shops in Gerson station were low-end and utilitarian. There were no luxury goods being sold on this station, at least that I could see. Apparently, people this far out from the rest of humanity didn't need fancy luggage, purses, or perfumes. They were good with packaged fried foods and cheap booze. My kind of place.

The signs stenciled on the corridor bulkheads led me to the station's central hub, where three cylindrical lifts clustered together to take people to different levels. I boarded the one facing me and keyed in level three using an old-style button after my implant failed to find a connection to the lift's controller. How quaint.

Two minutes later, I was off the lift and stepping through the door into the outer room of the Naval Commander's Office. This part of the station *did* look like every other station I'd been on, all standard naval issue. The carpet here was a little more worn than usual, and the reception desk had a few extra chips in the cheap plastic veneer, but otherwise, it could have been a station in orbit of Prometheus itself.

I eyed the spacer behind the counter, a young man who watched me back with barely concealed interest. He was trying very hard not to gape at me and frown at my sloven appearance, and he was failing miserably at both.

"Can I help you, Captain?"

I fought the urge to sigh. The kid had to know precisely why I was there. His passive-aggressive question just showed that I was to be afforded no respect befitting my rank. Six months ago, that would have ended with me pulling the boy up and dressing him down while conducting a point-by-point inspection of his uniform while I questioned his parentage. Now...I couldn't even muster up enough righteous indignation to care.

"Captain Mendoza to see Captain Wainwright," I said in what I thought was a long-suffering tone. But it sounded monotone to my ears. I'd had a hard time expressing any emotion in my voice lately. Everything just came out flat.

"Of course, sir. I will inform the captain of your arrival. If you would please take a seat, I will show you in as soon as she is ready."

Now I did sigh. I just couldn't help it. Wainwright, whomever *she* was—at least I knew her gender now—had summoned *me*. Which would imply that she'd known I was coming and had planned this encounter. Making me wait now was either a clumsy power move or a calculated insult. Either way, it didn't bode well for the meeting I was about to have.

I dropped my day bag onto one of the empty chairs and flopped myself down in the one next to it. Pulling up a game on my implant, I moved a bunch of stupid shapes around to try and get them to fit in a stupid box. It was mindless, but it was about the most complex thing I could get my brain to tackle these days. And at least it kept me from thinking about anything for a few minutes here and there. Thinking was generally dangerous for me.

After ten minutes or so, right about the time I had restarted the game for the sixth time trying to beat my daily high score, the spacer at the desk stood and cleared his throat. "This way, uh, Captain."

I stood, leaving my bag where it was, and followed the young man to one of the doors behind his desk. He opened it and gestured for me to enter, which I did reluctantly.

Captain Wainwright was a sour-faced blond with her hair pulled back into a severe ponytail that made her forehead look huge. She had eyes the color and luster of puke, and her gaunt features made me worry that the Navy's ration shipments to Gerson must be a few months behind schedule. She frowned as I entered and threw her a salute that was only slightly less sloppy than the one I'd given my former father-in-law the last time I'd seen him—when he'd ended my naval career in all but name.

"Captain," I said expectantly. Well, I tried to sound expectant, but I think I just sounded bored…or maybe medicated, even though I hadn't been able to get a drink on the station yet.

"Captain," she replied, her frown coming through twice as intensely in her voice. I pretended to ignore it, which was easy because I really didn't care.

Without waiting for an invitation, I moved further into the small office and plopped down in one of the two spindly chairs that faced her across the desk. I was gratified to see her frown even more deeply at my impropriety. I'd had so little joy lately, but seeing her upset gave me just a hint.

"What can I do for you, Captain?" I asked.

She waited a tick, though her eye twitched noticeably at my continued lack of decorum. I almost smiled. When she spoke again, her voice was heavy with her disapproval.

"I would welcome you to Gerson, but maybe we can dispense with the pleasantries and get straight to business."

I shrugged and said nothing, my thoughts turning again to the bottle of scotch in my footlocker. I'd passed at least two liquor stores in the station on my way here; maybe I could pick up another bottle or two. There was no telling how long I'd be onboard my new ship before there would be another opportunity to stock up.

"I'm sure you're aware of just how irregular this all is," Wainwright said as I daydreamed of an alcohol-induced stupor.

"Irregular?" I asked, seizing on the word.

"Yes, quite," she responded, then studied me again. She was starting to remind me of Admiral Oliphant, which didn't necessarily endear her to me. Even when things had been good between me and Carla, Terrible Terrence and I had never exactly gotten along. He had tolerated me so long as his daughter was in love with me, but the second she'd come to her senses, he'd dropped all pretense of liking or respecting me. At least Wainwright was skipping straight to the disdain and dislike. No pretense here.

When I didn't say anything else, she sighed and continued. "Normally, command in the system would go to the senior most captain, as you well know. But my orders are different in this particular case." She paused, eyeing me expectantly.

I thought about her words for a long moment, unsure of what she was getting at. Then a strange and rare moment of clarity hit me. I mentally commanded my implant to bring up Wainwright's service record and specifically asked for her date of latest promotion. Sure enough, she had been promoted to captain three years before, almost a full year after my own promotion date. So that made *me* the senior captain in the room. Awkward.

"Am I going to have a problem with you, Captain Mendoza?" she asked when I still said nothing. I think she was trying to sound stern, but her voice cracked a little at the end of the question, and in another startling moment of clarity, I realized that at least a portion of her cold demeanor toward me had to be from her own nerves. After all, it wasn't every day you met the most hated man in the Promethean Navy and realized that he *should* have been your commanding officer.

"Probably," I replied, shrugging again. "Everyone else seems to have a problem with me."

Her eyes widened in surprise. Whether that was from my frank admission or my rakish good looks as I threw her a lopsided smile, I decided not to wonder.

She frowned again, which based on the lines etched on her face, must have been her default expression even when she wasn't sitting across from the Butcher of Bellerophon. But lucky for her, she had me in the flesh now, and I was giving her a real reason to frown. It must have been a fulfilling experience for Wainwright.

"I won't lie, Captain, you're nothing like I expected based on your service record," she said through her latest frown. "At least, your record before…the incident." She said the last word like she was suddenly sucking on a lemon, which might have been a better look for her.

I decided to say nothing again. Let her draw her own conclusions; they would be far better than the truth in almost any event. Me opening my mouth was unlikely to make much of a difference.

"Anyway," she said after a long moment, "I will be your commanding officer while you're here in Gerson. As I'm sure your orders have already made clear to you." They probably would have if I'd read them. For now, I'd have to take her word for it.

"I will expect weekly reports from you during patrols and daily reports while on station. Is that understood?"

I raised an eyebrow and almost smiled. I could tell she was expecting me to argue. After all, I was more senior, and the stated expectation of regular reports should have insulted me. Oh sure, it was standard procedure for me to give reports on a similar schedule to any commanding officer, but there was a fiction to maintain that I would do it out of my own courtesy rather than as the result of a direct order from an officer of my same—lesser really—rank. I decided to let it slide. I was just having such a hard time caring.

"Of course," I replied evenly. "Now, if I may be excused to report to my new command?"

She frowned again—her upside-down smile was growing on me by now—and nodded. "Dismissed."

I gave a jaunty little salute and left without saying another word. But as I grabbed my day bag and left the small office area, I felt my already low mood sink even further. Oliphant and the admiralty had not only sent me to Gerson, the veritable butt crack of human space, to command the worst ship to have ever flown His Majesty's colors, but they had added insult to injury by suborning me to a more junior captain.

Not that I could blame them. It really might be better for all involved if I just quit. I'd even started drafting my letter of resignation during the journey from Prometheus to Gerson on the transport. The only thing that had kept me from sending it was the image of the smile it would put on Oliphant's face.

THREE
WHAT HAVE I GOTTEN MYSELF INTO?

"Captain on deck!" the young ensign hollered as I stepped through the inner airlock door of *Persephone*. I winced. In the short walk from Wainwright's office to my new ship—which may or may not have involved a stop at a liquor store and a quick shot, or three, at a station bar—I had developed a headache. The ensign's shrill voice was like an ice pick in my temple. I already disliked the kid.

"As you were," I said, trying hard to make my voice not sound annoyed. I failed.

"Captain Mendoza," the boy said, lowering his rigid salute. "Commander Lin sends her regards and apologizes for not being here to meet you. We had expected you an hour ago, and she had to head down to engineering to confer with the Cheng about an issue with the ion drives."

'Cheng' was the near-ubiquitous shortening of 'chief engineer' that had been used on naval ships since time immemorial. It had probably originated on Old Earth even, but no one knew for sure. Besides, I'd only met even a handful of folks in my life who had ever seen Earth, much less knew anything about its naval history and traditions.

"Understood, Ensign..." I squinted down at his nametag, but he beat me to it.

"Stevens, sir. Ensign Peter Stevens. From Kipling. This is my first assignment, sir. And happy to be here."

No, he wasn't. Unless he was dumber than I was. But he was an ensign, so maybe he *was* stupid. Only time would tell. I just grunted at his fake enthusiasm.

"Very well, Ensign Stevens. I assume you can show me to my quarters?"

"Of course, sir. If the Captain would follow me?"

And follow him I did. It took all of four minutes to traverse half the ship to get from the airlock to the captain's cabin. And when we arrived there, I was underwhelmed. I'd seen larger officer cabins on modern patrol boats. The idiots who had designed the Poseidon class obviously hadn't even considered the comfort of their commanders. I'd been in showers bigger than the outer office of my new quarters. And I'm pretty sure I'd seen dog beds larger than the bunk in my new bedroom.

Shaking my head, I dismissed the overeager ensign with a wave of my hand and tossed my day bag onto the bunk. At least my footlocker was already in place on the shelf below my closet, though no one had bothered to remove and hang up my uniforms. I should have cared about that, I suppose, but made no move to unpack my things.

Looking around, I almost reopened that letter of resignation on my implant. But I had the fleeting mental image of the admiralty gleefully stranding me in the Gerson system by refusing me return transport to Prometheus on a naval ship, and I decided against giving up my commission quite yet. After all, I hadn't even had time to come to loathe my new ship yet, though it was certainly off to a strong start.

I looked at my day bag and was tempted to take out one of the bottles I'd purchased on the station. Stevens had no doubt smelled the alcohol on my breath from my stop at the bar, but he'd been wise enough not to say anything. Still, I was already feeling a bit buzzed, and even a screwup like me knew better than to show up to my station on my first day of a new command *completely* drunk. I'd wait until that evening.

A knock at my cabin door interrupted my heavy contemplation of the proper procedures of command.

"Come," I mumbled, but the hatch opened before the person could have heard me. I stepped—and it indeed was just about one big step's distance—out of my bedroom and back into the outer office to see a large brute wearing an enlisted man's garb, with the chevrons of a petty officer on his skinsuit sleeves, which were rolled up against regulation to reveal beefy, hairy forearms. The guy had to be at least two meters tall, abnormal for a spacer. I imagined he hit his head all the time on the tops of hatches throughout the ship. He was also handsome, in a way that made me feel oddly threatened, with a square chiseled jaw covered in just enough stubble to enhance his appearance—I would have killed to look that good without shaving; I just tended to look...well, like an alcoholic. He had blond hair perfectly combed and slightly longer than regulation, above cold blue eyes. He reminded me of my high school bully.

"Captain Mendoza?" he asked in a voice that would have sounded belligerent if I hadn't known any better.

I looked around the cabin incredulously. Who did he *think* was wearing the captain's uniform in the captain's cabin?

He didn't wait for my response. "I'm Jacobs. I'm sure you've read my file." I had not. But that didn't make him special. I hadn't read *any* of the personnel files attached to my orders.

"So, you know who I am and what I'm all about," he continued, unaware that I most decidedly did not. "And I just wanted to talk to you early to...set expectations."

I frowned. "Spacer, you're bordering on insubordination," I said in my best attempt at a stern voice. It took a lot these days to make me feel any emotion, but this guy had instantly rubbed me the wrong way.

He smiled! "I don't care, Captain," he said flippantly, and my mouth dropped open. I'd always thought that was just a turn of phrase, but my mouth *literally* dropped open in surprise. Go figure. "Listen," he continued, "everyone knows who you are and what you did. They don't send captains they like to the *Phony*. So, I'll give it to you straight. You stay out of my way, and I'll stay out of yours.

"But don't think you can intimidate me with your rank, Mendoza. No one is going to listen to a performance writeup from the Butcher of Bellerophon." He was the first person ever to use that nickname to my face. I knew what they called me behind my back, of course, but the audacity!

"Stay out of my way Captain. And we'll get along just fine."

My mouth was still open, and I was debating how to respond when the big man turned heel and left back through the outer hatch, which he almost slammed closed behind him.

Stunned, I sat down hard in my tiny desk chair, staring at the hatch and picturing the man's receding back. Never in my fifteen years of naval service had I even *heard* of an enlisted man talking that way to a *captain*. Oh sure, stories abounded of senior chiefs and petty officers dressing down shiny new ensigns and even the occasional lieutenant who got too big for his britches. But a *captain*? Never!

I wanted to be furious. I wanted to call the man back, read him the riot act, and then throw him in Gerson Station's brig for insubordination. But I was still so shocked by the encounter that I just sat there, staring at the closed hatch and wondering just what in the depths of Hades I'd gotten myself into.

FOUR
JESSICA LIN

Five minutes later, I was still sitting mouth agape at my desk when another knock came at the cabin door. I jumped in my seat, involuntarily picturing the massive Jacobs having returned to spout more insults and maybe even break me in pieces with his hairy forearms.

But I overcame my shock when the knock came again; it sounded *timid* of all things. Definitely not Jacobs.

"Come," I said, and the hatch opened slowly.

In stepped one of the most gorgeous women I'd ever seen. Have you ever seen one of those women whose dimensions are so perfect that it hurts? And whose face is so wonderfully proportioned, with smooth unblemished skin that never needs an ounce of makeup, that it makes you forget your wife—well, ex-wife for me?

Me neither. But the woman before me came as close as anyone I'd ever seen on both counts. I'd always loved Carla and thought she was as beautiful as any woman in the galaxy. And maybe it had something to do with her telling me she hoped I'd die in our last conversation with each other, but the King's officer I laid eyes on now put Carla to shame! Her short hair was jet black and straight, a sign of her obvious Asian ancestry, along with the slight hint of epicanthic folds around her eyes. She wasn't overly tall—probably around 175 centimeters—but her thin waist and legs made her look taller than she was, while her curves offset them in an incredibly pleasing way.

"Captain Mendoza," she said crisply, throwing an equally sharp salute as she brought that perfect figure to full attention in a way that made me want to bless the King's Navy for designing its uniforms to double as decompression skinsuits. "Lieutenant Commander Jessica Lin, reporting for duty. Welcome aboard, Captain."

I stared at her, my mouth open—twice in one day!—before I finally mumbled, "At ease, Commander."

She dropped her salute and put her arms behind her back, shifting her stance wider on the deck and keeping an expression of professional calm on her face that at least didn't look like she had noticed the drool on my chin.

"I'm sorry I missed you coming aboard, sir. Chief Engineer O'Malley requested a conference with me. I came as soon as I was able to leave engineering."

"Uh," I said. Real smooth. Did she know how great she looked in that skinsuit? She had to, right? "No problem, Commander. Ensign… Stevens," I think I said the right name, "showed me to my quarters. And I've already met some of the crew." No need to tell her about the aggressive and surreal encounter with Jacobs yet, not before I had a better handle on the obvious personnel issues on this horrid little ship.

"Thank you, sir," she said with a hint of a shy smile. That had to be affected; there was no way a woman who looked like *that* could ever really be shy. Then her smile disappeared. "I trust that the crew is being accommodating thus far?"

The way she asked the question, with a mix of trepidation and hopefulness, made me think that she had already guessed or even heard about the encounter with Jacobs. But I decided to play dumb for now. "All in order," I said instead.

"Very good, sir. May I give you a tour of the *Persephone*?" She said the name without the disdain I usually heard it imbued with.

"Of course, Commander," I said reluctantly. "Lead on."

I didn't get much from the tour. The alcohol I'd already imbibed that day had mixed with the shock of the encounter with Jacobs to put my mind into a haze. I couldn't recall later the name of a single person Lin introduced me to or much of what she said about the ship or its capabilities as we roved through its corridors and stopped at the various duty stations.

I pretty much spent the entire time looking over my shoulder for Jacobs, irrationally fearful that the big man would jump out of a hatch at any moment and club me over the head with one of his beefy fists. Any time not spent looking over my shoulder was spent admiring Jessica Lin's exquisitely formed backside as she led the way through the ship. At least there was one bright spot so far in my exile.

I was still staring at her when we stepped through a large hatch into an oven, snapping me out of my trance and making me look around for the first time with some semblance of alert attention.

"And this," Lin said to me, "is engineering. Apologies for the heat, sir. The climate controls down here are a bit temperamental."

"And the blasted ion drive gives off more heat than my mother-in-law's temper," a man's voice said from behind a bank of controls. A broad ruddy face peered around the console, and I found myself looking at the polar opposite of Petty Officer Jacobs. The man now in front of me couldn't have been taller than 160 centimeters, with drab brown hair and pasty white skin blotched with red. But he had laugh lines around his eyes and a smile on his face that instantly made him more likable than the bully giant I had encountered in my quarters earlier.

I threw a quick look around the room to make sure Jacobs wasn't there with us—he wasn't—then turned my attention back to the short man in front of me.

"Sorry, Captain, I'd salute, but I'm trying to fine-tune the reactor's containment field, and if I take my hand off the dial, we may all regret it."

I laughed lightly; I didn't find the man's banter funny, but I knew he would be worried if I didn't at least chuckle. But by the confused look on his face and the semi-horrified look Lin shot my way before she composed her features, I guessed that maybe he *hadn't* been joking after all.

"This is Lieutenant Commander Kelly O'Malley," Lin said, nodding toward the short man.

"Kelly O'Malley?" I asked incredulously.

The man shrugged with one shoulder, hopefully not the one supporting the hand still adjusting the reactor's containment field, and smiled. "I know, huh? Could I be any more Irish?" Then he ducked back behind the control panel ostensibly to keep fiddling with the reactor.

"Just give me a second, Captain," he said in a muffled tone. "And... got it!" He emerged fully now from behind the bank of controls, brushing his hands together as if to remove dust or grease from them. I liked him almost instantly, which is saying something. For the last six months, I'd hated pretty much everyone I'd met.

He reached out one of his hands, and I shook it. "Good to meet you, Cheng. I heard there's a problem with the engine." I tried to keep the hope out of my voice. My orders—at least the little I had read—said we were to leave the station by 0700 tomorrow morning for a long patrol around the outer system. But if the engines were down, we'd have to stay in dock longer, which meant access to the station's bars.

I guess I did a good job hiding my desires because O'Malley smiled and shrugged. "Don't worry, sir. She's a bit temperamental, but these ion engines got a bum rap. They're not so bad once you learn their quirks. We'll be ready to leave dock tomorrow as planned."

Lin beamed proudly at the man's statement, and the smile on her perfect face put one on mine, which O'Malley misread as pleasure at his report. Oh well, that wasn't a bad thing, I supposed.

"Good, Cheng. I, ah, assume there are department reports I can read up on to learn more about the engines and their quirks." Yeah, right; like I was going to read boring engineering reports. But the question made Lin smile again, and I was all for that happening as often as possible.

"Of course, sir. I'll have them sent to your implant." O'Malley's face took on an expression that reminded me of hope. It mirrored the expression Lin suddenly had as well.

Oh no. These poor fools thought *I* was a source of hope? They'd learn. It also meant their last captain must have been a royal loser. But I still bet I could be worse.

"Captain, it's nearing dinner time. Perhaps we can retire to the wardroom to meet the rest of your officers?" Lin suggested lightly. There went my plans to suggest that she and I have a working dinner *alone,* to help me learn about the ship…and about her.

"Sounds good, Commander," I replied grudgingly.

"If it's all right with you, Captain," O'Malley said with a frown. "I'll stay down here and keep working on the engines so we don't miss our departure time tomorrow. I can have dinner brought down to me."

"Carry on, Cheng," I said with a nod. At least that meant one less interloper to distract me from Jessica Lin.

It took us about five minutes to get back up to officer country, or what passed for it on the *Persephone.* With such a small ship, there weren't the natural divisions of territory you would get on a ship of the line or even a modest size cruiser. The little frigate made my last command, *HMS Lancer*, a battlecruiser, look palatial by comparison.

The wardroom was no exception to that. Space was at a premium on any King's ship, but the small room Lin led me to looked barely big enough to hold the two people waiting there for us. I had no idea where the commander and I would squeeze in, and I had a warm but fleeting mental image of Lin sitting on my lap at the head of the table and feeding me grapes. Carla would have slapped me for being a misogynistic pig. She'd be right, but that didn't stop me from smiling at the fantasy.

The two officers already in the room stood up awkwardly—the table's benches were so close to the bulkheads that they couldn't stand behind them, so they stood uncomfortably bent in the even narrower space between them and the wardroom table—as we entered.

"As you were," I said, more out of habit than out of any genuine care for their comfort. They sat down gratefully anyway.

"Captain Mendoza, allow me to introduce Lieutenant Junior Grade Petra Yesayan," she gestured toward a mousy-looking young woman with dirty blond hair and an anachronistic pair of glasses on her face. "And Lieutenant Senior Grade Richard Ingbar," she nodded toward a slightly pudgy-looking man with a receding hairline and a double chin.

I nodded at both of them. Lin hesitated as if waiting for me to say something. When I didn't, she continued. "Lieutenant Yesayan is our helm officer, and Lieutenant Ingbar is our tactical officer."

The man nodded back at me. "I also double as our sensor officer. Small ship, sir. We all have more than one job."

I nodded back as if I cared.

"And I double as our navigator," chimed in Yesayan in a surprisingly high and squeaky voice—well, maybe not that surprising given that I'd already described her in my head as 'mousy'.

"And you've already met Ensign Stevens," Lin continued. "He's on bridge watch right now and won't be joining us for dinner."

I almost scoffed at that. Bridge watch while *docked*? Sure, regulations demanded it, but I hadn't expected to find a bunch of rule followers on the worst ship in the King's Navy.

I took my seat at the table's head while Lin sat to my right next to Ingbar, and unfortunately, not on my lap. I cleared my throat and asked the first lame question I could think of. "And how long have the two of you been on the *Persephone*?"

Lin frowned in my peripheral vision, and I realized my mistake. As captain, I should have already *known* the answer to that question. It would have been included in the briefing packet attached to my orders. Oh well. Hopefully, they would all just think I was trying to make small talk.

"I've been on the ship for three months," Yesayan answered simply.

"And I've been on the *Phony* for almost a year now," Ingbar said with a small frown. Lin shot him a sharp look that could have powered the ion drive if the reactor ever went down.

"The *Phony*?" I asked, causing Lin's frown to deepen. But I couldn't help myself.

Ingbar shot an apologetic glance at my XO, then shrugged. "Sorry, sir. It's the crew's nickname for *Persephone*. Fitting, too, if I'm not too bold."

I chuckled. Here was the first person I'd encountered on the ship who wasn't either threatening me or trying to make me forget I was on the laughingstock of His Majesty's pointy-ended spear. Of course, Ingbar looked rather old for a lieutenant senior grade, so I'm sure he was just as much of a loser as me, but that might make him easier to deal with.

"It has a ring to it," I admitted.

Lin frowned more fiercely. But it was Yesayan who spoke first. "We've been trying to keep the crew from using it; it's disrespectful. But so far, we haven't managed to stamp it out completely." She threw a look at Ingbar that rivaled the one Lin had given him a few seconds ago. I almost laughed again.

"Well, sometimes it doesn't hurt to let the crew have their fun," I said with a lopsided grin. As I expected, anger flashed on Yesayan's face before she composed herself and nodded once to acknowledge my comment.

Lin shook her head but didn't seem quite as offended as Yesayan.

"In any event," I continued. "Tell me about your departments." It was the question they would be expecting from me. And it launched both junior officers into monologues about their few personnel and systems.

I let them talk while a spacer brought in something that looked like it *might* be dinner. It tasted worse than it looked, but I hadn't eaten since lunch on the transport, and the alcohol I'd had earlier was no help. While I ate, I nodded along and made small sounds of agreement at some parts to make them think I was listening. At one point, I thought Lin might have caught me staring at her a little too closely, but I quickly moved my head as if I'd been panning my gaze around the table and not drooling over her curves again.

All in all, the first dinner in the wardroom wasn't a total disaster. Too bad the rest of the night would be.

FIVE
TRYING TO FORGET

I'd hoped to dream about Jessica Lin when I hit my bunk that night. But I dreamed about Carla instead, back to the first time I'd seen her after the Bellerophon disaster. In the dream, I arrived home on a fast naval transport, a courtesy extended to a man of my rank, though I'd clearly been summoned back to Prometheus to stand trial for what had happened. People on the transport had treated me a bit oddly, as if they weren't sure what to do with me.

Carla was waiting at the airlock on Home Station One when the transport docked. She ran up to me the second I disembarked, wrapping her arms around me and burying her head in my chest.

"Brad, I'm so glad you're home," she said in a voice that sounded like she meant it.

I knew better. I wasn't coming home after a simple deployment or to get another promotion or even attend another of the endless military balls where her father would beam at his daughter and cast disapproving glances at me.

No, I was coming home because I might be losing my freedom. And I wasn't sure how I felt about that. Part of me resented it, of course. No one *wanted* to be court-martialed and possibly imprisoned. But the other part of me knew I deserved it. After all, my actions had resulted in about five hundred people—five hundred and four, to be exact; all innocent civilians—dead.

I pushed Carla away, refusing to meet her gaze. I said nothing, not trusting my voice, and instead gently moved her aside so I could continue walking down the corridor toward my fate...

I woke up from the dream with the same sense of futility I'd felt when I'd gotten off that transport. Except now, I felt a double sense of frustration. Because that had been the moment when I'd first pushed Carla away…when I'd first made her feel that she was no longer my wife.

Not that I could have done any differently. I didn't deserve her, and I knew it. My biggest regret was that I hadn't pushed her away more directly. What I should have done was file for divorce the second I'd arrived home on Prometheus, freeing her to move on with her life without any guilt or backward glances. After all, there was no way her dear old dad was going to let her stay married to the Butcher of Bellerophon. I knew it, and she must have known it too.

But instead of doing the brave thing and telling her right then and there it was over, I stayed silent, letting her stew in uncertainty as I turned away from her and never once let her back in. It hadn't even surprised me three months later when I'd found her in bed with Vice Admiral Clarington's son. By then, it was finally clear to her that there was no future with me.

Now I lay awake in my bunk, reliving *that* wonderful moment in my head. Even though I'd pushed Carla away and had even decided that I needed to cut her loose for her own good, it had still hurt to find her in bed with that empty-headed idiot Clarington. Without his daddy's influence, the guy wouldn't have risen to command even a transport. But apparently, a battleship captain who got his post purely through nepotism was still a better option for Carla than a disgraced murderer. I couldn't argue with her logic. Though, seeing her with another man had hurt far more than I ever could have imagined.

It was the worst mental image I retained in a long line of horrible ones from the last six months of my sorry life. And that was saying something! I'd killed a few hundred children, after all.

There was no going back to sleep now. With nothing else to do and needing a distraction, I eyed my footlocker. Getting out of my bunk, I stumbled the two steps over to it, keying it open with my personal code; it took a couple of tries, given the sleep in my eyes.

Once it was open, I reached in and pulled out a bottle. I had almost done this when I'd first returned from dinner in the wardroom. But exhausted from my travels—I never slept all that well on transports—I had exercised a modicum of self-control and gone to bed instead, telling Lin I was not to be disturbed so that I could catch up on reading the myriad of reports she and the other officers had already sent me.

Like I would *ever* read those.

Now, though, sleep fled, and I almost frantically twisted open the top of one of the bottles I'd purchased on the station, a cheap tequila. Not bothering with a glass, I lifted the entire thing to my lips and took a swig. It burned horribly going down, and I almost gagged, but I took another sip afterward and then another. I'd always hated tequila, but the pain was oddly comforting now.

I lost track of the number of swigs I took, but it at least helped me mostly forget the image of Carla in bed with Clarington.

I have no idea when or how long I passed out, but I woke up to find myself on the floor of my cabin, lying in something wet. I groaned when I saw the tipped-over tequila bottle, the contents I hadn't drunk all over the floor near my bunk and soaking into my skinsuit. There was a little vomit mixed in as well. That bottle, along with the other two I'd brought aboard, needed to last me for the entirety of the three-week patrol me and the *Phony* were set to embark on in the morning. But just like that, a third of my liquor supply was gone.

Suddenly, a pair of shoes appeared in front of my face. My first panicked thought was that Lin had found me passed out in a pool of alcohol and puke. That would surely hurt my chances with her. But even in my fogged and drunken state, I recognized the big feet of a man. Wincing at the pain it caused in my neck, I peered upward to see an older salt with graying hair and an enlisted man's uniform frowning down at me.

"Who the...?" I started to ask, but a fit of coughing cut it off.

"Sir, I'm Warrant Officer Hoag," the intruder said in a deep baritone voice. "Ship's supply officer...and your steward."

"My what?" I knew what he'd said. But ships the size of *Persephone* usually didn't warrant a warrant officer *or* a steward. 'Warrant a warrant officer.' I might have laughed at my own internal play on words if my brain weren't so foggy.

"Your steward, Captain Mendoza," the man said with a pronounced grimace. "I'm sorry I wasn't on board when you first arrived. I was securing the last of our supplies from Gerson Station Control, and I just returned to the ship a few hours ago. I was coming to get you for breakfast, but you didn't answer my knock."

"Well…" I started. But then I trailed off; I really had no idea what I was about to say. And I was still lying on the ground, not my preferred position from which to say anything pithy.

"Sir, we're due to leave dock in a little over an hour. With all due respect," funny how people who said that usually didn't say it with even a modicum of actual respect, "we need to get you cleaned up and on the bridge."

I didn't argue. I was too wasted to do so. Instead, I let Hoag lift me off the floor and help me into my personal head, where I promptly vomited again, missing the head but spraying his shoes quite liberally. Minutes later, I was naked in the tiny shower, with no memory of how I'd gotten undressed.

Shortly after that, I was drinking a cup of the blackest, strongest coffee I'd ever tasted, all under the watchful and blatantly judgmental eye of Warrant Officer Hoag.

He said little else to me that I can recall. But somewhere around my third cup of coffee, I remembered to feel at least mildly embarrassed for the state he'd found me in. I even mumbled an apology for throwing up on his shoes.

Hoag left after that and returned a few minutes later with a plate of breakfast. Given how terrible dinner had been the night before, I was loath to even try anything on my plate, but my new steward slash overseer wouldn't let me get away with skipping breakfast. Using few words but many stern looks, he made it clear I was expected to eat *everything* on my plate.

So, I did. And it was shockingly good. Maybe they'd executed the cook who had dared to serve us the slop for dinner last night and somehow replaced him with a magical unicorn who used the black arts to turn the Navy's powdered eggs into something that tasted better even than the real thing. Either way, I didn't care. I'd shoot the other cook myself if it paved the way for whoever had prepared this breakfast to take over all cooking duties on the Phony.

Before I knew it, I had cleaned the plate. Then I barely made it to the head before I threw up again. Lovely.

SIX
SOMETHING IS SERIOUSLY WRONG HERE

I groaned inwardly as I stood on the bridge of my new command, looking forlornly at the tiny space with only four duty stations in addition to my command chair. I'd once served as the tactical officer on the expansive bridge of a Hera-class fleet carrier. *Persephone's* entire bridge could have fit into just the space I'd had for my tactical station there.

And it was kind of dirty. Dust covered some of the controls, and there was an unknown grease on one arm of my chair and a weird-looking stain on the floor next to it. I saw Commander Lin blush when she noticed me studying it.

Hoag had gotten me mostly sober and on the bridge before the scheduled time for us to depart the station. But semi-sober didn't mean free of a massive migraine that had me squinting at the bright lights on the bridge.

"XO, tell Gerson Control we are retracting docking clamps and moving away on thruster power."

Lin acknowledged my command—I'd learned she included comms officer amongst her many duties on the bridge—and crisply relayed the message.

"Helm, fire port thrusters at ten percent," I commanded, and

Yesayan confirmed the order after a slight hesitation. I knew what was bothering her. Ten percent power was a bit much for an undocking procedure; usually, five percent was more than enough to move a ship far enough away from a station to light up its main drive. But I'd ordered ten percent *because* I knew it would bother Yesayan. I had so few joys left in life.

"Captain, message from Gerson Control," Lin said with a weird measure of excitement in her voice. "Happy hunting, *Persephone*."

I wanted to snicker. It was the traditional send-off for a ship leaving station, and I had heard it hundreds of times before. But it suddenly struck me as ridiculous in this situation. First of all, a piece of junk like *Persephone* wasn't going to be *hunting* anyone. The best we could do if we encountered trouble was to call in reinforcements and run the other way while we hoped the finicky ion drive didn't crap out on us. And second of all, there would be nothing *happy* about this voyage.

But I sensed that actually laughing out loud would break Lin. She looked so eager and shiny about leaving port that I could almost believe she *wanted* a dull patrol of the outer system. But whether it was affected or not, she looked spectacular while she sat at her station and watched the forward viewscreen, so I decided just to enjoy it and not burst her bubble.

"Engineering," I called, the bridge's AI automatically relaying my voice down to the ship's depths. "Is that ion drive ready for me, Cheng?"

"Yes, sir!" came the overly enthusiastic reply from O'Malley, and I couldn't help but shake my head slightly. "Ready when you need her, Captain."

Fine, even if I had been praying that we'd have a last-minute malfunction that would keep us on station for another day or two. Heck, if I was lucky, we would have had a catastrophic failure that would have put us in dry dock for the next three months. But apparently, I was cursed with a good chief engineer or just the worst luck of any captain in the history of the King's Navy.

Either way, we were due for our date with some random dust cloud out past Gerson's asteroid belt. Maybe we'd see smugglers if we were really lucky. Or unlucky, from my point of view.

"Very well. Helm, prepare to go to one-third power on the main drive," I said reluctantly.

Lin twitched at her station as if I'd slapped her. "Uh, sir. Don't you think you should say a few words to the crew before we light up the main drive? Maybe tell them our orders…or introduce yourself."

Ugh. Lin may be hotter than most movie stars I'd ever seen, but she was starting to get a little annoying.

"Oh, of course," I answered lamely. "Open a ship-wide channel, please, XO."

She nodded and motioned to me that it was done. I hesitated, then started talking.

"Ladies and gentlemen, this is Captain Brad Mendoza speaking. I have taken command of *His Majesty's Ship Persephone* as of…" I checked my implant, "1700 hours yesterday. Our orders are to embark on a routine patrol of the outer system for the next three weeks, after which we will return to Gerson Station for resupply and redeployment. That is all."

I motioned for Lin to cut the channel. She did so, but I could see from her face that she was disappointed in me. What had she been expecting, some grand speech? As if it would mean anything to the screwups on *this* ship. That thought quickly made me picture the massive Jacobs laughing at any speech I did try and make. I promptly thrust that image aside and focused back on my XO. She was still looking at me and frowning.

Oh well. I couldn't please everyone. Maybe she would want to talk about it later, in private, maybe in my quarters.

That mental image I did my best to keep around, all the way to the outer system.

Dinner that evening was significantly better than it had been the night before. I learned that Hoag was normally the cook on *Persephone* but that he'd been gone last night, as he'd told me, securing the ship's final supplies. That had left a spacer second class to cook dinner in his absence, and the results had been abysmal. But now that Hoag was back, I had to admit that this voyage might have a bright spot, apart from Lin's extraordinary derriere. My new steward was an excellent cook, somehow turning even boring and semi-disgusting naval rations into something that wasn't just edible but actually enjoyable.

Lin was silent at dinner. Apparently, my less-than-inspirational speech when we'd left station had upset her more than I'd counted on. She wouldn't even meet my gaze.

Yesayan, on the other hand, was glaring at me. I'd pegged her right for a rules stickler, and my little stunt overpowering the thrusters to undock had her tied in knots. At least I'd been able to crush the hope they'd both had in me; better to set expectations early.

I was making friends all over the place. Luckily, O'Malley joined us tonight, along with Ensign Whats-His-Name—the dumb one who seemed happy to be on the *Phony*. Ingbar had the bridge watch. So, the gregarious chief engineer did most of the talking, prattling on about some fine-tune adjustments he was making to the ship's artificial gravity. Something about gaining a few extra g's of acceleration on the upper end with better inertial dampening. I tried to pay attention; I really did. But it had been a while since I'd had to keep to a fixed schedule. Drinking myself into oblivion in the months since my court martial hadn't exactly required me to be up at a particular time in the morning.

So, I barely made it through dinner without falling asleep face-first in my pasta. Which would have been a shame. Hoag had somehow gotten his hands on *fresh* tomatoes to use in the sauce. Where he got those on an orbital station was beyond me, but I wasn't going to argue with the man's results.

Dinner finally ended, and I stood up and made a weak excuse about paperwork I needed to get done. There *was* paperwork—it was an eternal struggle for ship commanders to keep ahead of the virtual piles of it—but I had no intention of actually doing any of it. I just desperately needed to sleep.

Unfortunately, my XO had other ideas. Lin followed me out of the wardroom, and I was halfway back to my quarters before I realized she was right behind me. Turning to face her, I tried not to let my exhaustion and frustration show. I'd daydreamed of her following me back to my cabin, but by the look on her face, this was *not* the circumstance I'd been fantasizing about.

"Yes, Commander?" I prompted, raising my eyebrows both to look inquisitive and to keep my eyes open.

She stopped in her tracks, looking momentarily abashed but then visibly squaring her shoulders and looking me in the eye. "Sir, I wonder if you and I might talk? In private?"

Inwardly I sighed. But outwardly, I nodded. "Of course, Commander. Let's use my office."

I thought an impromptu confrontation with Lin would be the worst of my problems that night, but just before we reached my quarters, we ran into Petty Officer Jacobs.

I must admit that in the last day since taking command, I had largely managed to irrationally convince myself that I wouldn't often run into the man on the ship. Ridiculous—there were only twenty-four of us on the entire *Persephone*, after all. This wasn't a battleship with its crew of two thousand or even my old battlecruiser with its crew of eight hundred. This was a tiny frigate, and the only thing smaller than the crew was the space for that crew. We were all literally living on top of each other.

Jacobs was coming down the corridor in one direction as Lin and I approached from the other. Upon seeing us, he sneered and seemed to square his shoulders to take up *more* of the narrow corridor. I was suddenly left with two undesirable options. I could either make way for him by pressing myself against the corridor wall—as the ship's commander, that would be directly against protocol and a terrible precedent to set. Or I could meet him, engage in a contest of wills, and see if I could get him to make way. If he did, I would win a small victory. If he didn't, things could escalate very quickly.

I have to admit I almost immediately settled on the first option. Better to lose a little face than escalate things, I guess. But then I happened to glance back at Lin and saw that she had cast her eyes down to the deck and turned a shade or two whiter. She had gone from the posture of a somewhat confident—or, at least, angry—and beautiful woman to one very reminiscent of a dog I'd once seen whose owner regularly beat it. And seeing that transformation made my blood suddenly boil.

In the last six months, I had lost virtually all of my self-respect. But seeing a pretty girl threatened still managed to ignite some righteous indignation in me. I suppose it was the last little part of my honor I hadn't managed to snuff out.

"Ah, Mr. Jacobs," I said firmly as the man approached. His sneer didn't go away. "I'd hoped to run into you." Now he looked confused but managed to keep a disdainful grin that no longer reached his eyes.

"What of it, Mendoza?" he asked belligerently. It was an odd response. What of what? But I rolled with it.

"Mr. Jacobs, you will address me as 'Captain' or 'Sir' as long as I am your commanding officer. That aside, your behavior in my cabin yesterday was completely unacceptable. You are to report to the mess at 0400 tomorrow morning to clean it, top to bottom. I *will* be inspecting it."

He faltered for a second; then, his face turned red.

"You can't…" he started to say, but I cut him off.

"I can, and I will, Mr. Jacobs. And unless you'd like this to become a daily chore for you, you will carefully watch your next words." I didn't know I still had that in me, but old command habits apparently don't go away completely just because said commander turns into a worthless screwup with no self-respect or future.

He frowned, but I could tell he was considering all the angles. I had reached him now, and we stood in the corridor squared off with each other, less than a meter separating me from those vice-like hands and forearms that could surely crush the life out of me. Luckily for me, he chose not to argue. Then he did something that surprised me. He gave way, moving to the side of the corridor with his back pressed to the bulkhead so we could pass, which I did, careful not to meet his hateful gaze.

I had moved past him and heard Lin's footsteps behind me. Then I heard something else that was completely out of place in the corridor of a warship. It sounded like a smack. But it wasn't the sound of someone hitting a bulkhead as they tried to move around another person in a corridor; it was a sound that even my foggy brain almost instantly identified as a hand against cloth-covered skin, specifically in a fattier part of someone's body.

I whirled, and by the look on Lin's face, I knew my impression was accurate. Jacobs had slapped Lin on the butt when she'd passed him! I opened my mouth to reprimand him, my anger rising, but then I saw the pleading look in Lin's eyes and shut my mouth just as quickly. Jacobs just leered at her from behind.

I turned and proceeded the remaining distance to my quarters, my XO following behind still like a beaten dog. Something was seriously wrong on this ship! And I was going to find out what.

SEVEN
SO MANY MISTAKES

We got into the outer office in my quarters, and the hatch shut behind us. I didn't even take my seat or invite Lin to take one; I whirled and regarded her from just half a meter away—that was all the standing room there was in the small space.

"OK, Commander," I said. "Spill it. Just what is going on between you and P.O. Jacobs?"

She looked down, refusing to meet my gaze. For a long moment, she said nothing. Then she shook her head. "Nothing, sir. Just a personal matter. It's none of your concern."

It was my turn to shake my head. "*Everything* that happens on this ship is my concern, Commander Lin."

That was a mistake. She looked up at me now, a fire in her eyes and a hard set to her mouth. "Really, sir? Permission to speak freely?"

"Granted." My second mistake.

"With all due respect..." Again, how come people only use those words when no actual respect is implied? "...how can you say that when you don't seem to care about *anything* happening on this ship? Do you realize you called Ensign Stevens by the wrong name three times at dinner tonight? Or that the punishment duty you just gave Jacobs isn't a punishment for him at all? That mess will be sparkling clean by the time you inspect it, but I guarantee Jacobs himself won't be the one to clean it."

I wanted to stop her there and dig into that, but I didn't speak up fast enough and missed my opening. My third mistake. She continued.

"You don't seem to care about yourself or anyone else on this ship. You think I couldn't smell the alcohol on your breath this morning on the bridge? And if I smelled it, so did the other officers. I realize you may not respect yourself, but please do us the courtesy of respecting this ship and its crew."

"Are you done?" I asked the question with a lot more anger in my tone than I'd intended. My fourth mistake.

"Yes, sir!" She said it with such vehemence that it momentarily left me speechless.

When I found my voice, it lacked its prior confidence. "He smacked you in the hallway, didn't he?"

She grimaced, confirming it for me. "Again, sir. It's a personal matter. I will handle it."

I raised an eyebrow. Not everyone can raise just one, you know. I'd always been proud that I could do it quite well. "Commander, that's a major breach of protocol. Enough for a court martial."

"You would know," she muttered under her breath, but we were close enough for me to hear it. I chose to ignore it. Probably the first thing I'd done right in this entire terrible conversation.

"Commander Lin. Is there something going on between you and P.O. Jacobs? Some sort of romantic entanglement?" Ugh. My fifth mistake. By the anger and shame that flashed across her face, I'd hit the nail on the head. But she violently shook her head.

"Sir. There is nothing you need to concern yourself with."

"Really, Lin? *Him*?" Uh-oh. Sixth and, by far, my biggest mistake, and I knew it as soon as the words left my mouth.

Her face turned even harder, and she took a step forward, forcing her to look up at a sharper angle right into my eyes. "What, sir? Mad because it's not you? Note from a woman subordinate: you've spent more time looking at my chest and butt than my face since you came aboard, so you can't be one to talk. Who I choose to get…entangled with is none of your business!"

That wasn't true, strictly speaking. It was a major breach of naval regulations for Lin to be romantically involved with *any* subordinate, including P.O. Jacobs. That I'd been hoping forlornly for the same kind of relationship with her myself—an even bigger breach of regulations given my position as captain and hers as my XO—was beside the point right now. But how to tell her that? I was so shocked by her brazen calling out of my leering gaze that I was left speechless. And extremely embarrassed on top of that.

I mean, I suppose that it shouldn't have surprised me that a woman can tell when a man is undressing her with his eyes. But I'd never been called out on it before, so guess I'd fooled myself into thinking that the women I looked at that way didn't notice or that perhaps I was good enough at hiding it that they never caught on. And I'd managed to largely stop doing it at all after I'd met Carla, at least with women other than her.

But apparently, I was wrong. And I'd managed to turn what was actually a semi-well-meaning intervention—by the way Jacobs had made her cower in the corridor, it was clear that any relationship between Lin and the brute was not weighted in her favor—into an indictment of my own actions.

That hurt. No good deed goes unpunished, I suppose. But Lin was right; I'd lost any moral high ground from which to judge her actions.

She didn't wait for me to respond or even to dismiss her. She spun on one foot, threw the hatch open, and stormed out of my office and into the corridor, slamming the hatch behind her.

I caught myself watching her rear end as she did so. If I could have punched myself out, I would have done so in that moment.

EIGHT
THE DETOUR

"Captain, we're on station at the first waypoint," Lt. Yesayan said from the helm.

I'd managed not to come onto the bridge this morning smelling of alcohol. Not because I hadn't drunk myself into oblivion the night before. I was quickly draining my supply of liquor. I imagined that, on a ship with *Persephone's* reputation, the enlisted spacers probably had a hidden still somewhere. But the last person they were likely to want to share its output with would be their captain. It was going to be a serious problem. Bad things happened to me when I didn't drink.

No, I didn't smell like alcohol this morning because I'd remembered to take one of the anti-hangover pills I'd brought onboard in my footlocker. Technology had come a long way in the thousands of years since man had first invented alcohol and drunkenness, and those pills were probably my favorite invention of that whole period. Not only did they do a fairly good job of driving away the headache and nausea that were common after a bender, but they also managed to mask the stench on one's breath, but only if I remembered to take them *before* I started drinking.

I'd also shaved this morning for the first time since coming on board. But that hadn't been my idea. Hoag had made it clear when he'd woken me up that if I didn't shave myself, he would do the honors...with a straight razor he kept soaking in pure rubbing alcohol. I think he mentioned using salt as an aftershave as well. I knew he was messing with me—maybe—but it was enough to make me elect to do my own shaving.

The man had even managed to press my uniform. I was almost insulted. It took a lot of work to make a *skin*suit look rumpled and wrinkly. I was mildly proud of my capabilities in that area until Hoag ruined my streak.

"Thank you, Lieutenant," I responded to Yesayan. My words only slurred a little; the stupid pills didn't take care of that little problem as well as I thought they should. "Lieutenant Ingbar..." Had I gotten the name right? "Please conduct a full scan of the area, protocol four. Once done, we will move to the second waypoint."

Boring. Seriously, nothing was more tedious than an outer system patrol. Space was *huge.* And the chances of us happening to stumble upon a pirate or smuggler in the vast expanse of an outer star system weren't just low; they were virtually nonexistent. The only thing an outer system patrol was really good for, everyone knew, was to show the flag. The idea was that the mere presence of a warship on patrol would send the pirates and smugglers scurrying away with their tails between their legs.

I'd dealt with a few pirates and smugglers in my time. They *weren't* the type to be worried about the infinitesimally small probability that a single warship on patrol would see them, much less be in a position to catch them. And even if they were, I couldn't imagine *anyone* being the least bit intimidated by the *Phony.*

"Captain, may I suggest we randomize our pattern?" It was the first thing Lin had said to me in the three hours since we'd all been on the bridge for the day watch. Even as she said it, she didn't look over at me. I'd been careful to keep my eyes off of her, mostly. It was far more challenging than it should have been. I was pretty sure that at some point in my life, I'd had far more self-control than this. After all, I'd once been a happily married and entirely faithful husband.

But a lot can happen to you after you kill five hundred innocent civilians and drive your wife into the arms of another man.

"Explain, Commander," I prompted. It wasn't unheard of for a warship to vary its patrol pattern away from the fixed waypoints and timings, but it also wasn't the norm.

Lin didn't respond immediately. I wasn't looking over at her. I'd found a spot of discoloration on the opposite bridge bulkhead that I had spent a large chunk of the morning studying intently for that very reason. I was really scrutinizing it now. It kind of looked like a jellyfish.

"Sir," she finally said, her voice brimming with uncertainty. "I have no confirmation of this, but there have been…rumors that our patrol patterns have been leaking out of Gerson Station."

Now I *did* look over at her, but I was proud of myself that my entire focus was on her face—her perfect face with those stunning eyes and plump lips…

I literally shook myself in my seat, like a dog, drawing a sharp look from Yesayan. Lin ignored me. Ingbar was either too busy doing his sensor sweep, or he was playing a game with his implant. Either was equally likely.

"That's quite an accusation, Commander," I said. "Any evidence to back it up?"

She finally looked over at me, frowning, and for a moment, I thought she might back down and retract her suggestion. But she seemed to find a modicum of inner strength instead. "No, sir. At least none worth sharing. But even the rumor makes me think we should take precautions. If we vary our pattern even a little, we might catch whoever is trying to use the information to get through our patrol cordon."

Unlikely. We could completely randomize our pattern and still have almost no chance of seeing anyone. Or…

"Helm," I addressed Yesayan. "If someone knew our patrol pattern and schedule and wanted to enter or leave the system in the furthest possible place from where we are *supposed* to be, while also avoiding other patrols and the planetary sensor network, where would they go?"

I could see the woman's eyes go out of focus as she interfaced with her implant. It only took a few moments before she refocused and looked over at me.

"There are three possibilities, Captain," she said, her squeaky voice somehow crisp and professional. How did *she* end up on the *Phony*? I had my suspicions, but that's all they were. "First option is an approach between Hellguard and Heavengate." Those were the names of two gas giants in the system. I quickly checked my own implant and saw that they were at one of the closest approaches to each other in their respective orbits. A ship approaching the system between the two of them would be able to use their bulks to mask its sensor signature from a good portion of the system's scanners.

"Second option would be to approach from the leeward side of Gerson itself." That made sense and was pretty standard. Approaching from the 'leeward' side of the system's star would put that star's heat and bright fury between the approaching ship and the sensors of the one inhabited planet in the system, Gerson 3. Funny that they gave the creative names to the gas giants and not to the actual settled world.

"And the third?"

Yesayan hesitated as if she were having second thoughts about sharing her conclusions with me. But then she continued. "Well, sir. If it were me, I'd approach straight through waypoint eight."

I frowned. "And why is that?" Something nagged at my sleep-deprived and still somewhat drunk mind. I felt like I should *know* the answer to my own question—that I *would* have known it just six months ago—but it wasn't coming to me now.

"Sir," she responded. "When most patrol ships randomize their patterns, they still follow the same general direction around the system. Waypoint eight is a quarter of the way around the system from where we are now. And we're not scheduled to be there for another two and a half weeks; it's the last stop on this patrol pattern. *If* we're dealing with someone who has our schedule, what better way to ensure we won't be in their way than by choosing the place where they *know* we won't be now? But because we *will* be there later, we're likely to discount it in our after-patrol reports. So, it means they can continue to use that route because it would tacitly be declared 'secure' by system command."

She'd only done a passable job of explaining herself. Too many words and the circular reasoning made my head spin. But she also made sense, even to my sluggish brain. I thought that maybe I'd misjudged my helmsman and navigator. I'd pegged her as a rule-following stickler, but she was showing some creative thinking right now that surprised me.

"Commander Lin, your recommendation?"

Lin looked surprised. Had the last captain—I suddenly realized I'd never even bothered to learn the previous captain's name—never asked her for her opinion? Or was she just surprised that *I* was asking for it?

"Sir," she hesitated only briefly, "I think we should proceed to waypoint eight."

I shrugged. "Ok."

Both of the women looked at me with shocked expressions. And I was almost certain at this point that Ingbar *was* playing a game on his implant; I'm not even sure he knew we were having a conversation.

"Finish up the scan here and then proceed to waypoint eight, three-quarters speed." That would put us at the other waypoint, which was pretty far away, in oh… Never mind. One of the first skills I lost when I became a drunken failure and murderer was the ability to do math in my head. Luckily, Yesayan apparently still remembered how to do it, or she cheated and used her implant.

"Yes, sir. At that speed, we will arrive at waypoint eight in thirty-one point-five hours."

"Very well." I stood up from my chair. "I'm going to catch up on some administrative items. Commander Lin, you have the conn."

I wasn't actually going to go do paperwork, but a sandwich sounded pretty good right about then.

NINE
A TERRIBLE DISCOVERY

I'd almost forgotten about the punishment I'd inflicted on Jacobs the day before, but I was hungry, and thinking about the mess reminded me that the man was supposed to have cleaned it. I decided to kill two birds with one stone and made my way there.

When I arrived, Jacobs wasn't there, but four spacers were. I vaguely remembered seeing one of them somewhere before on the ship, but the other three were new faces to me. All four stood in surprise when I entered the mess. Technically, this area was for the enlisted men and women. My being here bordered on a breach of protocol, though more so of tradition than any actual regulation. The enlisted spacers needed a place they could go where their captain wouldn't be looking over their shoulders.

"As you were," I waved them all down. They sat hesitantly, not taking their eyes off me.

Hoag appeared out of nowhere, wiping his hands on a towel and giving me a look that clearly conveyed that *he* wasn't pleased to have me there and that he recognized the breach I'd worried about. But whatever; it was my stupid ship.

"Chief," I nodded to him. "I asked Petty Officer Jacobs to clean the mess this morning." I looked around. The room *looked* pretty clean, but never having seen it before, I had no reference point to know if it was always like this or cleaner than usual.

"Aye, sir," Hoag responded. "The mess was cleaned this morning."

The way he said it recalled to me Lin's comment from the night before.

"Chief, did Mr. Jacobs clean the mess as ordered?"

Hoag didn't respond immediately but glanced over at the four enlisted men who were trying very hard to listen to every word without *looking* like they were listening to every word.

"Sir," he said slowly. "It is my understanding that Petty Officer Jacobs' duties required him to be elsewhere this morning, so he delegated the duty of mess cleanup."

I was afraid of that, and I couldn't say that Lin hadn't warned me. Of course, *delegating* a disciplinary duty like Jacobs had done was grounds for a charge of insubordination. Technically, I could now throw him in the brig. But the expression on Hoag's face and the way his shoulders tensed, along with the anticipatory smiles I saw on the faces of two of the enlisted men at the nearby table, threw up warning signs that could even get through my special brand of stupidity. There was something at play here that I wasn't fully aware of.

"Very well, Chief," I said. "I am glad to hear the mess was cleaned. I will be sure to…extend my thanks to Mr. Jacobs for his work."

Hoag's shoulders visibly relaxed, and one of the two smiling enlisted men smirked.

Just what was happening on this Crown-forsaken ship? Did I want to know? Did I *care* to know? I wasn't sure.

But I was sure that I was hungry. So, I asked Hoag to make me a sandwich. I have no idea how that man made dehydrated turkey and cheese taste so good, but I was seriously thinking that if things didn't work out with Lin, maybe I could marry my steward. At least then I'd never go hungry. I took the food and headed back to my cabin.

The surreal experience with Lin and Jacobs the night before, along with the strange energy of the enlisted mess, finally convinced me it was time to actually read the personnel files that had come attached to my orders. Heck, maybe it was even time to read my *orders* in their entirety.

I started there and was interested to find that my orders were pretty explicit on not only the waypoints I was supposed to patrol but the order and timing in which I was supposed to patrol them. These weren't part of the original orders but had been appended by Captain Wainwright. I'd actually never seen patrol orders that gave so little latitude, and that technically meant that I was now insubordinate for following Lin's recommendation to vary our pattern.

Oh well, what were they going to do to me, assign me to the *Persephone*?

But it did make me think that maybe there was something to Lin's concerns about leaks. If all the patrol orders in this system were so strict, anyone with access to those orders could pretty much come and go as they pleased without risking entanglements with the Navy. It almost made me curious.

Next, I read the personnel files. Delaying the inevitable foray into Jacobs', I decided to go by descending order of rank. I thought that would mean starting with Lin, but O'Malley was actually senior to her by date of promotion by almost two years.

His file was boring. He'd done little of note, either positive or negative, in almost twelve years of naval service post-Academy. Reading his file actually put me to sleep for a little while.

When I woke up, Lin's file was next. Early on in reading it, I was confused by why she was on *Persephone* in the first place. She had high marks in the academy, scoring well in both command potential and tactical capabilities. She'd served with distinction on the battleship *HMS Hood* for her noob cruise just after graduation.

She'd been promoted quickly from ensign to lieutenant and had served in the Combat Information Center (CIC) of *HMS Faraday*, a heavy cruiser, where she had seen actual combat against pirates in the Ophelia system.

Her third assignment had been as a tactical officer on the destroyer *HMS Ordney*, where she'd also been promoted to lieutenant senior grade, a full year ahead of the normal schedule. But then, abruptly, her rise to the top had halted.

For reasons that had been redacted from her file, even for me, she'd been transferred from *Ordney* to a station desk job in the Lightman system. She'd stayed there for two full years, an unheard-of amount of time on desk duty for any officer worth their salt. She'd returned to combat duty on *HMS Ulysses*, another destroyer, where she'd eventually been promoted to lieutenant commander. But as far as I could tell, that promotion had been based not on merit but on simple tenure. She'd reached enough years as a lieutenant senior grade that naval regulations and tradition demanded she either be promoted or drummed out. The powers that be had chosen promotion but then almost immediately transferred her to *Persephone*. She'd been on the dead-end ship now for almost a year and a half.

What had she done on *Ordney* that had halted her career advancement so drastically? And why had it been scrubbed from her file?

Before I could wonder too much at the question, my implant pinged me. It had found supplemental files on Lin in the previous captain's personal logs on *Persephone*. As the new captain, I was granted access to those files by default. Did I want to amend those to her record?

I accepted the prompt, and the first thing that popped up was a video file. My implant asked if I wanted to play it, and I accepted again.

I had picked up a cup of coffee as the video started to play. I dropped it pretty quickly, spilling it all over the floor of my cabin but barely noticing.

I won't describe the video. I wish *I* hadn't had to watch it, but I had to be absolutely sure what I was seeing. Even so, I had my implant scan forward several times to avoid some of the more sordid details.

Needless to say, I now had ironclad proof that Jessica Lin was sleeping with Petty Officer Jacobs. And from everything I could tell, it *wasn't* consensual.

And it wasn't just Jacobs. My implant had helpfully supplied a second video, which showed much the same with another man I had never seen, but whom my implant helpfully identified as Commander Yancy Jessup, *Persephone's* former captain.

For some reason I couldn't fathom, Jessica Lin had been assaulted by both men, and I had the proof. And as more video files popped up to attach to her file, it became apparent it hadn't been a one-time thing.

I may be a mass murderer, but in my humble opinion, this constituted another level entirely of pure evil. And even in my twisted and broken sense of morality, it was shocking in the extreme. My first inclination was to immediately throw Jacobs in the brig and then send a message to Wainwright to have the Navy find and arrest Jessup wherever he might be. But I stopped myself, fighting to bring my rising anger under control. Because I knew that something like this needed to be approached with a certain measure of caution.

The admiralty may try and sweep it under the rug, and they certainly didn't put it on recruiting posters, but sexual harassment and even rape of this kind was a very real problem in the Promethean Navy. I imagine it had been in every military institution for thousands of years, even back when naval ships had traveled exclusively on water. Honestly, I wasn't sure I even believed those legends; why restrict a ship to only be able to move on water?

I'd been peripherally involved in two prior cases of rape. One had been pretty clear-cut. A commanding officer had used his position to take advantage of a young female lieutenant on his ship, threatening her with a poor performance review if she didn't go along. Scared, she had acquiesced. A friend and fellow junior officer had blown the whistle. The captain had been court-martialed and sent to the stockade. But the lieutenant had resigned her commission in shame; the rumor mill of the Navy was often far worse than any legal penalties. So even though the captain had been the one found guilty, the poor woman had suffered in probably greater measure.

I knew about that particular case only from the news stories and because I'd had a friend on the same ship who had given me some extra details. It had all horrified me.

The other case had been less clean, if the first could even be called that. I had actually served on the court martial panel for this one, as its most junior member. An ensign had been raped by a chief warrant officer on her first post-academy cruise. He'd been drunk and had accosted and assaulted her on a space station when they were both on liberty. She had immediately reported it, putting her trust in the system that she believed would protect her.

The system had failed her tragically.

It had been her word against his. And his story had been that *she* had forced herself on him and demanded that he go along or face disciplinary action. She was technically his commanding officer, even though no ensign with half a brain would ever dream of giving an order to a chief warrant officer, and that automatically cast suspicion on her. Still, things should have gone her way, and I had argued vehemently in the court that the chief be convicted of all charges and dishonorably discharged with a recommendation of the maximum prison sentence.

But then politics had intervened. The warrant officer came from a family that was very well-connected in the Promethean Navy. In the end, the rest of the panel sided with him, and the woman had actually been convicted of the crime for which she'd been the victim. It was a travesty of justice and had been the first time in my naval career that I had been ashamed to wear the uniform. When she had killed herself less than a year later, I had written my resignation letter, and only Carla and my then-father-in-law Terrible Oliphant had stopped me from following through with it.

Even then, had the military judge not put the court members under a gag order, I would have taken the fight to the press. I still almost did but chickened out at the last moment. I justified my silence by telling myself I could do more to change the system from within the Navy and that getting myself discharged would help no one, including the dead woman.

It turns out that even back then, I was cowardly scum and just didn't know it.

So now, I was in a quandary. To me, the video evidence of Lin's abuse was extremely unambiguous. But none of the videos had sound—part of me was extremely grateful for that—and so I was largely making my judgment off of facial expressions and body language, which I thought made it clear that Lin hadn't been a willing participant in the encounters. But I'd seen good defense attorneys twist evidence like that around pretty handily. The experience with the unfortunate ensign whose career and life I had failed to save as a member of the court had taught me not to take anything for granted when it came to situations like this.

Plus, there was the strangely confident behavior of Jacobs himself. A man who would storm into his new captain's quarters and tell him off on day one and then smack his XO's butt in front of the same captain wasn't a man who feared being caught. He must have *something* he felt would keep him out of trouble and out of the brig. But what?

I was about to open up Jacobs' file and find out, but I couldn't bring myself to do it. The *last* thing I wanted right now was to study more about that man, especially after what I'd just seen. I told myself I'd get to it later.

Instead, I went to my footlocker and pulled out one of the bottles still stashed there. It was still the early afternoon, but now there were new things that I needed to forget.

TEN
CONTACT!

We had just arrived on station at waypoint eight, over a day later, and I was having an incredibly hard time not looking at Jessica Lin. Except it was for very different reasons than before. Now, when I saw her perfect features, all I could see in my mind was the abuse she'd sustained at the hands of at least two different men. If I could have wiped those videos from my memory, and not just my implant, I would have done so in a heartbeat. But even the alcohol wasn't obliging me in that respect.

My guilt was overwhelming, as was my shame. Not just for what I'd seen done to her but for the fact that I had been leering at her almost nonstop since boarding *Persephone*. It made me feel just as dirty as the men who had raped her. I had already known I was a good-for-nothing loser, but I felt I had now sunk even lower.

Beyond the obvious, one other thing bothered me about those videos. I'd only known Lieutenant Commander Jessica Lin for a short time, but she didn't strike me as the type of woman that would *let* those types of things happen to her. Despite some of her timidity on the bridge and with her fellow officers, she'd boldly called me out on my own leering looks at her. The type of woman who would call out her *captain* for inappropriate looks didn't strike me as the type who would let herself be abused by a man under *her* command, even if her former captain was involved.

It just didn't add up. It was like I was seeing two different people. There was a strong and direct woman who had called me on my crap, contrasted with the beaten down woman who had looked like a dog about to be hit in front of Petty Officer Jacobs in the corridor. And somewhere in the middle was the timid woman who had still had the courage to suggest the change to our patrol pattern.

I had rehearsed and discarded dozens of different ways to broach the topic with her. None of them felt even close to right. I found myself desperately wishing Carla was there so I could get a woman's perspective, but alas, I was on my own.

"Sir, beginning sensor sweep," Ingbar said lazily from the tactical station. I still hadn't been able to force myself to read Jacobs' file, but I had, after waking from my bender, read Ingbar's and Yesayan's, mostly as a way to distract myself from the terrible things I'd learned about Lin.

Ingbar's had been more of what I'd expected to see for an officer assigned to *Persephone*. Low marks at the Academy, a lackluster service record afterward, and his promotions only coming for time-in-rank, never for performance or merit.

He was a dead weight on His Majesty's Navy. Pretty much like I'd become, though without the killing of hundreds of innocents.

Yesayan's record was a bit better, but at least some of my initial assessment about her had been right. She'd gotten good grades at the Academy and even had some merit awards since. But every one of her commanding officers had arranged to have her transferred as soon as they could justify it. Several of them cited issues of 'cultural fit'. One was blunter: 'She is the most frustrating junior officer I have ever served with'. The general story was of a rigid rule-follower who harassed her commanders by spouting regulations and challenging them openly when she felt they weren't following the book to the letter.

She pretty much just annoyed anyone who came into contact with her until they were willing to give up a kidney to get her off their ship.

It even seemed that some of her promotions had come mostly so they could justify sending her to another post.

"Very well, Lieutenant," I replied to Ingbar. I was starting to like him. He almost made me look good by comparison, and he was refreshingly uncomplicated and boring. Definitely not the guy you wanted to be in your foxhole, but more like the lazy uncle who still lived in your grandparents' basement and would help you score weed as long as you left him alone. Simple. I needed more of that right now.

My head hurt, even a full twelve hours after I'd woken up. I'd drunk a *lot* last night, even for me. Not even my magic hangover pills could keep up. Hoag had to splash water on my face this morning to even get me out of bed.

It could have been humiliating, but I was too shamed already by what I'd seen to care about the added indignity of an uppity, judgmental warrant officer who knew his captain was a raging alcoholic.

At least the whiskey had helped me somewhat forget those videos, even for just a few minutes at a time.

My internal shame parade was broken by an uncharacteristic exclamation from Ingbar. "Sir! Ship detected, bearing oh one oh mark fourteen at point oh three c. Range, four point seven three light seconds."

I perked up. A ship? Seriously? Diverting to waypoint eight had seemed like a great way to break the rigidity and monotony of our mission, but I hadn't expected to actually *find* anything.

"Class?" I asked.

"Unclear. It's running a sensor jammer."

Now I was really alert. Only those with something to hide even had sensor jammers installed on their ships. Probably a smuggler.

"Helm, set a course to intercept," I ordered Yesayan, who looked excited now. Even Lin managed a smile that looked almost predatory.

I hoped they wouldn't get too worked up. If this contact proved to be anything other than a pleasure yacht with a slingshot, it probably outgunned *Persephone*. This patrol could end real quick if we encountered a genuine pirate out here.

ELEVEN
RETREAT!

"Captain, we have visual."

"Show it," I commanded, and Ingbar dutifully threw the imagery of the ship we'd been chasing on the bridge's main forward viewscreen.

My jaw dropped open. It had been doing a lot of that lately. Next to me, Lin gasped. Even Yesayan grunted in surprise. Ingbar must have returned to his implant's game; I heard no reaction from him.

I'd assumed the ship we'd been closing with for the last three hours had been either a pirate or a smuggler. But it was neither. We were looking at a full-fledged warship, bristling with weaponry, burning its way toward the inner system.

An armed pirate or smuggler would have been a challenge for the lightly armed and armored *Persephone*. But the ship we were seeing now looked to be at least of light cruiser size. And it wasn't Promethean. It was hard to tell at the distance we were at—even the most advanced cameras could only zoom in so far without losing resolution—but it reminded me of Koratan designs.

Koratas was the nation that bordered Prometheus to the galactic north, or Coreward, on the opposite side of Promethean space from

Gerson. Koratas and Prometheus had been in a state of cold war for the better part of three centuries now, but it had never risen beyond that except for a few skirmishes with only warning shots fired. The last of those had been twenty-eight years ago.

So, what was a Koratan warship doing this far away from its borders in a worthless system like Gerson? It just made no sense.

What was clear, however, was that *Persephone* would never survive a battle with the enemy ship. This wasn't some storybook where the heroes always won by figuring out some insane scheme to clutch victory from the jaws of defeat. This was real life. And in real life, the bigger ship pretty much always won.

Trying to interdict the Koratan ship would be pure suicide.

"Helm, full stop on the main drive. Execute turnover and burn at full military power back along our current vector!" I commanded.

"But sir," Lin started to argue as I felt the g forces ramp up and press me in my seat. Full military power was obviously a bit more than the inertial compensators could fully suppress.

"Keep it to yourself, Commander," I snapped, too late realizing that I was taking out my frustrations at what I'd seen earlier in those videos on their very subject. I'd entered the bridge this morning already stressed out of my mind; the enemy warship this evening was just the latest thing to send me spiraling. I tried to recover by at least explaining my order. "That ship could destroy us with barely an effort. The vital thing right now is that we get away to report the sighting and keep our ship and crew alive."

She didn't argue, so I continued in a softer tone. "Send a packet with the sensor logs and a brief summary of the contact to Gerson Station...please."

"Yes, sir," she replied, subdued. It made me feel like a bigger loser than normal.

Pushing aside my self-loathing, I turned to Ingbar. "Lieutenant, is the enemy contact changing vectors to follow us?"

"No, sir. Not to follow, but she is changing to a perpendicular vector and burning back to the outer system."

"Ok," I nodded in relief. "We obviously spooked her, and she's giving up on whatever it is she's doing here. That's good. But let's keep running for a while before we slow our burn. And keep a full sensor sweep going. She might have friends."

If I'd known how prophetic that statement would be, I might have just let that first ship kill us. It would have been so much easier that way.

TWELVE
30% CHANCE OF DEATH

I swore loudly as Lin finished giving her report. The enemy ship may have been burning on a vector away from us, with the gap widening rapidly, but it had apparently launched a probe behind it that was still close enough to jam our comms. Every attempt to send a message with the contact report to Gerson Station had failed thus far, and Lin had been at it for a full hour.

That meant one of two things. Either the captain of that fleeing ship was worried we might have reinforcements nearby and didn't want us calling them in before he or she could get away, or…

…or they wanted to keep us quiet so that they could kill us before we could report their presence. Which meant there had to be another ship out there. But that same probe was doing a pretty good job of jamming our active sensors as well. So, any other ship might be closer than we thought.

We found it twenty minutes later.

"Contact bearing one seven four mark three relative!" shouted Ingbar in a very unprofessional tone. He must have lost his little implant game; either that or he was actually paying attention to our predicament now. Without being asked, he threw the long-range camera image of the new contact onto the viewscreen.

I swore again. This also looked to be a Koratan warship, but it wasn't a light cruiser. Even my alcohol-ravaged brain recognized it as a Scimitar-class destroyer. It had an acceleration at least twenty percent higher than *Persephone,* and though smaller than the cruiser we'd first seen, it had enough armament to destroy us about fifteen times over before it even had to recharge its weapons.

It would be on us in four hours at current speeds and vectors. It would be in weapons range roughly forty minutes before that. My implant told me all of this; I still wasn't doing math in my head.

"Cheng," I opened a channel to engineering.

"Yes, Captain?" O'Malley responded, stress evident in his voice.

"Can you give me anything more out of those engines?"

His long pause wasn't confidence-inspiring, but I waited the man out. I needed him to have time to think through options. Odd how I was falling back into old habits of command. I'd have to watch out for that. I couldn't delude myself into thinking I was anything more than what I knew myself to be.

"It's risky, Captain," he finally said. "But remember when I was telling you I had some thoughts on increasing the efficiency of the artificial grav and inertial compensators?"

I vaguely recalled ignoring something to that effect at dinner a couple of nights ago. "Sure, Cheng," I lied.

"Well, I haven't tested it yet, but the ion drive itself is capable of another twenty-four percent thrust. We don't go above the set military power only because the compensators can't handle it. But if my plan works, I can probably eke enough efficiency out of the compensators for us to ramp up another sixteen percent or so."

My heart sank. "Cheng, I don't like hearing 'probably' in that sentence."

Another long pause. I knew what he was thinking because I was thinking it too. If he tried what he was proposing, and we ramped up acceleration, and then the compensators failed or even went back to normal levels, we'd all be reduced to jelly stuck to *Persephone's* bulkheads. We wouldn't even have time to process our impending deaths.

"Captain, it's risky, like I said. But I'm seventy percent confident it will work."

Well, seventy percent wasn't great, but I was a hundred percent confident that Scimitar would blow us to bits as soon as she got in range.

"Ingbar, how much time would that buy us? Enough to reach help?"

The tactical officer shook his head. "It would buy us another twelve hours. But only if we stayed on our current vector, which is aimed only slightly toward the inner system. We'd never get close enough to Gerson Station or any of the other set patrol patterns for the Navy to aid us."

Left unsaid was that the only other two ships out on patrol right now were system patrol boats barely larger than *Persephone,* and even if we had all three of us, the Koratan destroyer would have little trouble turning us all into dust. Gerson Station itself would be hard-pressed to turn back the destroyer and would be absolutely outmatched if that light cruiser joined in. And that assumed those were the only two enemy warships in the system.

But still, it would buy us some time, and the first rule of space warfare was that time meant hope. Besides, I'd wanted to die for a while anyway. I focused on that flippant thought, trying very hard not to think about the other twenty-three people I would be taking down with me.

"Do it," I told O'Malley, and we were committed…with a 30% chance of instantaneous death.

THIRTEEN
PAST SINS

Well, we weren't dead. But we were in a lot of pain. O'Malley's adjustments to the inertial compensators were enough to keep us alive, but we'd been experiencing the equivalent of seven g's for the better part of six hours now. That, coupled with the fact that we'd all been awake for close to twenty hours, made it very hard to think of ways to stay alive.

So far, my command team and I had come up with and rejected a dozen different ideas, all of them focused on escape, not engagement. None were viable.

Finally, after those six hours, I called a break, ordering a temporary decrease in acceleration below what the compensators could handle. This would give us a small amount of time to recover our over-stressed bodies and get something to eat. Ingbar stayed on the bridge, and we called Ensign Roberts up to assist him while I took Lin and Yesayan to the wardroom so we could get a change of scenery.

Hoag brought us our meal there. Unfortunately, for high-g maneuvers, regulations called for a special slurry of high-vitamin liquid rations. Not even my intrepid steward could make *those* taste good.

While we ate—or rather drank—we kept talking through the problem, ignoring the fact that we needed a mental break as much as a physical one.

"What if we reconfigured a probe to mimic our ship's signature and launched it on our current vector, then revectored our thrust and went perpendicular?" Yesayan suggested. It was a variation of two previous suggestions we'd considered and rejected.

"That's a Scimitar class," I replied for the third time. "Latest intel on its sensors suggest it would see right through the ruse, and it could then easily catch us after the vector change."

"Oh, right." It was hard to blame her. We weren't exactly a crack crew of tactical geniuses to begin with, and so many hours at high g's with an accompanying lack of sleep—it was the middle of the night now—were enough to muddle anyone's brain. Luckily the liquid rations had drugs and supplements that should counteract that for a while. The crash, later on, would be spectacular and painful, but they'd been designed with just this type of occasion in mind. I could already feel my brain clearing slightly, though my bar for that was pretty low these days.

"Korgal Manuever?" suggested Lin.

"No," I said. "We don't have any phase torpedoes."

"Right."

"Jacard's Gambit?" Yesayan again.

"No Karatan uniforms on board," Lin said with a frown.

"What about a Chitoran Slide?" I suggested with a hopeful tone, though I knew the answer. It was important to keep the flow of ideas going, even if a real option seemed out of reach.

Lin shook her head. "*Persephone* doesn't have cold reaction thrusters." I knew that, of course, but I'd hoped that maybe someone had installed them without updating my briefing packet or that maybe it was in the part of the packet I still hadn't read. No such luck, apparently.

"Sir, do you mind if I go back to my station? Sometimes I think best when I can view the vectors in a familiar setting?" Yesayan asked.

I nodded to her. "Of course, Lieutenant. Commander Lin and I will join you shortly."

Lin threw me a look but didn't argue, and we waited in silence while Yesayan exited and closed the hatch behind her.

I knew what I wanted to talk to Lin about, though why I felt the need to do so in the middle of a combat situation I couldn't explain even to myself. But I just couldn't figure out how to start.

Finally, she got sick of waiting and spoke first. "Sir, can I ask you a question? And will you give me an honest answer?"

Uh oh. "Depends," I hedged.

"Why are you here?"

It wasn't the question I'd been expecting, though it was related.

"What do you mean?" I asked, playing for time, much as we were doing with the Koratan destroyer.

"I think you know, sir. You were exonerated of all wrongdoing by the court. And you were on a fast track to flag rank, by all the stories I've heard. But obviously…"

She left the rest unsaid, but it was clear. Obviously, I was now a drunken has-been with no hope for further advancement and no shred of remaining dignity or self-respect. She was right on that, even if she didn't say it out loud. She was wrong about the exoneration.

"Commander," I started. "There's too much to explain. And now really isn't the time."

I saw her frown and hoped she'd drop it. She didn't. "Sir, with all due respect, now may be the only time. And I need to understand. You didn't do anything wrong. The military court said so. So why are you here?"

I grunted in frustration. When I spoke, my voice was sharp and angry, almost a shout, which surprised even me. "Blast the court! They got it wrong, Commander. All wrong. They swept it under the rug because my father-in-law called in some favors, not so that I could walk free but so that he wouldn't be tarnished by association with me. Is that what you want to hear? It was a coverup, all of it. I'm a murderer, plain and simple. Happy?"

"No. You're not." She spoke the words with such conviction that they surprised me and stopped my tirade in its tracks. "I had a friend on *Lancer*. If you hadn't fired when you did, the station could have been destroyed."

"It was a *refugee* ship, Commander. Over five hundred innocents dead. It doesn't matter why I fired, only that I did, and there are families who are gone because of it."

How many times had I tried to articulate that same fact to Carla before she'd left me? It had been my greatest argument that she *should* leave me, even if I wasn't prepared for the way she'd finally done it with that fop Clarington.

"Sir," Lin just wasn't going to let this go. "They wouldn't respond to your hails, wouldn't even use their lights to signal you with flash code. You had no way of knowing it was a refugee vessel, and their captain had put them on a suicide vector with Bellerophon Station. How were you supposed to…"

"A captain is supposed to know!" I cut her off in exasperation. "There were signs I missed that should have told me what I was dealing with. A ship matching her description fled Langosta space a few weeks before, loaded with Rotingan refugees. If I'd been current on my briefings, I would have known that. They had a sputter in their right engine that no self-respecting pirate or smuggler would have allowed for. And they certainly weren't a warship!"

I stopped, breathing hard, both from the topic and the long hours in heavy gravity. I'd meant to use this time to interrogate Lin about her treatment at the hands of Jessup and Jacobs, but she had somehow turned this around on me to discuss the one topic I most didn't want to discuss with *anyone*.

"But sir…"

"That's enough, Commander!" I snapped. Then I said something monumentally stupid, even for me. "While we're bringing up bad memories, want to tell me what is going on between you and Jacobs? Or Commander Jessup?"

I saw her freeze in her seat next to mine. The color drained from my face, and I wanted to kick myself. I'd meant to bring the subject up lightly, but I'd lashed out, doing anything it took to avoid discussing my crimes. Classic Brad Mendoza move, and another sure piece of evidence that I was one of the worst human beings alive.

After several silent moments, I spoke again, doing my best to soften my voice. Now that the topic had finally come up, I needed to know.

"Why didn't you report them, Jessica? Why let them do those things to you?"

"You wouldn't understand," she mumbled, almost under her breath. No denial, just resignation in her tone.

"Try me."

Another long pause. I resisted the urge to keep talking and waited her out. Maybe I still had half a brain left.

"They were going to destroy me," she almost whispered. I waited again, silently willing her to say more.

"Jessup knew about my past—about why I was sent to *Persephone*—and he threatened to tell..." she stopped with a choking sound. Tears streamed down her face. "And Jacobs...well, he's..." She trailed off, shutting her eyes hard.

"Tell what?" I prompted, seizing on the first thing she'd said.

She shook her head. "Sir, you never should have listened to me about that patrol pattern change. I'm broken, and I'll only get you and everyone else on the ship killed. That's just what I do. And I deserve whatever I get."

I opened my mouth to either argue or ask what she meant, probably both. But then the ship shuddered around us, and the vibration of the deck halted. We had stopped all acceleration and were flying ballistic through space.

FOURTEEN
A REALLY STUPID PLAN

Remember earlier when I talked about how unreliable the experimental ion drives on the Posiedon-class frigates always were?

Well, up until now, I had dared to hope that *Persephone's* drives were the exception to that rule. Turns out I was wrong to hope for anything when it came to that blasted ship. Just at the moment we needed her most, she betrayed us.

"We burned out the impeller, Captain!" O'Malley was shouting, even though I was standing right next to him. Apparently, the sound of an ion drive impeller burning out is fairly loud, enough to have seriously damaged the man's hearing.

"How long to fix?" I shouted back, though I knew the answer wouldn't be good.

He shook his head. "We have a spare, but it's not rated for full military power, just enough for us to limp into a shipyard. They made it that way so that it would take up less space in our emergency stores and because the parts are expensive. And *Persephone* is a strictly in-system patrol craft, so they figured we'd never be that far from a station if we got stuck."

In my head, I cursed the Navy and its obsession with saving space and money. I cursed the designers of the Poisedons and, most-of-all, I cursed whatever possessed me to go along with Lin's recommendation to change our patrol pattern. She'd been right about it, but she'd also been right about the fact that it had killed us all. Or rather, *I* had killed us all by agreeing to it. My ship; my fault. I wasn't so far gone I'd forgotten the responsibility of command entirely.

"How long?" I pressed my chief engineer.

"At least four hours for the swap. Have to take apart the starboard conversion bank just to get at the thing."

It was terrible news. In *less* than that time, the enemy would be on us, and *Persephone* and all of us on board her would be so many unconstituted atoms floating in space. It wasn't an exaggeration to say that it would only take that Scimitar-class destroyer a single clear shot, maybe two, to completely destroy us.

"Well, guess I better get to the bridge and see if we can run up the white flag," I said reluctantly. Because we all knew that there was no way that enemy warship was going to let us live. They hadn't responded to any of Lin's communication attempts. They continued to jam us, so it wasn't even clear if they could hear us. It was possible they might relent and accept our surrender now that our acceleration had ceased and if I used the running lights to signal our surrender in flash code. But I doubted it. We were inconvenient witnesses to whatever it was that two Koratan warships were doing in an out-of-the-way system on the edges of Promethean space, far from their own border.

Ironically, now that it was pretty much certain we were dead, I finally had some time to think about just what that might be. Why were these enemy warships so deep in our territory? And why Gerson? It was a worthless system, even in comparison to the other Fringe systems this far from Sol. Most of the people in Prometheus would never see Sol or Earth; it was a six-month journey, even in a top-of-the-line jump ship, just to get there. The general rule was the further you got from Sol, the less value a system had. And Gerson was about as far away as you could get.

The other question that came to mind was just who was *helping* the Koratans. They obviously had our patrol patterns, and our orders were written so rigidly that it was clear to me that someone intended to prevent us from doing exactly what we'd done in varying our pattern so that these Koratans would have a free path into the system.

That suggested Wainwright was in on it. She'd been prickly when I'd met her, but she hadn't struck me as a traitor. But then again, that was the assessment of a mass murderer, so I wasn't a reliable judge of character.

I said my goodbyes to O'Malley, who couldn't hear me over the ringing in his ears and was already shouting—way too loud—orders to his engineers to start swapping the impeller. It would be too little too late, but at least it gave them something to do while they waited for death. It was good to have hobbies.

It was only a four-minute brisk walk from engineering to the bridge, and in that short time, I came up with nothing even marginally satisfactory to answer my two questions. When I arrived back at my command chair, Lin glanced up at me. By the look in her eyes, I could tell she already knew about the impeller and our hopeless situation...and that she was blaming herself.

"I tried hailing them again, sir," she almost whispered. "No response. And they're still jamming our distress calls. Should we strike the colors?"

"See to it," I said. That was the order to start flashing our running lights in code, signaling our surrender. As I'd already concluded, it wouldn't work. But it was standard operating procedure, and we lost nothing by trying it. Besides, not doing things by the book would probably give Yesayan a coronary and kill her even sooner.

"Any change on that destroyer's vector?" I asked Ingbar. Another long shot. Maybe they'd gotten bored and turned away.

"No, sir. Two hours and twenty-seven minutes to weapons range intercept."

Great. We had just under two-and-a-half hours left to live. Surprisingly, in that moment, I found myself missing Carla again. When you marry someone, you sort of expect that you're in it with them until the end and that when that end comes, you'll go out together, preferably holding each other to the last second. And even though I'd driven her into the arms of another man, destroyed our marriage, and she'd been clear that she never wanted to hear from me again, it just seemed wrong to be facing my looming death without her by my side. At the same time, I was vastly relieved that she *wasn't* here to die with me and that she would live on. Weird. I figured a team of Navy psychologists could write a fairly thick book about my messed-up brain.

"Any creative ideas, folks?" I asked my bridge crew, shaking off thoughts of my ex-wife.

All four of them—Ensign Stevens had slunk quietly back onto the bridge behind me and was sitting at the usually unoccupied survey console—stayed silent, staring down at their consoles or their hands and refusing to even meet my gaze.

"What if we launched Jacobs at them?" I asked, trying to lighten the mood. Lin flashed a look that I couldn't interpret, but it otherwise fell flat.

Well, this was it then. For six months, I'd more-or-less wanted to die, and the universe had finally heard and was going to give me my wish. Too bad that I would be taking twenty-three other spacers with me. Well, too bad about twenty-two of them; I was actually quite glad Jacobs would die with me after what he'd been doing to Lin. Maybe I could convince her to shoot him a few seconds before we all died, just to get some closure before the end. Probably not; she didn't seem like the type who would want to close out her life with an act of revenge. Maybe I could shoot him, just for fun. Where I was going, a five-hundred-and-fifth murder to my name wouldn't matter all that much.

"Uh, sir?" Lin broke the silence timidly. Then she fell quiet. She'd changed since our confrontation in the wardroom; gone entirely were the glimpses of the confident woman I'd seen on other occasions, as if being confronted about her victimhood had brought that aspect of her personality front and center.

I sighed; what a time for her to get shy on me. "Yes, Commander?" I prodded.

"Well, I…uh. Never mind."

I resisted the urge to shake my head and an even greater urge to kick myself. I'd broken her when I needed her the most. Whatever idea she had in her head was probably just as dumb and unworkable as every other one we'd come up with so far, but that didn't mean we shouldn't hear it. And I was *not* going to let Jessica Lin face her death broken like this. She needed to share her idea for her own sake if nothing else.

"Spit it out, XO," I barked, imbuing my voice with all of the command authority it had once carried so naturally. Surprisingly, it worked. Lin looked up at me in something approximating shock, and I watched as her own brain went into command mode as an almost Pavlovian reaction to my order and its tone.

"Yes sir," she answered crisply. "What if we sent full power to the ion drives?"

I furrowed my brow. "What do you mean? The ion drive is broken." What I wouldn't give for a jump drive right then, but the designers of *Persephone* had neglected to install one on such a small warship. It had to be carried attached to a larger ship between systems.

She frowned, and I could see the uncertainty creep back into her face. But she forged ahead. "No, sir…I mean, yes, sir. But if we sent full power to the drive and bypassed all the safeties without an impeller, it would create a feedback loop and a fairly large explosion."

"Okay," I said, trying not to let my doubt through in my voice. "Explain, Commander."

"It could be big enough to destroy that enemy ship."

I shook my head. This really was a dumb idea. Too bad. "And big enough to kill us. Besides, there's no way that destroyer gets close enough to us to even have their paint scratched, no matter how big of an explosion we make."

"What if there was a way to get them to come closer?" I could see her face harden at my challenge. Good girl. At least my talent for pissing other people off was doing something positive before I finally died.

"OK, I'll bite. How would we do that?" I was now genuinely curious, even though I was still pretty certain it was a stupid plan. But we'd already discarded all the good and even semi-good plans. So stupid was really all we had left.

"What if they thought there was something on board worth getting their hands on, sir?"

I thought about that, examining it from different angles. For a second, my brain fell into old patterns from back when I'd actually been a good captain. Before all the murder and drunkenness. But it only lasted a few seconds and didn't yield anything. I sighed. "Any ideas on how to do that?" I asked her.

"Uh, no, sir," she said sheepishly.

"Well," I said. Maybe I could at least build her confidence up, even if the plan itself was trash. "It was a good attempt. But…"

"King's Cross!" she cried out abruptly, interrupting what would have surely been an uninspiring attempt on my part to console her on her failure. My XO now had a look of wide-eyed excitement and stared around at all of us as if what she'd said should have had obvious implications.

It probably did, but I wasn't picking up on it. King's Cross was the name of a small group of elite intelligence operatives that His Majesty used throughout his kingdom to take on the really sticky messes. But I doubted one had ever seen the need to even get close to Gerson. "Explain, Commander," I ordered again.

"What if the enemy thought we were carrying vital intel that they wanted?"

I wasn't sure where she was going, so I stayed silent, watching the wheels turn in her head.

She started speaking faster. "What if they thought we had a King's Cross operative on board? They would want to capture that operative, not kill them. There are only a handful of King's Cross agents, and each one of them has access to and knowledge of the highest level of Promethean military plans and secrets."

"True," I said, still not getting it. "But how do we convince them we have a King's Cross agent on board when they won't even talk to us? Besides, there's no way a King's Cross agent would ever let themselves be captured. They'd kill themselves first."

"Exactly!" shouted Lin, slamming her hand down on the comm console in front of her so hard I was surprised she didn't break it—it looked like it had been repaired and patched together so many times, like the rest of *Persephone*, that I was amazed it could even stand up to normal use much less her blatant assault on it.

"The King's Cross," she continued, "wouldn't let themselves get captured. They would self-destruct the ship. Which is exactly what we're going to do."

Now my head was spinning. This felt like a whole lot of circular logic; we were right back to the problem of getting the enemy close enough before they destroyed us for our self-destruction to do any good by maybe damaging them.

Luckily, Lin chose to ignore my confused look and kept talking. "If we can somehow show the enemy that we plan to blow ourselves up, it might make them think that we have something to keep away from them."

"I don't know," Ingbar said for the first time, somehow managing to sound just as bored as he always did. "It would be a huge leap of logic for them to see our self-destruction as a sign we have a King's Cross agent on board."

"Not if we broadcast the Death Cry," Lin said with a grin.

Silence. I'd call it stunned silence, but for me, it was more of a confused silence. Until it wasn't, when the little light inside my brain finally sputtered to life.

"It just might work," I muttered. The King's Cross Death Cry was a thing of legend. I wasn't even sure it was real. But supposedly, when a King's Cross operative was about to die, they broadcast a very specific message that served two purposes. First, it told their enemy whom they had bested, like a sign of respect. Second, it told their enemy they only had a short time left to live. Because, again, based on rumor, the Death Cry was also a signal to all other King's Cross agents to hunt down and destroy whoever had killed their brother or sister.

Even had we had a King's Cross agent on the ship, the Death Cry wouldn't really work when all our comms were being jammed. But if the enemy was leaving just enough of the jamming open to listen to our attempts to communicate, even if they refused to respond, it might work. Assuming, of course, that the Koratans had also heard the rumors about the Death Cry. There were a lot of 'ifs' in this plan.

"So," I said slowly, "we broadcast the Death Cry and then make it look like we're going to blow up the ship, which should be somewhat easy because we really *do* plan to do that. And we hope they fall for it and disable and board us instead of just destroying us and being done with it?"

"Yes, sir!" Lin almost shouted again in her enthusiasm. It was the polar opposite of the woman who had reacted like a beaten dog in the corridor with Jacobs and who had been sulking in silence the last few hours on the bridge. And suddenly, I had insight into what had made Lin such a great officer before whatever it was that had ended her career progression…and a glimpse of what she could be *again* if given the chance. And I could tell that she was thinking along similar lines. It felt strangely good to see her confidence flourish like that.

"And then when they get close enough to board us, we *do* destroy the ship and take them with us?" I asked.

Despite her enthusiasm, it wasn't a stupid plan; it was a really stupid plan. But it was also the only plan I'd heard today that might actually work. Besides, a stupid plan for a stupid ship and its stupid captain was probably fitting.

"But how will we destroy the ship if they've already disabled us?" Ingbar objected. His voice made it clear he really didn't like the plan. But it was a legitimate question. "And how do we get off the ship before it blows up without them seeing the escape pods?" Another very legitimate question, unless Lin was as suicidal as I sometimes got.

I looked over at my XO to see how she would answer. She was grinning widely. "Come on, Captain, Lieutenant; you expect me to come up with *all* the ideas?"

Seeing what Jessica Lin could be made me hate Jessup and Jacobs even more for what they had robbed her of, and disappointed for whatever had happened on *Ordney* that had derailed her career. Just as important, seeing her enthusiasm lit something inside of me that I'd tried very hard to forget about over the last six months.

"Someone get O'Malley up here," I said. "You may need to shout."

FIFTEEN
NOT THE WAY I PLANNED IT

You know how when a beautiful girl is happy, she gets even more beautiful? Well, Lin was absolutely breathtaking right now. I hadn't seen her happy since I'd boarded *Persephone* just days before, and now she was practically giddy. It suited her.

With some prompting from me, O'Malley had filled in one other part of the plan for us. If we shunted all reactor power to the backup batteries, he'd surmised, we should be able to store enough charge to overload the ion drives at the right time, even if the reactor itself was disabled.

So, the first problem—how we would blow up our ship and the Koratan destroyer—was mostly solved. And the solution to the second problem, that of how we'd get off the ship undetected *before* blowing it up, surprisingly came from Ingbar.

One thing we'd all more-or-less forgotten was that *Persephone*, for all her faults and weaknesses, was, in fact, a warship. She would have no chance in a standup fight with any other warship, mind you, but she *did* have missiles in her magazines. Ingbar's idea was simple: launch a broadside toward the enemy destroyer. The enemy would easily swat the missiles out of space, but it might provide just enough distraction and sensor scatter to hide the launch of our escape pods.

The only problem was that someone would have to stay behind. The ship couldn't destroy itself, and if we didn't destroy it, we wouldn't be able to damage or destroy the Koratan vessel, and it would easily then find and hunt down our escape pods.

That might have been the easiest problem to solve so far. I would stay. As the only mass murderer on the ship *and* as her captain, it only made sense. However, I surprised myself. For all of my self-loathing and even genuine desire over the last six months to end it all, I found that wasn't the reason that I readily volunteered to be the one to stay behind. In fact, I found myself oddly melancholy at the idea of my impending death.

No, the real and surprising reason I so readily agreed to go down with my ship wasn't so that I could die. Rather, as I looked at Lin, O'Malley, Yesayan, Stevens, and even Ingbar, I realized almost with chagrin that what I really wanted was for *them* to live. It was a strange epiphany for someone who had killed over five hundred innocents, to be willing to give up my own life for the sake of five people I'd only known for a few days.

In fact, my only real regret was that I couldn't keep Jacobs on the ship with me. He'd probably find a way to mess up the whole plan if I tried.

Which wasn't to say I wasn't going to do something about the man. As Lin and the other officers worked out the finer points of the plan—even Stevens had a few mildly helpful suggestions—I used my implant to compose a note to my ex-father-in-law. Oliphant might be an ogre with no redeeming qualities, but he *was* an admiral with a duly sworn duty to His Majesty's Navy. My note outlined the situation with Jacobs and Lin, as well as the involvement of Jessup—I learned from the notes in my orders that said scumbag was still alive and commanding a destroyer in the Linford system. To my note, I attached the video evidence from Jessup's logs. I still didn't know why the man had recorded the encounters, and I really didn't *want* to know. I could only hope it was enough proof to put Jessup and Jacobs away for a very long time and keep any blowback away from Lin herself.

I loaded the note onto the memory of two of the escape pods with auto-routing instructions so it would reach someone at naval headquarters and hopefully be forwarded to Carla's jerk of a dad.

Now, all that was left to do was to wait. We had twenty minutes before the enemy reached weapons range, and we had to time things just right. If we made signs of self-destruction and broadcast the Death Cry too early, it would give the Koratan captain time to think things through and realize how unlikely it was that a King's Cross agent would be traveling on a piece of junk like the *Phony*. If we broadcast it too late, the destroyer would have already launched a set of ship killers at us, and we'd be dead.

Eighteen minutes passed, simultaneously the longest and shortest eighteen minutes of my life. Then the last two minutes became very frantic indeed.

"Send the message," I commanded, and Lin pressed a single button on her console. We'd already drafted the fake Death Cry message, full of all sorts of fun little threats against the enemy on behalf of the King's Cross—Ensign Stevens surprisingly had quite a foul vocabulary—and loaded it in the buffer so it was ready to send.

Then, O'Malley sent a surge from the reactor to the ion drive. It was a big enough surge that it would show up on the enemy destroyer's sensors. But it was just under the threshold—we fervently prayed—to actually overload the broken drive and kill us all. The enemy would hopefully see it and interpret it as a failed attempt to self destruct.

The power surge didn't kill us, and we all breathed a collective sigh of relief. Now though, we had to see if it worked. We held our breath again as the Scimitar entered weapons range.

"They launched a scrambler!" Ingbar cried out in the most animated voice I'd ever heard him use. That was good; a scrambler was a disabling weapon meant to target and disrupt our reactor's containment field, shutting it down. The physics of how they work is complex, but they work quite well, especially against lightly armored ships. It meant the enemy had taken our bait. We'd have about three minutes until it hit us.

"Fire full broadside," I ordered, my voice a bit calmer than my tactical officer's. It helped that a full broadside for *Persephone* was only three missiles, and they were small, short-range anti-ship missiles that wouldn't do much damage to anything larger than a lifeboat.

The second-to-last part of the plan had arrived. We'd already loaded everyone but the officers into the pods. O'Malley was down in engineering making the final arrangements for the real self-destruct sequence, which I would have to go to engineering to execute. He would shortly board an escape pod near his station with the rest of his engineers.

Now it was time for my bridge crew to board theirs. Only Lin and Ingbar were left. I'd already ordered Stevens and Yesayan to a pod over their protest.

This was the awkward part. Or I assumed it would be, and I was half right. Ingbar threw me a sharp salute but said nothing as he left the bridge to board the pod that already held the other two officers. That left me and Lin alone.

Lin had tears in her beautiful eyes. Mass-murderer-about-to-die-and-go-straight-to-hell I may have been, but if I had to go out, I guess going out with those eyes crying for me was about the best I could hope for.

She said nothing but stood ramrod straight and saluted. Then she broke down into a vocal sob and threw herself at me, surprising me with a hug.

It was over quickly, and she rushed off the bridge and into the pod with the others before I could say anything. It was a bit disappointing to be robbed of any heroic last words, but I probably would have screwed them up anyway.

Now, I turned to leave the bridge myself and made my way to engineering, but not before checking to see that all of the escape pods had launched. Only one remained, and it showed empty; even had I wanted to, I would never have the time to reach it after I executed the self-destruct. The ship would be gone in seconds.

The lights cut out as the scrambler hit *Persephone* and took out the main reactor. I navigated the darkened corridors, lit now only by emergency lamps, so it took me a couple of extra minutes to get to engineering. At least the dim lights had their own energy storage and wouldn't steal power from the backup battery. We'd need all of that to keep our sensors going and then blow the ion drive.

O'Malley had rigged a repeater display down in the engine room so I could see the sensor picture. That way, I could time *Persephone's* destruction at the exact moment the enemy ship closed to boarding range. With luck, it would destroy them along with us. At the very least, it should damage them enough that hunting down our escape pods would be the least of their concerns. And that light cruiser was far enough away now that it was unlikely to reach us before a rescue from Gerson. If our comms couldn't reach the station, the light of an ion drive going critical surely would.

Engineering had no chairs—stupid designers—so I sat on the deck with my back to a low console to await the arrival of the Koratan destroyer and my well-deserved death.

I heard the footstep behind me only an instant before I felt the crushing blow to my skull, and everything went dark.

SIXTEEN
AN UNLIKELY HERO

I woke up to a flashing red light through my closed eyelids and the really annoying sound of something beeping. My first thought was that it was way too early for my alarm to be going off. My second thought was that I must be waking up after a bender. Any moment, I expected to feel the cold splash of water on my face as that sadist Hoag forcefully roused me before breakfast. That thought made me hungry.

It took a minute or two for me to clear my head and open my eyes. I had a massive headache, and my scalp felt funny, as if something was caked on it. Like blood? My mind cleared a little, and I remembered just enough to expect to find myself in engineering when my vision finally cleared. But when I blinked the tears away, I was shocked to see the spartan accouterments of a standard Navy escape pod.

What in the…?

Panic surged through me. If I was in an escape pod, that meant no one had been there to destroy *Persephone*! And without that, the enemy ship would surely kill all of us any second. I scrambled to the viewport but could see nothing through it but the dark of space and a few scattered stars, even after blinking several times to try and further clear my vision.

Then the red flashing light caught my attention. The comm. I pressed it, if for no other reason than to stop that incessant blinking and beeping.

"—tain? Captain? Do you read? Captain Mendoza, do you read?" I was overjoyed to hear Lin's voice—at least someone else out there was still alive—and I felt an oddly warm surge at the obvious concern in her tone before I realized that concern was probably for my failed mission and our impending doom rather than for my well-being.

"I'm here, Lin. What happened?" It was a stupid question. At least I was consistent.

"Captain!" she exclaimed, relief filling her voice and sending a warm feeling through me. It doubled when I remembered the hug she'd given me on the bridge before I was to selflessly sacrifice myself to save her and everyone else.

Then I went cold again. Something with that plan had obviously gone very wrong. However...

"It worked!" Lin was saying. "It was Ingbar. He knocked you out, dragged you to the last pod, and then launched it right before that destroyer got close enough to be damaged by the self-destruct. Then he blew up *Persephone* and took the Koratans with him."

"Ingbar?" I tried to ask, but Lin kept talking over me.

"We thought your pod had been destroyed too. It took us an hour to find its sensor return through all the wreckage. But its status shows as damaged. You lost some of your oxygen."

"Ingbar?" I asked dumbly again. Of all the people on *Persephone* to play the hero, he was the *last* one I would have expected. The guy hadn't seemed to have a motivated bone in his body.

Surprising. Somehow inspiring. I sort of both loved and hated him right now.

"With that destroyer gone, so is the jamming," Lin continued, probably having figured out by now I wasn't going to say anything intelligent in response. "Gerson Station dispatched rescue ships four hours ago, and they should be here before the pods run out of air."

Wait, hadn't she just said my damaged pod had lost some of its oxygen reserves? Maybe I would get to die after all.

But it turned out I wouldn't get my grand exit from mortality. With only one person on board, my pod had just enough air to get me rescued.

I found I wasn't all that disappointed.

SEVENTEEN
THE KING'S CROSS

I sat quietly in the outer waiting room of the naval offices on Gerson Station. I'd been released from the med bay after a quick treatment for the nasty head wound Ingbar had given me—for a hero trying to save my life, he sure came close to killing me—and had been immediately summoned to Wainwright's office.

But I arrived to find the normal spacer at the reception desk gone. The entire place looked deserted. I could hear muffled voices in Wainwright's office, but no one answered when I knocked. So, I sat down and waited.

My entire crew, minus Ingbar, had come through our ordeal safely. Even Jacobs, though I had other plans for him.

Technically, none of them were my subordinates anymore; we no longer had a ship to be captain and crew of, but I felt oddly protective of them nonetheless. Even the ones I'd not even met in my short time on *Persephone*. So, I'd checked on each and every one of them in the med bay of the station before I'd let the doctors treat my head. The only one I hadn't been able to find was Lin, and no one knew where she was. Members of the crew thought she'd made it to the station OK, and I had seen her briefly hovering over me in my few lucid moments on the rescue ship, but she had never arrived at the med bay. It was strange and more than a little concerning, and it occupied my thoughts as I sat waiting.

The door to Wainwright's office finally opened, but it wasn't the grumpy captain I saw standing there. It was the red-headed civilian woman from the transport that had brought me to Gerson just days before—the one who had given me the look of death when she'd caught me checking her out. She was pretty, but now that I'd seen Jessica Lin, there really wasn't a comparison.

"Ah, Captain Mendoza," she said with a nod. She stepped out into the antechamber, and I was shocked to see Wainwright exiting behind her, or more accurately, *being* exited. Two burly enlisted men held the captain by each arm and bodily dragged her from her office and through the outer hatch. I was too surprised to say anything, and Wainwright didn't meet my startled gaze.

"Captain, if you will?" the red-haired woman said, gesturing into Wainwright's office.

Stunned into silence, I stood and followed her in. She took up position in Wainwright's chair and indicated I should take the chair across from her. It was surreal, as she was wearing civilian garb and sitting in a naval station commander's chair.

"Who are you?" I finally found my voice. My head was pounding still, but the question didn't sound quite as stupid as was the norm for me.

She smirked, a sort of half smile that reminded me of the proverbial cat who had just eaten a mouse. "You caused quite a stir over the last few days, Captain Mendoza," she said, ignoring my question. "First, you disobeyed direct orders and took your ship to the wrong waypoint. Then you discovered a Koratan incursion into the Gerson system. Then, somehow, you managed to take out a destroyer ten times your size with a broken-down ship. I have it on good authority that was *Persephone's* one and only verified kill in her seventy-three years of service, and it was the first enemy naval warship kill for our entire *Navy* in the last decade! And after all of that, you managed to get yourself knocked out and thrown into an escape pod for a last-minute rescue."

She stopped, letting all that hang in the air. It was a fun little recap of what I already knew. But I decided to keep my mouth shut and wait her out.

The redhead smirked again. "Don't worry, Captain. You're not in trouble, at least not with me. That was some bravery and ingenuity the likes of which I can appreciate. If you weren't the Butcher of Bellerophon, you'd probably be getting a medal after all this."

She paused again, eyeing me with a raised eyebrow. I guessed it was my turn to speak.

"Who are you?" I repeated my earlier question. So much for not sounding as stupid as usual.

"Tell me, Captain," she asked, ignoring my second attempt to interrogate her, "whose idea was it to use the King's Cross Death Cry to trick the Koratans? Was it Commander Lin?"

"Depends on who's asking," I said cautiously. I wasn't about to throw Lin under the bus if this strange woman had some issue with how we'd stayed alive.

Now she smiled with *both* sides of her mouth. "Relax, Captain. As I said, I'm not here to get you or Lin in trouble. Though some of my colleagues don't like it when someone else pretends to be a member of our little group, you're in luck that I actually got a kick out of your approach. Be sure to tell your XO that I'm impressed and that she should consider this redemption for what happened on *Ordney*."

I seized upon that and opened my mouth to ask her to explain what *had* happened to Lin on *Ordney* that had derailed her career, but then I stopped. Had this strange woman just admitted that *she* was an agent of the King's Cross?

Now, her expression turned serious. "In all honesty, Captain, you and your crew did exceptionally well. I was already here investigating rumors that someone in Gerson was passing on top-secret information to the enemy, and you solved the case for me. I shouldn't be telling you this, but just a few months ago, there was a large deposit of stellarium discovered in Gerson's asteroid belt. We'd managed to keep it quiet, but the Koratans somehow found out and were keen to move in and take the system."

My mouth fell open; that was my go-to move now. Stellarium was the rarest metal known to humanity. Just an ounce was worth enough to buy a modest-size *town* on Prometheus. And it was the absolute best material for the manufacturing of warship hulls; it had properties that made it resistant to energy weapons and even allowed it to absorb a small nuclear detonation without breaking apart. The entire Promethean Navy didn't have a single ship with a Stellarium hull; it was rumored no one did in the Fringe systems. The only known deposits were all much closer to Sol.

If Gerson had a deposit of the metal, and depending how large, it had just gone from the most worthless system in all of humanity to perhaps the most valuable.

I had so many follow-up questions, but my head hurt too much, so I just sat there with my mouth agape.

"I see I have your attention," she said wryly. "We kept this thing so secret that not even the Navy was supposed to know. We knew that the second we moved a fleet toward Gerson, it would alert everyone in the Fringe to our discovery. The plan was to quietly move a few ships into the system over the next two months and then send Third Fleet by on their normal patrol of the outer territories and have them stay here.

"But we got intel that someone in the system had leaked the discovery, though we didn't know to whom they were leaking it. It appears now it was to the Koratans. And your decision to divert from your patrol pattern and actually *find* the enemy, along with the strangely strict wording of your orders, pointed us toward Wainwright as the turncoat. She just confessed…after some persuasion. Somehow, she'd found out about the stellarium and decided to cash in and reap some of the massive windfall it will create by selling us out to the enemy."

I said nothing. I was getting unexpectedly good at looking like an idiot with my mouth open, so I decided to keep practicing that skill.

"Well, Captain, I can see that I've rendered you speechless." Then her smile abruptly disappeared. "But we have another problem that I need to discuss with you: Lieutentant Commander Lin's future."

My heart sank. I should have known something was wrong when no one had seen Lin since arriving on the station. It was enough to break me from my silence.

"Where is she? What have you done with her?" I used my command voice.

The King's Cross agent wasn't impressed. She smiled sadly. "I've done nothing with her apart from sequestering her in a cabin on the station where no one will find her. It's actually *you* who has done something to her."

"Me? What are you talking about?" I demanded, my voice losing its professional tone.

"That message you loaded into the escape pod memories," she said with a frown. "It was downloaded into the station naval computer and read by multiple personnel here *and* forwarded to the outer communication beacon before I could intercept it."

"So what?" I asked angrily, surprising myself at how worked up I was getting, even in my half-dazed state. "The Navy needs to know what's been happening to her. It's wrong on so many levels. I did what I did to make sure she gets justice, and I would do it again. Even the King's Cross can't suppress that kind of information." They probably could, but I was pretty ticked off right then.

"Calm down, Captain!" she snapped, all smiles gone. "Remember to whom you speak!" Her command voice was better than mine. Then her tone softened. "Besides, I'm trying to *help* you and Lin, not hurt you. But unfortunately, the Navy already knew what was happening on *Persephone*."

My mouth fell open again. Yes, again. I was becoming predictable.

She frowned and nodded. "You really didn't read the personnel records for your new command, did you? Petty Officer Nedrin Jacobs. Except that his mother's maiden name is Worthington."

My heart fell into my stomach. "You mean...?" I couldn't even finish the question.

She nodded sadly again. "Yes, *those* Worthingtons. Nedrin Jacobs is the nephew of our Royal Highness, His Majesty King Charles the Eighth of the Royal House of Worthington, Defender of the Realm, and Lord of the Federated Systems of Prometheus. And my boss."

Oh no. I was screwed.

EIGHTEEN
A MURDERER'S DEATH

So, I guess that being a scoundrel and a rapist was enough to get you knocked from an officer's rank down to enlisted, no matter who your mommy was, but not enough to get you court-martialed or even stopped from continuing your crimes...at least if you're the King's nephew.

Now, Jacobs' blatant approach to me on that first day on *Persephone* made perfect sense. Except, idiot that I was, I'd never actually read his file. So, I had no idea the fire I was playing with when I'd exposed him and Jessup for what they'd done to Lin. By the way, it really had been Jessup who had started the whole affair, using some sort of leverage he held over Lin to force her into his bunk, but he'd convinced Jacobs to join in, mostly to keep himself safe by association. Then he'd filmed it all probably to make sure Jacobs couldn't weasel out of charges without also getting Jessup free. And it had worked.

And as Agent of the King's Cross Heather Kilgore had pointed out to me in Wainwright's former office, by accusing the King's nephew of rape, I had quite literally guaranteed my own death and that of Lin. The accusation needed to be quieted quickly, lest it become a scandal for the Crown. In fact, Kilgore told me she expected to receive the orders herself to kill the two of us as soon as the King got wind of my message to Oliphant. That was if Oliphant didn't order it himself first. There was already a fast courier ship on its way to Prometheus with the news, along with an urgent request for reinforcements against the Koratan incursion.

I suppose it should have surprised me that my ex-father-in-law was in on the whole thing; he'd known for months what was happening to Lin, and other women, at the hands of Jessup and Jacobs, and he'd done nothing. It *should* have surprised me, but I'd never liked Carla's dad, even when I'd been crazy about her.

All that was highly unfortunate. But there was one small way in which fortune smiled on us. Heather Kilgore had a conscience. Or perhaps, as she'd said, Lin had just really impressed her with the genius plan to save the crew of *Persephone* and destroy that Scimitar. Either way, Kilgore had decided to help us, so long as we were out of her sight and reach before she got the official orders to kill us, that was.

Apparently, her morality only extended to bending her orders, not breaking them.

And that's how Captain Brad Mendoza and Lieutenant Commander Jessica Lin died, me from complications related to my head wound, and her from radiation poisoning from *Persephone's* destruction that somehow hadn't affected anyone else in her escape pod.

It was strange being dead. After sort of wishing for it for a while, it was surprisingly anticlimactic. I imagine there was a small service of some kind. Maybe Carla even cried into Clarington's shoulder. I hope it soiled his dress uniform.

But I guess that either way, it didn't matter to me. I wasn't in attendance. I was dead.

Funny, though, just a few hours after my meeting with Kilgore, a small merchant freighter left Gerson Station. More accurately, it was stolen by parties unknown. On board were two individuals with identity papers that proved they'd never been part of the Promethean Navy.

One was an absolutely stunning young woman with a still-secret and complicated past, and now a new confidence and zest for life after she'd saved the lives of twenty-two others with her brilliance. And the second was an unshaven drunk. Did I mention he was also a mass murderer? Or maybe he wasn't anymore. I'm not actually sure how new lives work. Do past sins carry over?

Luckily, the Navy didn't have any ships handy at the station to send after the stolen craft, or I might have found out. And then another funny thing happened. No one could actually figure out to whom the stolen ship had belonged in the first place. It was a nice ship; it even had a jump drive, a rarity for a craft so small. But its registry and prior ownership were nowhere to be found. And without a wounded party, no one could really muster up the enthusiasm or even a good excuse to chase it.

Apparently, the King's Cross really can do just about anything they want.

My only regret in the whole affair was that I didn't get to add a five-hundred-and-fifth murder to my tally. Jacobs got to live and apparently keep doing terrible things to people. But at least Lin was free of him, and her spark was back. And maybe I'd find him someday and shoot him anyway, just for fun. Murderers get to do stuff like that. Or better yet, maybe I'd simply hold him while Lin shot him.

Either way, life would never be the same. But my old life ended terribly anyway. Maybe the second time around would be better.

But let's be honest; I'm pretty sure I'll find a way to screw it up.

THE END OF BOOK ONE

THE WORST SPIES IN THE SECTOR

BOOK TWO

PROLOGUE

"Brad, you're an idiot."

How come people always feel the need to tell me that? It's not as if I don't already know! As I've said many times before, my stupidity is an incontrovertible fact!

Yet nearly everyone in my life seems intent on reminding me of it at every opportunity. My ex-father-in-law, the illustrious windbag Admiral Terrence Oliphant, was always especially fond of explaining to me in very colorful ways how little he admired my intelligence. My ex-wife, Carla, toward the end, said it not with words but with her eyes. I know that sounds dramatic, like something out of a cheap romance novel. But Carla had a way of conveying entire *epic poems* with just her eyes. I used to love that about her until those poems turned into indictments against me.

Even my own mother, the day after my divorce was finalized, told me straight to my face just how dumb I was for driving my wife into the arms of another man. Gee, Mom, I'm pretty sure Carla had something to say about that choice. But listen to Paula Mendoza tell it, and I may as well have physically pushed Carla into bed with that dandy Horace Clarington, and somehow, in the process of falling, she lost her clothes along the way!

Yes, many people have called me dumb, stupid, idiot, and a host of more colorful synonyms in the last six months, but *none* of them hurt me as much as these four simple words do now.

Perhaps it's because the person who just called me an idiot is quite literally the *only* person in the galaxy I can now count on as a friend, partner, or even acquaintance! After all, everyone else, even my mother, thinks I died in the Gerson system three days ago.

So, I look up from where I'm sitting on my bunk on board our new ship, the *Wanderer*, at the lithe but somehow looming figure of Jessica Lin, who just finished giving that simple yet scathing opinion of me. I've known her now for a very long and eventful week, yet every time I see her, it still takes my breath away. She's shorter than me, about 175 centimeters, with straight black hair and other Asian facial features. And *everything* about her, from her face to the curve of her waist into her hips, is absolutely *perfect*. But she's mad at me right now, so she's… crying? Wait, why is she crying?

I was expecting Jessica to be glaring angrily at me and the nearly empty bottle of scotch I just finished downing in a vain attempt to escape the reality of my death. But I'm surprised to find no anger in her expression. Instead, her stunning face is wet with tears that run in rivulets down her cheeks.

Now, any heterosexual man will tell you, at least if he's being honest, that few things can evoke emotion in a man more than the sight and sound of a woman crying. I know it sounds sexist, but it awakens some kind of primal instinct in us from way back in the day when we lived on only one planet, and men were expected to defend the honor of their women by throwing rocks at each other or slapping each other with little white gloves. Or something like that; I never listened in history class. If it didn't have anything to do with flying through the stars and shooting stuff with really big lasers, I was never all that interested.

But now, I get to feel a new and exciting emotion! One that I haven't allowed myself to feel in quite some time:

Shame.

I get unsteadily to my feet and look again at the bottle in my hand. There are a few last milliliters of scotch left sloshing around in the bottom, and they call to me with their sweet promise of oblivion and forgetfulness. I yearn to take them up on their offer.

But then I look back up at the tear-streaked face of Jessica Lin, and I reach out to her with the hand holding the bottle. She understands, taking it from me and putting it behind her back, where its siren song doesn't call out to me quite so strongly.

"OK," I say, trying extremely hard not to slur my words. "Let's go figure out what we're going to do now that we're dead."

ONE
THINGS COST MONEY

Do you know how much it costs to run a starship? I didn't.

When your entire adult life is spent in the Navy, trivialities like the cost of operating the ships you serve on don't often come up. When you need fuel, a tanker is there to provide it. When you need more missiles, a tender comes alongside, and you're good to go. When your uniform wears out, you get a new one from the quartermaster. When you need booze, you find whatever still the enlisted spacers have set up, and you 'confiscate' it and the product. And on and on and on.

Oh sure, I had my life outside of the Navy with Carla while we were still married. But she handled all the money, and we always seemed to have enough of it. I always suspected that good ole Terrible Terrence was giving her money on the side to augment my meager officer's salary. The Oliphants are kind of a big deal in Promethean society, and they have a lot of money from mysterious sources. They didn't always, but somehow Carla's dad went from rags to riches, all while on a government salary. Sketchy, I know.

OK, honestly, I *knew* that my father-in-law was giving us money on the side. I just never wanted to admit it, even to myself. There's an aspect of pride to being an adult where you really do want to provide for yourself and your spouse without accepting anyone else's charity. But I also knew when I married her that Carla had expensive tastes. She had *so* many shoes in her closet and still bought new ones all the time. So, she obviously took her daddy's money and didn't tell me, and I never asked. And we both lived more-or-less happily with the fiction of it all.

Until we didn't, but it wasn't money that drove us apart. It had more to do with me becoming a mass murderer. But I digress.

Anyway, what I really mean to say is that I'm realizing now that I more or less have no *clue* how the real universe works. I don't know how to pay bills or even what those entail for running a starship. And the thought of learning about that stuff gives me a headache…or maybe that's still the hangover from yesterday or the day before. They all blend together sometimes.

Either way, I'm not about to go build some spreadsheets or something boring like that to figure out just how broke Lin and I are. Because running a starship is *expensive*. I know enough to be daunted by that. There's fuel, water, foodstuffs, thruster reaction mass, toothpaste, soap, and booze. We can't forget the booze. Agent of the King's Cross Heather Kilgore, when she let us steal *Wanderer* from Gerson Station—I suspect it was a ship set aside for her personal use while there—was kind enough to leave a few bottles of the good stuff in the galley. But what I haven't already drunk, Lin has dumped down the sink.

But booze or not, we need *money*! Otherwise, our new lives as Ben Lopez and Jennifer Kim are going to be short and impoverished. By the way, I hate the new name Kilgore chose for me; my high school bully was named Ben.

It's only been a day since Jessica took my last bit of scotch, but all this thinking about money reminds me why I hate being sober.

"All I'm saying, *Captain*," Lin says to me now in the small ship's galley, breaking me out of my thoughts, "is that the only way this is going to work is if you take charge and *be* the captain."

I regard her across the table and the steaming plate of dehydrated potatoes that desperately make me miss Warrant Officer Hoag's cooking from *Persephone*. I honestly never thought I'd miss *anything* from that ship.

"Well," I respond, spearing another soggy potato with my fork and pointing it at her for emphasis, "the thing is, I'm not a captain anymore. And you're not a lieutenant commander anymore, Jessica. We're no longer in the Navy, so we don't have to think in those terms now. We can be anything we want. Like clowns."

She looks at me incredulously. Which, of course, means I need to explain myself. I feel like I have to do a lot of that with her.

"No, seriously. I went to the circus once with my mom when I was a kid. I saw like fifteen clowns get out of a tiny rocket, and I thought to myself, wouldn't it be so cool to be a clown and travel the galaxy in a tiny little starship with fourteen of my closest friends? For something like two years, all I wanted to be was a clown until someone told me that the Navy would let me shoot things. Clowns don't get to shoot stuff."

She's still frowning, trying to decide if I'm being serious—which I am—or mocking her—which I also am. So, I do what most guys do when they've put their foot in their mouth with a pretty girl: I double down.

"Come on, Jessica. Didn't you ever want to be anything other than a naval officer? Or did you come home from the hospital saluting your parents and spouting naval regulations?"

She shakes her head. "I don't know. I can't remember back that far."

Ugh. If she's going to insist on having no sense of humor, this new life will end up being *really* long for both of us. Actually, never mind, because we'll die first from starvation when we run out of food and have no money to buy more. But we'll be bored the entire time we're starving.

"Listen, Brad," she says my name for the first time since she called me an idiot yesterday. It sounds foreign coming off her tongue as if she's totally out of place calling anyone anything other than 'sir, yes sir, right away sir!'.

"I don't remember what I wanted to be as a kid," she continues, "but I know what I am now. And even though I've been...ripped out of the Navy, I'm still a naval officer at heart. And so are you. And if we don't stick with what we know, then…"

She trails off, and I can see her eyes starting to water up. And I don't particularly want to feel like a horrible human being for making her cry a second day in a row. Even mass murderers have to draw the line somewhere. So, I decide that surrender is the better part of valor.

"Fine. I'm the captain again. Happy? But you can't be the XO, not on a civilian ship. People will get suspicious. So, you're my first mate. Got it?"

She nods, a look of relief on her face that tells me that she genuinely is grasping for a lifeline with this whole 'act like we're still in the Navy' thing. Maybe being dead is easier for me; after all, my naval career all but ended six months ago. And with Carla, I at least had a life outside the Navy for a little while. But, as far as I can tell, Lin hasn't known *anything* outside the Promethean Navy for her entire adult life. So perhaps I just need to give her this.

"Got it," she finally responds.

"Good," I say, and then I have a wicked thought. "And as my first order to my new first mate, I need you to go and figure out what it's going to cost to run this ship and keep food in the galley. Report back to me at 0800 tomorrow with your findings. Scratch that; make it 1100. I want to sleep in."

She frowns.

"Fine," I say begrudgingly. "Oh nine-thirty, and not a moment sooner!"

I've never seen anyone so happy to be ordered to go and build a spreadsheet.

TWO
PICKING A NEW CAREER (LIN RUINS EVERYTHING)

"Three weeks? Really? That's all we have?"

I try and fail to keep the frustration out of my voice. I haven't had a drink in two full days now, and going that long without has me seriously on edge. Not to mention, I slept terribly last night, knowing that the first thing I got to do upon waking was review a depressing spreadsheet. And I wasn't disappointed!

"That's what the numbers say," Jessica says hesitantly. "I can recheck them; maybe I made a mistake somewhere."

"No, no, no," I say, waving her down as she starts to get up from the small table in *Wanderer's* galley. "I'm sure your math is fine. I'm just not used to having to worry about where my next meal is coming from. It kinda…"

"Sucks?" she finishes for me with a timid shrug. "At least we have three weeks if we keep our jumps to a minimum and don't eat huge meals. I'm sorry."

I don't know why she's apologizing, but it's not a good sign. I badly need 'Confident Lin' right now, the woman who devised the plan to destroy a heavily armed Scimitar-class destroyer using the barely-spaceworthy *Persephone*. What I *don't* need is for her to go back to doubting herself. Because at least one of us needs to be intelligent and decisive, and it sure isn't going to be me.

"It's not your fault, first mate," I say in my best imitation of my old command voice. "It's just the reality of the situation. So, what do we do about it?"

She sits up straighter. I'm quickly learning that Confident Lin usually emerges when she sets her brilliant mind to solving a problem. It's why I asked her to take on the task of figuring out our finances; well, that and because it was a great way to pay her back for forcing me to keep pretending I'm a captain. But either way, Lin needs problems to solve as much as I need alcohol to drink.

"We have to stop thinking like we're still in the Navy," she says slowly, directly contradicting what she told me yesterday. I'm smart enough not to call her out on it.

She continues, "And that means we have to figure out what skills we have and how to monetize them, and quickly."

"I can play chopsticks on the piano," I say with a half-smile, trying to lighten the mood. She throws me an irritated frown like my mother did when she caught me trying to light the drapes on fire when I was eight. It turns out Confident Lin also comes out when she's annoyed with me. Great, that should be easy to maintain.

"I can drive and fight a ship," she says through her frown, "but I don't know much about keeping it running."

"Neither do I," I admit. "At least, beyond the basic engineering courses from the Academy, but you and I both went the tactics and command track, so they didn't exactly spend much time teaching us to maintain a reactor."

She nods. "But we *can* drive the ship. And probably better than most merchant pilots out there."

"Might make us good smugglers," I say, only half joking.

Lin frowns again. "No, we need to try and stay on the right side of the law; avoid attention." It's a naïve statement, considering we're in a stolen ship with fake identity papers, but I get where she's coming from. Neither one of us has the makings of a criminal mastermind.

"OK, what do you suggest then?" I need to keep her working the problem and not focusing on what we *can't* do. I don't think either of us is coping well with our sudden and unexpected deaths five days ago at Gerson, but this is the most animated I've seen her since then.

She thinks for a long moment, and I let the silence go on while I watch her mind work. Finally, she nods. "Maybe not smugglers, but we *can* be merchant spacers. This ship has a good-sized cargo hold for its tonnage. If we can haul high-margin goods, it should cover our living and operating expenses and then some."

Wanderer—it's not the ship's real name, but it's the one we've decided to use—looks about like what you would expect for a smallish merchant freighter. It's essentially two large boxes laid end-to-end for a total length of about fifty meters and an overall width of around ten. The forward box is the cargo hold. The aft box contains the main drive, with exhaust nozzles coming out the stern. It also holds the reactor and the jump drive, the latter of which is a rarity for a ship this size. On top of both boxes and running the length of the ship is the crew area, where we are now, narrower than the boxes and shaped like a flattened cigar with tapered ends.

In other words, our ship looks like a very pregnant whale. But be it ever so humble, she's home.

And Lin's right; the box that makes up our cargo hold is large for a ship this size. I've stopped enough smugglers in my day to have plenty of reference points for comparison.

So, we should be able to make a living, I suppose, by hauling cargo. It just sounds so...*boring*. While I know I should be grateful to be alive after all that happened in Gerson, like Lin, I'm facing the harsh realization that my old life as a Navy captain is over, and my new life as a civilian is off to a terrible start. Besides, the life of a cargo hauler is one of the last I would have ever chosen for myself. They don't even get to shoot stuff!

"What about hiring out as mercenaries?" I suggest hopefully. When I was a teenager, my favorite series of books was about a daring mercenary outfit who managed to save an entire star system from pirates and were paid enough to literally *buy* their own small planet. Then their leader, the dashing Billy Firebrand, managed to parlay that into building a more extensive fleet, hiring more troops, saving a princess, marrying said princess, and eventually being named the monarch of a coalition of systems that could rival anything in the Inner Rim worlds. All while he fought for truth, justice, beautiful women, and lots of money.

It was a ridiculous story, but that didn't stop fourteen-year-old me from absolutely idolizing Billy Firebrand and wanting for all the universe to grow up to *be* him. And besides disappointing my father, those stories were a big part of why I joined the Promethean Navy.

But from the expression on Lin's face, she must have missed reading the *Adventures of Firebrand's Marauders'*. Too bad; she'd make a great Princess Nikita Starshine.

"We have a few extra cabins," she says, not even entertaining my fantastic mercenary idea. I'll have to suggest it again later and see if I can wear her down. "We could haul passengers along with cargo."

I nod and don't express my deep disappointment at not being the next Billy Firebrand. "That could work. And aside from food and water costs, it would be pure margin on top of the cargo. I think it's a great idea." What I'm actually thinking is, 'Stupid Lin and her stupid non-Billy Firebrand practicality'. But even I realize I'm being petulant, so I keep those thoughts to myself.

Then she lights up at my compliment, and all thoughts of playing mercenary flee my head. Lin is stunning at her worst. In those rare moments when she's happy about something, she's absolutely breathtaking. Enough to make me forget all about Billy Firebrand, Nikita Starshine, Scooter James, and the rest of the Marauders.

"OK," she says as if it's all settled, "but the next question is where do we go to get a cargo?"

I consider her query and order my implant to bring up a map of nearby star systems in share mode so Lin can see it, too. I scan the names of the closest systems, not recognizing most of them, until one jumps out at me.

"Kate's Hope," I say.

She nods in agreement. "Independent system, known for a pretty laissez-faire government, and a shipping hub for this sector. Intelligent choice."

I nod as if I were thinking all the same things and not as if I simply picked Kate's Hope because it sounded...well, hopeful. I'm not familiar with this part of space; few people know much of what's outside their home *system*, and far fewer know of what's outside their entire star *nation*. In the Promethean Navy, we mainly studied star nations, systems, and planets we might have to fight, and nothing out this direction was ever on that list. But Lin often shows surprising depths of knowledge, and I can see why she was such a fast-rising star in the Navy before whatever happened to her on the destroyer *Ordney* ended all that.

"All right, first mate," I tell her. "Set a course for Kate's Hope and jump the ship. I'm going down to engineering to see if I can make any sense of things in case we have a problem."

She gets up briskly and leaves the tiny galley to head toward the bridge—really more of a cockpit—of our small ship. And, alone finally, I start rummaging through the galley cupboards to see if that bottle of scotch from two days ago has a brother somewhere that Lin hasn't managed to find and throw out.

If this were a story in *The Adventures of Firebrand's Marauders*, I, the hero, would have sworn off alcohol after the events on *Persephone*. I would be a fully redeemed and changed man. But, as Lin just painfully drove home, this isn't a Billy Firebrand story. And while I do feel much better about myself than I did a week ago, when I first arrived at Gerson and met Jessica, none of that has rid me of the cravings. Frankly, I'm not even sure I *want* to stop drinking. Reality is just terrible these days.

THREE
HOPE DASHED

"What do you mean we can't take your cargo?" I ask in what I have to admit is a much more frustrated than professional tone. But the guy sitting at the big desk in the tiny office off Hope Station's main concourse deserves it.

"Listen," I continue, jabbing a finger in the air toward his chest. "You have stuff, and you need to get that stuff from here to the Mondez system, right?" I don't wait for him to respond, but now I jab the thumb of that same hand into my own chest. "I have a ship, and that ship can take your stuff to Mondez, for which you can give me money. You get your cargo to Mondez; I get paid. Everyone wins. So, what's the problem?"

The shipping broker holds out his hands and shrugs, though I can tell he's annoyed that I've been speaking to him like he's a particularly dull kindergartner. "Like I told you, Captain...Lopez, was it? You haven't been able to provide me with a cargo hauler's bond or even a ship's registration. Without those, no one will trust you to haul their cargo, and you're lucky if the local constables haven't already impounded your ship over lack of ownership papers. We respect the law here, you know."

It's already been a long and frustrating day. Still, I'm not proud to say that this is where I start yelling at the guy, using some language that no proper stuffy Promethean Naval officer would ever admit to having in his vocabulary. However, I've heard my ex-father-in-law yelling at the screen during football games, so I know better. I also recently learned some new words from a really annoying but very creative ensign on *Persephone*. I try out some of those now.

Luckily, Lin grabs me by the arm and drags me out of the tiny office before I can get too deep into questioning the broker's parentage and implying some pretty terrible things about his mother. My own mother would have slapped me, but I was just getting started. Ensign Stevens would be proud.

I'm about to shake Lin off and turn around to head back into the office and deliver a devastating zinger I just thought of about the hairy mole on the guy's chin, but my first mate's grip tightens around my arm, and I look to find her staring not at me, but at something across the concourse. I turn and follow her gaze, the mole-chinned broker forgotten for the moment.

The main concourse is the largest open area of the station, and it's pretty crowded this close to the local lunch hour. But I have no trouble picking out the guy Lin is focused on, mostly because he's the only person in the place staring openly back at me. Then he starts walking toward us, his eyes riveted on mine.

My first thought is that he's a member of the constabulary that the broker we just left not-so-subtly threatened to call on us. But nothing about him screams 'cop'; not that I've had a whole lot of interaction with the police outside of Navy cops and MPs, and they're easy to spot from a kilometer away. They walk funny because they have sticks surgically implanted…well, you know.

But still, I don't think this guy's a cop because about halfway to me, he breaks eye contact and looks around furtively as if he's *also* worried about the constables. So, I decide to stay put and let him come to us. This could be interesting.

Lin doesn't think so. I can tell she's itching to run. So now I have a moral imperative to stand my ground and show her I'm not afraid. After all, as she likes to point out, I'm the *captain*.

The guy stops just a meter away from us, his eyes still on mine, though they quickly flash to Lin so he can give her a quick once over. Who wouldn't? But she's totally out of his league; I mean, the guy is shorter than she is, and he looks like his nose has been broken and poorly reset more than once. He's also bald, but not in the cool way some big muscular actors are bald; more like an accountant who wears a funny straw hat so the top of his hairless head doesn't burn in the sun.

I'm picturing the guy now in a straw hat holding a calculator when he finally speaks. "Excuse me, might you be the owners of that ship docked at airlock B32?" He speaks in a lazy, almost disinterested tone at odds with the intense way he's looking at me.

"Depends on who's asking," I respond, trying to match my tone to his like I'm already bored with the conversation.

"Owen Thompson," he says, reaching out a hand toward me and taking a small step forward.

Throwing caution to the wind, I reach out and clasp his hand with my own. If he's a cop, this would be when he uses the handshake to pull me closer and slap cuffs on my wrist. But he doesn't do that. Instead, his cold, dry hand gives mine a quick shake and then releases it.

His eyes dart around again, maybe still checking for constables. "I hear that your ship is available for hire. Cargo and passengers."

It sounds like it should be a question, but he doesn't phrase it like one.

"You hear a lot for someone we've never met," I say skeptically. Next to me, Lin stiffens at my tone; leave it to her to take offense on behalf of a random accountant who's clearly stalking us or something. But I was intentional with my statement and my tone. I want to see how this guy reacts when thrown off balance. It will help me learn more about him.

Not *everything* I do is stupid.

Owen Thompson, to his credit, takes it all in stride. Maybe he's not an accountant after all. "I make it my business to hear things," he says calmly. "And I may have an opportunity for you."

"Listen," Lin starts, "we're not interested in anything ill—"

"What my first mate means to say," I interrupt her—I'm so going to pay for that later, "is that we're pretty confident of finding a standard cargo to a nearby system. So, we're not looking for anything…special right now."

Owen Thompson doesn't visibly react. He's a cooler customer than he looks.

"Then we're in luck," he says, "I have a legitimate business proposition for you. I'm looking for passage for me and a few friends to Namora, and I wanted to inquire if I might hire you and your ship."

My first inclination is to tell him no. There's something definitely off about the guy. But then I remember just how much money we have —which is zero—versus how much we need—which is a lot—versus how many shipping brokers have already told us no today—which is also a lot.

"How many friends?" I ask.

"There are four of us. And a small bit of cargo."

I consider this. It is the best—well, the only—offer we've gotten today. I honestly don't know how we'll even pay the docking fees that this station extorts out of ships that stop here.

"And you said to Namora. Straight shot?" I quickly check my implant and see that the Namora system and its namesake planet are only two jumps away.

But he shakes his head. "No. Our cargo is in the Fiori system. We'll need to stop there on the way and pick it up."

Another quick check of the implant shows that Fiori is one of three inhabited systems that sit roughly between Kate's Hope and Namora, one jump away from each. But it's the furthest out of the three, so it's a stretch to call it 'on the way'."

Owen doesn't wait for me to argue. "What are your rates?" he asks as if I've already agreed to consider taking his business. Presumptuous of him, even if he is right.

Before we got off *Wanderer* and onto the station, I had Lin do more spreadsheet work and figure out what we need to charge to make any profit off various trips of different lengths. She loaded her dumb little spreadsheet onto my implant, so now I can look up the correct rate. But I've always been terrible with spreadsheets, and I'm struggling now to find the right number.

"Nine thousand credits," Lin says from beside me, and I barely stop a sigh of frustration. Even without her cells full of numbers and equations, I know that's *way* more than we need to charge for such a short hop. She obviously doesn't want him to...

"Agreed," Owen says without pause, sending more alarm bells through my head. Definitely not an accountant. An accountant would know better than to accept a deal like that. I'm about to open my mouth and argue, but he keeps talking. "My friends and I will be at your docking bay in an hour. I trust you'll be ready to go then."

Without waiting for a response to his sort-of question, he turns and walks away, just like that! Not even a backward glance. Leaving me and Lin to stare dumbly at each other.

FOUR
THE GIANT I WANT TO PUNCH

True to his word, Owen shows up precisely an hour later at *Wanderer's* airlock, three others with him, each carrying a small duffel bag and nothing more. He steps forward and rings the airlock chime while his three 'friends' hang back in the corridor.

I study the three I haven't seen before through the external camera before I open the hatch. Two are men, and one of those is quite possibly the biggest guy I've ever seen in person. He makes my old nemesis, Petty Officer Nedrin Jacobs, back on *Persephone*, look puny by comparison. He's tall, muscular, and pasty white with a flat, red-mottled face. I take an instant dislike to the guy. The other man is about my height and of average build, with dark skin and hair, and he looks like he might have some Indian ancestry. He's dressed sloppily, and his hair is a mess. I don't hate him quite as much as the big guy.

The third and final of Thompson's friends is a woman. She's shorter than Owen himself and has a feisty look about her, as if she's searching for an excuse for a fight. She's slim and trim with brown hair and olive skin. I like her, predictably, I suppose. I'm a sucker for a pretty face. When she turns to say something to the big guy, I catch her profile. She has a nice butt, though not nearly in the same league as Lin's.

I open the hatch and step out. "This everyone?" I ask with false joviality as I once again grasp Owen Thompson's hand. Same as before, it's slightly cold, but at least it's dry.

"This is Tucker," he motions toward the big guy first. "And that's Harris and Jules." Both men meet my eyes, but only Harris, the dark, sloppy one, gives a slight smile and nod. Tucker may as well be considering how I might taste for lunch. He probably needs a lot of calories every day.

The woman with the decent butt, Jules, just frowns when I meet her gaze as if she's evaluated me that quickly and has come away disappointed. That's good; it gets the awkwardness out of the way. I eventually disappoint *everyone*, so it's better if they know it's coming up front.

Lin isn't happy that we're taking this job, though even she had to begrudgingly admit that we really have no other options. But she's still mad at me and decides at this moment to ignore my order to stay on the ship while I negotiate the final particulars. I hear her step through the airlock hatch behind me, and the eyes of all three of Owen's friends flash to her. The big guy, Tucker, grins in a way I especially don't like.

"Well," I say to draw their attention back to me. "If you're ready to go, let me show you to your rooms. We only have three open bunk rooms, so two of you will need to share."

I'm half hoping that this revelation will make them reconsider hiring us; as much as we need the money, nothing feels right about this. But no such luck. They all seem to take it in stride.

Owen picks up the small duffel from the ground at his side and starts to walk past me through the outer hatch, but I put a hand on his chest to gently but firmly stop him in his tracks. I pretend not to notice Tucker bristle at this. Owen, for his part, shows no reaction but looks at me calmly. That lack of expected emotion sends a weird chill down my spine.

"There's, uh, the matter of payment," I say uncertainly. This is literally the first time in my life I've had to negotiate a business deal, and I'm not even sure what the protocols are.

"Of course," the probably-not-an-accountant responds as if he were expecting the question. "Half now; half when we arrive with our cargo on Namora."

I nod, though I don't know enough to decide if that's a good deal.

My implant pings me then that it's been offered a connection from Owen's. I accept and watch 4,500 credits magically appear in the new blockchain account Lin set up as soon as we got in range of the planetary internet earlier today. I fight not to show my relief that we are no longer destitute.

"Do you need to fuel up before we go?" Owen asks.

I shake my head. "We've got plenty. Foodstuffs too. We can be underway as soon as you're all on board."

He looks down at my hand still on his chest meaningfully, and I lower it sheepishly. I've faced down self-proclaimed pirate *admirals* and even actual admirals in the Promethean Navy, but being here now, out of my element, has me feeling like a new midshipman all over again. I'm unsure of even what to do with my hands now, so I hook them on my belt.

"You gonna show me to my bunk, sweetheart?" Tucker speaks for the first time, leering at Lin's chest.

I instantly feel a wave of anger, and I remove my hands from my belt and ball them into fists. I'm opening my mouth to call the whole thing off when Owen beats me to the punch.

"Tucker!" he snaps in something akin to my old Navy command voice. It's the first time I've seen him show emotion, and it startles me. "That is an unacceptable way to speak to our hosts. Apologize, now!"

Owen may be a petite accountant-type, and Tucker three times his size, but the big man instantly looks cowed. Staring down at his hands and refusing to meet Owen's gaze, he mumbles an apology in Lin's general direction.

I turn my gaze to Owen and see a frown on his face. But he gives a curt nod, then turns and resumes walking through the open airlock. Looking back at Tucker, I see him glaring at me, hatred almost brimming over in his eyes and the hard set of his mouth. But he breaks eye contact first, picks up his bag, and follows his boss—because what I just saw makes it abundantly clear Owen *is* the boss here and not just some 'friend'—into the open airlock.

Behind him goes the woman, Jules, without even glancing my way. I still watch her butt for a second or two as she passes. It's growing on me. That leaves only Harris, the one who smiled at me earlier. But he's not smiling now; instead, he's watching Tucker's retreating back with an expression of concern. Then he looks at me and Lin. "Watch yourselves," he says in a low voice. "That one…" he nods toward where Tucker has now disappeared into our ship, "Well, don't let yourselves get caught alone with him."

Before either Lin or I can ask any clarifying questions, he hurries off after his compatriots. I share a look with my first mate and shrug. She frowns, and I can see she's shaken, but she only nods in reply. I think we both have the distinct and unsettling feeling that the time when we could have backed out of this deal passed us stealthily at some point, and now we're in whether we want it or not.

But at least we have one thing going for us. Unless Owen is somehow magically familiar with all members of the Promethean Navy on sight, he can have no idea who he's dealing with.

Of course, that goes both ways. We have no idea who or what we're dealing with, either. For sure, it's not a group of traveling accountants.

FIVE
AN UNAPPRECIATED PRANK

It doesn't take much cajoling, not after the way Tucker acted toward her, to convince Lin to go to the cockpit while I show our new passengers to their cabins. I decide to take Harris' advice to heart, so I show him and Tucker to their shared room first, with Jules and Owen in tow.

Each of our crew cabins has a bunk bed, so I could have theoretically chosen any of the three to put the two men in. But I chose this one because it's the furthest from mine and Lin's cabins. There is also another…bonus to this room.

"Hey," Tucker complains loudly as he surveys the small space. "How am I even supposed to fit in that bed?"

I try not to laugh but keep an innocent expression on my face as if I have no idea what he's talking about—as if I don't notice there's a floor-to-ceiling wardrobe closet right at the end of the bunk that will prevent a tall person from letting their feet hang off the end of either of the small beds. And Tucker is *tall*.

"Tucker, you'll be fine," Owen says in a lazy voice, but it's enough to shut the big man up again. He angrily throws his duffel onto the lower bunk, glaring at Harris as if challenging the dark man to argue about being relegated to climb a ladder into bed.

Harris doesn't seem to mind, and from the small grin he throws my way, I can tell he's appreciating my unique sense of humor.

I take that opportunity to leave and show Owen and Jules to their rooms. We drop off Jules next. She doesn't even wait for me to show her the room's amenities but enters as soon as I key the door open and then shuts it behind her.

That leaves only Owen, and he frowns at me as we take the two steps down the corridor to his room. "You know," he says, his voice still casual, "you really shouldn't antagonize Tucker like that. He's actually not that bad of a guy. You just caught him in a sour mood. But I promise you there will be no trouble from him."

I try and look surprised, as if I have no idea what he's talking about. He shrugs like he doesn't care one way or the other.

Like Jules, he doesn't wait for me to show him the room. He bids goodbye at the door and then closes it behind him, leaving me in the corridor with my emotions hovering somewhere between glee at the thought of Tucker in the fetal position, trying to fit on the tiny bunk, and worry that maybe I've poked a bear once too many times. But mostly, I'm confused and worried by Owen. Something is unquestionably off about the guy, but I can't figure out what it is.

Lin is in the cockpit when I arrive, and she's even locked the door. I enter my captain's code to open it, and she turns at the sound, jumping a bit in her seat.

Now, I don't know everything that's happened to Lin in her past. I know she was a real up-and-comer in the Promethean Navy before *something* ended all that during her time as tactical officer on the destroyer *Ordney*. There was a point, while we were on *Persephone* and running from the enemy destroyer, where I thought she was about to share with me what had happened, but we were interrupted by the stupid ship's ion drive failing. Then, we were too busy saving our own lives and those of our crew to resume the conversation. Since then, I haven't found the right time to ask her.

What I *do* know is that she was being raped by her former captain *and* Petty Officer Nedrin Jacobs, the King's own nephew, for several months on *Persephone*. So, it's no surprise that a man like Tucker, who could be Jacob's larger cousin if it weren't for his gutter accent, would set her on edge. I mean, the guy puts *me* on edge, and I don't have nearly the emotional baggage that Lin has, at least not in that particular area.

"You OK?" I ask.

"I'm fine," she answers a bit too quickly. Nice try, but I used to be married. I know exactly what 'I'm fine' means. Or rather, I know exactly what it *doesn't* mean.

"I was thinking about ship security," I say as casually as I can. "I don't think we should give our new passengers access to the bridge. But, as captain, they will expect to have some access to *me*. So, my thought is that you should stay on the bridge as much as possible, with the door locked, and I'll tend to the passengers and their needs. Except when we're making a jump or docking or some such, then we should both be up here. Sound good?"

She regards me for several slow seconds, and I'm worried that she's going to argue and pierce the flimsy fiction I've set up around my reasons for the suggestion. But I'm relieved when she finally nods.

"Oh, and one more thing," I add as if it just occurred to me. "I don't think we should leave the bridge unattended, so I can bring you your meals here, and you and I can sleep in shifts." The implication is clear, despite my clumsy attempts to be nonchalant about it. This way, Lin will always be behind a locked door, either the one here in the cockpit —I keep calling it the 'bridge' out of habit, but it so isn't one—or the one on the hatch into her quarters. Safe and sound.

She nods again, with less hesitation this time, and I think I see a flash of gratitude in her green eyes. It turns out that, every once in a while, I can do something right.

I just hope she doesn't get used to that.

SIX
UNDERWAY AND OVERWHELMED

The next time I see our passengers is when I announce dinner through the intercom. I cooked. Yep. It's going to be horrible.

Not that Lin is any better of a cook than I am. Again, being Navy our entire lives, we didn't exactly make our own meals very often. And Carla and I ate out a lot, undoubtedly using her daddy's money. So, I haven't learned to do much other than rehydrate something using the auto-cook, which is exactly what I did for dinner tonight. By the way Lin wrinkled her nose when I took her plate into the cockpit, my rehydrated spaghetti turned out precisely how I expected it to.

Now, our four passengers file into the small galley and take seats around the even smaller table as I serve them their supposed meals. I'm half worried Owen will renege on the rest of our fee once he tastes the fare. But, surprisingly, none of them complain. Harris thanks me for the food. Jules grunts in my general direction. Most surprisingly, Tucker doesn't say anything at all, even though I literally handed him something to complain about on a plate!

They eat quickly and efficiently, not that there's any need to savor a meal like this. It may as well be Navy survival rations. Tucker asks, through a series of grunts and hand motions, for seconds, and I refill his plate. I don't even spit in it this time; I totally did on his first helping.

When they're all done eating and at some unspoken signal from Owen, the other three get up from the table and file past me back toward their cabins. A few seconds later, I hear a dull thud and the sound of a deep voice swearing, and I have to hold back a laugh. There isn't a ship in the galaxy designed for anyone as tall as Tucker, and his pain brings me a measure of joy.

Owen is still waiting there at the table, so I grab my own plate and sit across from my new and hopefully very temporary employer.

I have to say, my first bite of what I've cooked makes me marvel even more at Tucker's ability to keep his mouth shut all through dinner, and *especially* at his bravery to ask for seconds. It's terrible! I reevaluate my earlier thought: this is *worse* than Navy survival rations.

So, I'm half expecting Owen to complain about the food now that we're alone, but he watches me eat for a few moments and then broaches a different topic.

"How many hours to Fiori?"

I shrug and quickly check my implant. "We're still in Kate's Hope. Just under six hours more to the Fiori jump point and then another seven in transit. After that, depending on where your cargo is in the system, anywhere from four to forty hours to rendezvous and pick it up." I leave the implied question hanging in the air.

Luckily, he either takes the bait or was planning to tell me anyway. "It's at Fiori 2, on the Skytran Orbital."

I nod and consult my implant again. "So, about twelve hours from the jump point on the Fiori side. Do you mind me asking what the cargo is?"

He frowns, which is about the most severe facial expression I've seen him make since we met. "It's nothing too special," he responds. "Just some computer components we plan to sell in Namora. Pretty small crates that will fit easily in your hold. Is that going to be a problem?"

As if I have a choice at this point.

"No. No problem. As long as it's not dangerous and shows no signs of being dangerous," I almost add 'or illegal' but stop myself because I'm not sure I want to know.

"Good," Owen answers simply, then gets up and heads back to his room.

He leaves me behind with a bad feeling deep down in my gut. Because the chances that Owen is some sort of computer parts salesman are about as high as the chances of him being an accountant. There's something he's not telling me about his cargo, and I'm positive I'm not going to be happy when I find out what that is.

I look down at the remains of what is supposed to be spaghetti on my plate. I push the noodles around with my fork, but my appetite is suddenly gone. Then my implant alerts me that it's time for me to take my shift in the cockpit and let Lin get some sleep. So, I trash the remains of my plate, shove down my growing anxiety, and head to relieve my first mate.

SEVEN
STORY TIME

The next morning, after a fitful half a night's sleep, I'm back in the cockpit with an equally sleep-deprived Lin. Seems neither one of us is doing well in that department these days. In fact, I can tell that she's a nervous wreck, but she seems to calm down the longer she's locked up here in the cockpit with me. Maybe I need to suggest that tonight she just sleep in the co-pilot's seat next to me while I take my shift, but I'm unsure of how to propose that without sounding over-protective.

We made the jump successfully at the end of my shift last night, and Lin took over most of the time in jump space before I joined her this morning. We'll emerge from our jump into the Fiori system in just a little while. She keeps asking me about the cargo, and I keep dodging the subject. No need for both of us to worry, though I can tell I'm not fooling her.

So, I decide instead to tell her about what I did to Tucker, putting him into the bunk that will make him contort like a pretzel to fit. To my surprise, she's more horrified than amused.

"Ben," we've agreed to use our new names this flight, even in private; no use risking a slip in front of our sketchy passengers, "why do you insist on antagonizing him like that? He already doesn't like us."

To my further surprise and hers, I bristle at the question. "And what should I do?" I ask. "Jess…Jen, if we don't stand up to bullies like that, they'll walk all over us. The best thing we can do with that giant is to keep him off balance. That way, he always has to ask himself what we know that he doesn't that gives us the confidence to spit in his eye." I don't tell her that I actually *did* spit in the man's spaghetti dinner.

She shakes her head, and I know that she's thinking. Or, at least, I think I do. She's thinking of Nedrin Jacobs and everything he did to her. I have no idea if she ever tried to stand up to the man or if whatever happened on the *Ordney* broke her so badly that she gave in without a fight. But I am sure that if she did try to stand up to him, it ended poorly for her. And Tucker, as I've mentioned, gives off major Jacobs vibes.

"Listen, Jen," I soften my tone. "They'll be off the ship in a couple of days, and their payment will give us enough profit to go and figure out how to get the registration and bonds that all those brokers were so worked up about at Kate's Hope. Then we can start hauling cargo on the up and up. You'll see. Things are going to turn out OK."

I can tell she's unconvinced, but my head hurts this morning. It's now been *four* days without alcohol for me; I didn't even have the cash to buy more on the station in Kate's Hope. So, instead of continuing to try to reassure her, I once again change the subject.

"Did I ever tell you about the time I took down an entire pirate flotilla on *Lancer*?"

It's such a weird segue that I can tell I caught her off guard, and she only shakes her head.

"We were on an extended patrol in the Corpus Christi cluster; you know how those go: running around and showing the flag. Battlecruisers like *Lancer* are good for that. Large enough to project power but a lot cheaper to operate than a battleship."

Of course, she knows all of this, but I say it anyway. It's my story, so I get to tell it how I want, and it's one I've told countless times at the stupid dinner parties Carla used to make me go to, so there's a rhythm to it. I lean back in the *Wanderer's* pilot seat, clasping my hands behind my head and staring at the stars outside the forward viewport with a little half grin on my face as if I don't have a care in the galaxy.

"Anyway, we're on our third stop, in a little Podunk system called Poe. You ever pass through there on a patrol?" I don't wait for her to answer. "Terrible little place. One station and only a few million people, mainly in the asteroid belt. It's a mining system with pretty much nothing else going on. The one inhabited planet is barely big enough to hold atmo. So, it all seemed like a pretty dull assignment, and I was more or less using it to rotate some of the junior officers through bridge duties and give them some hands-on training.

"Well, we're about two-thirds of the way through the system when we get a distress call from one of the nearby asteroid mining operations. Turns out a pirate flotilla, six ships ranging in size from heavy cruiser to destroyer analog, had exited jump space pretty close in and were burning full bore toward their little rock and broadcasting demands that they surrender or die. Somehow, the idiots hadn't seen us yet, or maybe they weren't looking.

"So, I had us cut acceleration and revector on thrusters so that our drive plume was hidden behind the bulk of our forward hull. Then we went full stealth mode, cutting off all EM and vectoring our drive nozzles to minimize our thermal signature. It helped that we could largely keep the asteroid between us and the pirate fleet for most of the trip in." I throw in the extra details I usually leave out at dinner parties because Lin will actually know what they mean. And I put my feet up on my console now, trying harder to look like a man who isn't being eaten inside by stress and ulcers. I doubt I'm fooling her, but she seems to be relaxing just slightly.

"They didn't see us until we were almost right on top of them, and by then, they had already turned over and were close to zero-zero intercept with the mining station. Well, we pop around the asteroid, and we're on them, and I mean within spitting distance. But even *Lancer* didn't have an even chance against all six of them."

As I always do, I pause there for dramatic effect and wait.

"So, what did you do?" Lin finally asks. She speaks! Victory!

I smile wider at her.

"Simple. I broadcast in the clear. Something to the effect of, 'All task force units attack on my mark; deadly force is authorized'. Now, they can only see *Lancer*, but the way we snuck up on them, I knew their leader had to be thinking about what *else* he might have missed out in the big dark. So, he doesn't waste any time but orders his ships to full burn back along their original course. And my tactical officer uses the big, bright thermals of their exhaust to put a trio of ship-killer missiles each right into the drive nozzles of their two largest cruisers."

I look over at her, grinning stupidly. I love this story. I heard they even made it a case study at the Academy, but that would have been after Lin graduated. And I can see just a hint of interest in her eyes, so it's working as intended. I keep going.

"Well, with their two biggest ships gone and their leader along with them, it took a few minutes for the remaining four ships to decide who had the authority to surrender on their behalf. But surrender they did. You should have seen the looks on their faces when they realized *Lancer* was all alone out there. But by that time, they'd shut down their reactors and couldn't put up a fight even if they'd wanted to. We disabled the rest, and our Marines barely encountered any resistance when they boarded each ship in turn."

I stop again and wait, watching her with that stupid grin still on my face. And slowly but inexorably, I see the corners of her mouth twitch up. Then she's smiling back at me, and I have to try hard not to shout for joy. And not just because Jessica Lin is the most beautiful woman I've ever seen, and double that when she's happy. But because I also know what a dark place she's been in since, and even well before, our deaths. So, at this point, I'll take even a single smile as a major win.

"Good story," she says without a hint of irony. "But not as good as the time my captain made me lead the Marine boarding party on Cantralla 7's orbital refinery to rescue hostages being held by the Fringe Alliance terrorists."

"Oh, I've got to hear this," I tell her with genuine enthusiasm. And it turns out to be a great story, though not as good as my pirate one.

Still, it's opened the floodgates, and Lin is talking to me and laughing more than she has...well, ever. In fact, I'm reasonably certain that I've never once heard her laugh before now. I'd remember if I had; it's the most fantastic sound in the world. Like church bells on a Sunday afternoon mixed with the wind chimes at my grandpa's farm growing up. It reminds me of summer and puppies.

From there, we keep going with the stories well into the hours after we emerge from jump space into Fiori and pause only for a quick announcement on the intercom that we've arrived in-system. I tell her about the time I let a greased pig loose in Oliphant Hall at the Academy, and she tells me about putting itching powder all over the toilet seats in a men's dorm after one of the midshipmen there dumped her roommate for a first-year.

We talk and laugh until we're a third of the way toward our target station, when I finally decide, with great reluctance, that it's time for me to go make lunch for our passengers. I already let them fend for themselves regarding breakfast, and they're probably not too happy.

As I get up to leave, Lin surprises me by reaching out to grab my wrist. Looking down, I see her smiling up at me. "Ben…Brad. Thanks," she says and then releases my hand. I nod and smile back, and then I have to almost drag myself the rest of the way to the hatch because now I *really* don't want to leave.

Outside in the corridor, I take a moment to lean against the nearest bulkhead and collect myself before making my way to the galley. And in that silent moment of solitude, I finally admit to myself something that has been building in the back of my mind since the day I first stepped foot on *Persephone*.

I'm in love with Jessica Lin. But there's no universe where she will ever love me back.

EIGHT
THE OTHER SHOE

Lunch is a largely silent affair, just like dinner last night. This time, the meal is simple sandwiches using some relatively fresh ingredients that Heather Kilgore or someone else left in the galley fridge when we took the ship. Even Tucker appears to enjoy the meal more, though I did manage to spit in his sandwich again.

"How much longer?" Harris asks, drawing an undecipherable look from Owen.

"We're just under eight hours out," I tell him, ignoring Owen altogether. "We'll turn over in another two hours to make our deceleration burn."

"Excuse me for just one moment," Jules says, getting up and leaving the galley. It's the most I've ever heard her say, and I watch her —or rather her butt—go but make no move to follow. Tucker and Owen strike me as the real threats, and I'm convinced now that Owen is the one I need to watch the closest.

He finally chooses to speak. "Will Miss Kim be joining us?" At least he hasn't learned Jessica's real name.

I shake my head. "I'm not comfortable leaving the cockpit unattended. Too many things can happen to a ship that a steady hand on the controls can react to far better than an AI."

He nods to acknowledge my response but says nothing more. I set about making a sandwich for myself and then join the three other men in eating silently.

Owen finishes the last bite of his sandwich and regards me again. "Ben, there's been a slight change of plans."

It takes a second for the words to register. My mind is elsewhere, on the beautiful hours I just spent swapping stories and laughing with Jessica. But when I finally recognize what he said, I cock my head in confusion. Then I see Tucker smile and Harris squirm in his seat.

Uh oh. I'm pretty sure the other shoe just dropped.

Owen doesn't wait for me to recover from my surprise. Instead, he keeps talking, though now more to himself than to me. "Let's see, right about now."

As if on cue, Jules reenters the galley, except now she's holding a pistol in one hand and the arm of a terrified Jessica Lin in the other.

"What's the meaning of this?!" I shout, but Owen ignores me, regarding Jules instead.

"Any problems?" he asks her.

She smiles and presses her gun deep into Jessica's ribcage, drawing a pained grunt from my first mate that almost has me leaping across the room to strangle the short woman, gun or no. "Not a one," Jules says. "The door lock was a simple hack, and I don't think the two of them even have any weapons on board. Fools."

"Owen, what is going on?" I demand again.

This time, he turns his cold eyes toward me. "As I said, Ben, there's been a change of plans. Or should I call you Captain Brad Mendoza?"

I already have my mouth open to shout another question at him, but hearing my real name uttered from his lips stops me cold. Then, my heart sinks even further as he turns his icy gaze to my first mate.

"And it's very nice to formally meet you as well, Lieutenant Commander Jessica Lin."

NINE
MOTHER WARNED ME ABOUT DAYS LIKE THIS

If this were an *Adventures of Firebrand's Marauders* novel, the next thing that would happen would be Owen monologuing about his evil plan for twenty minutes, during which time Billy Firebrand would figure out his weakness along with those of all his cronies. Then, at the end of the monologue, Billy would say something clever and proceed to subdue and incapacitate each and every one of them…using only a toothpick.

But I'm not Billy Firebrand. I blame Lin for that. If she'd just said yes to us being mercenaries, we wouldn't be in this situation, and I'd be well on my way to emulating my boyhood hero.

But instead, I'm Brad Mendoza, the helpless idiot.

"Put her in her cabin," Owen says to Jules, and before I can object, the two women are gone. Now I look back over to the three men still seated at my galley table, Tucker still contentedly munching on his second sandwich and reminding me of a particularly large pig my grandpa used to have on his farm.

"Owen, what is the meaning of this?" It's the third time I've asked a variation of the question and this time, he actually responds.

"Sorry, Captain Mendoza, but I find myself in need of your particular skillset, and I couldn't think of a better way to get your cooperation. Your first mate will be fine as long as you do *exactly* what I say." Tucker frowns at this in disappointment, but Owen ignores him.

"And just what exactly do you want from me?"

He takes in a deep breath and blows it out through pursed lips as if he's contemplating a rebuilding year for his favorite football team. "Well, you see, Brad—I can call you Brad, right?" I don't respond, so he takes it as a yes. "Brad, I need a Navy man for a particular job I've been hired to do. What's more, I need a senior naval officer who understands both the Prometheans and the Koratans. And, as you can imagine, there aren't too many of those just bumming around this sector of the Fringe."

"How do you know who we really are?" Wow! Maybe I should have, you know, denied being Brad Mendoza. Instead, I've just given him ironclad confirmation, just in case he had any doubts that maybe he's taken over the wrong ship crewed by two ex-Promethean Navy officers.

"That's not important," he says with a dismissive wave of one hand. "What's important is that you're going to help us with a little job here in Fiori. And if all goes well, you'll drop us off at Namora as planned and never see any of us again. You and your former XO can go your merry ways all safe and sound. But if things don't go well..." He pauses for dramatic effect, much as I did earlier telling my pirate story to Lin. "Well, let's just say that Tucker here would really like some alone time with Miss Lin."

Tucker grins widely at that comment, which lights a fire in me. So, I do something really foolhardy. I step across the room and land the most brutal punch I can right in the big man's face, smashing his sandwich in the process.

Before I even have the satisfaction of seeing him bleed—assuming I even hit him hard enough for that; his face felt like I was punching a steel bulkhead—I hear a whoosh and simultaneously feel a hard punch to my gut. I have just enough time to register the pistol in Harris' hand and the apologetic look on the dark man's face before several thousand volts of electricity from the stun round embedded in my stomach course through my body, and everything goes black.

TEN
SO MUCH FOR BRAVERY

I wake up slowly and painfully. It takes me a moment to figure out where I am, but I finally determine I'm on the hard metal deck of the *Wanderer's* galley, staring at the ceiling. Owen and his thugs just left me lying where I fell after the stun round hit me. So nice of them.

My other senses slowly return from the sheer overload inflicted upon them, and I feel a wetness in my pants. I groan. I've never actually been hit by a stun round before now, but I fired a few at pirates during boarding actions when I was a junior officer. About seven times out of ten, the person stunned suffers a very embarrassing release of the bladder. Apparently, I'm now one of the seven. This day just keeps getting better and better.

Good, you're finally awake." A face appears in my view, peering down at me. Owen isn't smiling or gloating; he's just looking at me with the same bored, almost disinterested expression he's mostly worn since I first met him.

I open my mouth to respond, but whatever comes out of it just sounds like a series of mumbles. So, I stop talking.

"You'll be fine in a few minutes, Brad, though I can't say the same for Jessica."

I yell this time, even though it's still incoherent, and I try to sit up but can't make my arms move.

Owen waits patiently for my unintelligible raving to stop. Then he raises his eyebrows and shrugs. "Sorry, Brad, but there have to be consequences when you disobey me. It's the only way we're going to have a productive working relationship. And that means hitting you where it hurts the worst—meaning Miss Lin."

My eyes frantically search the room, hoping beyond measure that I'll find Tucker there so I can confirm he's not with Jessica right now. Owen understands what I'm trying to do and shakes his head.

"Don't worry so much, Brad. I'm not a monster. Our dear Jessica has a couple of broken ribs courtesy of Jules. I'd never set Tucker loose on the poor woman unless…" He leaves the rest unsaid, but the implication is clear. And in that moment, so is my realization that I will do *anything* this man tells me to.

ELEVEN
THE JOB

When I'm recovered enough to walk, Owen has Tucker escort me to my quarters. The big man watches with an evil grin as I quickly shed my pee-soaked clothes and shower in the room's small bathroom. He forces me to leave the door open to make sure I'm not going for a weapon that I hid in the toilet or something. Then he pulls out a random shirt and pair of pants from my closet, demonstrating his complete lack of fashion sense as he pairs plaid with stripes. It would be funny if I weren't the one looking so ridiculous…and if my only friend and the woman I love weren't sitting under gunpoint somewhere, nursing cracked ribs or worse.

Finally, dressed like a clown—and definitely not appreciating the irony of that after my previous discussion on clowns with Jessica—I'm led back into the galley where Owen is waiting for me along with Harris, who at least still looks embarrassed for having shot me.

"Are you ready to tell me what's going on?" I growl as Tucker shoves me down into one of the seats surrounding the small table.

"Of course," Owen says, taking no notice of my tone. "You see, there is a man here in the Fiori system who has some information that my employer wants very much."

"And just who is your employer?" I interrupt.

Owen frowns and shakes his head. Then he picks up a small short-range comm that I hadn't noticed before and speaks into it. "Jules, it seems that Captain Mendoza needs another lesson. Go ahead and—"

"No!" I shout, trying to stand up but encountering a brick wall as Tucker shoves me back down in my seat. "I'll stop asking questions. Just don't hurt Jessica!"

Owen regards me coldly for a long moment, the radio still at his lips. Finally, he speaks again. "Jules, wait a bit. I think our dear captain is finally starting to grasp the realities of his situation."

He clicks off the comm without waiting for a response, leaving me irrationally worried that Jules didn't hear him and may even right now be hurting my first mate. But I hold it in, knowing that if I voice my concern or ask another question, then Jessica is *guaranteed* to be harmed further.

Owen seems to read my thoughts and nods once. "Good man. Now, where was I? Oh yes, my employer wants the information this man has. And they are willing to pay me handsomely for retrieving it. But I cannot do so without your help. Which brings us to our present situation."

He pauses as if daring me to ask a question. When I don't, he continues. "The man in question, like you, is a member of the Promethean Navy. But he's offered to sell out his nation and share some very sensitive information with the Koratans for quite a lot of money. What I need from you, essentially, is to help us ID the man—you know, one Navy man recognizes the habits of another—and then convince him that *you're* the Koratan handler he's been told to expect. You'll get the information from him, give it to me, and then we'll all part ways as friends, with you another 4,500 credits richer. Any questions?"

I don't speak, sensing a trap. Owen sighs and shakes his head. "I mean it, Captain Mendoza. You can ask whatever you'd like now—within reason—and I promise Miss Lin won't be harmed."

"OK," I say slowly, not trusting this man's promises but also unwilling to upset him by not following his instructions. "What if he recognizes me? I'm not exactly an under-the-radar figure in the Promethean Navy."

"Terrific question," Owen says as if talking to an exceptionally bright preschooler. "And it's simple. He served exclusively as an enlisted man in the Layton System Patrol. The chances that you ever crossed paths are minuscule, as your records show you were never stationed at Layton. Furthermore, just in case he recognizes you from the media firestorm around the Bellerophon disaster, Harris here is going to make you look much different than you do today. Any other questions?"

"Yes," I say hesitantly, not sure if I should take the risk. But I decide to push forward. "You said I need to help you ID the man. But you have his file, right? So why do you need me for that part?"

"Another good question. I suspected reports of your stupidity were exaggerated." If only he knew. "While the changes Harris will make to your appearance will be temporary, we have it on good authority that the man we're after has made some very permanent changes to his. We're talking extensive cosmetic surgery and enough bioengineering that even military-grade biometrics won't work to identify him. All paid for by the Koratans, of course, as part of their deal with him. He only agreed to give up the information they wanted after that was done. So, he's not a complete imbecile, even if he is a traitor."

He pauses again, inviting more questions.

"Where exactly is he?" I ask, hoping the answer is what I think it will be. Because I have the beginning of a plan forming in my head, but it will only work if this all goes down in a big public place…

"All we know is he's on the Rishi Paradise Casino Orbital above Fiori 2."

Jackpot!

I've never been to the Fiori system before. All I know about it now is the little I found and read on my implant while alone in the cockpit last night during Lin's turn to sleep. Since I never expected to visit this sector of human-controlled space, the information I had loaded was pretty sparse, but it might be enough.

For example, I know now that the system has a population of five billion spread across two inhabited planets. It's part of the Leeward Republic, a collection of relatively wealthy systems with a strong enough navy that not even the Federated Systems of Prometheus would dare upset them. And Fiori is no exception to that wealth. Especially since it's one of the rare systems that can boast more than one planet capable of supporting human life, meaning most of its five billion citizens are doing pretty well for themselves.

I also know that the system's biggest export is grain; one of the planets—Fiori 1—has incredibly fertile soil and fairly stable weather and seasonal variations. You can grow almost anything there, which they do. Then they sell it, for lots of money, to pretty much everyone else.

I also know that they have a supposedly democratic local government, that their national tree is something called a Fiori Fern—sounds pretty boring to me—and that their national bird is some kind of local animal that looks like a flying badger—not so boring

But that's about it. Oh, and I know that Fiori 2 isn't as fertile, at least not in terms of soil and weather. Instead, that planet's largest export is broke tourists who return home poorer from their stays in one of the planet's many orbital and surface-level casinos. And that, I hope, is how I'm going to get myself and Lin out of this mess.

"And the casino," I say to Owen, "has how many guests at any given time?"

He shrugs. "Five thousand, give or take."

"And you expect me to just saunter in there and find this guy out of five thousand people, right?"

"We do. As I said, we believe that as a Promethean Navy man yourself, you will be able to recognize patterns of behavior that we may otherwise miss." It's a dumb idea, but I'm not going to be the one to tell him that.

"And how much time do we have to find him?"

"Two standard days before his *real* Koratan handler shows up. We've managed to delay them, but only for that long. And *they* know what he looks like even with his new face. They did pay for it, after all."

"You know," I say, mentally crossing my fingers that this will work and not upset him again, "that what you're asking me to do is nearly impossible, right?"

He shrugs again. "I don't care how hard it is, Captain Mendoza.

You will figure out how to do it, or Miss Lin will suffer the consequences. I trust in your resolve to do whatever it takes to keep her safe, if not in your ingenuity."

"Oh, I'll do it," I assure him. "But I can't do it alone."

His eyes narrow. "If you're suggesting that—"

I am suggesting what he's about to say, but I need to unbalance him a little before he can shut down the idea entirely. So, I take my biggest chance yet and interrupt him. "Do you know, Mr. Thompson, how to best draw out a Promethean Navy man? It's with a beautiful Promethean Navy woman. I guarantee you, if you let Jessica work with me on this one, your man will come to us."

He considers this for a long time, but I hold my tongue, not wanting to jinx it. That he doesn't immediately shoot down my idea is the best sign I've had yet in this conversation. Especially since I'm making this up as I go along and really have no idea how to accomplish what I just promised. But finally, almost as I'm about to lose my mind, Owen shrugs in that infuriatingly casual way he has. "Fine. Miss Lin can accompany you onto the station."

Uh oh. He gave in on that *way* too easily, and now I have to wait for the other shoe to drop...again.

TWELVE
THE OTHER OTHER SHOE

I don't have to wait very long this time. Within minutes, Jessica is brought to the galley, Jules again holding tight to her arm with a gun pressed into her ribs. By the pained look on my first mate's face, I can tell they're the same ribs the sadistic, shorter woman broke less than an hour before. It's all I can do not to punch Owen this time or leap across the room and try to kill Jules with my bare hands.

No, I need to stay calm now. It's our only hope…even if it means watching the woman I love suffer for a time.

Love stinks. Someone should write a song about that.

Shortly after Jules and Jessica enter the room, Owen motions to Harris, who gets up from his seat at the table and walks around behind the two women, his customary apologetic expression on his face. Before I can even ask what he intends, he reaches up and presses something to the back of Jessica's neck, and I hear her gasp in shock and pain.

"What did he do to her?" I ask, almost shouting, but I at least hold myself back from doing anything more rash than that, even if only barely this time.

Luckily, Owen seems to have anticipated this reaction and doesn't take it personally. Instead, he calmly explains. "Now, you didn't think I was going to just let you and Miss Lin disappear into a crowded casino with only your word that you'll do what I need you to do, did you?"

I absolutely hoped so; it was a critical part of my fledgling—and, in retrospect, stupid—plan. But I'm not going to give him the satisfaction of confirming it for him. He continues.

"What Mr. Harris has just injected into Miss Lin is a subdermal implant, though on a much smaller scale than the ones we all carry around in our brains. This one is rather dumb, in fact. It only does one thing, but it does it very well. If I don't send an hourly ping to it, it will trigger a small but very deadly explosive charge that will sever Miss Lin's spinal cord from the base of her brain, killing her instantly. Do you understand?"

I nod silently, not trusting my voice but not wanting to find out what he'll do if I refuse to answer. He seems satisfied with that, though I can see the horror in Jessica's eyes as she looks at me with a pleading stare. I force myself to look away from her and back at Owen, whose expression still looks bored.

"Good then," he says. "We understand each other. One important note. Try to dig the implant out, it will explode. Try to tamper with it in any way, it will explode. And since the casino has a dampening field to prevent cheating amongst players, I can only reset it if I have line-of-sight to Miss Lin."

"What about when she needs to sleep?" I ask, instantly regretting the query.

"Now that's a dumb question," Owen says, then nods at Jules.

Jessica screams in pain as Jules pulls back the hand with the gun and then jabs it fast and hard back into my friend's already busted ribs. This time, it's too much for me, and I do leap toward them, only to have Tucker's iron fist explode against the side of my head, dropping me to the deck. Thankfully, I don't lose control of my consciousness or my bladder this time.

"Even though it was a dumb question," Owen says, a hardness to his tone that wasn't there before, "I'll answer it. You only have two standard days—49 hours, to be exact—before mission failure. If I were you, I wouldn't even *think* about spending any of that time sleeping. We will provide you with a room to refresh yourselves and change clothes, but at least one of us will be there at all times so that you can't use it to conspire against us or do anything else to jeopardize the mission. And if you somehow still manage to be just as much an idiot as the media reports suggest you are, then the cost will be Jessica Lin's life. Do I make myself clear?"

This time, I sense a simple nod won't suffice. "Crystal," I say from the hard deck where I still sit after Tucker's punch. And I see Owen Thompson smile broadly for the first time.

It's not something I ever hope to see again.

THIRTEEN
RISHI PARADISE

Owen lied when he said we would have forty-nine hours to find our target. We burn six of those hours just getting to the Rishi Paradise Casino Orbital (say that five times fast) and two more hours waiting for a docking slip. Apparently, the place is wildly popular.

So now, as Jessica and I enter the station, with Owen and his cronies right behind us, we only have forty-one of those hours left.

Our first stop is the cashier's office at the front of the casino, where Owen procures various denominations of chips representing currency since we can't use our implants inside the casino itself.

Our second stop, at my insistence, is a clothing boutique in the casino's shopping center. There, I procure a few things that we'll need. Anything to get myself out of the plaid and stripes that Tucker put me in. I also explain to Jessica what I'm planning and have her pick something for herself. She's silent throughout the process, and I'm worried about her, but Owen doesn't give us any chance to be alone so I can't try and talk to her about it.

We reach the register with our new clothes, and I raise an eyebrow at Owen. He frowns, but he's obviously impressed with my genetic ability to raise a single eyebrow because he steps forward and pays the bill using some of his chips. Which is good because Jessica's new dress would have eaten deeply into the 4,500 sitting in our bank account.

The next stop is the check-in desk, where Owen gives the reservation details to a pretty blond who is dressed in a toga, of all things. Apparently, the Rishi Paradise has some sort of weird neo-Roman theme. Parts of the station interior are even decorated with fake stone pillars interspersed with bright neon lights. It looks horribly cheesy and cheap to me, but based on the dress of the other patrons and the prices we—well, Owen—paid at the clothing store, I'm guessing that Rishi caters to a more upscale clientele.

That's good, in a way. It should make our Navy enlisted man stand out like a sore thumb. Still a sore thumb that we have to find in a crowd of five thousand other thumbs, but I'll take what I can get.

The good news is that there's no chance the guy will recognize me, even if he watched my court martial live on a huge screen or has a poster of me above his bed. Harris is that good. He spent a significant portion of the remaining flight to Rishi going over both Lin and me with a wide variety of tools, liquids, gels, and gadgets. I hardly recognized myself in the mirror afterward. I have blond hair now, and my cheekbones are more pronounced. Even my eye color has changed.

Jessica looks more like herself; the chances our target might have ever seen a picture of her are far lower since she's not a mass murderer like me. But the goal with her, per the plan I explained to Owen, is to actually make her stand out. We *want* our man to notice her. According to Owen, our target has never met his Koratan handler and doesn't even know their gender. So, my brilliant plan is to make him think *Jessica* is the handler, not me.

That means I need her to be noticeable because I'm banking that a lowly enlisted man will be expecting this spy stuff to happen like it does in books and movies, not in boring real life. And every good spy movie has a stunning femme fatale, right? Sure, it's a stupid plan, but I haven't exactly been given all that much to work with.

We finally arrive at the room Owen arranged for us. He and his entire entourage accompany us inside. At least they let us go into the bathroom to change our clothes in private, but only one at a time, and after Tucker has checked the room for anything that can be used as a weapon. Which is too bad; I was really hoping the prior occupant left behind a crowbar or a Series T-1000 laser assault rifle. At this point, I'd even take a particularly sharp toothpick.

I go first, and I have to admit, I like the new suit I've purchased for myself. It has a lot of pockets, something that was always lacking in Navy-issue skinsuits. I don't have anything to put in those pockets, but just knowing they're there gives me a sliver of happiness despite our situation.

But when Jessica emerges from the bathroom a few minutes later, I lose all interest in my pockets.

Up until now, I've only seen Jessica Lin in two types of clothing. First, her Navy skinsuit, which, despite being very flattering to her figure, didn't exactly go for aesthetics otherwise. Second, a series of casual outfits, mostly simple pants and t-shirts, during our time on *Wanderer*. After all, Heather Kilgore didn't provide us with a whole lot of variety, though I was pleasantly surprised to find she had somehow magically stocked *Wanderer* with at least a few clothes in both our sizes.

But now…I've never seen anything more breathtaking. The dress Lin picked out in the boutique is bright red with lines woven into the fabric that shimmer and catch the light as she walks. It has a slit up the side, though not too high, leaving plenty to the imagination. The top of the dress is sleeveless but actually quite modest. Nevertheless, the way it hangs on her accentuates every one of her curves and makes my mouth drop open in awe. As she walks toward me in the small room, I'm having a hard time remembering that we're fighting for our lives here.

I mean, Jessica Lin would look amazing in a garbage bag. But this is a whole new level of beauty that I didn't even know existed.

Despite that, Harris isn't happy. In my efforts to make Jessica stand out more, I'd had the man turn her hair a bright blue on the voyage in. Now, he's dissatisfied with the way it clashes with the red dress. I expect Owen to tell him to drop it, but surprisingly, the man lets his minion work. It only takes fifteen minutes and a strange electronic doodad that I've never seen before today, and then Jessica's hair and dress match perfectly. I have to admit, for a guy who dresses like a hobo, Harris knows his way around cosmetics and fashion.

"Wait," he says as Jessica turns to walk away from him and the hotel room's small vanity. And from nowhere, he produces jewelry.

In the Navy, women don't wear jewelry. You don't wear anything that can get stuck on a vacsuit or helmet. Not if you want to live. But somehow, Jessica dons the diamond studded bracelet, choker, and earrings that Harris produces like she's born to them. And I suddenly realize that I don't really know all that much about her background before the Navy. For all I know, her parents were insanely wealthy, and she wore jewelry like this to grade school.

I will tell you this: if I wasn't already in love with this woman, I would fall hopelessly now. But seeing her this way at this moment is actually quite depressing because I know there's no chance for us to be together, even assuming we survive the next forty hours.

FOURTEEN
SEARCHING IN VAIN

Fifteen minutes after Harris pronounces us both good to go, Jessica and I walk arm-in-arm through the hotel lobby and into the casino proper of the Rishi Paradise. Somewhere behind us are Owen, Harris, Tucker, and Jules, but they're far enough away that they can't hear. And the blanket jamming that the casino uses to dissuade cheating means that they can't listen in even if they've planted microphones on us, which I don't think they could have. That's the other reason I purchased new clothes for us and then never let those clothes out of my sight until we got them on.

I just have to hope that Owen is right about him still being able to get a signal to Jessica's new and terrible implant, as long as he has line-of-sight to her. Otherwise, she'll be dead within an hour. Cheery thought.

But I can't worry about that now, as much as it tears at my heart, because I need to focus on the few things I *can* control. For now, that means doing everything I can to complete our impossible mission successfully, which means adding one more accessory to her outfit.

"Here," I tell her once we've entered the noisy casino floor. I hand her a small silver pin.

She looks down at it in her hand. "You're joking, right?" Harris put lash extensions on her and a shimmering dark eye shadow that makes her eyes 'pop'. That's the word he used, but it fits because even now, looking at me with incredulity, those eyes are amazing.

"Hey, why not?" I ask.

"Because it's too obvious. There's no way the guy falls for it," she argues.

"Trust me, one look at you, and he'll be willing to believe just about anything for an excuse to get close. And this will be like a beacon to him."

She frowns but doesn't argue further, though she does decline my offer to help her pin the thing on.

"There," she says once it's securely fashioned to her dress right above her left breast. "Happy?"

"Yep," I try and say nonchalantly, but it catches in my throat and sounds more like a frog croaking. Real smooth, Brad.

The pin, small though it is, is unmistakable to anyone who knows anything about Fringe navies.

"Where did you get this anyway?" Lin asks as I start to lead her through the casino again.

"I took it off the body of a Koratan officer I killed in hand-to-hand combat."

She stops dead in her tracks, yanking her arm out of mine and folding it with the other across her chest. "Brad, stop it," she hisses. "I need to know you're taking this seriously. Our lives are on the line!" A few patrons look our way as Lin's voice rises loud enough to be heard, but I smile and nod at them as if it's all some big joke, and they quickly go back to their slot machines and keno games. Except for a few old guys who keep staring at Jessica, but it's hard to blame them.

"Sorry," I say, offering my arm back to her. She takes it, but only after hesitating a moment longer than I would have liked. "I make jokes when I'm nervous. And when I'm hungry. And when I'm—"

"Brad," she hisses again. I take the hint.

"Sorry. Again. I won the pin in a poker game on the Harper Line."

The Harper Line is a sort of neutral zone between Promethean and

Koratan space. Both nations claim the three inhabited systems there, and they regularly send their respective navies through to patrol them and show the flag. But someone forgot to tell the inhabitants of those three systems that they belong to either nation. So, what you essentially get is disputed territory where the denizens cater equally to both nations' navies. Add on top of that the fact that few people in those navies actually want to get into a shooting war with each other, and you end up with a sort of uneasy and unspoken truce on the Line. Sometimes, you even find a good underground poker game where you can rub shoulders with officers from the opposite side of our little cold war.

She accepts my answer this time, which is good because it's the truth, and I feel her relax, but only slightly. She's still wound so tightly she could probably *push* the *Wanderer* to the next system over.

"Listen," I tell her, "I'm working on a plan, but I need that brilliant mind of yours. The best thing we can do until we come up with something better is to find the guy Owen is looking for and get whatever information from him that Owen's employer wants. Then, hopefully, we can get out of this system and away from him and the rest of them and never look back."

She's silent for a while, walking beside me, and I'm trying very hard not to be too conscious of her arm through mine. When she speaks again, I have to strain to hear her near whisper. "That's if they're telling the truth about letting us go when this is over."

She has me there because I'm almost certain they're not. Especially because I'm starting to get a pretty strong suspicion of who Owen's mysterious employer likely is.

But, without anything else to do until we come up with something better, and needing very badly for Owen to keep sending his hourly signal to Jessica's new implant, we have no choice but to look for the traitor from our old Navy.

So, we keep walking around the casino floor, hoping vainly that some guy sees Jessica and notices the pin on her chest and pops up and yells, 'Hey, I'm the traitor you're looking for'. He doesn't. And after six *hours* of walking around, sometimes with Jessica alone out in front—

which has *every* guy in the casino trying to talk to her—and sometimes arm-in-arm—which has every guy in the casino giving me dirty looks—I have to admit defeat.

We only have thirty-three hours left.

FIFTEEN
A NEW APPROACH AND A FANTASTIC FAILURE

"I'm hungry," I announce as we finish our latest full circuit around the casino floor.

"Really?" Jessica says next to me. We're arm-in-arm again; it was slowing us down way too much to have to stop when she got hit on every five meters. "How can you even think of food at a time like this?"

"I can always think of food," I say, and then drag her toward one of the many restaurants placed around the edges of the casino. This one is a bar and grill, and I feel Jessica pull against me as we near it. By our ship's clock, it's breakfast time. By Rishi's, it's just after the lunch rush, and the place is only half full.

"No, Brad, this is *not* the time," Lin says harshly, and I'm a little disappointed. Does she really think I would drink again right in front of her? No, I'd only do that behind her back.

"Relax," I tell her, though Carla used to tell me that was one of five words a man should never say to a woman. But I'm a slow learner, and Carla isn't here. She's with Clarington, hopefully crying into his pudgy shoulder about my death.

I shake off thoughts of my ex-wife. It's easy to do that with Jessica

Lin on my arm. "Relax," I say again. "I'm not going to drink anything. But you know what they say about station bars?"

She doesn't reply, but her resistance stops, and she lets me lead her into the restaurant, where a cute little hostess, also in a toga, leads us to a table. After she finishes telling us about the day's specials, I do my best to casually ask my planned question.

"Say, we're trying to meet up with a friend here at the casino, but we can't message him with the comm jamming. Any chance you may have seen him?"

The hostess looks at me with an expression that says, 'Do you know how many people I see daily? I'm going to forget you exist the second you let me leave this table'. But I forge ahead anyway.

"You'd recognize him. Ex-Navy guy. Probably telling all sorts of stories about his time serving over in Prometheus. Ring any bells?"

"What's he look like?" she asks. Shoot, the most obvious question but also the one question I can't answer. Luckily, Jessica saves me.

"So, this is a little embarrassing," she tells the hostess. "He's more a friend of a friend. We've never actually met him. All we know is that he's here this week, and our mutual friend said he could hook us up with some concert tickets we've been after for months."

The hostess nods dubiously but doesn't argue, and luckily doesn't ask the guy's name, because we don't know that either. "Doesn't remind me of anyone we've had through here. Sorry I can't help you."

I'm about to shrug it off when something hits my shin hard. I yelp, drawing a surprised look from the hostess, but I quickly figure out it was one of the high heels Jessica bought to go with her new dress; couldn't have her wearing her normal combat boots with that little ensemble. And Jess is looking at me now and motioning with her head toward the server. I look back in confusion, but then I finally get it.

"Well, if you do hear or see anyone who you think matches the description, please let us know." I hand her one of the twenty credit chips Owen gave me for walking around money while we search for our target.

The girl brightens and looks far more helpful now. "I'll definitely let you know. You may also ask some of the other staff. This is my first day back on station from a trip down planet, so they may have seen your friend while I was gone."

Great! Couldn't she have led with that? I just spent twenty credits on someone who has no chance of helping us.

"Thank you so much," Jessica says graciously, and the toga-clad girl bounces off back to the hostess station.

"Ow," I say once she's out of earshot as I reach down to rub my bruised shin. "What are those shoes made out of, hull metal?"

"You should try wearing the blasted things for the last six hours," Jessica says as she surveys the other diners around us. "That's real torture."

"Really? My ex-wife always said she liked wearing them." Another smooth move by Brad Mendoza. Here I am, sitting with the most beautiful woman in the galaxy, and I bring up my ex-wife. Nice. Maybe next I can tell her all about my last colonoscopy.

"No one actually enjoys wearing high heels," Jessica says, ignoring or perhaps even oblivious to my faux pas. "It's just something women pretend they like to please men."

"But," I argue, "Carla wore them long before she met me. And she kept wearing them even after I told her I didn't care. She was always buying new ones."

She looks at me now, breaking off her study of the other people in the restaurant. "Brad, sometimes you really are dense, aren't you?"

Her words are harsh, but there's no real bite to them. So, they don't hurt as much as when she called me an idiot just a few days ago.

"Enlighten me," I challenge her.

"OK," she turns her body more directly toward me in her chair as if settling in for an intense conversation. We're both just trying to distract ourselves from our current situation, but that's not such a bad thing. "How long were you and Carla married?"

"Six years."

"And in those six years, how often were you actually together, like in the same apartment or house, on the same planet."

I think for a moment. "Well, with my deployment schedule, I guess maybe only a quarter of the time."

"OK, so about a year-and-a-half of actual time together then?"

"Sounds about right."

"And when did you first catch her cheating on you?"

"Wait, how did you know that? I've never told anyone." I don't like how this conversation is going at all.

"Just answer the question, Brad."

"Three months after Bellerophon," I admit.

"And what did she do when you were on deployment? Did she sit around and pine for you in your apartment?"

"We had a house."

"Whatever. Answer the question."

"Well, no. She had a group of girlfriends she would go out with. But I was OK with it. They would just go to movies and stuff."

"Now. And this is important. How many pairs of high heels did she have?"

"Uh. A lot. Maybe twenty. Maybe more."

"You said she was always buying more. But did she ever throw any out because they were too worn or scuffed?"

I think hard, struggling to remember. "I think so. Yes, I'm certain. There were always new pairs when I'd get home, but I remember a few of my favorites—the ones I thought looked best on her—would be gone. I just figured she wanted to keep her wardrobe fresh."

"OK, last question. These friends of hers that she would go out with while you were on deployment. Did they ever hang out with her while you were around? I mean, did they come over to the house while you were there, or did she go out with them while you were in town?"

"Uh. No. Now that you mention it, I met a few of them at our wedding but never really saw them after that."

Her facial expression changes to a pained one. "Oh, you dear, sweet, stupid man. I'm so sorry."

"What? What are you sorry about?" I demand, sick of playing twenty questions and being called stupid. A few other diners look our way at my outburst.

"Brad, I hate to break it to you, but that time you caught Carla cheating on you…I'm pretty sure it wasn't her first time." She stops, letting that sink in.

"No, you're wrong," I argue, again a bit too loudly. "Carla was loyal. There's no way she was cheating on me before..." But I can't finish the sentence because, all of a sudden, things start falling into place. Three months before I caught Carla in bed with Clarington, the man had attended my court martial. I thought it was just because his daddy, the Vice Admiral Clarington, was one of the judges on the panel. But now I recall that I caught him staring at me a lot and nudging some of his friends and laughing as if there was some great joke at my expense.

Then, I remember a time before that when I got home from deployment a day early and thought it would be fun to surprise Carla instead of telling her my new schedule. I caught a cab home. Just as it pulled up and I was getting out, another car drove past the house slowly. At first, it looked as if it was actually going to turn into my driveway. But instead, as it got closer, the driver hit the accelerator and sped by.

When I went inside, I found Carla waiting by the front door, resplendent in a black dress I'd always loved on her, with spiky black heels to match.

The funny part was, looking back, she seemed genuinely surprised to see me but then made a big deal about how she had dressed up to welcome me home. When, disappointed at my failed surprise, I asked her how she even knew I was coming home early, she'd said, "Daddy told me."

The thing is, Admiral Oliphant had no idea I was coming home early. It wasn't planned, but my transport caught a rogue gravitational wave in jump space and rode it for several dozen lightyears, cutting an entire day off our travel time to Prometheus. When we arrived, Terrence Oliphant was in the outer system doing combat training exercises with First Fleet. Even if he had gotten the news that the transport had arrived early, he wouldn't have been able to get a message back to Carla until almost half a day after I actually walked in the front door.

Which means she wasn't waiting for *me* dressed like that.

Everything clicks into place now, and I feel hot tears well up in my eyes.

"I'm so sorry, Brad," Jessica says, reaching out to place one of her hands on top of mine. Usually, any kind of physical contact from her would electrify me, but not this, not now. "I'm so sorry. I figured you must know. I just assumed that was part of why you got divorced."

I jerk my hand back, not sure how to react to anything right now. She looks hurt for a moment, but it passes quickly.

"Listen," she tries to change the subject, "the idea of asking the staff here for information on our man is a good one. Let's keep throwing some of those chips around and see what it gets us."

I still say nothing, staring down at the table in front of me, reading the same line on the menu over and over again without remembering a single word, and fighting hard to keep the tears from falling. It feels like someone punched me in the gut and then pulled the floor out from beneath me.

"Brad, I'm so sorry. Maybe when this is all over, we can talk more about what a real, healthy relationship looks like."

Well, it's been a few hours since the last truly stupid thing I've done, so I'm due. But what I say next is perhaps the most monumentally dumb thing to ever leave my lips. I mean, we are talking Nobel Prize-level idiocy on this one.

"Like you would know."

I whisper the words, but Jessica hears them. She stiffens across from me, and a stricken look clouds her perfect features. Then, wordlessly, she pulls the napkin off her lap, folds it carefully, and places it on the table in front of her. She then deliberately and carefully pushes her chair back and stands up.

My mind is racing now as I realize what I've done, and I open my mouth to plead my case, apologize, anything! But the words just won't come. Instead, I watch mutely as Jessica turns and then walks briskly from the restaurant, leaving me behind. Every man in the place follows her with their gaze as she does so.

What. An. Idiot. But I guess I should stop expecting more from myself.

Our waitress picks that very moment to arrive, another bouncy little blond in a toga. There's a definite hiring trend at this casino.

"Is everything OK with your wife, sir?" she asks in feigned concern.

I shake my head slowly. “Just bring me your biggest bottle of scotch.”

SIXTEEN
SUCCESS, BUT AT WHAT COST?

Usually, after such a monumental act of sheer idiocy, I can't wait to erase my memory, at least temporarily, with copious amounts of alcohol.

I expect now to be no different, but twenty minutes later, I still sit here, staring at the glass of scotch in my hand, the one I first poured, that I haven't even taken a sip of.

There are so many things going through my head right now, few of them good. But one keeps coming back to the surface: if I get drunk now, Jessica Lin is a dead woman. With only thirty-three hours left, I can't afford to spend even a few hours of that time drunk and useless. And once I take one sip, I won't stop. Still, I *need* the drink so badly. So, I just sit there, unable to make up my mind, staring into its amber depths.

I'm in this state of startling conundrum when Owen slips into the chair Jessica vacated.

"What happened?" he asked.

Seeing him here, I frantically access my implant to check the time.

"Relax," he says, picking up on what I'm doing. "She's at the bar two doors down. I pinged her little implant before I walked over here to see what in Hades is wrong with you. She's got fifty-seven minutes before I need to ping it again."

I nod, not sure if it's appropriate to thank the man for not killing the woman I love. So, I say nothing. Instead, I give the glass of scotch one last fond gaze before I get up, leaving the glass and the bottle untouched on the table behind me, and walk in the direction Jessica went. I'll let Owen settle my bill.

I find her right where he said she'd be. Unlike the restaurant we were in, which was a bar pretending to be a grill with fancy food, this new establishment makes no such pretenses. It's just a bar, and the waitresses here wear togas even shorter and more revealing than any I've yet seen. It's also dark, and there's smoke in the air from several of the patrons who haven't been able to kick a habit that was proved to be deadly hundreds or perhaps even thousands of years ago.

She's sitting alone at the bar, an empty shot glass in front of her, which she's staring into and studying as if it holds the key to our predicament. Or maybe she's trying to forget what just happened between us. But I know better. All the booze in the world doesn't wipe away the memories we most desperately wish it would. Those are here to stay.

I stand there and watch her for a few minutes, unsure of how to proceed. In that time, three different men approach her. She sends the first away with nothing more than a cold look. The second, she sends scurrying onward with just a few words. But the third is more persistent. I'm about to go intervene, but the guy's hand on her lower back quickly results in her bending his finger so far back that I can almost hear it crack from across the bar. I admire her work as the third guy scampers past me out of the bar, holding his hurt hand in the other and swearing. She doesn't even watch him go.

When I slide onto the stool next to her a moment later, she looks up as if to tell another would-be Romeo to buzz off. But when she sees it's me, she says nothing and looks down at her empty drink again.

For several more minutes, neither of us says anything. But I can feel the angry glances of every other single guy in the bar directed at my back. If only they knew that she likely hates me more than even the guy she just sent running to a first aid station.

Finally, I work up the courage to speak. "Listen, Jessica, I'm—"

"I found him," she says, interrupting what I was hoping would be a truly heartfelt and heartstring-tugging apology from yours truly. But the moment is over, and now I'm no longer seeing Jessica Lin, the woman I love and who laughed with me and told stories in the *Wanderer's* cockpit. Instead, I'm seeing Lieutenant Commander Lin, the woman who, on the second day after we met—hard to believe that was less than two weeks ago—dressed me down for staring at her butt.

I'm afraid I've lost the other Lin forever. This one is all business now.

"Where? How?" I ask, letting myself forlornly slip back into my role as Captain Brad Mendoza, her superior officer who will almost certainly never be anything more.

"The bartender," she motions with her head, still refusing to look at me. I look over to see a tall brunette woman—finally someone who breaks the casino's staffing mold—cleaning a glass two meters away and flirting unabashedly with a couple of older men who keep flicking casino chips her way while simultaneously casting furtive glances toward Jessica. I can see from here that at least one is wearing a wedding ring. Real nice.

Funny, even after so many years among the stars, sometimes it doesn't feel like we as humans have evolved, not even a little bit. And I include myself in that.

"She says a guy was in here just last night," Jessica continues. "Got a couple of drinks in him and started bragging about being some big shot in the Promethean Navy. Tells this tall tale about being a daring captain who took out six pirate ships with a single battlecruiser."

"Hey, that's my story," I say despite myself. She doesn't acknowledge that I've even spoken.

"She says we can usually find him at one of the craps tables. He's blond with blue eyes and a chiseled jaw. Guess he was going for a look that he thought would get him more girls. Supposedly, he also wears a red rose in his lapel. She thought he was full of it and that he talked way too rough to have actually been an officer in any navy, but he was pretty liberal with the chips he was throwing her way, so she kept him talking."

With that, Jessica gets up to leave, and I scramble to follow. She tosses a chip on the bar for the bartender's trouble, then walks briskly out the door. I'm a few steps behind, but the opportunity—however brief—I had to apologize to her is now gone and over.

As is any opportunity for a future between Brad Mendoza and Jessica Lin. Because even I have to admit, if I were her, after all she's been through, I would never forgive me for what I said.

SEVENTEEN
FINDING OUR MAN

Now that we have a description, our guy is surprisingly easy to find. He's not at the craps tables, but he is right next to them, playing blackjack and losing quite badly, both at the game and with the pretty dealer he's clumsily flirting with.

As we get close, Jessica throws me a hard look, stopping me in my tracks. She continues forward, leaving me behind. That hurts more than anything else she could have said or done because she just made it clear that she no longer trusts me with her life. She's going to handle this herself or die trying rather than put any faith in me.

I sit, dejectedly, at another table where I can see the one our target is at. I mindlessly bet and lose a few hands as I watch Jessica at work, perhaps for the last time.

She's good. I have to give her that. She slides into the seat next to the guy. He looks her over, his eyes lingering in all the right places, but she pretends not to notice. Instead, she places some of Owen's chips on the table and asks to be dealt in.

I see the exact moment the guy notices the pin on her chest. It takes him a little while because it's on the side opposite him, but when he finally sees it, he goes rigid. After all, no one is expecting to see the

Koratan Medal of Valor on a supermodel, especially this far from Koratan space.

He's still staring at it when the dealer literally has to tap him on the arm to get his attention. He mumbles something at her, and she shrugs, dealing him another card. He busts. So do I, by the way. At this rate, I'll lose my remaining chips faster than Lin can land this fish.

But I don't have to wait long. He leans over urgently and asks her something. She pretends to notice him for the first time but places a hand gently on his arm and shushes him, like a teacher to a naughty student. It works. Sort of. He plays a few more hands, but he's shaking so badly and so distracted that he's just making random moves, and he busts quickly on two hands and then holds at nine on the third. The pile of chips in front of him is almost gone.

Lin chooses that moment to lean over and whisper something in his ear. He stiffens again but nods. Then she gets up, tosses a chip to the dealer, collects the rest of hers, and walks away slowly. The guy stays put for only a few seconds, nervously bouncing, until he gets up and follows my first mate—if she's even that anymore. But before he does, Jessica catches my eye and indicates through sheer anger that I'm to follow after him as he follows after her.

I get the message. I collect my own chips, toss one to the dealer at my table, and try to follow the target as casually as I can. Not that he would notice me even if I shouted in his ear. Between his nervous energy at finally making contact with his supposed handler and the fact that he can't take his eyes off Jessica's rear end—I've been there, buddy—a battleship would have to *hit* him for him to even notice it approaching.

She leads him to a relatively quiet restaurant, not one of the two we've already been in, gets a table, and invites him to sit with her. He's still bouncing. I wait outside; there's clearly not a third seat for me anyway. And frankly, I don't think she needs any help with this guy.

They talk quietly for a few minutes, breaking off only when the waiter—I didn't think the casino employed men—dressed like a Roman gladiator arrives to take their order.

I find a bench outside where I can see into the restaurant and keep an eye on things. I'm still there five minutes later, watching Jessica work from a distance, when Owen plops down beside me.

"Good job finding him," he says without preamble. "Now, let's hope your girl can seal the deal."

"She's not my girl," I say in return, not really wanting to put up with the guy's fake friendly crap for one more second.

"You know what I mean," he says calmly.

I look over at him now, meeting his eyes and staring so hard I hope I'll make his head explode. "Shut up, Owen." Then I get up and walk away.

EIGHTEEN
THE WRINKLE

"What do you mean it's not here?"

It's the first time I've seen Owen look genuinely angry since the time he snapped at Tucker outside *Wanderer*. But Jessica doesn't react. She wears the same impassive, stony expression that's been on her face since the moment I finished putting my gigantic foot in my mouth back at the first restaurant we went into.

"Just as I said," she explains calmly. "The information isn't here. The guy isn't a total fool, after all. He wants payment first, then he'll give us the location of the dead drop where he left the intel you want."

I now have the pleasure of watching Owen Thompson sputter and throw his hands up in the air in frustration and anger. It's a good look on him. I hope to see him frustrated more often moving forward, so long as it isn't directed at us. There's still that nasty little implant in Jessica's neck to consider.

Owen paces the hotel room where we've all met up again, muttering to himself. Finally, he stops and looks hard at me.

"Fix it," he says simply and definitively.

"What do you expect *me* to do?" I argue. "Just pay the guy, and you'll get what you're after." I don't even mention the fact that he should be talking to Jess, not me. *She's* the one who found the target; I don't feel like I've contributed much at all to this little mission. But better to keep the psychopath's focus off her and on me, I suppose.

"No." Owen says the word with such finality that it's not even worth arguing with him. I do, anyway.

"What do you mean, no? You told us to find the guy; we found him. Now she's telling you exactly how you can get the intel you're after from him. So just pay him, and we can all part ways happy."

"No," he says again, and he steps forward and jabs one of his sausage-like fingers in my chest. Behind him, I see Tucker smirk at me from where he sits on one of the room's beds. Harris and Jules are nowhere to be seen. "I told you to find him *and* get the intel for me. So, find me a way to get what we came for that doesn't involve me paying the guy twenty million credits."

Now, *that* catches my attention. On the flight in, Owen told me the guy was selling his intel for a lot of money, but *twenty million credits*? For that much, it has to be some explosively valuable information. But what could be so valuable to the Koratans that a lowly in-system spacer would know...?

I want to moan out loud when it hits me. Because suddenly, I'm pretty sure I know exactly what information the guy has. And it's not good. But the real question is, do I care?

And the answer is yes. But not because I care who actually gets such valuable intel. For all I'm concerned, King Charles, Lord and Ruler of the Federated Systems of Prometheus and uncle to a rapist, can rot. But I can't do anything that will put Jessica in more danger. And until we find a way to remove that explosive implant, that means I need to keep playing Owen's little game.

"Fine," I say through clenched teeth. "We'll find another way."

NINETEEN
THE OTHER WAY

Did you know implants are really spectacular devices? I remember hearing once, maybe in school, that the average implant can hold the entirety of what the internet contained a thousand years ago. Not bad for something small enough to fit in your head. Of course, as storage grows, so does the amount of information available, so we still have to be choosy about what we store in our implants. They can run out of space. But the space they do have is still astonishingly large.

For example, in my role as a captain in His Majesty's Promethean Navy, I've long had my implant set to automatically download any and all naval bulletins every time I come in range of a planetary internet node. Usually, I don't bother reading any unless my implant's AI tells me one of them has a direct impact on me or my ship. But included in those bulletins are alerts for any spacers or officers who occasionally go AWOL or otherwise disappear. And I have these bulletins stored in perpetuity, going back several years, last updated just eight days ago when I was in Gerson.

Owen told us that our target deserted from his duty station in the Layton system, where he served as part of the system patrol. But the funny thing is, I can't find a single bulletin in my implant about *anyone* deserting or going AWOL from Layton in the last five years.

But there *has* been a recently AWOL spacer from another system, and it confirms a suspicion I've had since the moment Owen revealed he knew our true identities. It also means that now I have a real plan to end this.

I quickly explain a portion of that plan, without revealing what I've learned from the records in my implant, to Owen, Jessica, and the rest. Then, I sit impatiently for thirty minutes while Harris undoes most of the changes he made to my appearance. My cheekbones are still a little too pronounced, but at least my hair and eyes are back to their proper coloring.

Even with all that, I'm ten minutes early to the place where Jessica arranged to meet our target, who told her his name is Jorge. He's already there, of course. When a woman like Jessica Lin tells you to meet her somewhere, you show up early to ensure there's *no* chance you miss your rendezvous.

I slip into the seat across from the traitor, who is too busy looking all around for Jessica to even notice me approaching.

"Uh," he says in confusion when he finally sees me there. "I'm expecting someone."

"Not anymore, Jorge," I say, channeling some of the bored psychopath tone that I've learned to love so much from good old Owen.

"I, uh, don't understand," he responds haltingly.

"That's because you're not thinking hard enough, Jorge," I say, this time a bit derisively. "Or, should I say, George Peterson?"

OK. I hate Owen, and I'd love to kill him and all his friends at this point. But I get it now: the big reveal he did in the galley when he told me he knew my real name. I get why he did it that way because the look on Jorge's face is absolutely priceless.

"How did you know?" he asks, his whisper way too loud.

"Come on, George," I say with a lopsided grin. "Don't you recognize me?"

His eyes search my face for several long seconds, and I can see it isn't ringing any bells with him. I sigh internally; I guess I'm not as famous as I thought, which is a major blow to my ego. It's the cheekbones that Harris couldn't fully undo. That must be it, right?

"Think Butcher of Bellaraphon," I say reluctantly.

That does it. His eyes go wide with recognition, and his mouth falls open in surprise. I do that a lot, too—the whole jaw dropping open when something surprises me—but seeing it now on another person, mouth agape like he's a whale after krill, makes me want to rethink ever using it again.

"You're Brad Mendoza!" Several heads turn at other tables, responding to his proclamation. Idiot.

"Keep your voice down, George," I hiss. "You know, you make a really crappy spy."

"But you're..." he starts to exclaim again but stops himself. "But you're dead," he says in what he probably thinks is a whisper, but to me, still sounds like rushing wind in a thunderstorm.

"Apparently not," I say.

"But how?"

"Come on, George. Hero captain with spotless record accidentally kills 504 civilians, then mysteriously dies in a place like Gerson? You don't really believe all of that, do you?"

"I... Wait, you mean it was all an act?" I love it when useful fools fill in the blanks for me.

I don't respond but raise my eyebrows, inviting him to keep speculating.

"But why?" Oh well. Seems like I'll need to do the heavy lifting for him.

"It's quite simple, really. I'm part of ProSec now."

If he looked shocked earlier at my identity, his shock doubles now. The blood drains from his face because, for a spy and traitor against the Federated Systems of Prometheus, the Promethean Security Service —'ProSec' for short—is his worst nightmare. It means he's been caught.

Oh, sure, he doesn't give up immediately. He stammers for a while, trying to explain his new appearance, what he's doing so far from his duty station, etc., etc., etc. But as he does so, he also lets slip a lot of very useful information, all of which makes me feel a whole lot better because it's more or less exactly what I expected. Then, it makes me feel a lot worse because it's more or less *exactly* what I expected. And what I expected is pretty scary. It means the stakes of the game Jessica and I are unwillingly playing in are as high as they can possibly get.

Finally, as he runs out of wind and lies to tell, I chime back in. "Listen very carefully, George, because you are in grave danger."

He looks like he wants to say something, but I don't wait for him to ask any stupid questions.

"That woman you met with earlier; she's not who you think. She was sent here to kill you."

His mouth drops open again, and this time, he reminds me of a fish I once caught. Yep, I definitely need a new go-to facial expression when I'm surprised.

"In fact," I continue, "the Koratans have been planning to kill you all along after you give them the intel you stole. You simply know too much for them to allow you to live."

It's all very believable to him because everything he knows about spies comes from movies and novels, just as I suspected. I can see it in the way he reacts. But, in reality, the Koratans probably aren't going to actually kill him; that would mean way too much paperwork. They're far more likely to put him in some secret prison somewhere and let him get killed by another prisoner. Cleaner that way.

"What do I do?" he asks, again too loudly, leaning across the table toward me.

"Well, you have two choices, George. First, you come with me. You take me to wherever you've stashed the information you were going to sell the Koratans; I suspect you're way too smart to have brought it to this meeting, right?"

He nods vigorously.

"Great. You take me to it, you give it to me, I give you a new identity, and you go on your merry way."

I pause, waiting. Finally, as anticipated, he breaks the silence. "And the second option?"

I lean back and smile, showing my teeth. "The second option is to see whether the pretty Koratan assassin or I get to kill you first. Because you screwed up George. By hiding the info where only you can find it, all I need to do is take you out of the equation, and then *no one* will ever find it."

Now, he really turns white.

"So, what'll it be, Jorge?" Who chooses a fake name that's just their real name in another language? Even spies and traitors should have higher standards than that.

I let the silence hang, not feeling any need to fill it with more words or threats. My new friend needs time to think, and I'm giving it to him, even though we both know what his answer will be.

He doesn't break the silence, but he nods.

"Good choice," I tell him. Everything is going exactly the way I told Owen and Jessica it would. I can see her sitting at a slot machine behind George but in my line of sight. I wink at her. She ignores me.

Yes, everything is going according to plan. But now comes the part that I didn't share with anyone else.

"Listen, George," I say, forcing him to meet my eyes. "There's one more thing I need you to do."

TWENTY
THE MINE

"It's right there," George tells me as I bring *Wanderer* in close to an asteroid that sits a relatively short flight from the Rishi Paradise. It's a small rock, mined and stripped clean of anything valuable centuries ago, with an ancient and decrepit abandoned mining station as the only evidence humans were ever here. At least on the surface.

Underneath the surface is a different story. The rock is so criss-crossed by mine shafts and tunnels that I suspect a single missile from my old battlecruiser, *Lancer,* would be more than sufficient to break the entire thing up into tiny little dust particles. But, as such things go, the warren of abandoned tunnels makes it an excellent place to hide something you never want to be found by accident.

I might have to revise my original estimate of George Peterson's intelligence.

"Where, exactly?" I ask him from the pilot's chair. He strains to look around the seat in front of him to see the scanner image—there was no way I was going to let him take Lin's co-pilot seat, even if it is vacant right now. He points toward one of the largest and most obvious tunnels, just off the central mining station.

OK, maybe I was starting to give his intelligence too much credit.

In a rock full of so many interesting hiding places, he went ahead and picked the most obvious *and* boring of the lot.

George thinks we're alone on *Wanderer*. Lin is currently locked in her cabin. Unfortunately, Owen and his cronies are jammed in there with her as insurance to keep me cooperating. To prevent them from all accidentally meeting George on the six-hour flight from Rishi to this rock, I've kept him in the cockpit with me, except for a few trips to the restroom and one to the galley for some terrible reheated rations.

I bring *Wanderer* close to the abandoned mining station and find a hopeful-looking landing pad that is slightly less crumbled and degraded than the others. Gingerly, I set my new ship down, hoping the ground doesn't collapse underneath it; it shouldn't with the asteroid's feeble gravity, but we're talking about a place that has more in common now with Swiss cheese than a planetoid.

Luckily, *Wanderer* settles into place without incident, and I put the engines on standby with a lock code only I know. With the talents he and his team have shown so far, I have little doubt Owen can still break the code and make off with my ship if he really wants to, but I'm not going to make things too easy for him. Then, I enter another command into the ship's AI that I hope no one will discover until it's too late.

George and I are already wearing decompression skinsuits from the ship's stores. I now help him affix his helmet and then do my own. We enter the starboard airlock and evacuate the atmo before opening the outer door and climbing down an extendible ladder to the surface of the rock. The gravity is light enough to keep us from floating away, but not much more, so we adopt a weird-looking leaping walk taught to all Navy men and women alike as we head toward the mouth of the target tunnel.

Behind us, I know that Owen and at least one of his goons are following. The agreement—I made a big stink about this before I agreed to contact Jorge and reveal my true identity so that he would lead me to the intel—is for Lin to stay behind on the *Wanderer*, but not before Owen resets her explosive implant. If it takes us more than an hour to get George's package and get back, we have other problems.

"It's about fifty meters in," the traitor tells me morosely through our helmet comms. He's become increasingly sullen the closer we've gotten to our prize. I think it's finally dawned on him that he won't be making the huge payday he was hoping for on this. All I've offered him is his life, but I've also been noticeably vague on how I plan to protect him from the Koratans. Because, truthfully, I don't care what happens to him; I'm only doing this to save Jessica.

"You first," I tell him, just in case he was smart enough to leave any booby traps behind when he hid the thing.

But alas, he wasn't that smart. It takes us about five minutes to get from *Wanderer's* airlock to a modest rockfall inside the tunnel where he's buried a small metal case. He opens it in front of me and shows me a portable memory drive inside, about the size of my finger. I ping it with my implant, using the code I also forced out of him, and I'm now looking at exactly what was so valuable that someone hired Owen to hijack me, my ship, and my first mate.

It's what I expected it to be, which isn't good at all. In fact, it's very, very bad. Because this information is definitely worth killing for, hundreds of times over even, depending on your personal moral code. But I've known choir boys who would probably kill a few dozen people for this particular tidbit. It's worth that much.

Which means, simply, that there is no scenario where Owen lets me and Jessica out of this alive. Or George, but again, I don't care all that much about the life of a traitor, even if I'm also technically on the run from the same government.

"So, this means I get to live, right?" George asks hopefully.

I glare at him through the helmet. Then, another voice intrudes on our comm channel. "Unfortunately, this is the end for both of you."

Owen.

George's eyes go wide, and he starts blubbering and crying in the helmet. He has no idea who Owen is, but he's already begging him for his life. Some of the promises he makes through the whining are pretty inventive, but it's all to no avail. I know it, and I suspect, deep down, even an imbecile like George knows it.

His annoying pleading stops as Owen cuts him out of the comm channel. "OK, Mendoza," he says to me. "Time to hand it over. You're a dead man, but we might be able to let Commander Lin live if you don't piss me off in the next few minutes."

I turn to regard the man. He and Tucker are both there, emerging from a slight bend in the mine shaft behind us. Tucker's hands are empty, but Owen is holding a pistol aimed squarely at my stomach.

"Hand over the drive," Owen says to me again.

So, I toss it to him. But as it's in the air, I drop a verbal bomb. "It's blank, Owen. I erased it."

I'm gratified to see just from his body language how enraged he is at the thought of coming all this way for nothing, though he does catch the drive and put it in his pocket. Before he can call back to the ship to have Jules kill Jessica, or worse, I speak again. "I copied it first. It's in my implant, behind military-grade encryption. If you want it, you'll need me and Jessica alive and willing."

George picks that moment to start running away, deeper into the mine. For an instant, Owen shifts the gun to aim at the fleeing man but then shifts it back to me, even holding out a hand to stop Tucker from pursuing the man. Without a ship to get him off this rock, the hapless traitor won't be going far.

The mercenary—because I figured out a while back that that's what Owen really is, though not the cool kind like Billy Firebrand, more the evil psychotic kind that always works for the bad guys—turns his eyes back on me through the helmet, and shrugs laconically. "No matter, we'll just kill you later, *after* we kill Miss Lin in front of you. So much for letting her live. Tucker will be disappointed."

I bite back my first response. I can almost *feel* Tucker's anger from the way he tenses next to Owen, but he makes no complaint. The muscle rarely does in outfits like this.

"Maybe," I say carefully, trying to keep my voice as equally unconcerned as Owen's. "Maybe not. You kill her, you'll never get what's in my implant. I'll delete it, and you'll lose. Good luck explaining *that* to your employer."

Owen laughs, which seems a truly inappropriate response at a time like this. But he *is* a psychopath, so inappropriate emotional responses are kind of his thing.

"Really, Brad? How about this? Turn the information over now, and Jessica dies quickly. Don't, and I let Tucker have his way with her first."

I can almost feel the big thug's anger turn into a stupid grin at his boss' words.

I shake my head. "No. This is how it's going to work, Owen. You're going to let me and Jessica go. And then I'll transmit the info to you. Surely, it's worth our lives, especially given what I expect will happen to you if *you* fail to deliver."

Judging by the man's hesitation before he responds, I've finally struck a nerve. But not enough of one because I can see him shake his head in his helmet. "Sorry, Mendoza. Not buying it. I'm thinking that you'll do just about anything to save your pretty little friend from what Tucker has in store for her. Especially if the rumors out of Gerson are true. So, here's my final offer. We all go back to the ship. You transfer the data to me there, then watch your girlfriend die quickly. Or you can watch Tucker teach her a lesson and *then* give me the data and see her die slowly. Your choice." The jerk isn't even meeting me halfway; some negotiator.

I take a step forward, slumping my shoulders as if in surrender. Owen follows my movements with the gun but otherwise holds his ground. I move to within a couple meters of him and Tucker, and now I can see their facial expressions clearly through their dimly lit helmets. Owen looks bored on the surface, as always, but I can see wariness in his eyes, and one of them is twitching slightly. Even he's feeling the pressure right now at the end. Tucker is more emotive, of course, and if his gaze could kill, I'd be dead a hundred times over. I wink at him just to upset him more.

Now I'm also close enough to see precisely what kind of gun Owen has pointed at my stomach. And suddenly, I have a sliver of hope. It's only a sliver, but I've bet on worse.

I stop moving and widen my stance on the mine shaft floor, with my right foot planted behind me relative to the two men. "I'm not going with you, Owen. So, shoot me now and lose the information, or send Jess out to join me *without* her explosive implant, and I'll let you take my ship and go with the information. Your choice, but I'm done negotiating with a psycho like you."

"Pity," he says without any such emotion in his voice. "But there's more than one way to get you back to the ship." He points his gun at my left thigh and pulls the trigger.

TWENTY-ONE
TUCKER MUST DIE

Nothing happens. Owen pulls the trigger again and again, but nothing. Confused, he looks down at the pistol. That's when I act.

In the Billy Firebrand novels, this is where the hero, me, would say something pithy about why the gun won't work and about how non-spacers should never go up against a real spacer like me in a low-grav vacuum.

But witty banter with the bad guy doesn't work in real life. It eliminates the element of surprise, no matter how satisfying it might be to point out the man's mistakes. So, instead of talking, I crouch down, bending my right leg so that I'm kneeling on it for maximum leverage, and I pick up a large rock—discarded mine waste—that's on the ground next to me and which is the reason why I chose to stop in this exact spot.

Before either of the other men can react, I pull the rock—about the size of a volleyball—to my chest and, with both hands, *push* forward as hard as I can, my low stance and the leg behind me keeping me from flying backward with the effort. Instead, the rock propels out of my hands and straight at Owen's transparent helmet.

Wanderer is a great little ship, but she's not a naval warship. And that means the vac helmets in the ship's stores are simple transparent plastic, not as reinforced and indestructible as what I used in the Navy. So, when the rock hits Owen's helmet, even though it's not moving terribly fast, it's got enough mass and momentum to crack the bubble around his head.

Oh, it's probably not a big enough crack to actually go all the way through the material and let his air escape, but he doesn't know that. He yelps in surprise as the rock hits him, its mass knocking him backward into a slow-motion fall to his butt. His hands fly to his face to cover the crack now right in front of his eyes, which must loom as large for him as a broken battleship spine. In the process, the worthless gun flies from his hand and begins its own slow-motion tumble toward the tunnel floor a few meters away.

"Tucker, take him out!" Owen cries, sounding terrified, as he gets his feet back under him and turns to begin a clumsy, loping run back toward the mouth of the tunnel and the relative safety of *Wanderer*.

I ignore him, focusing all my attention on the big man who is now dramatically cracking his knuckles through the gloves of his skinsuit. Seriously? I thought that was just a cliché in the movies.

Then Tucker takes a step toward me, and I forget to laugh. He truly is *enormous*. And now he's madder than I've ever seen him. So, he does what most big guys try to do at the beginning of a fight. After his first step, he lunges forward, both arms outstretched to grab me in a warm hug and crush the life out of me.

I'm still kneeling on the ground where I threw the rock at Owen, and I make no move to get out of Tucker's way. Instead, I lay down flat on the mine shaft floor. And, just as expected, Tucker overestimates the effect of the asteroid's light gravity and sails right over my head.

As a naval officer and not a Marine, I'm not exactly well-trained in hand-to-hand combat. But I *did* train extensively in low-and-zero g maneuvering. So, while Tucker would surely beat the life out of me in seconds in full gravity, here he's playing on my turf.

It also helps that most of my zero-g training in the Academy was in the form of being my dorm's team captain for slug ball. Think basketball, but with medicine balls in zero-g chambers, where the goal is to use the balls to hit the other team and knock them out of the playing area. It's a brutal game but an Academy favorite, with the instructors just as often betting on the outcome versus trying to dissuade a bunch of competitive eighteen and nineteen-year-olds from hurting each other. It usually resulted in a lot of cracked ribs, but it taught us all about how Newton's third law acts in low-g environments.

And while I don't have any medicine balls nearby now, there are a *lot* of rocks, just like the one I hurled at Owen.

After Tucker sails by overhead, I roll to the side toward another one of the stones I spied earlier. The big man slowly hits the ground behind me, and I can hear his anticipatory grunt through the comm. But it's just a reflex; the gravity isn't enough to even knock the wind out of him.

I make it to my rock and pick it up, rising up on one knee and pivoting to face Tucker, who is ponderously levering himself up and turning to face me.

I throw the rock, again from my chest, just as he launches himself toward me once more, aiming lower this time. That's not great; I was sort of hoping he wouldn't learn from his mistakes that quickly. I guess he does have a brain behind all that meat.

The rock glances off the top of his helmet—I aimed too high, not anticipating his low dive—and I don't have time to move before all of Tucker slams into me, knocking me back and wrenching my knee where I had it planted, as before, on the floor of the mine shaft for leverage.

Now that I'm in the big man's arms, he does just what I expected him to try earlier as we tumble slowly together to the ground: he squeezes...hard.

Full grav or none, it doesn't matter when a guy with arms like an anaconda gets them wrapped around you. I almost instantly lose the breath in my lungs, and any advantage I had over the man is gone.

We bounce once off the ground and then hit again, coming to rest near one of the tunnel walls, my body pinned underneath his. That's when I get supremely lucky. Still working off his normal, full-grav fighting instincts, Tucker momentarily loosens his grip on me and tries to reposition his arms for better effect.

Normally, that would work fine, as he's landed on top of me, and I wouldn't be able to get out from under his bulk fast enough to do anything with that one moment of reprieve. But in low grav…

I push up hard with both hands and bring my knees to my chest, propelling Tucker straight up toward the cavern ceiling. Even in the low grav, he won't fly high enough to hit it—the mine shaft is wide and tall, about five meters both ways—but that's OK because he does fly high enough for me to roll out of the way, so I won't be there when he lands.

A few seconds later, cursing loudly through the comm channel, Tucker hits the mine floor where I used to be and has no time to get his footing before another rock, hurled by yours truly, hits him in the side, sending him sprawling back down in another slow-motion fall before he can even get halfway up. I follow that up with another rock, this time connecting solidly with his helmet, just as I did earlier with Owen.

Like Owen, Tucker gets only a cracked helmet for my trouble, and he's not losing his atmo yet. But the momentum of the stone knocks him over again while I leap up into the air as high as I can go above him and to the right, toward the nearest mine shaft wall. Spinning in the air, I absorb the impact on the wall by bending my knees and then straighten my legs with a hard push, aiming back and down toward the still-prone Tucker, who is on his back and just starting to sit up again.

In my hands is one final rock, which I picked up just before my flying leap, held above my head. Just as I come close to Tucker's helmeted head, I violently slam it down. But I don't let go, adding the momentum and mass of my body to that of the large stone.

The result is exactly what I hoped for. I hear a loud crack through the comm and then another wetter one. The angle of the impact sends me in a sort of tumbling somersault over Tucker, and it takes me a moment to get my feet under me and make my way back over to finish the man off.

I needn't have bothered. Tucker's helmet is shattered, and so is his face. He's not dead yet, but he will be shortly as he tries to take deep, gasping breaths of nonexistent air through his crushed nose and open mouth. It's too late to save him, even if I wanted to.

I stand over him and watch him die. As a mass murderer who once killed 504 civilians, including women and children, and as an ex-Navy captain who has killed countless pirates and more mundane enemies in battle, this is the first time I've killed with my own two hands. It's also the first time I'm actually in a position to watch my victim die up close and personal.

It sickens me, and I have to swallow hard to push back the rising gore that threatens to erupt into my helmet.

Tucker is strong and takes a full minute, even in the vacuum, to fade completely. I could walk away; I *should* walk away—time is of the essence now. But I can't. Tucker is a pig and a bully and probably worse, but it somehow still feels wrong to make him die alone. Or maybe it's more that I feel the need to at least observe the consequences of my actions. Even for a man like me, killing should never be easy. Either way, I wait with him while he lives his last moments.

When the light and hatred finally fade from his eyes, and his gasping attempts at breath stop, I silently turn away, spend another minute or so searching the tunnel floor for one thing I need, and then start a loping run toward the tunnel entrance and *Wanderer*.

TWENTY-TWO
OWEN'S FOLLY

I find Owen right where I expected, outside my ship, standing clumsily at the top of the ladder to the outer airlock hatch and banging ineffectually on it with one fist. No one answers his frantic knocks, which I take as a good sign or, at the very least, not a bad one.

He can't hear me approach, but some sixth sense seems to warn him, and he turns and leaps down from the top of the ladder, landing lightly on the ground to face me, bouncing once as he fails to properly absorb the landing with his knees the first time.

"Hi, Owen," I say in a weird, almost friendly greeting. I'm a little off-balance, having just completed my first up-close kill, so I think I can be pardoned for not fully embracing the social rules of a situation like this one.

"You locked the ship," he says unnecessarily, so maybe I'm not the only one unsure of how to approach this new standoff.

I nod through the helmet. "Time lock programmed into the AI. It engaged right after you and Tucker left the ship, and only my code can open the airlocks any time in the next six hours. No one in or out without my say-so."

He nods back, though whether it's in acknowledgment of my statement or admiration for my forethought, I can't tell. Doesn't matter anyway.

"And what's to stop me from calling Jules inside and telling her to go ahead and kill Jessica Lin? Or simply waiting fifteen more minutes until her implant kills her without my signal?"

I shrug. "If you could have called Jules, you would have already done it." It's a good sign that he hasn't been able to reach her yet, though I'm not sure exactly what it means. "Besides, it's all game theory. You had to hurt Jessica before to show me you're serious, but the second you kill her, you lose all leverage over me. And I'm the only one with the intel you desperately want. At this point, it comes down to which one of us flinches first."

He nods, and I can see the hint of a smile through the local star's reflected glare on his helmet. "You truly aren't the idiot people make you out to be, are you?"

"No. I am. But you know what they say about resourceful idiots…"

He cocks his head quizzically inside the cracked dome.

I step forward, closing the distance between us, and jam the pistol I collected from the mine's floor—where Owen dropped it—right into the man's gut, grabbing his shoulder with my other arm for leverage.

"…there is nothing more dangerous."

I pull the trigger. And, unlike when Owen tried to use it on me, this time, the gun works flawlessly. I feel the buck of the pistol in my hand and see a cloud of red explode from behind his back, the mess of blood and other matter falling slowly to the asteroid's surface. It's disgusting and bile rises again in my throat, so I turn my attention back to him.

With my helmet right up near his, I can see his eyes go wide in pain and disbelief. And I just can't help myself. I'm not sure if it's the fact that this is only my second face-to-face kill or if I've read way too many Billy Firebrand novels. Or maybe it's because I think even a piece of scum like Owen deserves an explanation. Whatever my reasons, I monologue.

"You made a lot of mistakes on this one, Owen. First, you let on far too early that you knew who Jessica and I are. That gave me time to think about how you'd learned what the rest of the galaxy doesn't know.

"Second, you simply didn't grasp the magnitude of what you've gotten involved in. I do. After all, this particular mess is a big part of what killed me the first time around.

"But third," I shut off the comm and press my helmet to his so that he'll still hear me, but no one else can listen in. "You threatened the woman I love. And the second you did that, the only outcome of this was for one of us to die."

Then I take a step back and switch the comm back on. "Finally, you didn't do your research, or you would know that the X-421 Stinger," I raise the pistol for him to see, "has an extra safety for low-g use. It's to prevent an accidental discharge that could send someone tumbling through space if they don't know what they're doing."

I'm still close enough to see the moment Owen dies. And whatever strange sympathy I felt watching Tucker's life leave him eludes me now because I have zero doubt that the galaxy is now a much better place without Owen Thompson in it.

I search his pockets quickly and find a small transmitter with a single button. Its screen shows a countdown with six minutes and fourteen seconds left. Saying a silent prayer, I press the button, and the timer resets to an hour. I breathe a sigh of relief and slump to the asteroid's surface in exhaustion.

TWENTY-THREE
THE KING'S CROSS...AGAIN

I'm torn now between an overwhelming desire to sleep and an equally strong urge to climb quickly up the ladder, get inside the ship, and make sure Jessica is OK in there with Jules and Harris. I don't even dare call her in case Owen and his team hacked our implant comms.

I start getting up but stop myself from climbing to the airlock. There's one more thing that needs to be done first.

"You shouldn't have hired him," I say softly into my helmet comm.

A figure steps out from behind one of *Wanderer's* landing struts and walks slowly toward me.

"No choice," a woman's voice says without a hint of apology. It's a voice I last heard eight days ago in the Gerson system, threatening to kill me and Jessica if she ever saw us after that. Now, it's oddly comforting to hear it again.

"There's always a choice," I tell Heather Kilgore, Agent of the King's Cross, as she stops a meter from me. Her gun is aimed at my chest, though I've made no effort to point Owen's old gun in her direction.

She shrugs, the move making her military-grade helmet bob up and down a bit. "You're right, of course, but that doesn't change the fact that this was the best way. I needed the traitor and his intel before the Koratans got it, but I needed plausible deniability for the King in case the entire thing blew up; there's no way we can be caught operating in the Leeward Republic. You and Lieutenant Commander Lin were... convenient."

"And Owen?"

She shrugs again. "A mercenary I've used in the past. Willing to do whatever it takes, and usually very effective."

"Well, your plan failed," I tell her simply.

"Did it? I still kept the intel out of the Koratans' hands. And one more dead mercenary isn't—"

"Two," I interrupt her. "Two...dead mercenaries."

She cocks her head and searches my face for a long moment through our respective helmets, then she nods once but says nothing.

"What happens now?" I ask.

"Well, that depends on you. But tell me first, how did you know to have Petty Officer Peterson contact me?"

That was the last thing I'd told George to do back in the casino restaurant, instructing him to send a specific message to a comm code I'd found deep within *Wanderer's* memory on the first day I'd flown her away from Gerson. It was a gamble, but I suspected the code belonged to the ship's former owner. Turns out, I was right. And having George send the message would keep it a secret even if Owen had found a way to break my implant's encryption. He made the call as soon as we were clear of the casino's jamming.

But I don't tell her all of that. I just tell her the little that matters. "Owen said we were after a traitor from the Layton System Patrol, but there hasn't been anyone AWOL from there in over five years. But there *was* a George Peterson who went missing from Gerson several weeks ago. Idiot thought changing his name to Jorge was enough."

She nods, apparently impressed. "He was on loan to the survey corps ship that actually found the stellarium deposit in Gerson's asteroid belt. Wainwright may have sold the existence of the deposit to the Koratans, but Peterson could have told them its *exact* location."

"And if the exact location got out, the Koratans would send *everything* they've got to take it from Prometheus."

"Yes," she confirms; I'm on a roll here. "You saw first-hand what the Koratans were willing to do even just knowing there was a deposit *somewhere* in the system. Imagine what they'd do with the exact coordinates. Pure chaos. And if the information got out to other nations..."

I nod again, numb and not particularly caring if good ole King Charles loses the most valuable deposit of metal in the Fringe. "So again," I ask her, "what happens now?"

"Well, if you're asking if I'm going to kill you, I don't think I will. You and Lin proved valuable for a second time in just the last two weeks. And I may need to use you again, so keeping you alive is the best choice. Besides, why punish you for providing yet another valuable service to the Crown?"

I huff. Even after she let us go the first time, the idea of a King's Cross agent with a conscience amuses me. "And what's to stop you from sending the rest of the King's Cross, or the Navy, after us later?"

She smiles just a bit. "Think of it as mutually assured destruction. The King wanted you dead, so you're dead. If he finds out otherwise, he'll hunt you down ruthlessly across the galaxy. But also..."

"He'll know you lied to him," I finish for her.

She nods.

"Of course," I admit, "that still doesn't stop you from killing us yourself. And the whole thing about us being useful, I don't buy it. Because, like you said, having us alive is a threat to your life as well. If *anyone* finds out who we are," I look down meaningfully at Owen's corpse, "whether you tell them or they figure it out for themselves, you'll be as good as dead. So, tell me the real reason I'm not lying next to our friend right now."

There's a long silence, and I think she's going to refuse outright. But then I hear her sigh. "Like we talked about at Gerson, what happened to Jessica Lin on *Persephone* was wrong. And let's just say I have...firsthand experience with just how wrong."

I nod. There's no more explanation needed.

But she continues speaking anyway. "And what happened to her on *Ordney* was almost worse. She deserves better. Call it feminine solidarity if that makes you feel better."

"What happened on *Ordney*?" I ask softly.

She shakes her head. "Not my place to tell you. Only Lin can make that choice."

It's what I expected, but you can't blame a guy for trying.

"Now," she says, "speaking of Miss Lin, perhaps you'd better go and make sure she's OK. But not before you give me what I came here for."

I motion down toward Owen's body. "Right breast pocket."

She keeps her gun pointed in my direction but crouches and quickly searches the body, finding and pocketing the drive in her own skinsuit. I see her eyes go momentarily out of focus as she accesses it with her implant.

"So, you didn't delete it. You were *bluffing*?" She's apparently been listening in the entire time. Good of her to help me in the fight against the two mercenaries.

I shrug. "There wasn't enough time. But a guy like Owen expects a double-cross, so I gave him one to believe in."

"And the copy you made on your implant?"

"Another bluff. The drive was copy-proof." I give her temporary root access to my implant so she can double-check that I'm telling the truth. Left unsaid is that I could have still memorized the coordinates from it, but she doesn't ask, and I don't tell. "Besides, by now, George Peterson has no doubt gotten himself completely lost in those tunnels, but I'm sure a woman with your ingenuity and resources can find him and make sure no other copies exist."

She doesn't acknowledge my suggestion verbally but starts to walk toward the tunnel mouth, confident enough to leave me at her back with a loaded gun. But I'm done killing for today...well, almost. There are still two of Owen's team on my ship with Jessica, and they'll be getting antsy that their boss isn't back by now."

I start climbing the ladder to the airlock to punch in the code and enter my ship. But before I'm done, I hear Heather Kilgore's voice one more time. "You know, you'd make a halfway decent mercenary yourself. Expect a call from me in the future. I seem to find myself suddenly short of resources in this sector of space."

I don't respond directly, because she and I both know the truth. If she calls, I'll have no choice but to answer. Instead, I say, "I do have two requests before you blast off back to Promethean space." And then I tell her what they are. To my surprise, she agrees to both.

TWENTY-FOUR
THE REAL FEMME FATALE

I find Jessica in the *Wanderer's* galley. I have the pistol out and extended in front of me, struggling to remember what I learned nearly a decade ago when I participated in my last boarding action—before I reached too lofty a rank for the Navy to risk me behind a gun like that.

But there's no need. Jessica is standing with her back against the galley counter, a gun in *her* hand pointed squarely at me as I enter the room. She's still wearing the dress from Rishi, and one of the shoulders is ripped, but otherwise, she looks to be in one piece. When she sees it's me and not Owen or Tucker, she lets her shoulders droop as tension flows out of them, and she swings the gun back around to cover the two other people in the galley.

Harris sits calmly at the galley table, his hands flat on the tabletop where Jessica and I can easily see them. Jules, however, is tied to her chair with a gag in her mouth, glaring hatefully in turns at me, Jessica, *and* Harris.

I clearly missed all the fun, but I'm duly impressed. I almost died taking out just Tucker in an environment where I had a huge advantage. Somehow, Lin managed to subdue and capture two mercenaries seemingly without much trouble, though from the way she stands favoring one side, her broken ribs aren't doing too well. Also, the fact that Harris isn't even tied up indicates she may have had only one that actually fought back. Still, I'm impressed beyond measure.

"You good?" I ask my first mate.

"No," she says, a tremor in her voice. "The hour passed, but someone needs to get this *thing* out of my head." I suddenly feel terrible for not coming into the ship sooner. While I was chatting with Kilgore outside, Jessica must have been a wreck counting down the hour and not knowing I'd already reset the timer.

But maybe I can make up for that. I look over at Harris, and he nods once. So, I take a leap of faith and carefully hand him the transmitter I took off Owen's body. He fiddles with it for a second and then nods again. "It's inert now," he tells us. "You can dig out the implant at any time, but the explosive is no longer armed."

I see Jessica's shoulders drop further, and for a second, I think she might collapse in exhaustion like I almost did on the asteroid's surface. But she keeps her footing, and the gun in her hand never wavers from covering the two mercenaries.

I move over to stand beside her, my pistol now pointed squarely at Jules. Slowly, hesitantly, I reach up and put my other arm around Jessica's shoulders. And then, the floodgates open.

In a Billy Firebrand story, this is the part where the beautiful woman cries into the hero's shoulder. But this isn't a fictional adventure, and it's me now sobbing as I hold tight to Jessica, the pain, stress, frustration, and guilt of the last few days—perhaps even longer—coming out in choking, very unmanly sobs.

She cries a bit, too, and even leans her head into my chest, but I'm the one who ugly cries. And, you know what? It feels amazing.

TWENTY-FIVE
A NEW CREW MEMBER

Fifteen minutes later, Jules is sitting on the deck of *Wanderer's* airlock, still loosely tied up but dressed now in a decompression skinsuit. Next to her are a helmet, a long-range comm, and a few days' supply of extra air bladders. I crouch down in front of her, thankful she's still gagged, so I can't understand the very colorful grunts originating from her.

I pick up the helmet, but before I put it on her head, I lean forward and whisper so only she can hear. "You know, it would have never worked between us. Your butt is pretty nice, but not nearly good enough to make up for your terrible personality."

She glares at me and starts a whole new string of undoubtedly creative invectives rendered ineffective by the gag. I seal the helmet, further muffling her tirade.

Then I turn to regard Harris, who is also wearing a skinsuit and is about to put his own helmet on. I've reached a decision—an important one. But first, I look over at Jessica, standing outside the airlock, who gives me a nod of permission.

"Harris," I say, "you want a ride somewhere?"

He stops with his helmet halfway on. "Actually, I was hoping to sign on. Be part of…" he looks around as if to encompass us and all of *Wanderer* around us, "whatever this is. I like the way you operate."

I nod. I half expected that response. And given his skills with disguises, he'll be useful to two semi-fugitives on the run. Though we may have to work on his own atrocious appearance. Plus, of all Owen's team, he's ultimately the one I grew to hate the least.

He and I leave the airlock and go back into the ship's corridor, sealing the hatch behind us. Then, I override the controls, blowing open the outer hatch without first evacuating the atmo. I can't help it, and I laugh out loud as a still tied-up Jules is forcibly sucked out through the hatch and falls slowly and comically to the asteroid's surface. Even Jessica can't entirely suppress a snicker.

Of course, Lin wouldn't laugh if she knew what I know, that Jules won't be alive for long. Heather Kilgore will see to that after she finds George Peterson, and I doubt either of them will ever leave this rock. Part of me is sad about that fact, but I also recognize the expediency. They know about me and Jessica, and that's as much a threat to Kilgore as it is to us. Besides, one is a traitor who sold out his country, and the other is a sadistic killer who might chase us forever if she got free.

But I'm glad Jessica doesn't know. Best that only one of us has to live with their deaths on his conscience. I can at least protect her from that.

As I turn to head back to the cockpit to lift the ship off this horrid little rock, Jessica close on my heels, Harris asks, "So, any chance you can tell me what it is we'll be doing? What are we?"

I turn back as Jessica answers first. "We're mercenaries," she says, smiling in my direction.

"Nope," I say quickly, though it pains me to do so. "We're a legitimate cargo ship." I open a file on my implant, the one Heather Kilgore gave me in response to one of my last requests on the asteroid's surface, and I send it to Jessica's implant.

Her eyes widen momentarily when she receives the fully signed-over registration for the *Wanderer*, though under its original name, *Hornet*. She searches my eyes, probably trying to see if I'm serious about being a simple freighter captain from here on out now that we have the proper credentials.

Whether she finds in my eyes what she's looking for or not, I can't say. But she turns away from me and looks back toward Harris. "No," she says in the Confident Lin voice that sends good chills up and down my spine. "We're mercenaries."

"Wait! I'm Billy Firebrand?" I exclaim unable to hold my tongue or keep the excitement out of my voice. It's been a long day, and my normally modest self-control is pretty much gone at this point. "Like, for real?"

She turns back to regard me with a long-suffering expression. "Sure, Brad. You can be Billy Firebrand, whoever that is."

"And that makes you Nikita Starshine. And Harris is Scooter James. This is going to be awesome!" Apparently I get inappropriately giddy when I'm exhausted and just killed two men.

She sighs loudly and rolls her eyes; then she smiles and says, with laughter in her voice, "Brad, you're an idiot."

Those four words have never sounded better.

TWENTY-SIX
TO FORGIVE IS DIVINE

Later, Jessica and I are sitting in *Wanderer's* cockpit as we fly away from the little Swiss cheese asteroid. We lost no time leaving; I want to be well clear of the rock before Heather Kilgore finds George Peterson and Jules and then blasts off from wherever she's hidden her ship. Jessica, who still has no idea Kilgore was ever there, seems equally anxious to leave the place behind.

We sit there in silence for a long time, maybe a full hour. Harris is nowhere to be seen, probably in his new cabin sorting through his feelings at leaving his old life behind. I know what that's like, so I give him his space.

I've settled on and then rejected about a dozen things I want to say to my first mate—a dozen different lame but heartfelt apologies for what I said to her back on Rishi—but she's the one to speak first.

"I'm sorry, Brad."

Wait. What?!

"Uh, Jess. I don't mean to sound rude, but why are *you* apologizing to *me*?"

She looks at me, eyebrows knit in confusion. She still has the lash extensions and the eye shadow from Harris' makeover on Rishi, and they accentuate the effect. "For what I said about your ex-wife back in the casino. I was upset and jumped to some conclusions, and I know I really hurt you."

Now I'm speechless again. Literally. I'm opening my mouth, trying to get words to come out, but the only thing I manage sounds like someone is letting the air slowly out of a balloon. Super manly. Just like Billy Firebrand.

She looks confused again but says nothing as I choke on my words. Finally, I manage to eke out, almost in a whisper, "But…what I said to you. I…I didn't mean to hurt you."

Understanding dawns in those beautiful eyes, and she smiles at me. "Is that why you've been so quiet? I thought it was because of what *I* said to *you*. I mean, what you said about me not knowing what a healthy relationship looks like…well, it hurt, and I was really angry with you for a few hours, but you were right. And even if it wasn't the nicest thing to say…" she shrugs. "Listen, your entire world had just come crashing down around you; I can't blame you if you lashed out in the moment."

"OK," I say in consternation. "But you have to know that I'm sorry, too. And, for what it's worth, I'm pretty sure you were right about Carla." It hurts to say that, but just voicing it out loud somehow also seems to lift a small part of a massive weight from my shoulders.

She looks back at me now, graces me with another of her rare smiles, and reaches out a hand to place on mine like she did back at the bar and grill. It sends an electric charge through my entire body. For a long time, we just sit that way, enjoying the moment.

Lin is again the one who breaks the silence. You couldn't make me do it for all the stellarium in the galaxy.

"So, where do we go from here, Captain?"

I want to take her in my arms, kiss her, and say something smooth about how it doesn't matter where we go as long as we're together. But there are lines that, once crossed, can never be uncrossed. If she doesn't feel the same way, and I'm almost certain she doesn't, things will forever be awkward between us. And right now, I need her with me like I need oxygen to breathe, even if she isn't with me in the way I truly want. And even if it means no more booze…at least around her.

So, I keep it simple. "Well, we're mercenaries now. We look for someone willing to pay us to shoot at things. Should be easy; everyone wants something shot now and again."

She laughs and squeezes my hand, and it's the best I've felt about myself in the six months since Bellerophon.

EPILOGUE

I slam awake, disoriented and wondering where I am and what that infernal high-pitched wailing in my ears could be. Luckily, after so many years of Navy conditioning—not to mention almost a week without a drink—I gather my wits quickly and find myself in *Wanderer's* pilot seat with the alarm coming from the console in front of me. I check it quickly.

Proximity alert?

I'm alone in the cockpit, and a quick time check reveals it's been nine hours since we burned away from the small asteroid; we're still one hour short of the jump point back to the Kate's Hope system, where we collectively decided to return if for no other reason than to get out of Fiori space as quickly as possible.

I recall now that I sent Lin back to her quarters to sleep a few hours ago, and Harris is likely still resting as well. I must have dozed off because I didn't even notice…

My heart sinks, and I swear loudly as I see what's triggered the proximity alert. The sensor picture resolves at the same time the massive ship moves overhead and becomes visible in the cockpit's forward viewport, reversing thrust to match velocities with my little freighter.

It's a warship. And not just any warship. This is no simple patrol boat, but a full-fledged battlecruiser ten times longer than *Wanderer*. And while I might not immediately recognize its design, I don't need to know what star nation it's from to see the dozens of laser turrets that look like they're aimed right at my head through the cockpit window.

"*Merchant Vessel Wanderer*," a professionally cool female voice sounds from the comm, "this is the *Leeward Republic Navy Ship Dauntless*. This is a system patrol stop. Heave to and prepare to be boarded."

I immediately cut acceleration and send a quick acknowledgment. *Wanderer* can't outrun a battlecruiser, and all it would take is a twitch on the controls of one of those laser turrets to vaporize my ship and its small crew. I want the captain of that behemoth to be one hundred percent assured I'm not going to make a run for it.

"Jennifer! Harris!" I shout through the internal comm, using Jessica's false name in the event the *Dauntless* is already hacked into our shipboard transmissions. "We've got company! Meet me at the..." I check the sensor picture "...starboard airlock."

The ship shudders around me as the battlecruiser grasps us in a docking clamp. I unstrap from the pilot's seat and head out the cockpit door toward the airlock, making haste. My hand automatically goes to my belt where I've been carrying Owen's pistol, but it's not there, left behind in the cockpit. No matter; a simple handgun wouldn't be of any use against a ship full of trained spacers and Marines. Even having it might actually get me shot before I can figure out what they want.

I arrive at the airlock before either Jessica or Harris, which is fine. Better for me to face this first as the captain. That gives me pause; I'm not sure when I started thinking of myself unironically as the captain again. But old habits of command are once again kicking in, though they come with a sober lack of confidence that I'll be able to get us out of whatever this is.

I have no idea why a Leeward Republic Navy vessel would not only sneak up on *Wanderer* but then demand to board us with no preamble, but it can't be good. And it would be far too much of a coincidence for this *not* to be related to what happened just half a day ago on that lonely asteroid, which makes it doubly not good for us.

Further speculation on my part is cut off when the outer airlock hatch opens without protest, the boarding party entering a manufacturer's override code that my ship's AI has no choice but to accept. Not wanting to appear like we have anything to hide, I check the pressure and then key open the inner airlock hatch to save them the trouble.

Only to find myself staring down the business ends of four light assault rifles pointed straight at my face.

I automatically raise my hands. "Uh, hi," I say through a suddenly dry mouth, "can I help you?"

With an effort, I look beyond the looming rifles to see a bemused look on one of the Marines' faces at my question. There are three men and one woman, all dressed in identical uniforms that are foreign to me, but they are still instantly identifiable as Marines in their stance and the steady hold on their rifles. That and they each look like they could break me in half without a second thought.

"Are you the captain of this vessel?" asks the same stern female voice that ordered me to prepare to be boarded over the comm. Looking past the Marines, I now see an older woman in what looks more like a naval uniform. From the marks on her collar, I think she might be a rear admiral of all things. Now this *really* isn't looking good for us.

"Uh, yeah?" I respond to her. I didn't mean for it to sound like a question, but given I just woke up from a nap after fighting for my life for two days straight, I'm willing to forgive myself. You might think that after conducting so many routine boarding operations in my time in the Navy, I would know what to do here, but I've never been on *this* side of those guns. Besides, you don't send battlecruisers, battle-ready Marines, and a rear admiral for a routine inspection stop.

"Good," she says with a curt nod. "Where is the rest of your crew?"

I shrug without lowering my hands. "Coming, I think. We were all asleep."

She frowns as if I've just committed some cardinal sin by being asleep at the wheel of a starship, which maybe I have. I'm unfamiliar with the navigation laws in the Leeward Republic, but either way, I don't think she's the type to let me off with a warning.

Before I can open my mouth and ask the stern woman what's going on, an older man in an expensive-looking civilian business suit steps up beside her. He's reasonably tall, about my height, and Asian, with perfectly combed black hair that's graying at the temples, the only feature that betrays his age. His face looks even more dour than the naval officer next to him, giving the impression of a man who only smiles for corporate PR photos. He gives me a quick once over before looking past me into my ship. Then he speaks.

I can't understand anything he says; it's in what sounds like Mandarin to my untrained ear, but I could be wrong. I'm about to tell them so when I hear a familiar female voice answer in the same language from behind me.

Without lowering my hands, I turn my head to see Jessica stepping up next to me, staring at the older man, a grim set to her mouth.

"Uh…Jen?" I ask.

Lin shakes her head but keeps her hard stare on the man with the graying temples, matching his glare for its intensity. "It's OK, Brad, they know who we are. No use hiding it." Then she sighs loudly.

"Hello, father."

THE END OF BOOK TWO

THE WORST PIRATE HUNTERS IN THE FRINGE

BOOK THREE

ONE
INTERROGATED BY AN IDIOT

"Mr. Mendoza, you may be the dumbest man I've ever met."

You ever have one of those days when the hits just keep on coming? Seriously, I thought that day for me was just two days ago when Owen Thompson hijacked my ship and put an explosive implant into my XO's neck. But today is quickly inserting itself for the title of 'Worst Day Ever'. Or maybe it's just an all-around crappy week.

There we were, minding our own business, trying to get out of the Fiori system as quickly as we could while avoiding any official entanglements, when the mother of all official entanglements sought *us* out. I was rudely awakened from a nice nap, my ship was captured and boarded by a Leeward Republic battlecruiser, and then I got to sort of meet Lin's father—that was weird. And now I get to sit here and be questioned by this guy who looks like he just got out of high school and keeps telling me *I'm* dumb.

Of course, he's a naval intelligence officer—not in *my* Navy, but that doesn't really matter—so he has plenty of experience with stupidity. Whoever originally said that military intelligence is an oxymoron must have been thinking of this kid.

"What do you have to say for yourself, Mr. Mendoza?" he asks, rudely omitting my title. I may no longer be in the Navy, but I'm still the *captain* of a ship.

I shrug, mainly because every time I do, it ticks him off, and that's probably the only fun I'm going to have on this cursed day.

"I'll ask you for the last time: what were you doing in the Fiori system?"

I shrug again, gratified to see his face turn a slightly deeper shade of red. "I was shopping for some drapes. My cabin has a pretty cold aesthetic going on, and I thought I could liven the place up."

He slams both palms down on the table in anger at my flippant response. I don't react; that's the third time he's done that, so it's lost any small shock value it had ninety minutes ago when this little interrogation started.

"I warn you, Mr. Mendoza, until you answer my questions, you're not leaving this room."

Taking a moment to look around the small gray interrogation room, I shrug once again. "I don't know; it's not so bad. My drapes guy could do wonders with that two-way mirror over there; add in a few throw pillows and a duvet, and this space could be downright cozy." Ha! The joke's on him. I have no idea what a duvet is. I just remember my ex-wife, Carla, always talking about us needing a new one.

He doesn't appreciate my amazing sense of humor. But that's alright with me; I decided from the start that his opinion doesn't really matter. Besides, it's fun messing with him, so I lean forward conspiratorially. He can't help it; he leans forward across the table as well.

"Listen," I tell him soberly, "all joking aside, I was actually here smuggling drugs out of the system."

A look of triumph flashes across his face, followed just as quickly by skepticism. He suspects I'm playing an angle. Good.

"And just where would we find these drugs, and what exactly are they?" he asks cautiously.

"In my cargo hold, near the port bulkhead, in a crate marked 'baked beans'." I lean forward more, and he does the same as a natural response. "And I'd rather not say what kind of drugs they are."

He's getting excited, even though he must still suspect I'm pulling his leg. "I don't care if you'd rather say or not," he says with what he probably thinks is a calm, authoritative tone, but his voice cracks a little at the end. "You will tell me now what is in that shipment."

I shrug again and lean forward even more; our faces are less than ten centimeters apart now. "Fine, but I thought you'd want me to exercise a little discretion in a matter like this." I cast a meaningful glance at the two-way mirror behind him.

"Anything you say to me, you can say to the cameras and the other intelligence officers watching," he says.

"OK," I say with an apologetic look, "I was just bringing you your medication; you know, for that little problem you have." I look down in the direction of his lap meaningfully and then back up to savor his reaction.

For a moment, nothing happens; his face is stuck in the grim, authoritative expression he uses when asking me questions. But then, I see understanding dawn, and his eyebrows furrow as his mouth curves down in an angry frown.

I should stop now; I really should. But I'm having way too much fun. "It's nothing to be ashamed of; it happens to the best of us. But I think I got it here not a moment too soon. All the female Marines were talking about your…issue while they escorted me here."

That does it. I thought I made him turn red earlier, but now he turns a shade of almost purple, and I can see he's about to throw an apoplectic fit. Perfect! I lean back to enjoy the show.

But just as he starts opening his mouth to let forth a no-doubt bloodcurdling but impotent scream, the small room's hatch opens, and an older woman steps in, interrupting the show. I recognize her immediately as the rear admiral who led the boarding party that 'captured' me two hours ago.

"Daniels," the woman says calmly, addressing the stupid intelligence officer, "give us the room."

Admirals have a way of issuing orders without yelling but with no less emphasis, and her simple command is enough to instantly cut off any invectives the guy was about to throw my way. He turns heel without argument and leaves the room, not even giving me a backward glance, though I can tell by the way his shoulders are hunched and his hands balled into fists that he's still raging mad.

"Bye, sweetie!" I yell after him. "I'll see you after work. Don't forget about those pills!"

TWO
INTERROGATED BY A MASTER

The admiral waits for the intelligence officer to leave the room and for the hatch to shut behind him before throwing me a disapproving look that reminds me of my grandmother when she caught me trying to ride one of the dogs on her farm—it was a beagle, and I was nine, but I still thought it might work.

I say nothing but do a pretty good job of keeping a perfectly innocent and beatific expression on my face like I'm a favored student and not the little boy caught pulling the braids of the girl in front of me.

"There is a debate going on, Captain Mendoza," she says calmly—at least *she* remembers to give me my due title, "about just what I should do with you. Our intelligence section would like me to throw you in a very deep and extremely dark hole for the rest of your mortal days while we extract each and every piece of knowledge that may be rattling around in that brain cavity of yours. I suspect that Lieutenant Commander Daniels will be the first to recommend that the particular hole they throw you in be full of Visalian crocodiles."

She pauses, perhaps to give me the opportunity to respond. I choose not to. I want to see where this is going. And I'm still trying not to laugh out loud at the way Daniels left the room a few seconds ago.

To my surprise, she smiles at my silence. "Luckily for you, it just so happens I'm not convinced you would even know enough for it to be worth our trouble."

OK, now I *have* to say something. Because she just called me dumb in a much deeper and more meaningful way than Daniels did. Of course, what I end up saying isn't at all what I would have said had I taken even a moment to consider my words.

"Lady, I know things that would make your head spin." And just like that, it's as if all my SERE training about resisting interrogation never happened.

She raises an eyebrow. "Really? Like what, that big discovery in Gerson that your king is so convinced he's managed to keep under wraps?"

My composure breaks. I just almost died—twice!—to keep the secret of that stellarium deposit, and here she is mentioning it like it's yesterday's news. "You broke Harris, didn't you?" I demand to know. "I *knew* that guy wouldn't be able to hold up."

"The makeup artist?" she asks incredulously and then sits back in her chair and laughs. She's surprisingly casual and relaxed for a member of the admiralty; maybe they do things differently here in the Leeward Republic. "No," she continues. "I imagine he knows even less than you, but he did go into great detail about what he would change about his interrogator's approach to cosmetics. The look on the poor lieutenant's face when she finally realized he wasn't trying to get under her skin but was actually being serious…" She shakes her head and gives a short laugh.

"Then, Jessica?" I ask, my voice rising an octave because the thought of someone breaking her to the point that she would reveal such valuable information is distressing in the extreme to me.

"Relax, Captain," the admiral says, her tone not rising to meet mine. "Miss Lin hasn't been subjected to the ham-fisted interrogation techniques of our illustrious intelligence directorate. No, she has been with her father this entire time…catching up."

Oh, yeah. Her father. I'm still trying to wrap my head around that one.

As if sensing my thoughts, the admiral gives me a wry smile. "Yes,

I imagine you and Lieutenant Commander Lin will have a lot to talk about when you're reunited after all this."

"So, we *will* be reunited?" I ask, unable to keep the hope out of my tone.

She leans forward, and I subconsciously meet her halfway, almost kicking myself when I realize she just used the same tactic on me that I used on poor Daniels moments ago. "Oh, yes, Captain," she says with a thin smile, "you see, I actually have some need of you."

I'm going to ask what she means, but she quickly changes the subject, and I'm starting to realize that when it comes to subtle verbal sparring and keeping your conversation partner off balance, I'm in the presence of a master.

"Tell me, Captain, did you know that the Leeward Republic Naval Academy just added an entire section on your actions at Bellerophon?"

That actually surprises me. "What class, How-Not-to-Captain 101?"

She smirks. "No, actually. Military Ethics 304, one of the advanced classes for our command candidates. And it may not surprise you to hear that there are multiple schools of thought…"

She goes on for a few minutes, and it takes a little while for me to realize that she has cleanly distracted me from the fact that she *knows* about Prometheus' greatest secret, and she supposedly didn't hear about it from Harris or Lin, and she certainly didn't get it from me.

Then how?

"Anyway," she says, "it's an absolutely compelling case of the classic trolley problem; do you divert a trolley to hit one person on a side track to avoid killing five on the main track, or do you…"

I'm still only half listening as my mind races to try and figure things out. Because as near as I can tell, this is all-around *bad* for me and my crew. Not that I really care about good ole King Charles and his stellarium—I'd tell the Leeward Republic or anyone else about it in a heartbeat if I thought it would benefit Lin or me. But even if they *didn't* learn it from us, I know there are many, including one Agent of the King's Cross, Heather Kilgore, who will assume it *was* us who spilled the tea. And that is *not* a woman I want thinking I betrayed her.

But then I realize something else and want to hit my head with the palm of my hand repeatedly, but I refrain lest she think I'm having some sort of episode. She mentioned the *secret* in the Gerson system, but she didn't actually mention the stellarium.

She's fishing.

"...and I'm of the second school of thought, that you made the only choice you could have." She pauses, maybe for air or maybe because she's finally realized I'm not paying attention to her as she dissects the action that ruined my life six-and-a-half months ago.

"You're mistaken," I tell her bluntly. "What I did at Bellerophon was wrong, and there's simply no way to spin it otherwise. I made a bad choice. Period. And 504 civilians died as a result. Tell that to your classroom." The words come easy—strangely so—though I know my tone is bitter. The only other person I've ever said this out loud to was Jessica Lin. But something about the old admiral has put me weirdly at ease. It's the mark of an *excellent* interrogator, and even knowing that she's playing me like a fiddle doesn't change how I react to it.

She considers my response for a second, then shakes her head. "Even your own navy concluded you were innocent of any wrongdoing. Full acquittal."

I frown. "A farce," I say dismissively, having had this particular discussion *many* times with friends and family following the court-martial. "Admiral Oliphant didn't want me dragging his name or his daughter through the mud any more than I already had; he pressured the panel to find in my favor. Politics, pure and simple."

She looks at me, perhaps trying to see if I'm serious, but then surprises me by smiling. The admiral leans forward conspiratorially again, but this time, I stay where I am and don't meet her halfway. "You know," she says, "my father used to say the same two things to every poor boy who picked me up for a date when I was a teenager. First, he'd say, 'Son, there is nothing more powerful than a father's love for his daughter'. Then, he would add, 'Except, that is, for a father's hate for any man not good enough for his daughter'."

She lets that hang there between us for a while as if she expects me to respond. When I don't, she shrugs and stands abruptly. "Well, anyway, I assume you'd like to get back to your crew."

Surprised, I stand slowly, nodding.

She moves to the hatch, and it opens as she nears it, no doubt via some unseen signal to the Marines in the hall. But right before she leaves the room, she turns back to me, her smile gone. "I know you think your father-in-law lobbied for your acquittal. But we had a man in the room, as it were. Terrence Oliphant did, in fact, lobby the panel of judges. But it will surprise you, I imagine, to learn that he lobbied *against* you. Had Oliphant had his way, you would have been convicted and received the death penalty from the King. Something for you to think about."

Before I can respond, she's gone through the hatch, leaving me with my head spinning and with far more questions than answers.

THREE
THE DAMSEL IN DISTRESS

"She had a giant zit on her forehead, and she used the wrong shade of foundation to try and cover it up. She used Beige Dream, but she should have used Desert Sand." That strange fact enters my earholes courtesy of Harris, the newest member of my crew.

It's been three hours since the *Dauntless* stopped my ship and took us all into custody without much in the way of explanation. Now, at least, we're not in interrogation rooms anymore. Instead, a Marine showed me to a small conference room where Harris was already waiting. Since then, for about forty minutes, he's been describing in painful detail the various cosmetic shortcomings of the female lieutenant who tried to interrogate him. The admiral wasn't kidding. I only hope the poor young officer isn't still listening to our conversation, or she might develop a complex.

"Where's Jessica?" I ask aloud for about the fifth time. Harris ignores me—which is fine because I'm asking the microphones no doubt live in this room, not him—and keeps prattling on about his interrogator's split ends or something like that. I think the guy talks when he's nervous. Being woken in the middle of your sleep cycle by a massive battlecruiser capturing and boarding your unarmed ship will do that to a man.

Luckily for both of us, my question is answered promptly this time as the conference room hatch opens and Jessica Lin steps in, her face red and partially hidden by her straight, short black hair, which is hanging forward in a vain effort to hide the puffiness around her stunning green eyes. Despite all that, she's still the most perfect woman I've ever laid eyes on; even the rumpled shipsuit she must have thrown on as we were being boarded can't hide her beauty, nor can the redness of her face hide its perfect proportions or the smoothness of her unblemished skin.

Before I know what I'm doing, I'm out of my seat and standing in front of her, my eyes searching hers for any signs that she's been mistreated, and, finding none, I pull her into a tight hug. I feel her go abruptly rigid, and I quickly realize my mistake and start to unwrap my arms from around her, but suddenly, she grabs me and hugs me back tightly, burying her face in my shoulder.

"Uh, all OK, XO?" I ask.

"All good, Captain," she responds, pushing back from me and blushing as she does so.

We both awkwardly take seats at the conference room table, where Harris has blessedly stopped talking and is now eyeing both of us like we're the characters in some movie he's watching.

"So, what is going on? Why is your father on a Leeward Republic warship?" I ask Jessica.

She looks down at her hands, and I give her the time she needs to formulate a response. But when she finally does speak, it's not very satisfying. "Not here, sir."

I get her point; we have no idea who might definitely be listening in. So, I just nod and turn my attention back to Harris for lack of anything else to talk about.

"Regretting your decision to sign on?" I ask him.

He shrugs. "Owen changed over the years—got meaner and less principled. I wanted to quit his team for a while but couldn't think of a way to do it that didn't end with Tucker bashing in my skull or Jules putting bamboo shoots under my fingernails."

Lovely picture; makes me glad those two thugs are dead.

Harris shrugs again. The constant shrugging really *is* annoying; no wonder Daniels was getting so mad at me. "I mean," he continues, "I wish we weren't on a warship being held against our will and interrogated, but at least we're not doing anything that makes me feel ashamed to be me."

The monumental depth of that statement actually renders me speechless for a few moments as I try to think back to the last time *I* could say I wasn't doing anything that made me feel ashamed to be me. It's been a while, though there have been some brief moments of late.

"Did they mistreat either of you?" Jessica asks, looking back and forth between us like she's scanning for black eyes or tortured souls.

I shake my head. "No. They sent some young intel weenie in to interrogate me, and I'm pretty sure he's reevaluating his life choices now that I've forever ruined his dating life in the Navy." She looks at me funny, but I don't explain further. "But Harris here, he gave his interrogator a complex. She's probably standing in front of a mirror somewhere examining every pore in her face."

Harris grins. "She did have big pores, but she didn't like it when I started counting them. I was just trying to be helpful." This guy. He may seem absent-minded, but I'm becoming increasingly sure he's smarter than he lets on.

At least Jessica seems mollified by our answers, and some of the concern and worry on her face disappears. I'm about to say something to fill the silence when the room's hatch opens again, and the admiral steps in, trailed by a younger woman.

The two sit down without preamble, and the admiral turns to me. "Captain Mendoza, I failed to properly introduce myself earlier. I am Rear Admiral Walters of the Leeward Republic Navy, Fourth Battlecruiser Division, and you are on my flagship, *LRS Dauntless*."

I nod in reply and then motion to Jessica and Harris. As long as the admiral is being civil, I see no reason not to reciprocate. "And as you already know, this is my first mate, Jessica Lin, and our crew member…" I trail off, realizing I actually don't know Harris' first name.

"Harris," he says, not seeming to get the hint. Or maybe he doesn't have a first name, like a music artist. He is weird like that.

Admiral Walter's lip twitches upward in what might be a suppressed smile. But she cuts it off and turns to the young woman in civilian clothes next to her. "This, Captain Mendoza, Commander Lin, and Mr. Harris, is Kayla Carter."

The younger woman nods but says nothing. I study her now. She's short and blond and very attractive—not at the same level as Jessica, but few are. Still, Kayla Carter is quite pretty in a girl-next-door kind of way. She has a small nose surrounded by freckles under dirty blond hair that's pulled back in a messy bun, and her face and arms are tan, the natural kind like she spends a lot of time on the surface of a sunny planet. Her clothing is rough, mostly denim and flannel, and reminds me of the work clothes my grandparents wore around the farm growing up. She turns her head to meet my studying gaze and studies me right back without breaking eye contact, almost in a challenging way.

Admiral Walters continues. "I'm afraid that Miss Carter came to the Republic Navy with some rather disturbing news, and I'd like her to share it with you now."

At that, Kayla Carter breaks eye contact with me and looks around the table. When she speaks, her voice is a soft soprano. "I'm from a small planet called Carter's World. I know what you're thinking, and yes, it's named after one of my ancestors. My father is the current planetary president, but it's an elected position, not hereditary. It's just a matter of tradition that the post often goes to a Carter."

From her homespun clothes and sun-drenched look, I assumed she was an undereducated farmer—like I used to be—but she speaks with clear diction and a steady, confident voice, sounding more like someone educated at one of the universities on a large planet like Prometheus.

"I came here to Leeward Republic space to petition the Navy for aid. Our planet, for the last year, has been under siege by a ruthless group of pirates led by a very nasty man named Poulter. They started small, raiding the occasional freighter coming in and out of the system. Then, six months ago, they escalated things. They destroyed our only system patrol boat and then raided our orbital station, stealing most of the food shipments we had ready for export.

They've come back every few weeks since, raiding both the orbital and the planet's surface. They've even brazenly started visiting my father at the presidential mansion and demanding tribute payments. When our small planetary militia tried to stop them on the ground, they strafed our force from one of their ships and killed most of them."

She stops, frowning as if she's reliving that moment. "Now, with outside trade cutoff and our treasury depleted, we're essentially just growing food to feed the pirates and our own populace, but we're short on a lot of vital goods, like medical supplies, that we usually get through trade. If something doesn't happen soon, our people will start dying.

"I barely escaped in our last spaceworthy ship and came to the Leeward Republic," she throws a sour look at Walters, "to petition the Navy for aid, but they have refused to help me."

Walters remains a cool customer, ignoring the woman's piercing gaze. "If it were up to me," the admiral says, "we would take *Dauntless* and deal with these pirates directly. Unfortunately, Carter's World is not a member of the Leeward Republic, nor does it have a mutual defense pact with us. I have explained to Miss Carter that if she were to petition for membership, Republic law would allow me to intervene and help with her situation. But she has made it very clear that she is not empowered to petition on her planet's behalf."

Kayla Carter frowns. "Actually, I've made it clear that even if I could, I wouldn't. We've maintained our independence from the surrounding star nations for seven hundred years, ever since my first ancestor founded the planet. And we will not throw off the shackles of one petty despot for another, no matter how well-intentioned they may appear."

The admiral tactfully ignores the jab at her and her star nation and turns her gaze to me instead. My opinion of Walters keeps rising, and I'm not exactly the biggest fan of admirals in general, so that's saying something. "This is what I was referring to earlier, Captain Mendoza, when I said I had need of you. The Leeward Republic cannot intervene, but perhaps an independent party can."

I return her stare incredulously. "Seriously? What do you expect us to do?" Whether I feel respect for her or not, I can't keep the skepticism out of my tone.

Walters smiles. "Mr. Harris told his interviewer that you're mercenaries, are you not?"

I lean back, sensing a trap. "Well, yeah, but we're just getting started. And you're talking about a pirate force large enough to hold an entire *planet* hostage. I have..." I look around the table for emphasis, "...two officers, a makeup artist, an unarmed freighter, and two pistols. What do you expect me to do with only that against a force like the one Miss Carter describes? Besides having Harris critique their mohawks and nose rings until they run away in embarrassment, I can't think how we would do any good."

Walters smiles again, and I feel like she's in on a joke that hasn't been shared with me. "Oh, I'm sure you'll figure something out. You seem to be rather adept at that if all the rumors are true."

"And if I say no?" I leave that out there, watching the admiral carefully. Her smile doesn't disappear, but she does raise an eyebrow.

"Well," she says with no hint of malice in her voice, "given that you're foreign nationals in my star nation under false identities and in a ship of dubious origin, I may have to ask Lieutenant Commander Daniels and his intelligence division to dig a little deeper into just what you're doing here. That could take a while. I have a feeling that, in your case, he'll want to be especially thorough. You made such a good impression on him, after all."

She stops, still smiling, but with a look in her eyes that tells me it's my move, and she knows she's backed me into a corner. But I'm in a bad mood, so I open my mouth to argue.

"We'll do it," a firm and resolute voice says. It's not mine, and my mouth now drops open in astonishment as my XO agrees to take the impossible job. I'm going to vocally disagree until I see Jessica shoot me a pleading look, and that shuts me up. She's a sucker for lost causes, apparently, but I'm a sucker for her, so I'll go along with it... for now.

Admiral Walter's smile gets even broader, though Kayla Carter looks from Jessica to me and then to Harris dubiously. And just like that, we're pirate hunters.

FOUR
A FARMER'S BREAKFAST

It takes us five jumps and seven days to get to Carter's World from Fiori. For the first two days, we mostly sleep. For me and Jess, it's our first real opportunity to rest since we met Owen Thompson, and we've been running on adrenaline, caffeine, and sheer willpower for more than two full days as we fought for our lives. So now, finally—even if temporarily—out of danger and ignoring how badly I want to talk to her about her father, we crash.

Harris doesn't know how to pilot a ship, but Kayla Carter surprisingly does. Normally, I would never trust someone I don't know to pilot a starship I'm in charge of, but I'm too exhausted to argue. So, she takes on the lion's share of the pilot's duties those first two days while Jessica and I mostly sleep.

On day three, I finally wake up feeling more like myself than I have in a long time. I'm almost ten days without a drink now, not entirely by choice. And while the withdrawal headaches have been pretty severe, at least my brain is clear. Even though there are still a lot of things I'd love to forget, I'm seriously considering swearing off alcohol altogether. Or maybe I'm just trying to make myself feel better since I'm stuck on this ship for another three days without a drop of alcohol on board.

I leave my cabin and make my way to the galley for breakfast. As I near the room, I can hear someone already there and the sound of what I think is rummaging. Sure enough, I round the corner to find the refrigerator door open and someone bent over inside so that I can't fully see them, just their rear end sticking out beyond the door's edge.

Sure it's Jessica, I do my best to muster a cheerful "Good morning!" She stands up and looks back at me, but to my surprise, it's Kayla. She sees my surprise and misinterprets it, looking me up and down. "Were you just staring at my butt?" she demands sternly.

"I…uh…" My brain shuts down, and the words just aren't coming. Wouldn't you know it, less than three days into my first mercenary job, I've already mortally insulted our client. The worst part is, I wasn't even staring. Finally, I eke out a pathetic "No."

She frowns. "Pity. I've worked hard to make it look this good." My jaw drops open, and she laughs at my expense.

"Come on in," she says playfully, "I'll make you breakfast."

I sit mutely at the table while Kayla bustles around the small galley, and soon, smells that I didn't know could exist on *Wanderer* are making my mouth water. Fifteen minutes later, we're feasting on scrambled eggs and hash browns.

"Where did we get the eggs?" I ask between mouthfuls.

"The *Dauntless* transferred over a bunch of stores right after they fueled up your ship and put that crate in your hold."

Oh yeah, the crate. All Walters would tell me was that it contained some items we would find useful in liberating Carter's World. But it has a location-based lock that won't open for us until we actually reach Kayla's home system. I almost told the admiral to keep it out of suspicion and sheer stubbornness, but Jessica interceded, and cooler heads prevailed.

We eat in silence for a few more minutes, and I get up to grab seconds out of the pan. Kayla finishes eating first and leans back, regarding me with a small frown. "So, you're just starting out as mercenaries?"

I stop the forkful of eggs I was about to bite into and lower it back to the plate. She's trying to keep her tone casual, but from the way her body has tensed up, I know she's truly worried; I would be too in her situation.

"As mercenaries, yes," I admit, "but Jessica and I have plenty of experience fighting pirates in the Promethean Navy."

Kayla raises her eyebrows skeptically. "But didn't you have weapons and warships and even Marines back then?"

She's got me there. But I push the plate away from me and meet her gaze steadily. "We did, but the tactics are still generally the same." It's a lie, but I consider it a harmless one; she needs some sort of assurance right now, even if I legitimately have no idea how we're going to help her and her planet. "How many pirates are there?" I ask, turning the questions back to her.

She frowns. "We're not entirely sure. The most we've seen at any one time was only thirty or so."

"But enough to decimate your planetary militia?"

Kayla nods. "Yes. But you have to understand; besides the fact that the pirates had air support and we didn't, our planetary militia was basically a hundred farmers using weapons older than my great-grandfather. We're a peaceful settlement, and Carter's World has no native large animals, so we don't even hunt for food. And we're a relatively poor farming world, so trading for or buying more and newer weapons has never been a priority."

"Until you needed them," I say.

She sighs loudly. "Until we needed them. You're right. In some ways, we may have brought this upon ourselves by being an easy target. I don't know why we thought a single, barely armed patrol boat would be enough to turn away any trouble coming our way. It was incredibly naïve of us."

It's a startlingly self-aware admission and not one I'm used to hearing from victims. But it's also a self-defeating attitude if allowed to fester, so I decide to cut it off. "Listen, what pirates do, there's no excuse for it, regardless of who the victims are or how the balance of power lies. Besides, I've seen pirate gangs that have dozens of warships and hundreds of well-armed ground troops, so not even a fully-armed destroyer or modern weapons in the hands of a fairly well-experienced militia can hold off every threat. But maybe we can help you out with this one." I have no idea *how* we'll do that, but I'm hoping to at least reassure her.

She smiles now, and it makes her nose crinkle up and accentuates the freckles around it. It's nice and reminds me of my first girlfriend back on Denton III, when I was fourteen. Kayla reaches out a hand and places it on mine. "Thank you, Captain Mendoza. I hope you *can* help us."

Wouldn't you know that very moment, with Kayla Carter's hand on mine and a smile on her face, is when Jessica would show up for breakfast?

"I hope I'm not interrupting," I hear my XO's voice from behind me, and I quickly jerk my hand back, which is not the best move. It makes me look like I was definitely doing something wrong and not just comforting a woman whose entire planet is under attack.

"I…uh…Kayla made eggs. I saved some for you," I say lamely, and Jessica moves wordlessly over to the galley cupboards to grab a plate and start dishing up her breakfast.

Kayla is looking between me and Jessica now, an expression on her face that I can't decipher.

"Umm," I stammer, "I'm going to go to the cockpit and check our course." I get up from the table and beat a hasty exit. Sometimes, I've learned, retreat is the only tactical option a man has.

FIVE
WHAT HAPPENED ON ORDNEY

Later, I'm sitting in the cockpit when Jessica joins me, sliding into her co-pilot's seat. She looks as stunning as always, but there's a pensiveness about her that keeps me from opening my mouth. She has something on her mind, and she'll need to decide when it's time to tell me.

We sit like that for five long minutes while I pretend to be busy checking and rechecking and then rechecking our course again. Seriously, there's not much to do on a starship that's beating a straight-line course between jump points in an uninhabited system. So, I'm extremely relieved when Jessica finally decides to start talking and saves me from running a general diagnostic on the ship's systems a *third* time.

"So…about my father…"

I look over at her but say nothing. I try to keep my expression neutral as well, but I'm sure I'm failing at it. She's about, I hope, to answer some of the burning questions that have dominated my waking thoughts and even a few of my dreams since we were first boarded by the *Dauntless.*

"He's a real piece of work," she says. "I didn't even meet him until I was seventeen. He left my mother while she was pregnant with me."

I manage not to react audibly to that, but my eyebrows shoot up. If Jessica's mother is anything like her, a man would have to be crazy to leave her.

"He's not from Prometheus. He was there for two years as part of a trade delegation from the Leeward Republic. My mother was one of the cultural attaché's assigned to make sure he and the rest of the delegation got whatever they needed while in Promethean space.

"He and Mom grew close, and they even moved in together for his last year on the planet. She got pregnant with me just a few months before his assignment was set to end. I think that having the baby meant Mom naturally assumed he'd either stay with her on Prometheus or ask her to go with him back to the Republic. But..."

She trails off, and I can see pain flash behind her eyes. I want to reach out and comfort her, but I hold back, sensing it would break the spell that has her talking openly right now. This is the first I'm learning much of *anything* about Lin's past—at least, her past before *Persephone* and the little her military file had in it.

She starts talking faster, clearly just trying now to get it all out. "A month before he left, he told Mom she could come with him but that she wouldn't be living with him in the Republic. Turns out he had a whole other *family* there—a wife and kids—and my mom was just the mistress. And he made it abundantly clear she would never be anything more than that. It crushed her, and she told him where he could shove his offer. Then he left. He sent money each year for us, more than enough for us to live very comfortably. Apparently, he came from an extremely wealthy family, and his government work was just part of his training to take over the family business.

"At first, Mom would just send the money back. But as it slowly became clear to her that her government salary wouldn't provide the life she wanted for me, she started keeping the payments. She would spend every credit on me, never on herself. I had the nicest clothes, went to the fanciest private schools, had horse riding and etiquette lessons, and had a full-ride scholarship to the King's University of Prometheus. But it all felt so...claustrophobic, like I was stuck inside her dream for me."

She stops, frowning, and I'm wondering why anyone would *pay* for riding lessons. I can't even remember the first time I rode—I was probably still a toddler—but I'm fairly certain my grandpa just threw me in the saddle, slapped the back of the horse, and told me to hold on tight. I'm sure my father yelled at the old guy after that, but Grandpa never seemed to care what Dad thought, and vice-versa.

"When I decided to reject my scholarship and go to the Naval Academy instead, it nearly killed Mom. At the time, I thought it was her being controlling; now, looking back, I realize that she only wanted what was best for me. Turns out she was right.

"Because just after I accepted my appointment to the Academy, dear old Dad reached out to me for the first time ever." She says that last part bitterly. Still, the way her lip trembles, I can almost feel the hope that a young eighteen-year-old Lin must have had at finally hearing from her absent father.

It's funny how something as simple as a shared genetic code creates such strong expectations of a bond between two people. Even when my own father effectively disowned me after I joined the Navy, I never stopped loving him or longing for his approval. That he died five years later without us ever having a chance to reconcile haunts me to this day. So, I can understand how Lin, even though her father had never shown the slightest interest in her before, had felt so much obvious hope when he'd finally reached out. Unfortunately, I could already see that this story wasn't going to have a happy ending.

"He was on Prometheus for a trade conference, and he asked to see me during his short stop there. I snuck out to meet him because I knew Mom wouldn't approve. I met him at a restaurant near our home, and he was just so…I don't know, perfect, I guess. He said all the right things and even hugged me when he first saw me. I expected him to badmouth Mom, but he never did. He even seemed interested in learning how she was doing. And, unlike her, he was *so* supportive of my decision to join the Navy. I felt like…"

"…like you finally found what you'd been missing?" I finish for her when it's clear she's struggling for the words. Because that's the feeling I always longed for with my own father but never found.

She nods, and I can see she's crying now. Again, I long to reach out and comfort her, but I don't want to overstep like I did in the *Daunt-*

less's conference room. After all Lin's been through, and despite her briefly hugging me back on *Dauntless*, I know that she has to be the one to initiate any physical contact with a man, and I'm doing my best to respect that, though every part of me often yearns to take her in my arms.

Jessica takes a deep breath and lets it out slowly through pursed lips like she's struggling for oxygen. Then she turns and looks at me. "It was all a lie," she says so softly I can barely hear her. "He played me. We'd get together every six months or so, usually on Prometheus between deployments. He always seemed really interested in my naval service, but I didn't tell him anything classified or secret, and he didn't press.

"Then, one day, I got a note from him that he was coming to the Federation again and *really* needed to talk to me about something. He sent the note to Prometheus, and I got it a few days later, forwarded to me on *HMS Ordney* in the Kipling system, where I was deployed. In my return message, I told him that we would have to wait a couple of months until my next leave, but he wrote back so insistent. He said that what he needed to talk to me about couldn't wait. We went back and forth a few times until finally I gave him a day and time to meet me in the Hothan system, our next patrol stop. I thought it wouldn't do any harm."

Tears are flowing down her face now, and I'm practically holding my breath, unable to believe that I finally might be hearing about what happened on *Ordney* that ruined Jessica's career.

"He didn't show…" she says in a gasping sob. "He—"

An alarm sounds in the cockpit, causing us both to jump in surprise. My first thought is that *Dauntless* followed us from Fiori and is going to repeat its forced docking maneuver again—maybe that intel weenie, Daniels, finally convinced Admiral Walters that I'm too dangerous to roam free, or maybe she decided it was time to forcefully extract the information about Gerson from me—but a quick check of the cockpit displays dispels that notion.

The real reason for the alarm, however, is perhaps more concerning, even if it comes in a deceptively polite package.

"Congratulations!" I read out loud from the display. "Your Star-

Hauler model TK421 has reached a thousand hours of jump time. It's time for your first service appointment. To ensure your safety and the proper break-in of your advanced Gorendi 6000 jump drive, you only have one more jump before the drive will auto shut down until a licensed StarHauler service technician has certified that its one-thousand-hour maintenance is complete. Please proceed directly to the nearest system with a licensed StarHauler service center. And have a great day!"

Jess and I look at each other. And whether it's the fact that we just went from the grim to the absurd in no time flat or because we both just really need something to distract us, we burst out laughing together.

SIX
FIXING OUR DUMB SHIP

We're not laughing for long. Because now we have a really big problem. The service catalog on *Wanderer* apparently never assumed anyone would operate the ship this far out in the Fringe because it doesn't list a single licensed StarHauler service center within five jumps of our current location. And we only have one jump until the drive shuts down.

"Just override it!" Lin says in exasperation. Whenever she has a problem to solve, she transforms into Confident Lin, and right now, Confident Lin is taking all of the emotional frustration she's been feeling from reuniting with her father and instead directing it toward this problem. Unfortunately, that means she's taking at least some of it out on me.

"I thought of that," I explain, my own exasperation mirroring hers. "But it's a civilian ship, not a warship. And apparently, StarHauler's desire to keep its customers safe *and* bilk them out of money with required service overrode any concern the company had for its customers completing vital missions to rescue planets and damsels in distress from mean pirates."

Jessica grunts and reaches out to slap the console in front of her in frustration. It's the most violent reaction I've ever seen out of her, but I pretend not to notice. Instead, I peer more closely over her shoulder at the menu of options on that same abused console. We're in *Wanderer's* small engineering compartment, and so far, nothing we've tried has allowed us to bypass the ship's dogged commitment to shut down our jump drive after our next jump.

"What if we just yanked out all the fuses and forced the computer to reset?" Lin asks next as I try to read some incredibly small print about power conduits and fusion reactor maintenance. Unfortunately, every single paragraph I've read thus far ends with the same infuriating statement: 'Please do not attempt to service [insert random system here] on your own. Contact a licensed StarHauler service center'. Terrific.

"It won't work," I tell her. "Or it might, but it could also scramble the computer so badly that we won't even get that one jump. What's the largest inhabited system we could get to in a single jump?"

She consults her implant for a moment. "Jeffrey's Landing. It's got two stations, including a shipyard. Very promising. But it's in the Jutzen Protectorate."

I frown. Even in Prometheus, we've heard about the Jutzen Protectorate, and I'm not that keen on trusting my ship and my crew in a system controlled by jingoistic neo-Nazis. "Next," I tell her.

"Literally, the only other option big enough to have even basic repair facilities is Boral. But if we can't find what we're looking for there, we're completely out of luck. Are you sure you don't want to try the Nazis?"

"Oh yeah. One hundred percent sure."

She nods, which I take to be agreement. "OK. Boral it is, then. I'll lay in the course." She leaves to head back forward to the cockpit.

I spend a few more minutes going through more nonsensical menus on the engineering console, doing anything right now to distract myself from the fact that if we can't magically find a licensed StarHauler technician in Boral—and I've never even heard of Boral—then our little mission, and even our entire future as mercenaries or anything else, is over before it even had a chance to get started.

As I continue my frustrated scrolling, I hear someone enter the small room. "Forget something?" I ask, expecting Jessica.

"What are you doing down here? Is the ship OK?"

I look up in surprise to see Kayla. She looks like someone just woke her from a nap. Her blond hair is mussed, and she's wearing a soft-looking t-shirt, a pair of cutoff shorts, and no shoes. She looks oddly terrific.

"Uh, sorry," I say, flustered, "did we wake you?"

She nods but smiles to show there are no hard feelings. "What are you doing down here? Is everything OK with the ship?" she repeats her earlier question.

"Oh, uh," I look from her back down to the console and then back at her. "Sure. All good. We just have to make an unscheduled stop."

Kayla frowns and crosses her arms, pulling herself up to her full 162-centimeter height. It shouldn't be intimidating, but I have the sudden mental image of my grandma scolding me for throwing newly laid eggs at a target I drew on the side of the barn when I was eleven. "You're lying," she says simply. "What's going on, Brad?"

I'm honestly not sure when she and I got to a first-name basis, but I don't give it much thought. "Well…we kind of have a problem with the star drive."

Kayla says nothing but walks over to peer into the inner workings of the main engine. She fixates on a power conduit and follows it across the small room until it terminates in a large metal box. "Hmm, is that a Gorendi 6000?"

The question takes me aback. "Yeah, it is. How did *you* know that?" I don't mean to make it sound the way it does, but the question leaves my lips before I can stop it.

She raises an eyebrow. "What, because I'm a woman? Or because I'm a hick from a dead-end farming world where we only know about sheep, cattle, and kissing our cousins?"

"Uhhh." There's no answer I can give here that won't get me in trouble.

Then she surprises me by smirking. "Relax, flyboy, I'm just messing with you. I studied starship engineering at the University of New Rottendam. We do have starships in Carter's World—or we did before the pirates showed up. Someone had to keep them running."

She walks over to me, bumping me aside with one hip as she peers at the console readout. She starts manipulating the display and skimming through the text, grunting, nodding, and frowning at various parts. Then she looks back up at me with another smirk. "Got the old 'pay us tons of money to service the drive, or we'll shut you down' message, huh?"

I nod dumbly.

"And you were going to fly to the next system over and try and find a mechanic who could service it?"

I nod again.

She shakes her head and laughs. "And here I thought you were ex-navy and knew something about ships."

I shrug. "I know how to fly them and shoot things. We had engineers for all the other stuff."

She laughs again, and it's a good sound, especially after the gloominess that Jessica and I shared earlier and the sense of despair since the service message. "Boy, there's a sucker born every minute." She pecks at the console for another few moments, and I see her pull up some kind of root menu that I was never able to find and probably still couldn't even after watching her. Then, about a minute or so later, she looks back up with a wry smile. "And, done. No more drive shutdown. You can thank me by walking me back to my quarters, flyboy." I guess I have a new nickname now. I'm not sure how I feel about that.

Do you ever get the sense that you're completely out of your depth, like there's some big joke in the universe that everyone else is in on but you? That's how I feel every second with Kayla Carter. Sure, she's attractive, but I'm in love with Jessica, so I don't think it's that. It's more the way Kayla talks and teases me like I'm still the young farm boy with dreams of being a mercenary like my hero, Billy Firebrand.

So, I don't say anything but follow her dumbly out of the engineering space and the short distance down the corridor to the door to her quarters. And I have to admit, I'm watching her tan, toned legs a bit as she walks in front of me.

She turns right at the hatch to her quarters and smiles at me. "Thanks, Brad. See you at dinner? I'm cooking chicken cacciatore."

I nod, not trusting my voice right now, and she smirks again and reaches up to cup my chin in one hand like she's examining a small child with dirt on his face. Then she releases me and opens the hatch to her room, enters, and shuts it behind her without a backward glance.

I shake myself out of my stupor and make my way to the cockpit, all sorts of confusing emotions clashing in me, to tell Jessica she can return us to our original course.

SEVEN
EAVESDROPPING

The final two days of our journey pass uneventfully, even in boring fashion. I try a few times to get Jess to talk about her father again, but she changes the subject each time. Whatever moment we shared in the cockpit doesn't repeat. Instead, we spend a few hours here and there talking about old Navy missions or Promethean officers we both knew, but we run out of common friends quickly and often lapse into silence, both doing our best to pretend there isn't a massive elephant in the room.

Kayla, on the other hand, is a whirlwind of nervous energy the closer we get to her home system. She seems to deal with her nerves by cooking, pacing the ship's single long corridor, and generally trying to engage just about anyone she can in conversation.

Harris learns the hard way that he can't hold his own with her. A pretty shy guy normally, I can see that interacting with Kayla breaks his introvert brain, and he spends most of the last two days hiding in his quarters. And Jessica, who is reserved at the best of times, and this isn't one of those times for her, soon starts to avoid Kayla like a plague.

Which leaves me.

At first, I tell myself I should also be annoyed by the bubbly young woman. But soon, I find I can't even fake not enjoying it because Kayla is just so…different. We talk about so many things as she literally follows me around the ship that I feel like I know her almost as well as I ever knew anyone aside from Carla.

We spend a lot of time, in particular, talking about farming. And for a guy who literally joined the Navy so I *didn't* have to take over the farm from my grandpa or be an accountant like my dad, I find it oddly comforting to talk about something from my past life. Maybe it's because my past life is irretrievably over. I'm still legally dead, even if it seems everyone I come across knows who I really am.

As we go, I can feel something growing inside me. It's strange because my unrequited feelings for Jessica haven't diminished in the least, and I can't imagine life without her, even after less than three weeks together.

Still, with Kayla, everything is just so natural and easy. Even though I can see her worrying about her family and what we'll find when we arrive at Carter's World, she still seems so upbeat. She also flirts with me, a *lot*. And while I know it shouldn't, that makes me like being around her even more. It's nice sometimes to feel wanted.

So now I somehow have feelings for two women at once, and while I still, in moments of self-reflection, know that my feelings for Jessica are the much stronger of the two, I can't ignore what I'm starting to feel for Kayla. Which makes me, honestly, feel like a horrible human being. Am I really so desperate to be loved that I'll let my affections shift so quickly? Or that I'll go for another woman simply because she's available and willing?

It all comes to a head on our last night before we arrive in Kayla's home system. Jessica and I have been alternating sleep schedules again, so one of us is always awake in case something goes wrong in the cockpit, even when Kayla is flying the ship. It's about eight in the evening, and my next shift doesn't start for another four hours, but I awake in my bunk and can't fall back asleep. Maybe it's pre-mission jitters, or maybe it's just that I'm getting older and can't sleep on command at strange hours anymore. Either way, I'm awake, and I'm hungry.

My plan is to grab a snack, take it back to my quarters, and try again to sleep, so I don't dress or even put shoes on. I walk out into the corridor in stocking feet and make my way toward the galley.

Now, *Wanderer*, for all of her charm, is not a luxurious ship by any stretch of the imagination. And nowhere is that more apparent than her deck. The floor of the corridor is basically a two-centimeter-thick metal grate that covers conduits full of power cables and environmental systems. That means that you can usually hear someone walking from almost anywhere on the small ship. But in my socks alone, I make almost no sound as I approach the galley, making it quiet enough for me to hear the voices before they can hear me coming.

I'm surprised to hear that Jessica and Kayla are in the galley together. Apparently, Jess didn't manage to dodge the talkative young farm girl slash engineer, or maybe she just wanted some of Kayla's cooking badly enough to put up with her chatter.

No matter how it happened, it's happening, and I subconsciously slow and creep up to the door, listening in on their conversation.

"So, are you excited to see your family?" my XO asks our passenger.

"I am, well, mostly. It's just my dad, really. Mom died a few years back, and my brother died in an accident before I was born. So, I'm all he has, and I'm just not sure he can manage without me there."

"He obviously did fine while you were away at school."

I hear Kayla laugh at Jessica's observation. "Well, he didn't starve, if that's what you mean. But I also don't think he wore a matching outfit the whole two years I was gone. Some of his press conferences were…interesting. He looked more like a beggar than a president. But everyone is so in awe of the Carter family name that I don't think even his own staff were willing to tell him just how ridiculous he looked." She laughs again, and I can tell the memory is a good one for her.

"Well, I'm sure he'll be glad to have you home then." Jess's response is a little less enthusiastic, and I know she's probably thinking of her own father and whatever passed between them to destroy her relationship with the man.

Kayla doesn't seem to notice Jessica's sudden shift in mood. "It'll be so good to see him." Then, she abruptly changes the subject. "So…Brad?"

"What about him?" Lin's tone is suddenly guarded.

"Well, I'm not sure how to ask this, but...are you and he...?" The unfinished question hangs in the room between them, and I can almost feel the tension even without seeing the expression on either woman's face.

Jessica is slow to answer, and when she does, it's in the crisp, professional tone she seems to use whenever an overly personal matter comes up and she's trying to deflect. "No. We're not. It wouldn't be appropriate, given he's my commanding officer. And besides, he and I...well, I don't know. But no, we're not together."

The words spear me through the heart like a hot knife, and my knees go weak. I had thought that the whole 'no fraternizing between officers' had ended when we both literally *died* and left the Navy. But apparently, Jessica doesn't think that way. And the way she's so quickly dismissed Kayla's comment, it feels like she just shut the door forever on any possibility of us being more than what we are now.

Honestly, I've known since before the Rishi Paradise that Jessica was never likely to love me back the way I love her. But hearing her actually say the words is painful in the extreme, and I'm trying hard not to gasp for breath in the corridor and betray to both of the women that I've been listening in.

"Oh, that's..." Kayla starts but seems unsure of how to respond to Jessica's statement. Instead, she pushes forward awkwardly. "So, you wouldn't mind if I... Well, I like him. And I think he may like me, too. I just didn't want to start anything if you and he were...you know."

"Well, we're not," I hear Jess say with a painful, almost angry finality. Then I hear her stand from the galley table and start walking across the room. I beat a hasty retreat and duck back into my cabin hatch an instant before she enters the corridor where I was hiding.

Inside my room, I stand with my back to the hatch, fighting to control my breathing and my emotions. Because I feel like my whole world, the little that I've been able to reconstruct since the disaster at Bellerophon has now crashed down around me...again.

EIGHT
PIRATES!

Jessica and I are both quiet, engrossed in our own thoughts, when *Wanderer* exits jump space in Carter's System. It actually has another name on the star charts, but Kayla assures us everyone just calls the system the same basic name as the planet.

She's in the cockpit with us, too, and is abnormally silent herself. Harris is even here, though he looks lost. I guess there wasn't much time spent in ship cockpits for a makeup and disguise expert who somehow fell in with mercenaries. Though he's also mentioned a few times that Owen used him as a technology expert; I may need to unpack that with him.

"Scanning," Jess says crisply as *Wanderer* reenters normal space.

"Bringing the main drive back online," I reply.

We continue back and forth like that, falling into old habits and patterns that provide a sense of comfort to me. I'm still reeling from what I heard Jessica tell Kayla, and I'm wishing for all the universe that I had a bottle of scotch on board. But in the absence of my normal solace, I'm finding consolation in the mundane.

"Ship detected!" Jessica exclaims, breaking me from my concentration on spinning up our main engine. "Unknown class, bearing one oh four mark two relative."

I check the sensor picture and see the same thing she does. The ship in question appears to be burning hard on a vector from the outer system like it was waiting just behind the jump point for anyone exiting it.

We've been in Carter's System for all of thirty seconds, and the pirates have already found us.

Of course, we knew this could happen. There are only so many jump points into and out of any given system, and the number is pretty random, though the more populated systems seem to have more simply by virtue of being more heavily explored. But Carter's System only has two known jump points, which has made it very easy for the pirates to blockade the entire place.

In our favor, however, is the fact that through some quirk of celestial mechanics that no scientist has ever been able to adequately explain, a ship exiting jump space maintains the same velocity as when it entered the jump. And we purposefully set ourselves up to come in hot.

"Time to intercept?" I ask my XO, even though my own console would just as easily give me the answer. Division of duties is as important on our freighter as it was on the bridge of any warship we've ever crewed. It keeps us all focused on the right things and avoids duplication of effort that often can lead to disaster when other important items go unnoticed.

"If we go full burn, eight hours. We've got a velocity advantage on them, but they can outdo our acceleration by about seventeen percent, assuming what we're seeing now is their max."

"Great. Options people?"

I'm really asking just Jessica, but having learned how to conn a starship on the bridge of many a warship, I'm used to having a larger command crew. Luckily for me, Kayla takes my question literally.

"Big Ben," she says, causing both Jess and I to turn in our seats and regard her in confusion. "It's that gas giant over there," she continues, pointing through the forward viewport at a star that's significantly brighter than all but the system's own primary; it's also about as far away as you can get from the planet of Carter's World, but that's beside the point.

"When I was learning to pilot an in-system shuttle," Kayla continues, "one of the old salts told me stories of smugglers who used to come through back when we actually had a small system patrol fleet. Supposedly, they used to hide in Big Ben's upper atmosphere because the ionization wreaked havoc on the patrol ship sensors, and the dense gases hid them from visual scans as well."

I look over at my XO. Jessica consults her implant and nods. "At full burn, we can get there in a little over six hours. It's cutting it close, but unless they have long-range ship killer missiles on that little boat, we should be able to do what Miss Carter's suggesting before they can get within weapons or boarding range." She turns and regards Kayla again. "That is, of course, assuming you're right."

I can almost hear Kayla bristle behind me, and I do hear the deep breath she takes in as she prepares to argue, so I jump in before she can. "Let's do it. XO, set a course. Main drive is coming online now, and we'll go full burn. Kayla, you're the closest thing we have to an engineer, so I want you back with the engines in case something goes wrong." That'll keep her and Jessica separate for now. "Harris," I look back at him, "find a fire extinguisher or something in case we take damage."

Harris immediately unbuckles from his seat and heads aft to do as instructed. Kayla lingers for a moment, and I'm afraid she's going to object to being relegated to the engineering space. But after only a second or two, she unbuckles as well and follows after Harris, leaving me and Jessica alone.

"Any other options?" I ask now that Kayla is out of earshot.

Lin shakes her head. "No. We knew they'd probably be waiting for us, but I honestly didn't think they'd risk being that *close* to the jump point. It's reckless. What if we'd drifted that direction on exit? Either way, if they'd been just a little further out, we might have made the planet or even the other jump point before they could catch us, but now…" she shrugs. "Now we'll just have to hope Miss Carter knows what she's talking about."

I nod grimly. "Well, let's game out some contingency plans in case it doesn't work." But after thirty minutes of that, we both surrender and admit that we only have one option. Now, all we have to do is wait five and a half more hours to see if that option means we get to live today.

NINE
ANOTHER STUPID PLAN

Five and a half hours gives us plenty of time to examine the pirate ship chasing us, even with the *Wanderer's* commercial-grade scanning suite. What we see isn't encouraging. According to Kayla, the citizens of Carter's World have seen two different pirate ships at various times. A big one and this smaller one that's chasing us now.

But even though it's the smaller of the two, the scanner readings on the ship chasing us are enough to tell us that we've likely bitten off more than we can chew.

"Really, they have cold reaction thrusters?" I ask incredulously. What I would have given to have had those on *Persephone*, and she was a warship…well, sort of.

"And some pretty serious retro boosters," Jessica says solemnly. "Not to mention, those really look like missile tubes to me." She points at a few dark circles on the visual scan image.

"Agreed. This isn't the rough-and-tumble variety of pirates I was hoping to find, with ships cobbled together from spare parts. That boat looks like it probably started life as part of some system's patrol fleet. Maybe the pirates stole it somehow or just bought it surplus from a mothball fleet, but if that's the case, they've upgraded a few things. Whoever these guys are, they're well-financed."

Jessica is silent after that, and I can see she's working through some things on her implant. I busy myself rechecking a few indications on the sensor reading, giving her the time she needs to think. I've learned that Jessica Lin's brain, when engaged in solving a problem, is a truly beautiful and dangerous thing. I always considered myself a good tactician before I became a drunken mass murderer, but I've caught glimpses enough of my XO's brilliance that I have to admit she's better than I ever was. The problem is in helping her believe in herself enough to put that genius to work.

For the thousandth time, I find myself mentally cursing Commander Yancy Jessup, Lin's former commanding officer, and Petty Officer Nedrin Jacobs, the king's rapist nephew, for all they did to Jessica on *Persephone*. Likewise, I find myself cursing her father, who obviously had something to do with whatever happened before that on the destroyer *Ordney* that ruined her career and robbed her of whatever self-confidence she may have previously had.

I prod her gently. "What's going on in that head of yours, XO?"

We're nearly to the gas giant now, and in about twenty minutes will enter its upper atmosphere. We can't see it through the forward viewport, though, as we're turned over and facing away from Big Ben, letting our main drive burn hot to decelerate us enough from our mad dash so that we won't either skip off the atmosphere or break up upon entry.

"I was just thinking," she replies, her voice professional and firm like it was when she came up with the plan to take out that Koratan scimitar-class destroyer we encountered in the Gerson system. "Even if our ruse works, that pirate can almost certainly wait us out. All he has to do is position himself between us and Carter's World to intercept us. And if he calls in backup, a second ship could do the same with the jump point. We'd be stuck with no way out other than a run to the outer system, and he'll catch us with his better acceleration in any extended chase."

I nod. I've been thinking much the same thing but decided that was a problem for Future Brad. Present Brad is just trying to survive the next twenty minutes. But, as usual, Jessica is thinking four steps ahead. "So, what do we do about it?" I ask.

"What if we could make him think we didn't survive entry to the gas giant's atmosphere?"

It's a good thought but not concrete enough to take action on yet. "Go on," I tell her.

"I think if we jettisoned a few things out the airlock, we could make it look like debris from damage. Then we could flare the drive and simulate an explosion."

Whoa. The first part, I'm totally with her; but the second? It's pretty stupid. But, as usual, stupid may be all we have to work with. Fitting, considering our captain.

"Let me get this straight," I say slowly. "You want to purposefully light the atmosphere around us on fire?"

She grimaces but nods resolutely, and despite the sheer audacious idiocy of the plan, seeing Confident Lin make an appearance gives me a little thrill.

"OK, OK," I say. "But we'll need perfect timing, or we'll go boom along with the atmosphere around us."

"On it, sir. You get us to Big Ben in one piece, and I can make that pirate ship think we didn't survive entry."

TEN
LIGHTING STUFF ON FIRE

"Ten seconds, Commander Lin!" I call out, subconsciously reverting back to her old Navy title. "You ready?"

"Ready, sir!" she responds from the co-pilot's seat.

"Harris, you ready?" I ask through the intercom.

"We're ready," Kayla answers for the man. Seriously, if I don't find Harris something constructive to do soon, I'm not going to be able to justify even having him on the ship breathing our air and eating our food. It's surprising how *seldom* we find ourselves in need of a good makeup artist.

As the seconds count down, I quickly imagine what Billy Firebrand, my favorite fictional mercenary, would say in this situation. Probably something really cool and pithy right as we hit the gas giant's atmo. I need to come up with something just as good.

"Let's get some!" I call out as the timer hits zero. I hear a startled grunt from Jessica next to me, but she doesn't thankfully waste any time trying to figure out what I mean—which is good because even *I* have no idea what I was trying to say there—and instead cries out, "Harris, Kayla, now!" and then hits a button on her console to run a preprogrammed routine.

Three things happen in quick succession. First, our main drive cuts out. We've already turned back over to hit the atmosphere nose-first, so to the pirate behind us, it will look like a drive failure—we hope. Second, Harris—or probably Kayla—overrides the airlock controls and slams open the outer hatch, and the near vacuum still around *Wanderer* forcibly sucks out the air that was in the airlock, and with it, the various odds and ends we piled in there. Unfortunately, we didn't exactly have many things on the ship to start with, so the gas giant just got most of our dishes, some spare hull plating kept in the cargo hold for repairs, some canned foodstuffs, and most of our collective wardrobes. I say a silent prayer of thanks and farewell to the red dress Jessica wore at the Rishi Paradise. I'm going to miss that dress most of all. But hopefully, our improvised 'debris' is enough to help sell this.

Third and final, our drive roars back to life just as the airlock closes again. It's only on for a split second, but it's on at full burn, and burn it does. Because now we're just deep enough in the atmosphere that the heat and fire from our drive going at max thrust, even for a moment, is enough to ignite every particle of air within five hundred meters of our little ship.

I cringe as I imagine the fire engulfing us and burning *Wanderer* and then each of us to so much gooey slag and ash. Luckily, our forward momentum is enough to mostly outrun the maelstrom, and I keep us on a fixed course deeper into the atmosphere. Then, hopeful that we're deep enough to be out of sight and sensor range, I hit the retro thrusters and slow our mad descent into Big Ben's gassy depths.

We're alive, though maybe barely. Now, we just have to hope that it actually worked.

ELEVEN
A LOT OF GAS

In the movies, *Wanderer* would be able to hover in place, just at the right depth to prevent detection, while the heroes inside pat themselves on the back and have a good meal.

This isn't the movies, and sad to say, most starships aren't all that good at hovering, especially in the gravitational well of a gas giant with its wind speeds measured in the hundreds of kilometers per hour.

So, the only way we can maintain our little ship at the correct depth—just deep enough to hopefully be invisible to the pirates above but shallow enough to, at some point, be able to reach escape velocity and break the grip of the massive planet's gravity—is to fly almost recklessly fast in what is essentially a very low orbit.

With the high winds and the sudden increases and drops in atmospheric pressure that threaten to send us up and down by several hundred meters at a time, that means I'm in a constant state of white-knuckle panic at the wheel. It really sucks.

After four hours of it, my hands have cramped so hard that they're practically locked onto the control yoke, and the sweat is pouring down my face in veritable rivers. At that point, Jessica finally convinces me to let her take the helm.

It's not that I don't trust her, but when you're the captain of a ship

—any ship—you feel a responsibility to do the really hard stuff yourself, especially when so much is on the line. Strange, again, that I find myself falling back into those old patterns of command I thought I lost after Bellerophon.

I stumble out of the cockpit and head down the corridor to the galley. As tired as I am and as badly as I just want to fall into my bunk until I have to take over from Jessica in a few hours, I know my body needs nourishment as much as it needs sleep. My plan is to grab a few ration packs and stuff them down on my way back to my quarters, but I enter the galley to find Kayla there with a steaming plate of something that smells amazing.

I sit down at the table without a word, my body still shaking from the stress, and she sets the plate in front of me. I start eating ravenously, and I'm sure it's about the least attractive thing in the world, but she moves around the table and slides onto the bench next to me, sitting close. As I'm shoving food into my mouth, she starts to lightly caress my back with her fingertips.

It's always been an internal debate for me whether or not women understand what they're doing to men when they tickle or lightly scratch our backs. Carla used to do it absent-mindedly while we watched movies together on the couch during my rare times home from deployment, and it drove me crazy in a good way every time.

Now, with Kayla doing it to me here, it starts to relax my aching muscles ever so slightly, and I'm suddenly very aware of her hip touching mine as she sits so close to me. My brain is foggy, as if I've just drunk half a bottle of whiskey, and I'm so tired and stressed that I'm amazed I have any capacity left for rational thought. But the small part of my brain that is still capable of anything is screaming at me to think and not act.

However, it's only a small part, while the rest of me is looking for a release—any release—from the stress of the past few hours. Couple that with the aching pain I still feel at hearing Jessica last night in the galley telling Kayla there would never be anything between us, and I'm in a pretty vulnerable and raw state, I suppose.

I don't know who initiates it, but suddenly, Kayla and I are kissing. It's not for long, and I'm the one to break it off, but it ends with her snuggling into my side contentedly while I try to figure out what just happened and regain interest in the meal in front of me.

There's a voice in the back of my head now, whispering all sorts of things to me. If I listen to that voice, the next thing that will happen is pretty obvious. But there's another voice in my head arguing against that. It's my mother's, and I can hear her almost as if she were in the room, telling me what she told me on my seventeenth birthday when my girlfriend at the time and I were starting to get serious: 'Son, you can always wait, and if it's meant to be, it will still be there when you're done waiting. But if you act too soon, you can never take that back.'

And the truth is, I still love Jessica. Even after hearing what she said last night, I'm not willing to give up on her yet. I honestly don't know if I ever will be. Part of me wonders if that's because she *is* so unattainable, and I see some sort of challenge in that. But my mind also keeps going back to the night we laughed and told stories in the cockpit while transporting Owen Thompson and his crew into the Fiori system. Even in my conversations of late with Kayla, I've rarely felt so in sync with another person as I did that evening with Jessica. On top of that, even just in the three weeks since I met her on *Persephone*, we've been through an incredible amount together. Am I willing to throw that all away just for the chance of sleeping with a girl I just met?

No. I'm not.

So, with a little regret, I gently disengage myself from Kayla, carry my plate to the sink, and then mumble something about how tired I am before I leave the galley and go collapse in my bunk…alone.

TWELVE
BOMBS

Three hours later, my alarm jolts me awake, and I make my way out of my quarters and back into the galley. I'm equal parts disappointed and relieved that Kayla isn't there waiting for me, but she or perhaps Harris has recently started a new batch of coffee, so I help myself to two full cups to shake off the sleep. Then, I go up to the cockpit to check on Lin.

Jessica doesn't even acknowledge me when I sit down in the chair next to her. Her red-rimmed eyes are locked on the console in front of her where the instrument readings give the only indication of where we are; the swirling gases of Big Ben's atmosphere block any meaningful view out the forward viewscreen. Lin's hands, similar to mine before, are gripping her control yoke so tightly that her knuckles have turned stark white, and I can see tremors in her arms from the fatigue and stress of constantly having to adjust the ship's course to keep us at the proper altitude.

"Do you think they're gone yet?" I ask softly, mostly as a way to make sure she knows I'm even there.

"No way to know unless we want to risk popping up where we can see. But then they'll see us if they haven't left yet." Her voice is shaky, and there's a desperate edge to it that I can relate to.

I grunt in agreement. Reluctantly, I pull up the proper view on my console and then put my hands around the control yoke. With an audible gasp of relief, Jessica relinquishes control to me and slumps back in her seat, panting from the last four hours of exertion.

Ten minutes later, just as I'm starting to feel the pain from muscles already clenched too tightly in my shoulders, back, and arms, she finally seems to have recovered enough of her wits and motor functions to leave. She gets up and, using the backs of the seats for support, starts to make her way to the cockpit hatch.

"Jess," I stop her, "what happened on *Ordney* with your father?"

I'm horrified the moment the words leave my lips. I don't know why I've chosen this exact moment to ask it, but the words are out now, and there's no taking them back.

"I..." she trails off, and I wisely keep my mouth shut and don't prod her further. But she also doesn't leave the cockpit yet. I can't see her; I can't afford to take my eyes off my console readout long enough to even glance back at her, but I can almost feel her staring out the forward viewscreen at the roiling gases beyond. "I'm sorry, Brad," she says, but there's none of the expected anger or annoyance in her tone; she just sounds tired. "I might be able to tell you the rest of the story one day, but I'm just not ready to tell *anyone* about it quite yet. I hope that's OK?"

"Yeah, of course, Jess." Why is she asking me if that's OK? Seriously, she should be yelling at me for asking such a deeply personal question while we're both exhausted and chasing pirates.

But instead, I feel her hand land on my shoulder and squeeze it lightly. "Thanks," she says, and then she's gone.

An hour later, I hear someone come back into the cockpit, but I can't turn to see. Hands land on my shoulders and start massaging them.

"When do you think we'll be able to leave the atmosphere?" Kayla asks behind me.

I take a deep breath, letting it out, which she probably interprets as my exhaustion or a sign that I'm enjoying the shoulder rub. Truth be told, I definitely am. I would just enjoy it more if it was Jessica giving it. But as the knots work out of my shoulders, I'm very grateful, and in my frantically overwrought state, I start to have some more very warm thoughts about my cute passenger.

"I don't know," I answer honestly. "Maybe we can try in another few hours and see if they've left, but we'll only get—"

I'm cut off when *Wanderer* jolts to one side as a bomb goes off.

THIRTEEN
WE NEED A NEW PLAN

The explosion rocks the ship, almost sending our little freighter off course completely before I'm able to correct and prevent a dive deeper into the atmosphere. My first thought is that something has happened to the engines, and I have a flashback to the ion drive failing on *Persephone* as we made the mad run from the Koratan destroyer in Gerson. But this explosion feels different to me, and I soon ascertain why.

By that time, a second and then a third explosion have rocked the ship, and Kayla is no longer rubbing my shoulders. Instead, I hear her sit in the seat behind me and strap herself in. To her credit, she otherwise makes no sound and doesn't panic.

Lin rushes back into the cockpit and wordlessly takes her seat next to me. By how quickly she arrived, she must have been lying awake or even in the galley eating.

"Proximity mines," I say through gritted teeth.

Jessica swears, the first time I've actually heard her use that kind of language, and Kayla yelps in surprise as a fourth and then a fifth explosion hit *Wanderer* like the fists of an angry deity.

"They know we're alive then," Jessica says, and I nod rigidly.

"It's a pretty good bet."

"What are we going to do?" Kayla asks from behind us, her voice cracking from stress.

"We have to go deeper," Jessica answers for me. "They've obviously been able to see us, at least to some degree, and they've gotten ahead of us and mined our orbital path."

"Why don't we just shift our orbit laterally?" I hear Harris ask, though I'm unsure when he actually arrived in the cockpit.

"Can't," Jessica answers again. "Or rather, we can, but there's no guarantee they won't be able to see us again and do the same thing. We're obviously too shallow in the atmosphere, and they've been able to track us well enough to drop mines in our path, but luckily not enough for a missile lock, or we'd be dead already."

"Call it, XO," I say, every word feeling like a chore as I fight the control yoke to keep our abused ship from careening off course.

"Ten-degree dive, now," she says, her voice reverting back to the professional detachment of a naval officer under stress.

I comply, pushing the yoke forward until my console says we're at a ten-degree down angle aimed deeper into Big Ben's swirling clouds of noxious gases. A few seconds later, what looks like rain starts to pelt the forward viewscreen, though I know little of it is actual water—more likely, it's the liquid states of the gases all around us.

"Hull stress estimated at sixty percent," Lin says as if she's reading a daily weather report. "Any further down, and we may start to buckle the hull plates. You know, assuming the mines didn't already do that."

"If they did, we'd certainly know about it by now. But we're still breathing," I say in reply. Regardless, she's right; we can't risk going any deeper into the atmosphere, so I level off the ship. Luckily for us, the explosions have stopped, though now we have another problem.

"They won't leave any time soon," Jessica says what we're both thinking. "They know we're here, and they won't trust that those mines got us."

"Any damage?" I ask, dreading the answer.

Which, surprisingly, comes from Harris. Or maybe not, since the seat he habitually fills is next to the damage control console. "Looks like a failed pressure seal in the cargo hold and some minor damage to one of the drive exhaust nozzles, but the AI is saying that it's nothing to worry about, just to have a licensed StarHauler technician examine and repair it at our next scheduled service appointment. Do you want me to schedule it?"

I would look back at him in exasperated incredulity if I wasn't fighting so hard just to keep us on course and from going any deeper.

"What are you talking about?" Kayla asks, her tone mirroring my thoughts.

"Uh," Harris answers, "it's what's here on the screen. The AI wants to know if we want to go ahead and make an appointment with a licensed repair shop."

"No, we don't want to make an appointment!" Jessica yells from the co-pilot seat. "Just tell us if anything else breaks!"

"Uh, OK," he answers, and I feel genuinely bad for the guy. He's completely out of his element, though to be fair, I'm still trying to figure out what the guy's element actually is. What *does* he do when he's not dressing and putting makeup on other people? I know Owen used him as some sort of tech guru as well—at least when it came to the explosive implant he put in Jessica's neck, which is still there, by the way, albeit dormant—but that seemed more like a side gig for Harris.

"OK," I say to stop the parade of hits on my newest crew member—well, my only crew member besides Jessica. "A broken pressure seal isn't that bad, but we got lucky. None of those mines came particularly close; if they had, our little freighter would be a permanent addition to Big Ben's atmosphere."

"Or they don't want to kill us, just force us back to high orbit so they can capture us," Jessica says, and she's probably right; that many mine hits should have blown us to bits. The intensity must be dialed way down.

"But we can't stay down here for long," Jessica says, "or we'll lose enough hull integrity that we won't even be spaceworthy."

She's right. We're in trouble either way right now. "Commander Lin," I say, "now would be a really good time for you to come up with another crazy plan."

I can feel her glare even if I can't afford to turn my head to see it.

But she doesn't object, and I let her think while I continue to fight the controls.

Finally, she speaks. "Sorry, sir, I've got nothing."

Uh oh.

"Anyone else have any bright ideas?" I ask Kayla and Harris.

"I think we should just surrender," Kayla surprises me by saying. "It's better than death, right?"

I ignore her because she's wrong. One of the first things they teach you about anti-pirate operations in the Promethean Navy is that you *never* let yourself get captured. You fight to the death. Pirates aren't exactly known for their ethics on the subject of torturing prisoners, sometimes just for fun.

But because no one has any useful ideas, that means it's up to me to figure something out. We're so dead…again.

Then it's like a little light goes on in the recesses of my brain. This happens to me sometimes when I'm under stress, and all hope seems lost. It's like when I was in high school, and I had left an assignment until the last minute, and I pulled an all-nighter and wrote a pretty good two thousand-word essay on early human expansionism through the lens of early post-diaspora video games. Sometimes, I do my best work under pressure. Plus, at that point, I was an *expert* on video games.

"OK," I say, tearing my eyes off my instrument readouts just long enough to look Jessica in the eyes. "Here's what we're going to do."

FOURTEEN
ESCAPE AND EVADE

Fifteen minutes later, we're ready to implement my truly daring plan. And I say daring because I'm sick of calling every plan we come up with stupid and foolhardy. But it's all of those things, maybe even more. The last time we had to fight off a superior foe in space, our ship actually had *weapons* and armor and that sort of thing. *Wanderer*, for all her charm, is a simple freighter. And that pirate ship above us is a bonafide warship, which means I put our chances of this working at less than twenty percent.

"In three, two, one, now!" Lin counts down, and I pull back on the control yoke, sending us upward at a fifteen-degree angle while she pours more power into the main drive—not enough to reignite the atmosphere around us as we did before, but enough, hopefully, to break free of Big Ben's gravity.

Slowly but inexorably, the altitude numbers on my console start to tick upward. It takes another thirty minutes, but the gas in front of us dissipates, revealing scattered stars as we break free of the atmosphere.

Then, something occludes those stars as the pirate ship comes roaring downward to intercept us.

"Execute phase two...now!" Lin cries, and I poke a command button on my console's touchscreen that cuts out the main drive, then uses the thrusters to flip *Wanderer* end over end. It takes longer than normal, even with the scant air resistance at this altitude, but it still works. As soon as we're showing our engine exhaust to the pirate vessel, I jam the throttle forward again, stopping short of full power so I hopefully don't ignite the atmosphere like we did before.

"They're following!" Lin calls out as *Wanderer* skims above the upper reaches of Big Ben's gas clouds. The timing on this needs to be perfect, so I keep my eyes on my console and don't acknowledge her statement.

An alarm warns of an energy buildup within the attacking ship—I'm actually surprised our little freighter's scanners have that capability—and I use our thrusters to juke to the left just in time to miss a laser blast that comes way too close for comfort. A pithy remark about close shaves flashes through my head, but I wisely hold my tongue. I can only hope the sensor scatter caused by the gas giant is enough to keep them from getting missile lock, or we're really dead.

Just at the right moment, I push forward on the control yoke, angling my ship down and deeper into the upper atmosphere. I reach my desired altitude and maintain it for a little while. We can't see the pirates anymore; the same sensor scatter that's keeping us largely hidden from them is doing the same to us. But the last view showed them still hot on our tail and making a descent to stay behind us. And I'm praying they're still close enough on our tail to *see* us.

"Be ready!" Lin shouts unnecessarily; I'm watching a counter tick down on my console, the numbers turning from yellow to red as they near zero. When they reach it, I jam the yoke forward again and dive my ship. But this time, I take a much steeper angle. It's a huge risk but a calculated one. And for a moment, we are diving straight down into the heart of Big Ben. But then, slowly but surely, we pull out of the dive and loop back upward. For a second, our engines labor to take us on such a steep up angle, and I push the throttles to the max, igniting the atmosphere around me but pushing us just hard enough to win against gravity's unforgiving embrace and hopefully escape before the flames engulf us.

"Explosion! And another!" Lin calls out. We can't actually see the explosions, but we can *hear* them reverberating through our hull, conveyed via the planet's thin atmosphere, though the sound is much farther away—more like distant thunder—than when the mines nearly hit us before.

"Yes!" I cry out in triumph. I want to pump my fist, too, but I don't dare take even a single finger off the controls.

Once again, the roiling gases in front of us give way to stars and the big dark of space. By letting the pirates see and chase us earlier, we'd taken a very large risk, but we also had a pretty good idea of where their minefield was, having gone through it earlier ourselves. And we led them straight into it, diving out of the way at the last moment. Apparently, they didn't see our dive quickly enough and blundered right into at least two of their own mines.

But my triumph ends quickly as the rear cameras clearly show the pirate ship emerging from the gas giant only slightly off angle in their pursuit of us, though it does appear that part of their ship is venting atmosphere. I guess I shouldn't be surprised they're still behind us; after all, *we* survived the minefield. It's a miracle it did them any damage at *all*.

I curse just as Lin also uses another word I've never heard from her before.

"What now?" she asks, her voice still blessedly professional despite our near-certain impending doom.

We can't go back to the gas giant, not with that pirate between us and it, and regardless, we've already proven that approach won't work. So, our options are getting extremely limited…as in die now or die in a few minutes.

"We're too far off course to get to Carter's World," I say, still refusing to accept that I might die a second time in the last few weeks, and for *real* this time, "but maybe we can lose them in the gas giant's rings?" I phrase it as a question on purpose; flying as fast as we are through the rings of a planet is tantamount to suicide. All it takes is a few small rocks impacting our hull at speed to put holes in us.

"I think I'm going to be sick," Kayla says from behind me as I hear her frantically undoing her restraints and then running from the cockpit.

I look at Lin, and she shrugs. "I can't think of anything better," she replies, though I know she's also fully aware of the foolishness of the desperate plan, "and we should be able to get there just ahead of them."

I set in the new course and start praying in earnest, because religious or not, it's time to cover *every* base.

Two minutes later, however, Jessica cries out in surprise.

"What?" I demand, checking my console for any clue as to what shocked her. The last thing we need right now is an engine burnout or even a single thruster going offline.

"They're losing acceleration and changing vector!" she exults. "They're turning, breaking off pursuit!"

"Huh," I say in confusion. "Maybe we damaged them more than we thought?"

Jess is shaking her head but smiling ear to ear now. "Who cares, as long as they're not chasing us."

I nod in agreement. "OK. Lay in a course for Carter's World, full burn. Let's get on the right vector and get far away before they change their minds."

FIFTEEN
MEETING THE PRESIDENT

It's the dead of night on the part of the planet where Kayla directs us to land. We can't go straight to the capital city and meet with her father in the presidential mansion. According to her, they think some of the local populace may actually be working with the pirates, spying for them on the planet's surface. That seems farfetched at first, given the small size of the population and their common ancestry and tight family ties, but she explains that they get a good share of migrant farm workers that come to the planet only during certain regional seasons. A spy could easily hide among their number.

Still, it feels somehow wrong to meet with a planetary president on a dark piece of farmland with a single small house and a surprisingly large barn, big enough to accommodate our ship. We land on one of the plowed fields, almost breaking off our landing gear in the process, but then taxi slowly into the barn, directed by a man on the ground.

As Jessica and I do the post-landing checklist to shut everything down, Kayla is quite literally bubbling over with excitement at seeing her father. As soon as the ship stops in the barn, she jumps out of her seat and leans forward, kissing me on the cheek, and then bounds out of the cockpit to go open the airlock for us to disembark.

Chagrined, I look over to see Jessica frowning at me. "Really, Brad?" she asks. "Can we at least *try* to be professional?"

I shrug, embarrassed but also a little annoyed at her tone. Who is she to tell me who I can and can't date, especially since she's made it pretty clear she doesn't want to be with me?

I don't say any of that, of course. Paula Mendoza may have raised a screwup and eventual mass murderer, but even I'm not *that* stupid. I *was* married, after all.

Harris excuses himself from the cockpit next, mumbling something about changing his shirt. Judging by his usual appearance, he'll probably exchange one rumpled t-shirt for another and look equally dodgy in front of President Carter. But I don't say anything; he might put makeup on me in my sleep.

Right as I'm about to get up and leave as well, Jessica stops me. "Hold up," she says, her condescending tone from before lost. "Before we go out there, I don't think we should blindly trust Kayla and her father. We got away from that pirate way too easily."

"You call that easily?" I ask incredulously. "We almost died like six times!"

She rolls her eyes at me. "You know what I mean. No way a couple of those mines injured them enough to stop chasing us unless one was a *really* lucky hit. Something about this entire situation seems off to me. Just promise me we won't take everything they say at face value. Even if they're honest with us, there may be more going on here than even they know."

I'm hoping this is just her jealousy of my budding relationship with Kayla. However, despite only knowing Jessica for a few weeks, I'm already certain she wouldn't stoop to throwing suspicion at another woman, even if she is *jealous,* which I'm also pretty sure she isn't. "OK," I tell her, "We'll be careful."

We both strap on the pistols we took from Owen Thompson and his team and head out of the cockpit and to the airlock, where Kayla has already opened the hatch and extended the ladder.

I let Lin climb down first, and when I follow, I find a circle of three men facing me and the ship. Kayla is in the arms of the older man in the middle, apparently her father. He's hugging her tightly and talking in her ear; it actually looks a little too intimate for a father-daughter, but hey, this is a backwater world; maybe they do things differently out here in the sticks.

The president releases his daughter and extends a hand to shake mine. I step forward and take it, receiving a firm handshake that squeezes my hand just a little too tightly.

"Captain Lopez," the president says in a deep baritone through a salt and pepper beard—we agreed prior to landing we would use our false names; no use having the *entire* Fringe knowing who we really are, and Kayla agreed, "I want to thank you for returning my daughter to me and coming to help us. I know our plight seems desperate, and it is, but every little bit helps."

I nod in reply, but it's Lin who speaks first from our side. "President Carter, it's a pleasure to meet you, but do you mind introducing us to your friends?"

I'm worried for a second that the president will take offense, but he smiles and motions to the man at his left. "This is Wesley Adamson, my chief of staff and most trusted advisor. And this," motioning to the shorter, stockier man at his right, "is Norman Smith, the head of our planetary militia. At my orders, they are the only two men who know of your arrival here today. The rest of my cabinet, advisors, and what's left of our militia and police forces will only be told if they need to know. That way, we don't risk tipping off the pirates."

I study the two men. Adamson has a shifty look about him, like he's cheating at poker—classic politician. Smith is short and burly and has a hard look, more so than I would expect from a simple farm planet's militia leader, but maybe understandable given he's lost most of his fighting force to pirates in the last year.

Jessica frowns. "That's a good plan, sir, but we're afraid the pirates are already tipped off that we're here. We had a run-in with one of their ships in the outer system, which almost ended very poorly for us."

Carter frowns back and nods. "Yes, Kayla was telling me about that. I'm sorry it happened. But luckily, we've had a few smugglers brave enough to run the blockade to bring us medical and other off-world supplies at exorbitant prices. So we're hoping the pirates will just assume you're another of those."

Jessica is clearly unconvinced but doesn't respond, giving me a chance to finally butt in. "Let's hope so, but let's not count on it. We should get down to business quickly before they have a chance to regroup and think too hard about things. But first, is there somewhere we can get a cup of coffee? We're all running on fumes right now."

"Yes, of course," the president says, turning to his chief of staff. "Wesley, why don't you take them into the farmhouse and get them situated while I catch up with my daughter? Norman, go with them; they can start quizzing you on the situation if I'm not there when they're ready."

We follow the two other men out of the barn and across the yard to the little house we saw from the air. It has cheery orange light coming from the windows and reminds me a bit of my grandparents' farmhouse on Denton III, which instantly makes me feel simultaneously homesick and comforted. But I can see from the frown on Jessica's face that she's still worried about this entire situation. Well, Jessica is a worrier, that's for sure, though I promise myself I'll at least think about her concerns. After I get some coffee in me.

SIXTEEN
ROUNDTABLE

"And that's the long and the short of it," Norman Smith finishes his monologue. We've been sitting with him, President Carter, and Adamson for the last two hours, talking through the pirate threat while we fight to stay awake.

"And you're sure there are only the two ships?" I ask dubiously.

He nods. "Absolutely sure. We may not have much in the way of a planetary sensor network, but we do know where the pirate base is—it's not like they've felt any need to hide it from us—and we keep everything we have pointed at it. We've only ever seen the two ships coming and going."

I nod, but I still have my doubts. The pirates must expect that the planet is watching their base, and underestimating even a ragtag pirate gang—which this one certainly is not—can be extremely dangerous.

"We saw the one ship. What's the other one?" Jessica asks from the chair to my left. Kayla has planted herself to my right and moved her chair uncomfortably close, and I'm trying hard not to let it distract me.

"We've gotten a good sensor picture," Norman says with the first hint of excitement in the conversation, pushing a pad across the kitchen table with an image on it; apparently, the people of Carter's

World don't use their implants for a lot of things, assuming they even have them.

I look at the picture of the ship on the screen and whistle. "Koratan corvette," I say, shaking my head. How come it's always Koratan ships trying to kill me? "No wonder they took out your patrol boat easily. Those things are no joke." It's true; the ship I'm looking at probably last saw actual naval service five decades ago, but it appears to be well-maintained and well-armed, and the pirates have no doubt updated it, given what we saw of the other ship that chased us. I still can't believe such a well-equipped pirate gang is so intent on claiming a planet as small and worthless as this one.

Norman shrugs. "You would know better than me, Captain Lopez. All we know is that these two ships are enough to shut down trade almost entirely in the system. We can barely find smugglers anymore willing to run the blockade to bring us goods, and those we *can* find, we can't afford."

"You're a farming planet, so you should have plenty of food; what goods are you trying to get?" Jessica asks, and I want to groan. Leave it to a wealthy city girl to have no understanding of economics or what it takes to live in a backwater like this. Of course, my understanding isn't much better, but at least it extends to the things I used to hear my grandparents talk about at their farm on Denton III.

President Carter is the one to answer, and he doesn't seem offended by her question. "You're right, Miss Kim. We have plenty of food—a surplus, really, since we export most of what we grow—but we don't have manufacturing for basic goods, medicines, and other things that our people need to live. My advisors estimate that we have three months left before we start to see some easily cured but truly nasty diseases start to ravage the planet. But the pirates won't even let the necessities through. We have to put an end to it for the good of my people."

That sounds like a terrific campaign speech to me, but I largely ignore it. I'm still studying the image of the Koratan corvette. It's a little smaller than *Persephone* and probably would have presented my old frigate with a fairly even fight. My old battlecruiser, *Lancer*, would have been able to swat it out of space with barely a thought. But it's still a significant bit of firepower for this far out in the Fringe, so far away from any of the big star nations. It's no wonder the Carter Worldians… Carterians… Carterans… whatever…haven't been able to find anyone willing to risk taking it on.

"When do you expect them to show up for their next raid?" Lin asks. I've let her do most of the talking in this conversation, leaving me to absorb the information and maintain a bit of command separation from the 'civilians'. She takes to it naturally, as any good XO does, and I marvel at how easily we can always find a rhythm with each other in situations like this. Too bad we'll obviously never have the opportunity to find a similar rhythm in our personal lives.

"Tomorrow, if they hold to their usual schedule," Norman, the militia guy again, answers Jessica's question. "Should be right around lunchtime that they show up."

"Great," I say, drawing a few startled glances. "That gives us just enough time."

"For what?" President Carter asks.

"For Harris here," I motion to the man, who fell asleep with his head on the table an hour ago and now startles awake as I say his name, "to make me look like a different person and for you to get me onto your orbital station."

Now, they're all looking at me in confused silence, including my own crew. I just grin and pick up one of the tea cakes they set out with the coffee and take a big bite. They're quite good, and I chew around my grin, enjoying their flabbergasted stares.

SEVENTEEN
I'M GOING TO MURDER HARRIS

"Harris," I say through my comm bud, "when I told you to make me unrecognizable, this isn't exactly what I had in mind."

"Sorry, Captain," he replies in my ear, "You asked, and I delivered. I think it's perfect."

I frown. "You know how we talked about giving you a rank in our organization? Well, I *was* thinking petty officer, but I think you just convinced me to make you a spacer second class instead."

"That's good, right?" he asks somewhat eagerly. "Second class sounds better than petty."

Jessica breaks into our conversation. "Just ignore him, Harris. I think you did a marvelous job. And Brad, don't complain; you look beautiful." She's trying to joke around, but there's an undercurrent of stress in her tone.

I command my implant to change the comm to Lin's private channel. "You OK?"

"Sure," she answers shortly. "Why wouldn't I be? I'm the one safe behind a locked door, while you're the one being an idiot."

Ouch. She wasn't happy when I first presented my plan, and she hasn't really warmed up to it in the half day since. And when Jessica is annoyed with me, she becomes Confident Lin, the stern XO who doesn't pull her punches with anyone, much less her captain. Most of the time, I like Confident Lin, but not when she's angry at me.

"It'll be fine," I say with false casualness. "At least Harris got one thing right: I don't look *anything* like myself right now."

She grunts in reply. "I still think we should have done more intel gathering before we launched *any* operation."

"Come on," I say, "this operation is all about intel gathering. What better way to get information on the pirates than to get up close and personal? Speaking of which, our guests have arrived, so I'd better go."

I cut off the comm channel before she can reply and call me an idiot again and turn my attention to the guy who just walked into the small café on Carter's World's orbital platform. He's definitely a pirate. In fact, if you were to ask a fourth grader to draw you a pirate, he'd probably draw this guy. Not only does he have the stereotypical mohawk haircut, but every square centimeter of his exposed skin that *isn't* covered by tattoos seems to be hosting multiple very painful-looking piercings. Some of them look downright impossible, and I can't figure out how he eats. Heaven forbid he should ever try to kiss anyone or even blow his nose. A hard sneeze would probably kill him.

He walks in with the swagger and confidence of a guy who knows there's no one nearby to challenge him. He's wearing black leather pants and a mesh tank top underneath a matching leather jacket, and he has a shotgun held lazily in one hand and propped up against his shoulder. He looks ridiculous but also very scary. Like, I might laugh at him, but he'd definitely kill me for doing so.

Since I'm sitting near the café entrance, he looks at me first and swaggers over to my table.

"Hey, sweetheart," he says with a lewd smile. "Whatcha got for me under that dress?"

I shy away from him, pretending that I'm intimidated. But I'm really just uncomfortable. My pantyhose is riding up something fierce! How do women wear these things? And the high heels hurt *so* bad. Again, I silently curse Harris for disguising me to look like a woman. What was he thinking? And why didn't I put a stop to it before it got started? Morbid curiosity, I guess.

"Come on, sweetheart," the man says as he leers at my chest; I wonder what he would think if he knew those were just rolled-up socks. "Give us your name at least."

Ugh. He's not going to give up; I can see it in his eyes and the way he undresses me with them. Is this really how women are constantly being looked at by men? I suddenly feel guilty on behalf of my entire gender.

"Kiki," I say in a falsetto voice, giving the first name that comes to mind, which I immediately regret. Kiki? Really? Could it sound any more fake? But apparently, the guy likes what he hears because he slips into the seat across from me, ignoring the other patrons in the café.

"Listen, girly," he says, giving his best toothy smile that clearly demonstrates he's never met a dentist and makes some of his piercings stretch the skin in ways that make me want to puke a little. I want to kick him in his happy place under the table, but I refrain. "What's say you and I go somewhere a little more private? I might even let you keep that fancy jewelry afterward."

OK, now I'm literally going to murder Harris. He thinks I won't, I bet, but I *am* a mass murderer. I don't know why people keep forgetting that. They should be *way* more afraid of me than they are.

"I can't. I'm married," I say. Ugh, if this doesn't work, I *will* kick the guy.

He frowns but then seems to suddenly remember where he is and why he's actually here. He reaches out and grabs my left hand, roughly removing the fake diamond ring Harris put there. At least, I hope it's fake; if it's not, I'm going to have some serious words with my newest spacer second class.

After that, the big pirate empties out the purse I brought, finding the seventy-three credits we put in there for this exact purpose and shoving it in a bag with the ring. After that, he gets up and moves past me to start hassling the couple at the next table over. But as he does so, he paws my fake chest a bit as he roughly yanks the—hopefully also fake—pearl necklace off my neck. Then he's gone.

"Harris," I whisper into my comm. "You're a dead man."

"What?" he asks. "Did it not work?"

I don't answer; let him stew in uncertainty.

"He's kidding, right? Captain likes to joke around, right?" I can hear him asking Lin over the open comm as I try to subtly keep an eye on the pirate who accosted me, along with a few of his buddies outside the café shaking down people in the station's small concourse and the shops circling it.

As I watch, one across the way gropes a pretty blond girl, making her scream. When her husband or boyfriend tries to put himself between the pirate and the girl, he ends up on the ground with a broken jaw for his trouble. I itch to jump to my feet and intercede, but that would defeat the purpose for which I'm here today, which is just to watch, listen, and learn as much as I can about the foe we now face.

Unfortunately, knowing that I can't help those around me—that doing so now would rob my ability to help them later when it really counts—doesn't translate to feeling one iota better about that fact. So I watch, and I fume, and my hand twitches at my side for the pistol that isn't there.

The tattooed and pierced pirate finishes stealing everything he can from the café's customers and owner and then leaves out the front door. I watch his back as he goes and try to memorize everything about him so I can remember to shoot him the next time I see him.

EIGHTEEN
A GIFT FROM THE ADMIRAL

A half day later, I'm back in the tiny farmhouse where *Wanderer* is still hidden in the nearby barn. We hitched a ride to and from the capital city in the aircar belonging to Norman Smith, the militia leader, and then used the one-operating public shuttle to get to and from the orbital station itself.

I'm still fuming, and I had some truly choice words for Harris about the disguise he put me in. But then Jessica stepped in and reminded me that, as *captain*, I could have simply ordered the man not to do it. Stupid Lin and her stupid logic. In the end, I grudgingly apologize to Harris for yelling at him while my XO watches like the schoolteacher who made me apologize for kicking my bully in the groin in fifth grade.

I also feel like I need to apologize to every woman I see, but I haven't had a moment alone with either Lin, who rode with me and Harris to and from the orbital, or Kayla, who stayed behind on the farm with her father. Not that I would know what to say anyway. 'Hey, I'm sorry for being a man. We all really suck. Please forgive us.' Yeah, real smooth.

So, I'm a bit grumpy when we sit down for another annoying

strategy session with President Carter and his two advisors, this time in the farmhouse's tiny living room.

"What did you learn?" the president asks without preamble. Maybe he's just a no-nonsense guy generally, but his clipped tone could also have something to do with his short-short-wearing daughter sitting so close to me on the small couch that it's hard to tell where I end and she begins. I even try to move aside at one point, casually, but she just follows right along, and now she has an iron grip on my hand.

I really need to find time alone with her so I can somehow talk her out of all this. Assuming I really want to, which I'm pretty sure I do, but maybe there's a voice of doubt in my head. After all, Lin has made it abundantly clear that she and I are never meant to be. Would it be so bad to move on?

I'm so confused, though that's nothing new for me, I guess.

"We learned that the pirates don't operate as a unit," I say both to answer the president's question and distract myself from Kayla's other hand, now rubbing my back. "The ones I saw were disorganized and operated as individuals the entire time. I even saw a few folks on the station get shaken down by two or even three different pirates because they weren't even coordinating sections of the station to loot. How did it go on the ground?"

It's the president's chief of staff, Wesley Adamson, who answers. He's the one who was at the presidential mansion in the capital city while Carter was here with Kayla—I thought it was odd the president would send an advisor to take the heat, but apparently, Adamson insisted.

"They were upset the president wasn't there," he tells us. "But they still walked in like they owned the place. And after all the artwork they stole and loaded into their ship, they pretty much do. We couldn't pay their tribute in cash—no surprise there—but their leader, Poulter, said that we'd better have the money next time, with interest. And that was *after* he emptied the treasury vault of every scrap and credit we had, both the physical and digital."

President Carter frowns. "Next time, they won't be so generous. I have a feeling this is our last warning before things truly escalate. Captain Lopez, we'll need to move as quickly as we can."

I get his desire to do things fast, but they've been under these pirates for almost a year! Can't this guy be patient for a few more weeks?

Norman Smith takes his turn to speak up. "We shouldn't try and take them again on the planet's surface. Trying that with our militia was a mistake. We can't fight against their air support. That corvette isn't capable of atmospheric flight, but their smaller ship is, as we learned painfully last time."

I nod. All this I know, but I still haven't figured out a way to defeat our enemies. I need more time to think about it. Unfortunately, Jessica and I were both naval officers, not Marines, and even the ground assaults we did participate in as junior officers were planned and usually run by the gunnery sergeants while everyone *pretended* we were really in command.

"Even if we could fight them again with the militia," Norman is saying, "I doubt we could get more than a dozen of our people to show up. They're not professional soldiers, and they've been spooked by the eighty percent casualty rate of the last try."

"What if we could arm them better than the last time?" Jessica asks right before I can. We're on the same page.

Norman shrugs. "It would have to be a pretty good set of weapons to get them to leave their farms and go up against a serious foe again."

Honestly, anything would be better than the two-hundred-year-old bolt-action hunting rifles the militia normally uses. A big caliber hunting rifle with a kick like a mule *feels* like real power in your hands until you face down a guy with a laser or projectile assault rifle who can put a hundred rounds into you in seconds. Then you feel awfully small.

Not that I have any direct experience being the guy with the bolt-action rifle, but there were a couple of times I was commanding part of the guys with the assault rifles, so I can sort of imagine what the other side was feeling.

"Let me ask you something, Mr. Smith," I say. "How many militia members *could* you raise in a pinch, assuming we had the right weapons?"

He shrugs, which doesn't fill me with confidence. "I still doubt I could get more than two dozen, and even that would require that they *really* be the right weapons." His pessimism is starting to wear on me a bit. I mean, it's not like we're facing impossible odds and don't have a plan; well, yes, it is, but his defeatist attitude isn't helping.

I stand up, extricating myself from Kayla's grasp. "Well, let's go see what goodies are in my ship's hold."

In the excitement of our daring escape from the pirates, followed by the quick trip to and from the orbital to observe our foe in action, I'd pretty much forgotten all about the crate Admiral Walters had ordered put into our cargo hold. We head there now to check it out.

True to the admiral's promise, the crate unlocked once its internal nav chip verified we were in Carter's System. All it needs to open is my fingerprint. I only hope that the gases that got past our cargo hold seals in the atmosphere of Big Ben didn't damage the contents, but it all looks intact from the outside.

Without any hesitation or fanfare, I open the thing and peer inside.

I freeze, unable to believe what I'm seeing, but feeling a surge of hope for the first time since we started this impossible mission. Admiral Walters has given us some real toys to play with. And with them, we actually stand a chance.

NINETEEN
TWO AND A HALF SAMURAI

"I can see why she didn't want us opening the crate while we were still in Republic space," Lin observes as we study the contents, which are now laid out in neat rows across the floor of our otherwise empty cargo bay.

I grunt my agreement. With the arsenal now before us, we could start a revolution on most planets and probably win one on a small planet like Carter's World. And the pirates won't stand a chance against us if we can find enough people to wield the weapons.

In all fairness, it almost disappoints me. Not that I *enjoy* impossible missions, but daring and risky plans that somehow defy the odds have sort of become a thing for me and Jessica since we met. I expected this mission to top all of them, assuming it didn't kill us. But now, it just seems so *easy*.

Except for one thing: even with an array of weapons like these, they're all infantry or Marine arms. There's nothing that can help us take out either of the pirate ships. Especially that corvette. And our unarmed freighter isn't going to be any help in that department either.

"OK," Norman the militia guy says, rubbing his hands together like a kid in a candy store. "With this, maybe I can get you twenty-five troops. What's the plan?"

The plan. Yeah. Having one of those would be nice right now.

"Norman, have you ever seen a movie called *Seven Samurai*? It's an Old Earth classic." It was also my grandpa's favorite movie.

He shakes his head, looking confused.

"We're your seven samurai," I continue. "Well, two and a half if we're generous in how we count Harris. But the bottom line is, we're going to train and equip what's left of your militia to make those pirates run for the hills."

"Uh, we want them out of our system, not in our hills," he says, his eyebrows knit together.

I sigh. This guy really isn't any fun at all. "It's just an expression, Norm. We'll kick them out of the system. Happy?"

He nods doubtfully, but at least he walks off to start calling in some of his militia members.

Jessica steps up to me once he's out of earshot. "You don't have a plan yet, do you?"

I shake my head. "Nope. I was hoping *you* might."

She laughs at me and shakes her head right back. "Nope. Sorry, sir. Fresh out." It's another joke like the one about me making a beautiful woman; that's *two* in as many days. I'm slowly wearing her serious disposition down.

"Harris," I call to my spacer second class, who is staring at the weapons like they're foreign objects.

"Yeah, boss?"

"How about you? You have a plan?"

He looks at me for a moment, probably trying to figure out if I'm serious. Then he shrugs. "Owen used to always say, 'Take the fight to the enemy'. I never really knew what that meant, but he sure said it a lot."

I wasn't really listening to Harris—I didn't expect him to say anything constructive—but now I focus my full attention on him. "Say that again, Spacer," I demand.

"Uh, take the fight to the enemy."

"Harris, you're a genius. And you just got promoted to spacer first class!"

He looks over at Jessica in confusion. "Wait, I was a spacer second class, now I'm a first? Isn't one lower than two in the Navy?"

My XO just rolls her eyes at him. "Come on, Harris," she says, "let's get some lunch, and I'll explain naval ranks to you…again." They head through the internal hatch that leads to *Wanderer's* passenger area.

About that time, Norman walks back into the hold from outside. "I got five people already to say yes once I told them what we can equip them with. I should have another twenty by later today. They're coming from all over the planet, so they can be here in, say, two days. That work?"

"It'll have to," I tell him. "It's not like we have any other options for ground troops."

He nods and rushes off to make more calls, and I start working on my plan.

TWENTY
CAUGHT BETWEEN TWO ROCKS

It's ten at night local time, which means it's almost the start of a new day; whoever terraformed this rock didn't get the rotation speed right, so the day here is only twenty and a half hours long. Annoying.

I'm standing outside on the farmhouse's front porch after ending another four-hour discussion on tactics with Norman, during which I feel like I had to explain everything six times, which was particularly tough given I'm making it all up as I go. I'm exhausted, but I've been running ragged for days now, and I feel the overwhelming desire just to stand here and do nothing more than breathe in the scents of the surrounding farmland and forest. The smells here are different for sure, but they still remind me generally of my grandparents' farm on Denton III.

The creaking of the screen door behind me heralds the arrival of someone else. A pair of arms reaches around my waist, and someone hugs me from behind. Has to be Kayla, unless Jessica suddenly decided to throw out her principles.

Kayla releases me and moves to stand beside me, and the scent of loamy soil and pine needles is replaced by the smell of lavender soap. I look down. Her hair is wet, and she's wearing pajamas. It all adds to the homey feeling. And I have to say the worn cotton PJs look surprisingly good on her.

"Do you think we can win?" she asks me in an uncharacteristically small voice.

I consider the question for a moment, not wanting to answer too quickly so as to seem that I'm not taking her query seriously. "Yes," I say. "If the men and women Norman is gathering are as solid as he says, and if the pirates give us a week or two to train them, then I think we'll almost certainly win."

I can see her frown in the moonlight. "That's a lot of ifs."

Nodding, I keep studying the darkness of the tree line several hundred meters away across the fields. For a supposed farm, I sure haven't seen anyone working those fields while we've been here. I assume Carter sent them all away, or maybe he even owns the place himself, though it's strange it would be so far away from the capital, in an entirely different hemisphere.

"Brad," Kayla says, drawing my attention again, breaking the rules by using my real name. "Admiral Walters said something funny to me on *Dauntless* about you, and it's been bugging me."

Confused, I look down at her. "What'd she say?"

She frowns. "Something about you having some big secret that everyone wants, and something about a system called Gerty... Gerbon..."

"Gerson," I finish for her but realize instantly I probably should have just kept my mouth shut.

"That's the one!" she says excitedly. She puts an arm around me and leans into me, and the smell of lavender grows stronger with her hair now right below my face, and the wetness of it soaks through my t-shirt. "What," she continues, "could be so important in Gerson that everyone in the galaxy would be after it?"

On the surface, it seems like just an innocent question. And it most likely is. But it's not one I'm going to answer. "Listen, Kayla, Walters was probably just trying to talk me up and make me seem more important than I really am. Truth is, there's nothing in this head of mine that anyone wants. Trust me."

She looks up at me, and in a brief second in the moonlight, it looks like anger flashes in her pretty blue eyes, but I must have imagined it because she snuggles back into me and sighs. "Brad, tell me this is all going to work out."

I breathe in deep, savoring the smells of the forest and of Kayla, but when I let the breath go, it escapes as a sigh. "Kayla, all I can tell you is that we'll do our best. Aside from that, luck is going to play a pretty big role, as will good old Mr. Murphy if we're not careful. But I can promise our best effort to free your planet."

That seems to satisfy her because she says nothing else but just keeps hugging me there on that front porch as I gaze out over the fields. It starts to feel *really* good, and I'm trying to think of a polite way to extricate myself before I do something I might regret, when she looks up again. "Brad, I'm scared."

I reach up and put my arms around her, hugging her back lightly. "Nothing to be scared of," I lie. "Just some pirates. And we've got bigger guns."

"Let's leave. Now," she says, a sudden urgency in her voice. "We can get in your ship and fly away somewhere where there are no pirates and no worlds under siege. You can find Admiral Walters and sell her whatever information she thinks you have, and we can live off the money and just be together. Wouldn't that be wonderful, Brad?"

The sudden about-face from scared little girl to excited paramour has my head spinning, and I slowly push her away to look her in the eyes. "Kayla, think about what you're saying. What about your father? Would you just leave him here?"

"No," she says, then bites her lower lip and starts to tear up. I feel instantly bad. "But we could take him with us," she continues. "Maybe the pirates will leave once they realize we don't have anything more for them to take. But the thought of anything happening to you makes me..."

She throws herself back at me and hugs me tight, burying her face back into my chest, adding the wetness of her tears to my already-soaked shirt. I hold her like that for a long time, even though I know I shouldn't lead her on, but I have no idea how to get out of the embrace without being a jerk. She needs the comfort right now.

"Stay with me tonight." The invitation catches me off guard, and I look down in confusion to see she's craning her neck to look up at me.

"Uh..." I start to say, but my mind goes blank, and words fail me entirely. Slowly, I reach around and unwrap her arms from around my back and then take a step back from her. This time, I'm certain I see her eyes flash with anger, and her lower lip juts out in a healthy pout.

"Kayla, I'm not..." I try to say again, but I still can't form the words. Suddenly, she takes a step forward, grabs my head, and pulls it down, kissing me hard. Before I can even fight it, she releases me from the kiss and then steps back again.

"You know where to find me if you change your mind," she says coyly and then spins and walks back to the farmhouse door in a way that tells me she is one hundred percent sure I'm watching her go.

Then, as she reaches the darkened doorway, I see another person emerge from it: Jessica. The two women regard each other in a way that reminds me of two cats who used to fight all the time on Grandpa's farm, and then Kayla disappears inside, and Jessica steps out onto the porch.

"Uh," I say to Jessica because my brain has suddenly shut off... again.

She looks at me with a deep frown. "So, this is you being careful with trusting Kayla, huh?"

"I...uh...well...she kissed *me*," I stammer.

Jessica shakes her head in disappointment. "Brad, at least be man enough to admit that you like her."

"But...I..." I still don't know what to say. Because to any outside observer, I *should* like Kayla. She's cute, she's strong, and she clearly likes me. In fact, the only reason I can think of that I don't like Kayla is because I'm in *love* with Jessica. But I can't tell *her* that!

She shakes her head at me, grunts in frustration, and hisses something that sounds like 'men'. Then she storms off in the direction of the barn and our ship, leaving me standing there alone, trying to figure out how I've managed to drive off two women in one night without even trying. It might be a galactic record, and someone can send me a certificate that reads 'Humanity's Biggest Numbskull'.

I slowly walk in the same direction that Jessica just went, entering the huge barn and looking at my ship wedged inside. I stare at the ladder leading up to the airlock hatch, but I make no move toward it. Something tells me I should let Lin have the ship to herself tonight. Well, to her and Harris. He went to bed hours ago; there wasn't too much need for a makeup artist in our late-night tactics session, even though he was the one who provided me with the seed of the idea for our latest plan.

So, instead of walking toward the ship, I climb up a long wooden ladder to the hay loft high above, where I do something I haven't done since I was thirteen: I make myself a nest in the hay and lay down in it, ignoring it poking through my thin, still-wet shirt. There I lie, awake for at least another hour, turning the events of the evening over and over in my head until I finally slip into a fitful sleep without finding a single answer to why I'm such a monumental moron.

TWENTY-ONE
TRAINING DAYS

Luckily for me, Norman delivers the first sixteen of his hand-picked militia fighters a day early, and they start to arrive at the farm in small groups of two or three before I even wake up with the crowing of the rooster.

I find them all gathered, chatting excitedly, around the large table in the farmhouse's dining room. It's actually the biggest space in the small house, and it's perfect for a gathering like this, even though only about half of them can sit.

Almost to a person, they're in much better shape than I expected. When I think of a planetary militia, the image that usually comes to mind is a bunch of good ole boys with beer bellies, ball caps, and mullets who scream pig calls as battle cries. But not this group. They're lean and strong, and I can only guess got that way from hard work on the farms. But a few move in ways that remind me of Marines I've served with, and I have to upgrade my respect for Norman Smith's training methods. Maybe we can do this after all.

"This is Captain Ben Lopez," Norman introduces me as if I'm his best friend and his hand-picked savior. "He's a mercenary from off-world, "a few of them look at me a bit dubiously when he calls me a mercenary, "and is going to be leading our fight against the pirates. And he's got some surprises for all of you."

I try not to glare at him. I just got my first cup of coffee, and I haven't even had time to take a single sip. That, and I have hay in places no man should *ever* have hay, and it's the itchy kind. But I'm up, whether I like it or not, though I find myself wishing I had something a little stronger to put in my coffee this morning as my mind keeps going back to the events of last night.

"OK," I say to the gathered farmers-turned-militia-fighters. "You and the other nine people we're expecting are going to be the ones who drive these pirates off your planet and out of your system." I'm trying to sound inspiring, but it's early, and I just lost one, possibly two, loves of my life last night, so I come out sounding monotone. It doesn't matter. If they need me to inspire them to fight for their own planet, we've already lost.

"After breakfast," I tell them, "we'll head out to the barn and my ship, where we'll get you outfitted with the finest off-world weapons you've ever seen. You're going to want to start using them immediately, but we're going to train you up Marine style, which means you don't even load them without my say-so." There are a few mutters at that, but they can deal with it. Despite first impressions, I don't yet trust any of them not to shoot themselves, or worse, me, in the foot.

"We believe we have two weeks before the pirates' next raid. By then, I promise that you'll be the most efficient killing machines that Carter's World has ever seen." That's a really low bar, but it seems to make them stand up a little straighter. "But only if you listen to and do *everything* I tell you. Clear?"

Well, they're not military, so instead of a perfectly timed chorus of 'Sir, yes sir', I get back a smattering of 'Sure', 'Yes', 'Why not?' and at least one 'I guess so'. It'll have to do.

Five minutes later—I've never seen a group that large eat so quickly—we're out in the barn, and I'm bringing out weapons from the external cargo bay hatch on my ship. I haven't seen Jessica or Kayla this morning yet, and I'm very much hoping that lasts long enough for the caffeine to take effect.

It doesn't; halfway through my handing out of assault rifles and a few other special toys Admiral Walters included, Jessica enters the cargo bay from the inner hatch and starts helping me distribute the weapons, all while not meeting my gaze even once. Fun.

I suppose it shouldn't upset me as much as it does. I know I'm not any kind of a catch. In fact, I think Jessica would be insane to love me back the way I love her. She's an intelligent, caring, brilliant supermodel, and I'm...well, Brad Mendoza. It would defy logic for the two of us to end up together. Not to mention, I've only known her a few weeks! But no amount of rational thought will banish the feeling in the pit of my stomach every time I look at her and the worry that I may have lost her before I even had a chance to win her.

I'm moping, even though I know I shouldn't be. I was a senior *captain* in the Promethean Navy! I once defeated a pirate fleet with a single battlecruiser. I received the King's Star *four times* for bravery and for service above and beyond. I liberated Jalisco from a rebel blockade for crying out loud! I was one of the youngest officers in Promethean Naval history to attain my rank, and I was married to the daughter of a fleet admiral—even though he hated me—and was the envy of the stupid dinner parties she used to drag me to.

There's no way I should be acting like a teenage boy whose first girlfriend just dumped him for the quarterback! I should have more confidence than this. I should...

But no. Because while all of those accomplishments technically belong to me, I'm no longer the man who earned or deserved them. I'm Brad Mendoza, failure, murderer, drunk, and now...forever alone.

So, I do what any good officer does when his personal life is a mess. I take it out on the new recruits. And thus begins the worst two weeks of their lives, courtesy of the Butcher of Bellerophon.

TWENTY-TWO
THEY ALL HATE ME

For thirteen days, I make every man and woman that Norman Smith has gathered learn to hate every ounce of my guts. I'm fairly certain that, at this point, each one of them would happily kill me without a moment's remorse. But they learn surprisingly fast, and I'm now also certain that we now have a fighting force that can liberate Carter's World from the pirate threat.

If only I could convince President Carter of how we need to use them.

Kayla hasn't been around much the last two weeks—she's been on the opposite side of the planet tending to her family's farm near the capital—and I'm grateful for that. I know I need to take her aside and explain to her that I don't feel about her the way she obviously does about me, but I'm also dreading the conversation. I'm a coward, sure, but most men are when it comes to disappointing a beautiful woman, even when you're as practiced at it as I am.

Unfortunately, I don't think President Carter got the memo that I rejected Kayla's attempt to get me into bed that night, because he's been especially cold to me these last two weeks. And when I finally share my daring and genius plan with him, he's more than a little upset.

"Let me get this straight; you want me to *surrender* myself to the pirates?"

I smile tightly as he puts my proposal into the worst wording possible. "No, Mr. President," I say, really trying and failing to keep the impatience out of my tone, "I want you to *pretend* you're giving yourself up to them. We need them to think we're truly desperate, and this will be the best way to put them at ease by making them think you've given up all hope."

"It's insane," he says, shaking his head and throwing his hands in the air. Next to him, his faithful little lapdog, Adamson, nods in agreement.

"Mr. President," Norman Smith soothes from beside me, "Captain Lopez has shared his plan with me, and I think we ought to give it a chance."

Carter scowls at his militia leader but nods grudgingly, and I feel relieved again that I was able to convince Norman to back me on this.

"It's really quite simple, Mr. President," I say, imbuing my voice with as much respect and deference as I can. "You've already made it clear that we can't fight the pirates in the capital or on the orbital where civilians can get caught in the crossfire, and inviting the pirates to meet us on a farm like this one would instantly make them suspicious. There's also no way we can fight them in space; my ship has no weapons, and you have no more patrol fleet. So, that leaves only one place in this entire system where we can fight them."

"Their base," he finishes for me, and even though I already told him that was the plan, I'm glad he's starting to see the logic in it, even unwillingly.

"Yes, their base. It has the triple advantage of being the place where they'll feel most secure and relaxed, of being the one place we can ensure we get all of them together, and finally, it's the only place we can fight them on the ground without risk of civilian casualties."

"Except risk to the president himself," Adamson argues from his boss's side. I ignore him.

"Isn't the risk to one man, no matter how important he may be, worth it to safeguard and liberate the lives of every other civilian in this system?" Jessica asks from beside me. We may not exactly be hanging out a lot right now in our spare time, but we're still in sync enough that we can rely on each other in conversations like this. And anything said in her upper-crust Promethean accent and perfect diction just sounds so much more noble than the usual drivel from my mouth.

And it works because President Carter starts to look thoughtful.

I'm opening my mouth to try and bring this thing home when I hear Kayla's voice behind me.

"Do it, Daddy," she says sternly, and I turn in surprise. I didn't even know she'd come back today. She's standing there, looking her father dead in the eye with a determined stare.

I look back at the president, and I can see the moment he folds.

"Fine, I'll do it. But it had better work," he levels a finger at me.

I nod but say nothing, as nothing more needs to be said.

"OK," Jessica says, "then let's talk logistics. The militia will ride in *Wanderer*; she's not rated for that many passengers, but for a simple in-system hop, she should have more than enough life support, and there's plenty of room in our hold. But because she's such a small ship, the pirates will never suspect we're bringing a small army with us."

"Uh, yeah," Norman says uncomfortably, "about that..."

TWENTY-THREE
CATTLE

Do you remember how I had that little sense of weird disappointment when I first opened that crate of weapons in *Wanderer's* hold and thought to myself how easy this would all be with them? I felt it robbed me of the chance to pull another classic Brad Mendoza and Jessica Lin super risky stunt where we snatch victory from the jaws of a pit bull…or something like that.

Well, if I had a time machine and could go back and meet myself from that moment two weeks ago, I'd shoot myself in the face. Because this just got a whole lot more complicated.

"You're joking," Jessica says.

"I'm not," Norman Smith answers. "It's true."

"And *how* did the pirates get a life sign scanner?" I ask as I massage my temples to try and stop the headache that's quickly forming there. I've been sober now for *way* too long.

He shrugs. "We're an agricultural planet. Even one bug or rodent brought in from another planet's ecology could be enough to wipe out our crops. So, we had it installed in our orbital to scan incoming ships and their crews. The pirates took it the first time they raided the station. We assumed it was so that they could sell it—the things are *really* expensive; took us decades of saving to get one—but it's possible they've kept it until now."

I shake my head. "You realize this changes *everything*, right?"

Norman looks apologetic but just nods in reply.

This is bad, really bad. No one can scan a moving ship for lifeforms; life sign scanners rely heavily on thermals, and there's simply too much heat that comes off a starship in operation for even the best sensors to see through all that. But when a ship stops...

"You understand," Jessica says, "that as soon as we land, they will know our cargo hold is full of people? They'll blow us off that asteroid they call a base before we can even get your men and women out through the airlock."

Norman frowns and just nods, clearly upset and a little embarrassed. Good; he should be.

"What if they don't think they're people?" a new voice asks from the other end of the dining room table.

We all turn and look at the speaker, as if we can't believe Harris is actually talking in a planning meeting. He suddenly looks like a turtle trying to withdraw back into its shell.

"Harris," I bark, "if you have an idea, speak up. If it's a good one, I'll make you a petty officer."

He looks confused and glances over at Jessica.

"That's a good thing," she assures him. "A petty officer would be another jump in rank."

"Oh, ah, good. I guess. Anyway," he stammers, "what if the pirates think you have something else on board, like..." he trails off, and I can see he hasn't thought this through, but I wait him out anyway. "Like, I don't know, really big rodents?"

OK, giving him the time to think clearly wasn't helpful. But he is onto something.

"Cattle."

Now, everyone turns to look at me as if I just uttered something in a foreign language. "Look," I tell all the incredulous faces, "you've already said you don't have the money to pay him. But there are few things more valuable in space than fresh meat. Heck, I haven't had a steak in months. It might be enough of a draw, as stupid as it sounds, to make Poulter and his minions excited to let you come and visit."

I watch them all as they absorb this, and slowly, heads start to bob up and down. Kayla has moved up beside me and grabs my arm, and I can *feel* her beaming up at me. After the way Jessica has largely been looking at me the past two weeks, I have to admit I don't mind.

"OK," President Carter says. "I think we can round up some cattle."

TWENTY-FOUR
THE PIRATE KING

To my surprise, the pirate leader, Poulter, agrees to the president's proposal to bring the next tribute payment to them. They've made no secret of the location of their base on a small rock in the system's asteroid belt. And I guess it appeals to their naturally lazy side to let their loot and victims come to them. They even seem a little excited at the prospect of the cattle.

We actually did round up some cattle, loading them onto one side of *Wanderer* out in the middle of a field in case the pirates had someone watching even way out here. But we parked close enough into the trees that we hope they couldn't see the cows get right *off* the ship through the opposite cargo hatch. Either way, it's the best we can do. And Norman and his troops get on the ship through that same tree-masked hatch.

Of course, a life sign scanner isn't just going to see a bunch of thermal signatures shaped like humans and think cattle. But it's Jessica who comes up with the plan for that part. Once Norman and his people are on board, all wearing vacsuits and carrying extra air bladders, she activates *Wanderer's* fire suppression system and fills the hold with fire retardant foam. Our hope is that the foam will act as insulation and muddy up the heat signatures enough that the life sign scanner's results will come back as inconclusive.

Now, I'm piloting *Wanderer* on the last leg to their base. With me in the cockpit are President Carter, Harris, and Jessica. I actually tried to get my XO to stay behind and run our 'ground support', but she saw through my overprotective suggestion and utterly refused. Harris just happened to already be in the cockpit when I got there, as if there was never any question he would be coming. The guy's brave; I have to give him that.

"Hey, little freighter," a snide female voice comes over the comm as we get close to the rock. "Land wherever you can find a spot, but don't scratch the paint on either of our ships, or we'll have your president's skull for a salad bowl."

"Lovely landing control," I quip because I'm nervous. No one laughs.

My only comfort is that down in my hold—Kayla was able to work her engineering magic and fix our broken pressure seal—are twenty-five of what I believe are now the best-trained militia fighters this side of the Jutzen Protectorate. Plus Norman, and he can hold his own.

A few minutes later, I'm setting my little ship down between the big—by comparison—corvette and the smaller but still heavily armed patrol ship that escorted us in for the last tense hour of transit. Moments after I set her down, a docking tube extends and mates with our starboard airlock, allowing us to access the underground base the pirates have carved out of solid rock, though why they went through all the trouble for a system like this one is still beyond me.

It's just President Carter and myself who make our way through the tube, leaving Jessica and Harris behind to mind the ship. When we arrive at the airlock at the other end, two pirates roughly frisk us from head to toe. I'm pretty sure the one who searched me now knows more about me than my proctologist ever did.

Finally deciding that neither of us has a missile launcher or nuclear warhead hidden in our body cavities, the two men let us through to the next hatch, which opens into a surprisingly comfortable-looking lounge.

I mean, they even have a bar setup at one end, and it looks like it's fairly well stocked. I haven't had a drink in almost a month now, and I'm surprised by how my eyes insist on seeking out all the old familiar labels and how my mouth is suddenly watering.

There's a big man sitting on, of all things, an overstuffed bean bag chair in the middle of the room. He's tall, and metal studs cover just about every square centimeter of his head-to-toe black leather clothing. Despite all the spikey metal, the two women, one to either side, cuddling up to him, don't seem to have yet been impaled. They're each a sight to see on their own. One has a nose ring with a chain leading down to her belly button. What happens if she needs to look up or turn her head? Ouch. The other has a mohawk and a bionic arm attached to the stub of where her real one used to be. Neither is what I would call exactly modestly dressed. They make Kayla's typical short shorts look positively prim.

"Ah, Carter," booms the big man. "I see you've finally come to your senses and brought my money. You'd better have the full payment this time."

This is perhaps the riskiest part of the plan because there are two of us, unarmed, and I count a dozen pirates, including the leader and his two groupies, in the room. And they are *all* armed. And we're about to tell them we don't have the full amount.

"Sorry, Captain Poulter," Carter says next to me without breaking the big pirate's gaze. I have to begrudgingly admit, the president is built of sterner stuff than I expected; his voice only trembles slightly. "We only have half, but we'll have the rest in a few weeks if you'll just let us trade some of our goods off planet."

The pirate captain, Poulter, grins wickedly, exposing teeth that have been filed to sharp points like a shark. I'd love to hear Harris critique this guy's look.

"What do you take me for, Carter? You think I'm going to let you go for help somewhere, or try to hire some kind of mercenary outfit? Like anyone you could afford would be able to scare me." The guy doesn't know just how on the nose he is.

"Besides," he rumbles, "I've seen that daughter of yours around. I think I'll just take the other half out of her."

Carter tenses next to me, and I put out a warning hand to stop him from reacting, though I can tell he's right on the edge.

"*Captain* Poulter," I say, emphasizing his title and trying my best to sound meek. "If I may?"

"Who is this worm?" sneers Poulter, still looking at Carter.

"He's my trade advisor," the president answers through clenched teeth.

"As we told you on our way in, I believe we have a deal that will make up for our little shortfall, at least temporarily," I say without waiting for permission, doing my best to make my voice sound a little more nasally like every bureaucrat always sounds to my ears. "Do you like ribeye?"

Poulter regards me for a moment and then surprises me by breaking out into a smile. "I do at that. And fresh meat sounds better than the canned stuff. Maybe we can deal, but I'll just keep that little Kayla in reserve. She might like to finally meet a real man."

To his credit, Carter doesn't openly react, but he's as tense as a spring in a car's shocks, ready to explode at any second. I speak up quickly.

"We brought twenty head of cattle in our ship's cargo hold. At current market prices off-planet, they're worth about a tenth of what we still owe you, but we're hoping the value of a fresh cut of meat will make it worth far more than that since we've brought it to you."

He frowns but nods slowly. "What do you think, girls?" he asks, looking down at each of his groupies in turn. The one with the interesting nose-to-belly chain sneers in our general direction, but the other just nods eagerly.

"Very well, let's see just how good these cattle look before I decide if little Kayla is going to come out here and live with me. I'll have my fresh meat one way or another."

Uh oh, that does it. Carter explodes, rushing forward with a fist cocked. For an old guy, he moves pretty fast, but not fast enough. One of the other pirates lounging nearby, a tall guy with rings in places on his face I didn't know could support piercings—he makes the guy from the café look conservative—leaps out of his own lounge chair and clotheslines Carter before he even gets halfway to Poulter.

"Now, that was monumentally stupid," Poulter says in a low, menacing tone.

Then, pandemonium breaks out.

TWENTY-FIVE
PANDEMONIUM

On the flight in, Lin and I were able to capture some pretty good images of the pirate base. And we found what we were hoping for: a second entrance. Most places built underground have them. Otherwise, even the smallest cave-in would trap all the occupants inside with no hope of getting free.

And while we've been talking about cattle, steaks, and Kayla with Poulter and his merry crew, the rest of our passengers have been taking a long spacewalk around the backside of *Wanderer* and behind a short ridge to the other airlock into the base. And this is where Harris proves his worth. Because aside from being a makeup artist good enough to turn me into a woman, he was also Owen Thompson's tech guru. I find out later it takes him only twenty seconds to hack the airlock controls from the outside panel. Though I guess it's unlikely the pirates thought much about the possibility of a ground invasion and invested in a high-security lock.

Just as President Carter hits the ground and starts gasping for breath from the tall pirate's expert takedown, I spot movement in the mouth of a tunnel just behind and to the right of the bar. I leap down to the ground alongside the president, grateful that the artificial gravity inside the base makes me hit the floor quickly.

The sound of gunfire is deafening in the underground chamber, and so are the screams of the dying. We've taken the pirates completely by surprise, and few of them get off even a single shot before our boys and girls of the militia gleefully take them out.

About thirty seconds pass, though it feels much longer, before the last pirate slumps over with blood pooling on the front of his shirt. I wait another slow count of ten to make sure the battle is over, then I cautiously get to my feet and survey the carnage.

And it really is carnage. Those pirates that aren't dead are dying fast, and our militia boys and girls move in quickly and kick their guns away so that none of them will have a chance to avenge themselves with their last breaths.

My excitement at our successful ambush, however, fades when I turn my eyes to the beanbag chair at the center of the room, where I see the corpses of two women but no Captain Poulter. A quick count also reveals that we're one pirate short of what the room started with.

I swear loudly, and Norman Smith rushes to my side, his hair wet with sweat under the bubble helmet he's now removing from his head. "What's wrong?"

"Poulter got away!" I say louder than I intended. My ears are still ringing, but I hear Norman swear in response.

I look frantically around the room. I would have noticed if the big pirate had leapt over us to go down the corridor we entered from, and the only thing in that direction is the docking tube to our ship. But I scan the walls, searching until I find what I'm looking for.

The lounge is pretty gaudy, with sheets hanging from the walls like someone wanted to hide the bare rock or pretend they had tapestries or something. One of those sheets is moving now, swaying slowly back and forth. I sprint for it.

I think Norman is about to follow, but suddenly, more gunfire erupts. It seems the rest of the base's pirates have responded to the sound of the battle. Great.

That leaves me alone to follow Poulter to whatever hole he's fled to. I fling aside the sheet to reveal another tunnel carved out of the rock behind it. Without hesitation, I launch myself into the dark corridor and run as fast as I dare. It ends quickly at another open airlock and another transparent docking tube attached to it.

Without thinking or worrying about what might be on the other side, I run down the tube. I'm not worried about a random member of Poulter's crew getting away—they're likely to just go to ground and try to join another gang in another system. But if the pirate leader escapes, he'll come back someday for blood, with twice as many men and women to back him up. The future of Carter's World depends on stopping Poulter.

To my relief, the airlock at the other end of the tube is still open wide, and I very quickly find myself inside the Koratan corvette that I guess must be Poulter's flagship of his measly fleet of two. Guessing on instinct and general ship design, I turn left at a junction and run toward where I assume the bridge to be.

I find it a moment later, coming to a skittering halt as I enter the relatively small but open space to find Poulter staring me down along with five other pirates. That's when I remember I still don't have a weapon.

I am so dead.

TWENTY-SIX
NINJA LIN

Poulter smiles, though it's more of a disdainful sneer than anything else, and he momentarily reminds me of Petty Officer Nedrin Jacobs, the King's rapist nephew, back on *Persephone*.

"Well, well, well, if it isn't Captain Brad Mendoza of the Promethean Navy. I've been looking forward to this."

I frown. "Why does *everyone* know who I am in this blasted sector?"

He grins again, showing his teeth, but makes no response. I suddenly have the feeling that this entire time, I've been walking into a trap, though I can't fathom how the pirate leader could know me or know that I was coming.

At a sign from Poulter, a big pirate steps forward, covered in piercings and tattoos, and I recognize the guy as the one who stole my fake wedding ring, credits, and pearls when I posed as a woman on the orbital station. He moves toward me now, wearing a sneer a lot like his boss. I square my shoulders and ready myself to not go down without a fight, but the four other pirates in the room, all except Poulter himself and the guy approaching me, are covering me with their guns now.

My brain is racing, and I can see no path from this that ends with me alive. Still, I don't intend to go quietly, and when the big guy gets within a meter of me, I leap forward and hit him with a jab to the throat.

His hands fly to his neck as he suddenly can't breathe. It's a sucker punch, pure and simple, but I've done real damage to the guy's windpipe, and the scant satisfaction I get from that will have to be the last shred of happiness I get before I die…again. I brace myself for the feel of bullets hitting me; I've never been shot before, but I've heard it really sucks.

Then two things happen in rapid succession. First, Poulter cries out in surprise. Second, a gun barks from behind me, and one of the other pirates drops to the deck.

Then everyone is firing, and I lunge down to the deck next to the guy I just put there. He's gasping for breath and in a real panic, and I'm right there with him now as I can literally *feel* the bullets flying overhead.

Still, I manage to look up to see that just two of the pirates are still standing, plus Poulter, who is crouched behind a console now to one side of the small bridge. I crane my neck to look behind me and spot a completely unexpected figure taking cover behind the edge of the hatchway. Kayla!

She's dressed in the same vacsuit that the militia troops are wearing, and I can only guess she must have disguised herself as one of them and stowed away with them in the *Wanderer's* cargo hold. And now she's trying to have a gunfight with three pirates just to save my sorry rear end.

I've never liked her as much as I do now.

But regardless, she's outmatched and outgunned, though she must be a better shot than I would have expected, given that she's already downed two of the pirates. Even so, if I don't help her now, she's unlikely to get the rest.

I crawl over to the guy still gasping from my punch to his neck and grab the pistol from his waistband. He's turning purple and doesn't even notice. I raise the pistol and am about to fire at the pirate closest to me when the hatch on the other side of the bridge, behind the pirates, starts to swing open. I change my aim to center on that hatch.

If more pirates are allowed in, this could get ugly—well, uglier—real fast.

The hatch doesn't open wide, just a small bit, but a thin person slips through. I'm tightening my finger on the trigger when I recognize Jessica!

Right after I'd killed Owen Thompson and his thug Tucker on that galaxy-forsaken little rock in the Fiori system, I found Jessica safe on *Wanderer*, having already subdued the mercenary Jules with the help—or, at least, without the resistance of—Harris. I've wondered since what that fight must have been like because I've actually never seen Jessica so much as raise a hand in violence unless it was to hit a reticent ship's control console.

But now, my mouth drops open in shock as I see her lunge at one of the two pirates who remain standing and are shooting back at Kayla. Jess delivers a flying kick to the pirate woman's back like something out of a martial arts movie, knocking the pirate forward and causing her to drop her gun in surprise and stumble out from behind the small duty station she's been using as partial cover. I raise the pistol I'm holding and shoot the pirate right through the chest before she can get her feet back under her.

Jessica keeps moving, landing from her kick and using the momentum to pivot and fall forward into a somersault that brings her to her feet right next to the remaining pirate lackey. This guy sees her coming after watching his comrade go down, and he turns to point his pistol at her, but she knocks it out of his grasp with an open-handed slap, then crouches down and extends her leg as she spins, sweeping his feet out from under him. He gives a startled yelp as he falls and hits the deck hard, and the bridge gets suddenly quiet as all gunfire stops.

I want to look behind me and make sure Kayla is OK, but I can't tear my eyes away from my XO, who doesn't let the fallen pirate recover but stomps down hard with the point of her heel right into his chest, knocking the wind out of him, and then follows it up with a kick to his temple that renders him unconscious.

"Drop the gun!" Kayla shouts, and I look to see Poulter has partially risen from his crouch and is starting to point his pistol at me where I still lie on the deck. He scowls but obeys, dropping the gun and raising his hands as he finishes standing up.

He looks at me in disgust. "Really, Mendoza? You're gonna let your women do all the fighting for you?"

I get up from the deck and use the hand not holding the pistol to brush myself off. "Actually, I prefer to exclusively let women fight on my behalf," I tell him. "I'm very progressive that way." I smile at him.

"Now," I say, pointing my own stolen pistol at his gut, "tell me how you know who I am."

He sneers and stays silent. Oh well, that would have been way too easy. Kayla steps up beside me, her assault rifle also pointed at the guy, but a little lower down. What's that old saying? Hell hath no fury like a woman scorned. If Poulter's not careful, he'll lose any chance of bringing little pirate captains into the galaxy one day. His eyes widen when he sees her up close, and it almost seems like something passes between them. Then, to my surprise, the man appears to relax just a bit, though I'm not sure *I* could relax with a gun pointed at my family jewels.

"Brad? You OK?" Jessica asks, and I look over at her. She's barely breathing hard after taking down two very mean-looking pirates. I nod in response to her question. I think that she and I are going to have to have a very long talk about the seemingly hidden fact that she's some kind of ninja or something. To my questioning gaze, she shrugs and says, "Academy martial arts champ, two years straight." Figures. Does she have to be so good at *everything*?

A shot rings out, incredibly loud in my ear, and I whirl to see Poulter crumple to the deck. Then I look at Kayla, who is holding her smoking rifle and walking over to the now-dead pirate captain. She crouches down and comes up with a small revolver in her hand.

"He had a hideaway gun," she said. "I saw him reach for it when he thought we weren't paying attention."

I nod dumbly. Well, there goes my hope of interrogating the guy, but I'm grateful to be alive.

TWENTY-SEVEN
NO PRISONERS

There are no prisoners. Apparently, every pirate in the base—all thirty-four of them—chose to fight to the death. Unfortunately, we also lost six of our brave militia fighters. Norman takes it harder than I do, but I find myself surprisingly choked up about it as well. Even though I knew it was a likely outcome, I trained and worked with these people for two full weeks, and I feel the weight of personal responsibility for each one of their deaths. I add their names to the list I carry with me in my implant and my head, of every person who has ever died because of a decision I made.

It doesn't help to know that it was the pirates who chose violence. Often rational thought simply can't overcome the emotional response, no matter how hard we try. I honestly hope that never changes. The day I can rationalize someone's death—even those of my enemies—is a day that I think I'll sink even lower than I already have in life. I may be a mass murderer, but at least I feel terrible about it.

At the end of the day, I still have one more difficult situation to navigate: the ownership of the spoils. There is a wide variety of loot in the pirate base, and there are the two ships, the corvette and the smaller one. President Carter is obviously keen to get his hands on all of it, especially after the economic hardship the pirates have inflicted on his system. But he's also been unable to pay me even what Kayla originally promised.

Then, I remind him that as the military *leader* of the expedition and as the captain of the ship that brought us here, technically, *I* control the disposition of the spoils. He bristles at that, but he finds it hard to argue with thousands of years of interstellar law.

Luckily for him, I'm feeling generous, or maybe just sympathetic to the plight of his planet's citizens. In the end, I keep the corvette, which is what I *really* wanted as soon as I learned of its existence, plus enough loot to cover the operations for it and *Wanderer* for a few months. The rest of the loot, which is pretty substantial, plus the system patrol craft, I let the people of Carter's World have.

I'm such a good guy sometimes. OK, rarely, but I do have my moments.

Carter's not really happy, but his daughter glares at him when he tries to argue again, and he shuts his mouth.

The biggest question now is what to do given that I have two ships but only two pilots. That means no one to spell either myself or Lin, and that one of us will be alone on a ship while the other will only have Harris for company. I briefly consider asking if any of the militia fighters are interested in a career change, but I stop myself, worried that poaching some of his people might make Carter blow a gasket and try to renege on our deal.

Ultimately, I make Lin and Harris fly the corvette off the rock. Normally, I would be more keen to put myself in danger flying an unknown ship, but the pirates have surprisingly taken great care of it, and we even find the ship's command override code written on a sticky note on the captain's command chair. I guess pirates don't really worry about password security.

But actually, the reason I decide to have Jessica fly the bounty ship is so that I can fly *Wanderer* back to Carter's World with the president and his militia. I don't want them anywhere near my new ship, or my crew, if they decide to take a better deal through force, because I have the distinct impression that Carter—who I've never actually liked—would consider that.

I bid an awkward farewell to Jessica in the central lounge that we've used as a staging area for moving out the recovered loot to each of our ships. Carter and his people will have to make a few trips back in their small in-system shuttle to take ownership of the other pirate ship and get the rest of the spoils. But whatever we can fit in the hold while still making room for the surviving nineteen militia troops is going with us now.

"It was a good plan, Brad," Jessica says.

I nod. "Couldn't have come up with it without you…or Harris," I admit.

She chuckles, though it's a bit strained. "Yeah, that was a surprise. We might have to keep the guy around."

I smile, but it's also forced. "Sure. Well, I guess I'll see you at the jump point after I drop off the kids back at the farm."

"OK, Captain. I'll take a run through the outer system to play with our new ship and hopefully work out any kinks before we try to take her into jump space."

I nod, not knowing what else to do. "Uh, what do you want to call her?"

"Really, you're going to let me name the new ship?" she asks in surprise and her face lights up a bit.

"Well, yeah. Without your ninja skills on the bridge, we wouldn't have her. I was pretty much just lying there helpless before you and Kayla showed up." At the mention of Kayla, Jessica's joy abates. Stupid me.

But she thinks for a moment and then tells me the ship's new name.

"Really?" I ask in genuine surprise.

She nods resolutely. "Really. She did save us in the end, after all."

Then, with a few more awkward words, Jessica is gone, and I'm turning back to the tunnel that will lead me back to my little freighter and another awkward conversation.

TWENTY-EIGHT
THE LONG GOODBYE

I find Kayla, as expected, in the cockpit waiting for me when I get back on *Wanderer*. Surprisingly, her father and Norman aren't there, which is too bad, because I could really use them as a buffer right now. I can only assume that Carter is resting in his cabin after the ordeal of the day, and Norman is probably still down with his troops in the hold.

"Hey, flyboy," she says with a smile as I slide into the pilot's chair. She's sitting in Jessica's co-pilot chair, which actually bothers me, but I don't say anything.

"Hey back," I say lamely, my mind racing to find words for what I want to say to her.

Neither of us talks as I work to ready the ship. Jessica and Harris already have the corvette burning away from the rock; even though its unfamiliar, warships tend to be faster to warm up and get going than a civilian freighter like *Wanderer*. Kayla lets me work in silence, and fifteen minutes later our landing skids lift gently off the low-gravity surface.

"So, you need a new chief engineer for either of your ships?" Kayla finally asks.

"Uh, I think your father would kill me if I took you away," I say.

She smiles. "Yeah, he probably would. But that doesn't mean I have to listen to what he wants. You and I, we make a great team. At least, *I* think so."

I hesitate in my response, second guessing what I already decided to tell her before even saying my goodbyes to Jessica. "Uh, listen, Kayla, I..."

She surprises me by reaching across and putting a finger to my lips. "Quiet, flyboy. I'm serious about running away from this place with you. Let's go together, right after we drop Dad and his soldiers off, and let's go to a system where they've never even heard of Carter's World, or Gerson, or any of the other places we come from. We'll run cargo, maybe play mercenaries, and hold each other every night. And if you sell that info Walters thinks you have to her or the highest bidder, it'll be all we need to get started in our new lives."

I roll this over in my head for a moment, but not because I'm actually tempted by it. No, something just feels off about her offer. But I can't think what it is, so I just shake my head slowly. "Kayla, I can't."

She nods and smiles sadly, tears forming in her eyes. "I know. You love Jessica Lin. Any fool can see it, and she loves you back; any fool can see that as well." I'm going to argue that point with her, but I wisely hold my tongue.

She gets up, but before she goes, she leans down and kisses me gently, her lips brushing mine as if begging me to reconsider. Then she's gone and I'm alone in the cockpit.

TWENTY-NINE

THE REVELATION

Three hours later, when the corvette with Jessica and Harris on board is almost off my sensor scope, the comm chimes that I have an incoming hail. I answer it.

"Brad, can you hear me?" Jessica's voice asks over the cockpit speakers.

"I can, Jess, what's up?" There's an urgency to her tone that tells me this isn't just a social call.

"Put me on your implant so no one else can listen in," she says next, and my wariness spikes. I get up and close the cockpit door, then do as she says.

"OK, we're good," I say. "Now tell me, what's going on?"

"I don't know," she admits. "I just can't shake the feeling that we missed something. Did that whole mission feel, I don't know, too easy?"

On the surface, it sounds crazy, given all we went through to take out Poulter and his goons, but the same thing has been nagging at me. For all the many things that had to go right for our mission to succeed, it seems like it all went off without a hitch. We should have had at least one hitch—maybe three or four.

"Yeah, I think I know what you mean," I tell her honestly. Then, a thought hits me. "Jessica, what *exactly* did your father do while you were stationed on *Ordney* that makes you hate him so much?"

There's silence on the other end of the line, and I'm worried that maybe I've lost the connection or just lost her by asking the one question she's told me she won't answer.

"Brad..." she starts, but I jump back in.

"I know Jess, but I need you to trust me. I need to know. I can't explain why, but I just need to know right now."

Another long pause. When she starts talking again, her voice is subdued. "I told him where to meet me in the Hothan system, so he knew where *Ordney* was on our patrol. Brad, we were part of the *Intrepid* task force. So, he knew where the *entire* task force was going to be, and, more importantly, where it *wasn't* going to be."

She says the last part like it should hold great meaning for me. At first, it doesn't, but when the realization hits me, it's like a ton of bricks.

"The Yolandra Incident..."

"Yes," she confirms, in a whisper that I have to strain to hear even with my implant's direct connection to my inner ear. "Fifty-seven spacers dead, and a whole shipment of warship components lost."

And not just *any* warship components; these were components that King Charles had somehow managed to procure from a star nation in the Outer Rim, hundreds of light years closer to Earth than the Promethean Federation. Components more advanced than anything out in the Fringe, and that could have changed the whole nature of our cold war with Koratas and put Prometheus into the conversation with star nations like the Leeward Republic as a major player in Fringe power politics.

"They never found out who leaked the fleet's location or even who attacked the convoy," I protest, still disbelieving what she's telling me.

Another long silence follows my statement, but I'm dreading what I'm going to hear next.

"Yes, they did," she says morosely, "on both counts. But Naval Intelligence thought they would use me to keep feeding information—

the false information *they* wanted—to my father, and from him, to the Republic."

"He earned your trust and then double-crossed you," I gasp. "He gave you the thing you longed for most, and then used it against you."

And suddenly everything starts to fall into place.

"Jessica, let me call you back," I say before she can say anything else. Then I soften my tone. "And trust me, if anyone in the galaxy understands the guilt you've felt ever since then, it's me. We'll get through it together, I promise. But I have to make a really important call right now and confirm the one last thing for this entire mess to make sense."

"OK. But call back soon. I need to know you're OK, Brad. And be careful!" There's genuine concern in her voice and it warms my heart despite the sinking feeling in my stomach that's getting worse and worse with every new revelation.

I sign off and use my implant's interface with the comm to call another number. After fifteen minutes of making bold requests and subtle threats, I'm finally on the line with an older, gruff-sounding man, whose voice I've definitely never heard before.

"This is President Carter. Who is this?"

"Mr. President, this is the man who just saved your system from Poulter and his pirates."

"What? You did? We wondered about that ship that snuck out there. Was that you?"

"Yes, but I need you to stop asking questions right now and answer one of mine. Please."

Silence, so I forge ahead. "Do you have a daughter?"

"Yes," he says, though his voice is now filled with hostility and suspicion, "and if you even think about—"

"Please, Mr. President," I cut him off, though I already know the answer, at least partially, to what I'm about to ask next. "I mean her and the rest of your family and your people no harm. But I need to know; how old is she?"

A long pause. "Forty-two. She's married with her own kids these days. Why?"

"I can't explain. Only in a little while, you're probably going to get a call from someone named Jessica Lin, or possibly Jennifer Kim—she goes by both. She's with me, and I need you to promise that you'll do whatever she asks to help her. Do it in return for us liberating your system. Got it?"

"I don't know what you're babbling about, son, but if she calls, I'll listen."

"Thank you, Mr. President."

I cut the line and start to hail the corvette and Jessica again. But before I can finish, I hear the hatch behind me slam open, and then I feel the cold steel of a pistol's muzzle pressed to the back of my neck.

"Tsk, tsk, tsk," Kayla's voice says, though in a slightly lower register than before. "Now, Brad, you hurt my feelings once already today. Let's not make things any worse."

I turn slowly in my seat, mindful of the gun and keeping my hands where she can see them and look at the pretty little farm girl. Though she's no longer pretty or a farm girl. Her face is curled into a sneer, and she's wearing a black skinsuit with ballistic armor attached. On top of that, she holds the pistol like an extension of her arm.

"Kayla, or whatever your name is, just tell me what you want."

She rolls her eyes. "Come on, Brad, even you can't be *that* dense. I've told you already, several times. I want that secret in your head. I want the coordinates of that stellarium deposit out in Gerson."

Crap. So much for hoping she was just going off the little Admiral Walters may have told her, though I still don't know for sure if Walters was in on this or just a dupe like me; either way seems equally likely. It wouldn't surprise me that little Kayla has been ahead of me *and* the admiral this entire time.

"My name *is* Kayla, just not Carter. And you knew a cousin of mine, Jules," she growls, her voice hard and menacing. "In fact, I think you were the last person to see her alive, and I owe you for that."

I want to hit myself in frustration at my own stupidity. I'd left Jules, Owen Thompson's henchwoman, on the surface of that asteroid at Fiori tied up but with a long-range portable comm. I'd done it so that Jessica wouldn't know that I expected Agent of the King's Cross

Heather Kilgore to quickly find and kill the mercenary, but I should have at *least* disabled the comm. Apparently, the mean little woman got off at least one call before she met her end.

Now I'm positive that not even Walters knew what she was getting into when she set us up on this job with Kayla. Because Jules knew what Owen was after on that rock—the exact coordinates of the stellarium deposit at Gerson—and Walters would have *never* let me off her ship if she'd suspected I had that bouncing around in my head.

"And Poulter and his pirates?" I ask, though I already know the answer to that as well.

She shrugs. "We made a deal with him: help us get the info out of you and get a cut. They'd setup here in the Carter System as a convenient out-of-the-way base for raids in the Jutzen Protectorate.

"But you ruined everything! You were supposed to just surrender at Big Ben, or at least stay in the atmosphere long enough for Poulter's second ship to arrive and box you in. But you had to go and be all daring, so I had to call them off before you got us killed. Then we had to throw together the little operation at the farm on the fly and call in a bunch more of our team to play the roles of the militia because you just wouldn't give up or give sweet little me the information so we could run off together. You're a very annoying mark, Brad."

She grins wickedly. "But at least you helped us get rid of some troublesome business partners. Poulter kept pushing for a bigger cut of the prize when we finally sold those coordinates in your head. Now, my team and I will get to keep it all to ourselves. So maybe you're not worthless after all."

"Listen," I try to say in a reasonable tone, though I'm pretty annoyed. Why do the villains always insist on monologuing? I'm also, if I'm honest, more than a tiny bit terrified right now. "No one needs to get hurt. I'll share what I know, just let my crew go in peace."

Kayla sneers at me again, showing her teeth, and then looses a wicked laugh. "Sorry, flyboy," for a second, her voice goes back to the soft soprano she used as Kayla Carter, "I can't bear the thought of sharing your affections." Then her voice hardens again. "And I'm afraid I can't have your little trollop coming after us."

I turn back to my console in horror just in time to see the distant sensor reading of the corvette explode. Before I can even process what's happened, rage takes me, and I leap out of my seat with my hands outstretched as claws toward Kayla's throat.

The stun round hits me in the chest, and my world goes black before I even get halfway there.

EPILOGUE – JESSICA LIN; ANOTHER DEATH

The fire burns hot and bright, quickly consuming the oxygen around me. I can't breathe, for every time I try my lungs feel nothing but searing pain and heat. When I cough, the agony is so intense that I wish for all the universe to be dead, but I'm sure I already am.

"Jessica! Jessica!" a faint but frantic voice screams, and it takes me a second to recognize its owner.

Harris? What is he doing here in Hades with me? I always liked him. Too bad he had to join me in Hell.

"Jessica! You're alive!" That can't be right. He's delusional. Poor Harris; unlike me, he's never been dead before.

Something heavy comes off my chest, and I feel something soft press to my face. Cool air suddenly replaces the hot fires of perdition that have been scorching my lungs, and I gulp in great ragged breaths, desperately grateful for even the momentary reprieve.

"I think the ship is still flyable," Harris is saying, though I don't know quite what he's talking about.

"Just hold on, Jessica. They have Brad. We have to go after them!"

Brad. Brad. Brad. The name takes up in my mind like a drum beat, over and over again in time with the throbbing of the pain that still pulses through my body in agonizing waves.

Brad. I grasp onto the word and use it to fight my way up out of the dark fires that grasp me. My eyes fly open and I see Harris' face staring down at me through a haze that slowly resolves into smoke. He looks worried.

"Brad?" I ask, but the sound leaves my ragged lungs and lips in a mangled groan that is further muffled by whatever is on my face.

"They have him, Jessica. They have the captain. You need to live so we can go after him. They have the captain." He's frantically jabbering now, and part of me wants to reach out and slap him, but it's too painful for me to move my arm.

"Hold on, Jessica!" he pleads. "I'll get you to the auto-doc. The burns are so bad. Just stay with me for a few more minutes, please!"

I close my eyes as I feel him struggle to lift me from the hard deck of…the ship. *Persephone.* But that ship's destroyed… No. It must be our new ship, the one we took from…pirates? That's right. I told Brad I wanted to call her *Persephone.* Like the other ship…like…

"Brad!" I scream as my eyes fly open. But the pain is too much as Harris jolts and jars my body while he rushes down the corridor, and I feel blessed oblivion coming back to claim me.

But right before unconsciousness washes over me, I have one last desperate thought.

Brad, I'm coming!

THE END OF BOOK THREE

Read the thrilling fourth book now: *The Worst Rescuers in the Republic*, available on Kindle, Paperback, and Audible.

SKYLER RAMIREZ
THE WORST
RESCUERS
IN THE REPUBLIC

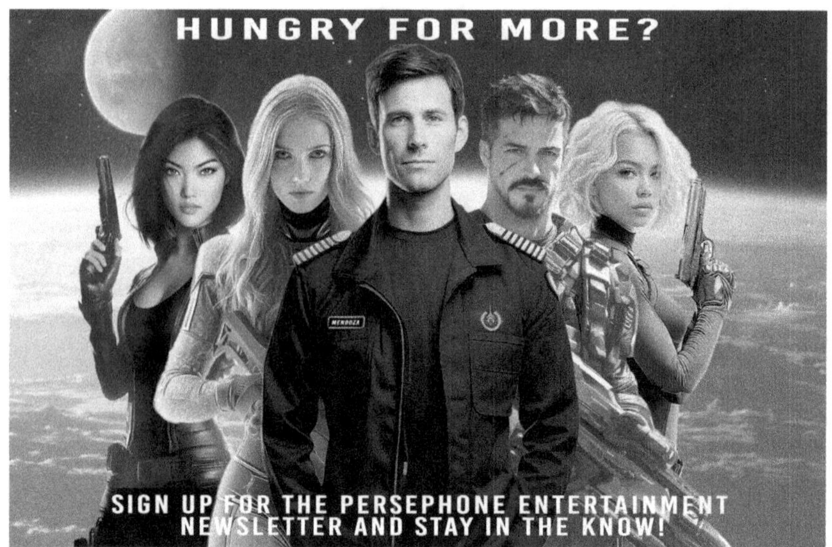

Don't ever miss a new release!

Sign up now for Skyler's newsletter and get access to new release updates, free content, and great deals.

Just go to
www.skylerramirez.com

BOOKS BY SKYLER RAMIREZ

DUMB LUCK AND DEAD HEROES

The Worst Ship in the Fleet

The Worst Spies in the Sector

The Worst Pirate Hunters in the Fringe

The Worst Rescuers in the Republic

The Worst Detectives in the Federation

The Worst Traitors in the Confederacy

The Worst Fugitives in the Star Nation

The Worst Mercenaries in the Border Systems

The Worst Admiral in the Star Cluster (Coming Soon)

A STAR NATION IN PERIL

Set in the same universe as Dumb Luck and Dead Heroes

Rogue Agent

Suicide Mission

Assassin's Flight

THE GALAXY'S WORST MERCENARIES

Set in the same universe as Dumb Luck and Dead Heroes

The Kaelen Extraction: A Billy Firebrand Adventure

The Calypso Enigma: A Billy Firebrand Adventure (Coming Soon)

THE BRAD MENDOZA CHRONICLES

Short stories in the same universe as Dumb Luck and Dead Heroes

Saving the Academy

Battle for Poe

Siege of Jalisco

Death Station

Bells and Bullets

THE FOUR WORLDS

The Four Worlds: The Truth

The Four Worlds: Subversion

The Four Worlds: Wrath of Mars

Ascension (Working Title; Coming 2026)

Revolution: A Four Worlds Story

BLACK SKY CLUB (WITH STEPHEN GAY)

Awakening

STANDALONE SHORT STORIES

Serena

TRANSLATIONS

Select books also available in:

German

French

Italian

Spanish

Japanese

Simplified Chinese

Hindi

ABOUT THE AUTHOR

I just love writing. My goal is to write books that my readers enjoy and that celebrate everyday imperfect heroes. I want to show that everyone, no matter how life has dealt with them or how they've dealt with life, deserves a second chance and can go on to do amazing things. Just look at Brad and Jessica in Dumb Luck and Dead Heroes or Jinny Ambrosa and Tyrus Tyne in The Four Worlds.

It's important to me that everyone be able to read my books, including my teenage children, so I purposefully leave out any swearing or graphic scenes, though I don't shy away from serious topics. In this, I follow a tradition set by many (far better) writers before me, most notably in my life, Louis L'Amour.

As for the personal side, I live in Texas with my wife and four children (and often a revolving door of exchange students), and I work for a major tech company in my spare time. But writing is my passion, and

I often toil into the early hours of morning, especially on the weekends, and it's all worth it when I see people enjoy my books.

Thanks for reading!

Skyler Ramirez

Visit me at www.skylerramirez.com

amazon.com/stores/author/B0BLM4MML2

facebook.com/skylerramirezauthor

instagram.com/skyler.ramirez.author

tiktok.com/@skylerramirez_author